P. Reau.

WHATEVER NEXT!

An engaging new role of life with the Hopkins family...

Billy is delighted to be retiring from teaching. He doesn't want to cross the Sahara Desert or take up mountaineering. No, all he wants is some peace and quiet, but it seems his retirement isn't going to be as peaceful as he thought. For starters, his children and grandchildren regularly come to stay, leaving a trail of disorder and confusion in their wake. Then there's the shock of realising that the young man inside isn't the man reflected in shop windows. When he writes his memoirs, though, and they become a bestseller, he finds himself having one of the biggest adventures of his life.

WHATEVER NEXT!

WHATEVER NEXT!

by

Billy Hopkins

Magna Large Print Books
Long Preston, North Yorkshire,
BD23 4ND, England.

British Library Cataloguing in Publication Data.

Hopkins, Billy
   Whatever next!

   A catalogue record of this book is
   available from the British Library

   ISBN   978-0-7505-2904-4

First published in Great Britain in 2007 by
Headline Publishing Group

Published in Large Print 2008 by arrangement with
Headline Publishing Group Ltd.

Magna Large Print is an imprint of Library Magna Books Ltd.

Printed and bound in Great Britain by
T.J. (International) Ltd., Cornwall, PL28 8RW

I dedicate this book to the memory of my own parents, Tommy and Kate Hopkins, and my parents-in-law, Louis and Mary Kinsler.

Acknowledgements

As with the first five books in this series, the present volume should be considered a work of fiction. The story has been inspired by true events but I have taken dramatic liberties in order to create what I hope is an enjoyable read.

There are many people whom I should like to thank for their help and advice. My own children, Stephen, Catherine, Peter, Laurence, Paul and Joseph for checking the manuscript and allowing me to quote some of their stories; Pirkko Soundy for reading through and making valuable comments on the first draft; Alec Adcock and Dr Darragh Little for putting me straight about Ireland; Steve Lovering for his help with research; Barbara McGahey for letting me see her mother's reminiscences on Collyhurst; and my brother Alf for checking out the chapter on early boyhood. As with all my books, however, my greatest thanks go to my wife, Clare, for her forbearance and encouragement when listening to my ramblings as I tried to make sense of my jumbled-up memories.

In the publishing world, my thanks go out to all those who have been involved in the production of my books. At the Blake Friedmann Literary Agency, to Isobel Dixon and support staff. At

Headline Book Publishing: to Publishing Director, Marion Donaldson, for her unfailing cheerfulness and help; to the unsung staff working in the 'back' office who have helped to make my books a success, from proof-readers and promotional staff to cover designers. I owe them all a debt of gratitude.

Last and certainly not least, I should like to thank all those people who have read my books, visited my website (www. billysbooks.info), written me letters or e-mails (billy@billys books.info) and generally given me their support and encouragement. They are very much appreciated.

There is a wicked inclination in most people to suppose an old man decayed in his intellects. If a young or a middle-aged man, when leaving company, does not recollect where he had laid his hat, it is nothing; but if the same inattention is discovered in an old man, people will shrug their shoulders and say, 'His memory is going.'
Samuel Johnson, *Boswell's Life of Johnson*

You don't stop laughing because you grow old; you grow old because you stop laughing.
Benjamin Franklin

The seven ages of man: spills, drills, thrills, bills, ills, pills, wills.
(Traditional)

Introduction

Growing Old

It was a beautiful spring evening and Billy Hopkins was sitting in his garden enjoying the sunshine and the singing of the blackbirds when his son Mark sat down on the bench beside him and said, 'I've been thinking, Dad. You've been retired now for over fifteen years and you've certainly kept yourself busy, trying this and trying that and writing your novels. How have you really found it? Is it something we should all look forward to or something to be dreaded?'

Billy chuckled. 'Retirement has its ups and downs, Mark, but if you're reasonably healthy and you've prepared for this momentous turning point in your life, I'd say that on balance it's something very much to look forward to. After all, no more joining the rush-hour traffic to and from work; no more ulcer-producing deadlines to meet, no more bosses ordering you around. Instead there's unlimited leisure and the possibility of travel to those faraway places you've always dreamed about. And, perhaps I should add, the chance to sleep late every morning if you're that way inclined. For me, Mark, retirement was a dream come true – something I'd longed for. I'd been in teaching for over forty years and now here was the opportunity to live life like never before.

15

And that's the way it was. At first. After a few months the novelty began to wear off and I wondered how I was going to fill the oceans of time now at my disposal. It's then that you're thrown back onto your own resources, and the interests and hobbies you've developed in your life become crucial. If you haven't developed any, then is the time to start.'

'I don't think I'll have any problem filling the time, Dad. But retirement usually means getting old and I don't fancy that one bit. How do you feel now that you're getting on in years? Do you feel out of touch with things or do you think sometimes you've seen it all before? Come on. What's it really like being old?'

'Cheeky bugger,' Billy laughed. 'Anyone would think I was ancient. But you'll find out for yourself one day, my lad.'

'I'll face that if and when it comes,' he replied. 'Life's too short to be thinking about my old age. Besides, who's to say I'm going to live that long?'

'I do, Mark, and it's no use being in denial. You ask what it's like being old. I'll tell you. There are compensations, like the feeling that there's no longer any urge to go rushing about trying to sort out the world's problems or to worry overmuch about what the morrow might bring. Every new day is a bonus.

'However there are a few downsides as well. Apart from the usual aches and pains and the difficulty in rising from a chair without groaning, there are still lots of people around with nasty ageist attitudes.

'Some folk consider you written-off, a nonentity, and your opinions count for nothing. Even the social survey ladies with their clipboards look straight through you and think your views irrelevant. And let's say you're in the company of younger people. To them you're a spectre and more or less invisible. Maybe someone asks you something and you hesitate for a minute because you're not sure what they mean or maybe you can't remember a name. Straight away they put you down as gaga and someone will step in and answer for you. "What he's trying to say is..." Or maybe you didn't catch what the other person said because *they* mumbled their words. "He's going a bit deaf," they explain. You admire a woman's figure and you're a "dirty old man". An elderly lady visits the beauty parlour and she's "mutton dressed as lamb". You express dissatisfaction with the government or a TV programme and you're a "grumpy old man". So it goes on. And then in advanced old age, they take away your independence and accuse you of being in your "second childhood". That's what being old can sometimes be like and, in such cases, you just can't win. There are lots of words and phrases bandied around to describe your condition. For men, there's codger, old fogey, old goat, geezer; for women there's biddy, hag, crone, old maid, and that's just a few of them. You attend a funeral and someone's bound to remark: "It's not worth your going home, is it?" Big joke. Some elderly folk are riled by those birthday cards with pictures of decrepit old couples and containing snide comments about being put out to pasture or being over the hill. Not me. Personally I don't object to these cracks because I believe that, in the pursuit of political correctness, we're in danger of losing our sense of humour altogether.

'Without trying to make a pun, mark my words, son. Your turn will come and you'll get old like the rest of us. And the way your generation treats its old folks will be the way your children will treat you.

'That's the meaning of Grimm's fairy tale when a peasant makes his poor clumsy old father sit in the corner to eat out of a wooden dish away from the family table. One day the son finds the little grandson assembling little pieces of wood. "I am making these for Father and Mother to feed out of when I grow big," says the child. Immediately the grandfather is given his place back at the family table and "they did not even say anything if he spilled a little upon the cloth."

'Another thing to think about, Mark, is that, thanks to medical advances and a healthier lifestyle, people are living longer and there are more centenarians around now than ever before in history. So that, even if you decide to work till you're seventy, you could still have twenty or thirty years of retirement left. Will you have enough money put by to live comfortably? And just as important as your savings, have you thought about what you'll do with all those new-found leisure hours?

'I like the story of the old lady who decided to spend her entire retirement taking cruises aboard the Princess liners. "It's cheaper than a nursing home and the service I receive is unsurpassable" she claimed. "I am treated as a customer and not a patient; I have luxury amenities, breakfast in bed and as many meals as I want; clean laundry every day, free toiletries, immediate medical attention and repairs to everything in my cabin; entertainments every night, a change of companions on each voyage, and visits to exotic places. And finally when I die, they'll simply dump me over the side free of charge, so saving funeral expenses." Makes you think.

'As you know only too well, Mark, I did not go for the permanent cruise option. But I did keep myself busy, although I took many wrong turnings and made lots of mistakes. But then the man who never made a mistake never made anything.'

Prologue

A Family Christmas

'What kind of computer did you have when you were a lad, Grandad?' asked young Jamie as he obliterated another alien monster on his Tomb Raider III. His attention was riveted on Lara Croft, the gun-toting, curvaceous killer heroine.

'Well,' Billy replied, 'we didn't have computers. Not even televisions.'

In his mind's eye, Billy went back to the Collyhurst of 1935 when he'd been a seven-year-old like Jamie. There'd been five boys in the family then and they'd all slept in the same bedroom, two in one bed and three, top and tail, in the other. Being the youngest, naturally Billy was always the tail and slept with his brothers' feet in his face.

On Christmas Eve, the five of them dutifully hung up their stockings on the brass rail at the end of the bed and waited for Father Christmas to put in his appearance even though they knew full well it was Mam playing the part as usual. But it seemed to make her happy and so they went along with it. As for Dad, he never took the role, preferring to celebrate the birth of Christ in the Queen's Arms at the corner of the street.

Around eleven o'clock, Mam tiptoed in and began stuffing the goodies into their stockings.

The five of them watched her every move through half-closed eyes. They'd hung up the largest football stockings they could find, not that it made the slightest difference, for every year they got exactly the same things. An apple, a tangerine, half a bar of Cadbury's Fruit & Nut, and a torch. Always a torch and always the same kind of torch from Woolworths, a flat case type with a large bulb and magnifying glass top.

They waited until Mam had finished distributing the presents and as soon as she'd crept out of the room, they leapt up to seize their prizes. By half past eleven they'd eaten the fruit and the chocolate, after which they turned their attention to the torches. First, they created a tent under the bedclothes and illuminated it while one of the older brothers terrified the living daylights out of the young 'uns with one or two ghost stories. Then it was competition time to see who could make the scariest monster face by sticking the torch under the chin and making a gruesome expression accompanied by spooky moaning noises. Finally, they spent an hour or two making animal shadows on the wall – following the detailed instructions from *The Hotspur* and *The Wizard*.

By the morning, the batteries were flat and since it was Christmas Day they couldn't buy any more – not that they had any money anyway. They found, though, that the appliance of science – a pinch of salt and a heating-up in the fireside oven – restored a little temporary life to them.

That was Billy's Christmas Eve and he couldn't remember it ever varying from one year to the next throughout his entire childhood.

Christmas today was a very different affair. It began some time in early September with the first carol in the supermarket. Billy often wondered if there was the same competition to report hearing the first carol in autumn as there was for the first cuckoo in spring. For him, the first jingle bell was the first alarm bell, signalling it was time to begin the task of identifying the current year's 'in' toy. This involved a close watch on children's TV programmes, especially the ads beamed at the kids. Which doll? Which monster? Which computer game? Which alien would be the 'must have' item that year? Every year, Billy asked himself the same old question: whatever next? In the early stages of the search, it was a matter of guesswork and it was only too easy to put your money on the wrong horse. To buy a reptile when it should have been a dinosaur (in that particular year, young Jamie had become one of the world's foremost authorities on dinosaurs), an Action Man when it should've be an ET, or a Pokemon. Sometimes, like the year when it was Tracy Island and Play-Station II, for example, the 'in' toys were virtually unobtainable unless you were prepared to take a return flight across the Atlantic. Once the TV ads had made their decision, it became an Anneka Rice-like chase across town to grab the prized item before supplies ran out. Naturally Grandad was the best bloke for the job, as being retired he had all the time in the world to run around the stores, even if he was hobbling around on crutches. One year it'd been dinosaurs, then Ninja Turtles, then Power Rangers, and Teletubbies. Another year, Tomb Raiders III, a Cabbage

Patch doll or a Furby creature and even by early November, local toy stores had run out of stock.

'We're expecting a fresh supply tomorrow at nine o'clock sharp,' the assistant said, 'but you'll have to be here early when the store opens to avoid disappointment.'

There'd been no choice but to join the queue the next day.

'Now we know how the Russians feel,' complained an old lady in the line which had formed at 8 a.m.

Billy didn't mind putting himself out for his two grandchildren; they had both developed into interesting – if at times mischievous – personalities. For example, when Jamie was five years old, he had been chosen to be one of the three wise kings in the school nativity play. And not any old king carrying common-or-garden stuff like frankincense or myrrh, oh no! He was the one with the task of delivering a bar of gold in a golden basket. Mark's wife, Tiffany, and the mother of Jamie and three-year-old Annie, had made a superb job of producing the royal gift and everyone was impressed. The whole family turned up at the school to see Jamie hand over the precious object. He was scripted to say: 'To the son of God I bring this gift of gold from the East.'

Simple enough. The family waited with bated breath for Jamie to deliver the immortal line. Micky Richards in the role of St Joseph came forward to receive the gold. Jamie hesitated and seemed to be taking a long time to say his piece.

St Joseph was becoming impatient.

'Gimme the gold, Jamie Hopkins,' he hissed.

Then Jamie made his decision and he was adamant.

'No, you're not getting it. My mam made it and so it's mine and you're not having it. So there!'

Consternation among the audience. Jamie was rewriting biblical history. His teacher had to step onto the stage and with urgent whisperings persuaded the reluctant king to hand over the loot.

Annie, too, was a character. Both children were keen followers of *Star Trek* which was being repeated on television. Both were fascinated by Mr Spock who was half human, half Vulcan and had pointed ears. But Annie was especially intrigued by the humanoids from the planet Klingon because of their long flowing hair and their ridged, furrowed foreheads. One day she was sitting on Laura's knee and, after studying Laura's wrinkles for a while, asked plaintively, 'Which planet are you from, Grandma?'

Billy loved it. It was a question that Laura had often addressed to him when he'd boobed and made a mess of something.

When it came to Christmas Day itself, Billy often felt that somehow he'd got sandwiched between two generations. It was like this...

In their early married life, when the children were still young, Laura and Billy always invited the elderly relatives to Christmas dinner. That was what Christmas was all about, wasn't it? Family spirit and family conviviality and all that. So they put up with old Aunty Agnes going on about how she couldn't eat a thing as 'she wasn't long for this world' and they listened to Grandad Duncan and his interminable anecdotes about

24

the 'good old days' and the exciting things that happened in his Inland Revenue office. No complaints – they'd simply been doing their duty by the old folk, making sure they didn't spend the big day alone. It was tradition. Sometimes it was heavy going but they had one consoling thought to buoy up their spirits. One day their own kids would treat them the way they'd treated their parents and aged relatives. How they looked forward to that time! It'd be their turn to be invited to Christmas dinner and they could then bore the pants off their grown-up kids with their trips down memory lane as they ate *their* turkey, *their* plum duff, and drank *their* sherry.

Pipe-dreaming. It was not to be. When well on into retirement, they'd moved to the town of Southport, the retirement capital of the north-west. A peaceful town with the second highest average age in Britain after Eastbourne. Every third house was a nursing home and the town abounded with the ancillary services required by the elderly: osteopaths, physiotherapists, retailers of Zimmer frames and wheelchairs and the like.

On the subject of Christmas, however, all of their progeny plus the four grandchildren descended on them en masse. They loved to see them, of course, and welcomed them with open arms. But they didn't come simply for Christmas dinner. Oh, no! They invariably stayed over for a few days and peace and tranquillity went for a burton. Their unmarried son John had even been talking about buying one of those motor homes, which Billy found really worrying. They loved their son and liked to see him from time to time but this latest idea meant he could simply drive up and live off them indefinitely. It didn't bear thinking about.

In their retirement, they'd settled into a quiet routine, which was how they liked it after fifty-odd years of marriage. Even now, after all those years, Billy could never believe his good fortune in having Laura as his wife. Looking back, he still wondered how he'd managed to be so lucky to win her hand in marriage. He often recalled how he'd first met her in the staffroom of St Anselm's School on his first day of teaching – when was it? 1947! Billy had been out with one or two girl-friends in his time, like the glamorous Adele, for example, but clichéd though it might seem, it had been a case of love at first sight with Laura. He'd fallen without a shot being fired the moment he'd set eyes on her. The courtship hadn't been easy, though. First he'd had to win her from her boyfriend, Hamish Dinwoody, not an easy task as Hamish had been favourite runner with Laura's father, Duncan, because of his glittering career prospects as an actuary. Funny how things had turned out because Hamish was now married to Laura's younger sister, Jenny, and living in Edinburgh with their grown-up family. But now that Billy was a father with a grown-up daughter himself, he could sympathize with Duncan's concern all those years ago. He'd been hoping his daughter might marry someone from the higher professions, like a lawyer, a doctor or an accountant. And what did she get? A working-class lad from Collyhurst whose highest achievement at that time had been to become a lowly assistant master in a secondary modern school. Then there'd been his own dad who opposed the match for opposite reasons.

'It's like oil and water,' the old, man had said. 'The classes don't mix. We're ordinary working-class people while your lady friend belongs to the higher-ups. That can only lead to trouble later on. We're best to stick to our own kind.'

'The daft ha'porth,' Billy muttered to himself now, fifty-three years later.

They each had their own sitting room, an arrangement decided when Laura accused Billy of making too many comments when they watched TV together. She said that when she was watching *Coronation Street,* he was in the habit of saying things like, 'A load of old rubbish' or 'They're all cardboard characters and not a bit like real life'. He couldn't remember saying those things and so he had to take her word for it. Anyway, the result was that she had her own space downstairs with her own armchair and TV where she studied the latest developments in cookery, gardening and social trends in the soaps and other wildlife programmes, while upstairs he had what the Americans called a 'den' with a sophisticated computer set-up plus TV and video where he viewed documentaries and made policy decisions about war, the environment, the economy and the Third World. For him, it was his Starship *Enterprise* and he became Captain Kirk in his own private cocoon. Sometimes, provided he promised to keep shtum, Laura and he watched a programme together if it was a costume drama like *Pride and*

Prejudice, *Vanity Fair*, *Emma*, or *Great Expectations*, when they would sit together and happily enjoy a sherry or two. It was an ideal arrangement, the two of them occupying their own little world and usually meeting in the kitchen around nine o'clock for Horlicks and cream crackers and to exchange views about the night's viewing and family matters. Who could ask for anything more? Pure bliss, it was.

The only thing they didn't see eye to eye on was the matter of ventilation in the bedroom. He loved fresh air and you could even call him a fresh air fanatic as he liked the windows and door open. Laura liked them closed. 'Keeping them open,' she claimed, 'causes coughs and colds and, besides, we've been warned that leaving the door open is a fire hazard.' They agreed to have separate rooms. Billy wondered if the fact that he had to pay one or two visits to the toilet during the night might also have had something to do with the new arrangement. For a Don Juan, this might have been a problem but not for Billy. Not at the age of seventy-five! Billy once asked an 85-year-old friend for his opinion about this.

'At what age does the sex drive finally cool down?'

'Eeh, you'll have to ask someone older than me,' he said.

However, every year at approximately eleven o'clock on the morning of 25 December, their serenity was shattered when the cars bearing their grown-up children and their progeny plus one or two of the family pets roared down the road and screeched to a halt on their pathway.

Boswell, their old, wise Persian cat, did a bunk and wouldn't be seen for the rest of the week. It took a long time to unload the paraphernalia that a modern family needed to survive for a week. Bottles, potties, trolleys, cots, sleeping bags, carrycots, quilts, high chairs, bedrolls, and a vast array of toys which Father Christmas had brought them. Billy was certain his oldest son, Matthew, and his wife Bernice had taken out a second mortgage to pay for the gifts that were required to keep their little horrors happy. Bernice was a lovely girl though she had given Billy something of a problem this year in the matter of gifts. She fancied herself as an artist and had offered to present him with a portrait of himself. Very kind of her except that he wasn't too keen on her work since her subjects were painted in the style of Graham Sutherland's portrait of Winston Churchill, which the great man described as 'an interesting example of modern art'.

'You can't turn it down,' Laura said, 'or you'll hurt her feelings.'

What about my feelings? Billy thought. 'OK. I'll have to accept it but I'll hang it in the attic stairway at the top of the house.'

'But we hardly go up there.'

'Exactly,' he said.

Within a short time of the family's arrival, their cosy nook was transformed into the Old Curiosity Shop. In the midst of the chaos and rumpus, Laura prepared and cooked a huge Christmas dinner for children, grandchildren, and the odd uncle, aunt and in-law who couldn't be left to eat alone on Christmas Day. Given the choice, Billy would gladly have volunteered to go to their homes to keep them company. Anything for a bit of peace and quiet, even if it did mean listening to Great-Aunt Edna and her detailed descriptions of her latest operation and the memorable funerals she'd attended.

As for the grandchildren, no sooner had they got through the door than they made a beeline for the TVs, the videos and the computer to experiment with their new PlayStations and monster games. Billy looked around the house for a quiet corner but there was no place to hide. John became occupied with the young 'uns in a game involving much squealing and shrieking, chasing round the house, and wrestling on the stairs. In the midst of the bedlam, Jamie came to report that the computer had crashed, explaining that four-year-old Annie had upset Ribena down the keyboard. The only copy of his 100,000-word novel which had taken Billy a year to write was somewhere on the hard disk. He prayed to the Lord that it hadn't been deleted by the gooey mess.

Some time before dinner, Billy tried to introduce a note of sanity into the melee by distributing glasses of sherry and port, though two or three of them were bound to be knocked over by John's madcap antics. Then followed a magnificent dinner which would have done the Pickwick Club proud. Their middle-aged children, behaving like young children, were ever on the watch for signs of favouritism, and they examined each other's plates like hawks in case one of them got preferential treatment.

The meal was somewhat marred by the insubordinate behaviour of their sons when Billy tried to give them a speech about how he'd first fallen for their mother.

'William Cobbett once said that when he first clapped eyes on a young woman scrubbing a floor, he knew right away that was the woman for him. In the same way when I saw that young lady with a smudge of flour on her nose and baking an apple pie. I knew right away, she was for me. And that's what made me fall in love all those years ago.'

Laura frowned, for she hated the story. The boys sitting around the table had anticipated it and they held up cards awarding him scores out of ten like they did at Olympic competitions: 3.6, 4.2, 2.1. Billy was most annoyed that the scores were so low for he was proud of his story-telling skill. They had done this to him once before many moons ago when he'd been telling them the meaning and history of April Fool's Day. Lucy, however, did not go along with it, he was happy to note. Instead she came to his defence.

'Most unfair,' she protested. 'Dad has a remarkable memory for the details of his childhood and his past and you should give him credit for it.'

'Sure,' Mark said. 'Pity he can't remember what happened yesterday.'

Matthew was a quieter and more thoughtful personality than his siblings. He reckoned that because he was the eldest son, he often had to behave more responsibly and more sensibly than the others. He hadn't always acted so. Though he was now a research physicist at Oxford, things hadn't looked so promising for him as a youth when he went off the rails by walking off his university course at Sussex in order to form a band. Though the band had prospered, it played only in the evenings, leaving him lots of spare time during the day which he'd devoted to the study of physics at the Open University. When the band finally packed up, he returned to academia where he'd obtained a doctorate in physics, something to do with cold lasers that Billy couldn't begin to understand.

Lucy, still into art therapy and oriental mysticism, had found her literary voice when she began writing for teenagers. She had since become a successful writer with a couple of dozen books published in several foreign languages. Being the only girl, she tended to worry about her brothers and their behaviour, claiming that the males in the family were more liable to acts of irresponsibility than herself. Billy suspected that there was a certain degree of friction, though nothing serious, with her older brother.

Mark was married (if you could call the bizarre, spiritual en masse ceremony he'd undergone marriage) to Tiffany and worked as an estate agent. He had moved from Kent to Manchester, reckoning that the property market in the south was overcrowded, besides which he felt he knew the Manchester scene better. He was undoubtedly the comedian of the family and seemed to view life as one big joke.

Youngest son John – perhaps trying to please his father and grandfather Duncan – had started off his university studies in medicine but was unhappy in that field because his real interests had always been in horticulture, no doubt due to Laura's influence since she was a keen gardener. He'd secretly switched courses and had recently achieved his life's ambition by becoming deputy grounds manager at a famous stately home in Derbyshire. Like Billy in his own family, he was still regarded as the 'baby' whose opinions were not taken seriously.

'He always gets special treatment,' Lucy, now forty-five years old, pouted, pointing to Matthew's plate. 'It was my turn this year for the wishbone. It's not fair – he's always been the favourite in this family.'

'Not only that, he's got more turkey breast and an extra roast potato,' whined Mark, the middle son and father of two children himself.

'Behave!' Billy barked in mock reproof. 'And be thankful for what you've been given. Otherwise leave the table.'

The grandchildren watched fascinated as their parents were scolded. Billy always got on well with the grandchildren. Maybe it was because they shared the same enemies, though he felt it was always wise to stay on friendly terms with his own children because, after all, they'd be the ones to choose his nursing home one day.

In the evening, when the young 'uns had been sent to bed (though none of them seemed to retire early), the adults played and cheated at parlour games, ate Laura's chocolates, and drank Billy's liqueurs and spirits. As the evening wore on and the drink took hold, the games became aggressive, and fiercely competitive. They began with Trivial Pursuit, a dangerous game as they bickered over the official answers and challenged their authenticity. To the question: who wrote *Hamlet?* Matthew claimed the authorship was still in dispute; it was either Edward de Vere or Christopher Marlowe.

'Rubbish!' exclaimed Lucy. 'Everyone with any brains knows it was William Shakespeare.'

'How do *you* know?' Matthew retorted. 'You've never read anything more challenging than a Mills and Boon love story.'

For Lucy, it was water off a duck's back. She countered with, 'Did you know that in the seventeenth century, Matthew Hopkins was a hated witch-hunter who hanged hundreds of women?'

'If he rid the world of a lot of crazy women, then he did a great service,' Matthew rejoined.

'Now, come along, you two,' Laura reproved, 'enough of this quarrelling. Calm down. Remember it's Christmas.'

They switched to playing Scrabble, perhaps better named Squabble, a more perilous game since it invariably ended up with fierce arguments about the acceptability of words like 'zambuk' or 'yuk'. Around eleven o'clock when Mark's normally quiet and amenable wife Tiffany turned on John in the middle of a round and called him a 'rotten swine', things threatened to turn ugly and Billy thought it was time to call it a night.

The next morning, Laura and he were up early ready to go for a walk on the beach – it was Boxing Day and the feast of St Stephen – though it wasn't easy to get dressed as they had to step over innumerable prostrate snoring bodies littering the floor in every room. The grandchildren, though, were bubbling with energy and eager to visit the seashore. Not so their parents who were still half comatose.

The rest of the visit continued in the same chaotic vein, as it did every year, their cosy, familiar routine being turned on its head. Being old folk, Billy and Laura were creatures of habit and had established routines. It was essential for them to know where every personal item was located. For example, Billy was forever losing things and so he possessed six pairs of reading glasses (an emergency pair in each room), three pairs of gloves, and two watches but after the family visit, he couldn't find a thing.

Then as suddenly as they'd descended on the family home, the visitors were gone, along with all their paraphernalia. Just like that. When they'd finally departed, Laura and Billy stood amidst the debris and the wreckage, the half-eaten packets of crisps, chocolate-smeared cushions, cakes with the cherries and the icing licked off, discarded sandwiches, abandoned drinks, overflowing ashtrays, and mountains of wrapping paper. It was as if a bulldozer had swept through the house. Upstairs in Billy's den, not only had the computer ceased working but the video had packed up as well. The £30-a-visit television engineer soon diagnosed the source of the problem – a Liquorice Allsort stuck in the mechanism. He got it working again only for Billy to find that his favourite video movie, *Gone With The Wind*, had been taped over with *Postman Pat*.

Whatever next! he sighed.

After they had waved goodbye and watched the last car go through the gate, they returned with a sense of relief to their home and to normality. Peace and tranquillity reigned once more but the tomb-like silence seemed somehow eerie and there was a depressing sense of anti-climax. And here was the strangest thing of all: Billy felt miserable and sad and missed them all terribly now they were no longer around.

He went back to his den and sat at his desk staring at the blank computer screen. How time had flown! It was hard to grasp that sixteen years had passed since he'd retired from his job at the William Pitt College of Technology (known to the locals as 'the Pit'). Since then, life had been one continuous roller-coaster ride of ups and downs, twists and turns, a zigzag of shocks and scares along the way. As he sat there, his mind went back to that fateful day when he'd finally shaken off the dust of a long, if undistinguished, career in education and entered a new phase of life, the so-called golden age of retirement.

Part One

Nothing Ventured, Nothing Gained

Chapter One

Retired At Last!

It was July 1985. Billy gazed up at the enormous building with its nine floors and its thousand windows and heaved a sigh of relief. It was the big day, a watershed in his life, and he couldn't get his head round it. He'd retired! At last! The enormity of the event began to sink in, and a shiver of joy ran down his spine. He'd left! Actually left! Finally got away from the William Pitt College of Technology.

What a nightmare of a job it'd been. Staff Development Officer in a college where no one wanted to be developed. He'd been appointed to provide education and training courses for the four hundred and fifty lecturers on the staff. He'd organized the courses all right but the problem was that the unions demanded time off from teaching duties in order to attend the courses. The authorities on the other hand were adamant. Releasing lecturers from teaching duties to attend his improvement courses was too expensive and staff would have to do so in their own free time. Result – stalemate. It was a conflict between two opposing forces and Billy was in the middle, between the devil and the deep blue sea. The broom cupboard which had served as his office was a symbol of the low esteem attached to staff development.

Now he was free. No more sitting in that

cubbyhole with the smell of floor polish and disinfectant; no more trying to persuade bolshie colleagues to take one of his improvement courses; no more having to bow and scrape to bosses who paid lip service to the need for his job. No more having to join the morning rush hour to get to work on time. No more being ruled by the demands of frenetic timetables and having to jump whenever some superior gave the command. Farewell to all that! Now he knew how a prisoner felt on the day of his release when he heard the gate finally clang behind him.

That morning he'd cleared his desk, such as it was, and packed up his things: his lecture notes, his personal files, his family photographs. At midday, he'd attended the special lunch arranged for the other four retirees and listened to the Principal's speeches about how they'd all be missed and about the great contributions they'd made to the life of the college and its achievements. Then they were each given a timepiece. Wally Simpson who'd put in forty-odd years at the place received the best, a gold watch (or so it was claimed), while the rest of them got carriage clocks of varying quality and value, according to the length of time they'd been there. As Billy had put in only five years there, having opted for early retirement, his was the cheapest looking instrument (certainly worth no more than a tenner). It amazed him that the authorities believed that their employees, who'd spent most of their lives being ruled and regulated by clocks, would now appreciate chronometers as going-away presents so as to keep a strict check of their leisure hours.

He dismissed such negative thoughts and turned his mind to relishing the notion that now it was all behind him and he was at liberty to go. He'd spent so much time dreaming about this particular moment and now here it was, come true. And it wasn't merely the end of the five years he'd been at this college that he was celebrating. He'd been working in the teaching trade, the so-called chalk and duster brigade, for thirty-seven years and the day heralded the end of a long career. But when it came to the awarding of chronometers, service in other places didn't count, it seemed. But no matter, all that was history.

As he drove away to join the usual traffic jam with its three-mile tailback he revelled in the prospects of his new life. From now on he could do whatever he pleased. Even opt to do nothing if that was the way he felt, though he doubted he'd be able to sit around on his backside contemplating his navel. His late father-in-law Duncan who'd long been his guide and mentor had advised him against it. As he stopped at the traffic lights on Regent Road, he could hear the old man's voice in his head.

'As you get older, you must abide by certain golden rules. First, never pass a toilet or you might come to regret it.' He was forever saying that God had mistimed things when it came to raising children. The best time, he reckoned, for looking after babies was when you were sixty-odd because then you had to get up twice a night anyway!

'Second,' he'd say, 'is to remember that, after you've retired, boredom is the big killer, so always have a project on hand. Keep busy! Be creative!

Never allow yourself to stagnate. Be like a youngster and be enthusiastic about everything. Look at things as if you've never seen them before or as if it's the very last chance you'll ever have. Don't wake up in the morning wondering how you're going to kill time because if you do, it'll be *time* that kills you. On the contrary, wake up every morning and be happy in what you do. Leap out of bed full of the joys of spring as you contemplate the wonderful things you've got lined up to do that day.'

Billy went along with the creative bit but he wasn't so sure about that leaping out of bed stuff, as the thing he was looking forward to most was being able to lie there and listen to the noises outside his window: the roar of the morning rush-hour traffic, the sound of honking cars as their drivers swore and cursed each other in frustration; the strident blare of the sirens as ambulances, police cars, and fire engines tore down the road to the next emergency. Best of all would be listening to the radio road reports. For instance: 'There are roadworks on Lapwing Lane causing long tailbacks. Avoid this area if you can. The traffic lights at the junction of Regent Road and Oldfield Road have broken down, so expect long queues there...' How he relished the thought that he didn't have to jump up to join the poor devils in their frenzied race to get to work on time. No more leaping out of bed. No, sir, he'd be snuggling deeper into his pillow and wallowing in the warm luxury of his duvet as the neurotic world outside went about its madcap business of making money and giving itself ulcers. Farewell to all that, he was done with it.

He was suddenly startled from his reverie by the flashing headlights and angry honking of the lorry behind him.

'Come on, grandad,' the driver bawled. 'Get a bloody move on. We haven't got all day. Some of us want to get home.'

For a moment, he was tempted to give him the finger but then thought better of it when he looked in his rear-view mirror and saw how big and burly the truck driver was. Discretion being the better part of valour, he mouthed the word 'Sorry' and moved forward, turning into Water Street towards the Mancunian Way.

Take the word 'retire', he said, continuing his inner monologue. What's it mean? If I remember rightly, the dictionary says it means 'to withdraw from society, office, or active life'. Made it sound frightening, as if it involved pulling out of life altogether and waiting around for the Grim Reaper to call. Maybe that was how it used to be when men worked till they dropped and there was no social security. But not any more; that was in the past. Today, they could expect to live longer and, if they were lucky, enjoy reasonable health. What was more, if his mam's age was anything to go by, he might last another thirty or thirty-five years, but how long anybody lasted after retirement was anyone's guess. Checking the obituaries of well-known people in the *Telegraph* gave you a rough idea of how long before you pegged out. More often than not, the deceased were pretty old and Billy felt bucked up at the prospect of having so many years left before he fell off his perch. But then the next day, things could even out if a few younger celebrities popped their clogs and he would wonder if he should take out more insurance. What was it that bloke Confucius said? If you want to live to a ripe old age, choose your parents carefully. Another thing he'd noticed in these obituaries was that when it was someone under the age of sixty, they gave the cause of death, for example: 'He died after a long courageous battle with lung cancer' or 'He died in a tragic road accident'. But if the subject was over sixty, no cause was given, as if implying, he was over sixty, for God's sake. What did you expect?

On Wilmslow Road in Withington, Billy stopped at a pedestrian crossing for an old lady struggling along with a Zimmer frame and, unbelievably, it happened again. Some hothead in the car behind him began beeping him. Somehow I seem to attract these bloody people, he muttered to himself. When he saw in his side mirror that the driver was a little bespectacled man in a battered Ford Escort, Billy got out of his car and knocked on the other's window.

'Look,' he said. 'If you want to come and run this little old lady over, be my guest 'cos I haven't got the heart.'

The little man made no reply but sat there staring vacantly ahead, thinking maybe that the man knocking on his window was an escaped lunatic. Billy decided to let it go; after all, this was the first day of his retirement and he wasn't going to let anything ruffle him. He got back in his car and went on his way.

He returned to his thoughts. Take that word 'retirement', it must be the ugliest word in the

English language. Retirement didn't mean you were written off and it was the end of everything; it could be the beginning of something new. Better to think of it as renaissance, rebirth, the start of a third career and a fresh start.

His little pep talk to himself came to an end as he reached home. He parked the car in the garage, picked up his things and went in.

Laura was waiting with a big smile, a pot of tea and a Dundee cake, his favourite and a particular delight that he and his hero, Winston Churchill, had in common.

'Well, Laura,' he said happily, 'that's it. Finito. No more job. In the immortal words of Robert Louis Stevenson: "Home is the sailor, home for his tea, and the hunter from Cheetham Hill." From now on, I'm all yours.'

She smiled brightly – or was it wryly? It wasn't easy to tell.

'Great news, Billy. A red letter day and the end of an era. It'll seem strange, you not going out to work in the morning. But I'm happy for you. You're done with that dreadful job. Tonight, I shall cook you a special meal to celebrate.'

'No, Laura. You'll do no such thing. Tonight, I'm taking you out for a slap-up dinner. I've booked a table at the Hotel Splendide. It comes highly recommended by Jules Dubois, the head of catering at the college.'

'Isn't that place a bit upmarket? I mean, can we afford it now you've retired?'

'I think we can just about manage it before we go into Queer Street.'

Chapter Two

A La Carte

The Hotel Splendide was located in the snootiest part of Manchester's city centre, not far from Kendal Milne's upmarket store. A good taxi ride from Didsbury but well worth it, according to Dubois, not only because of its reputation for superb cuisine but also for its opulence and its luxury. He forgot to mention the prices.

'I hope you know what you're doing booking an expensive place like this,' Laura said for the tenth time.

'Fear not, Laura. It's just a one-off before we go into economy mode. The storm before the lull, as it were.'

'Perhaps there'll be a reduction now you're a pensioner.'

'If a restaurant offers special reductions for pensioners, it will probably mean smaller portions not lower prices.'

They were met by an obsequious maître d' in an ill-fitting tuxedo. Billy gave his name and told him he had a booking for seven thirty.

'Ah yes, m'sieu. We have reserved your table. Meanwhile, you would perhaps like to wait in our little *salle d'attente*.'

He took them to what looked like a holding pen with a small bar where Billy ordered two dry sherries.

At the appointed time, the maître d' re-appeared. 'We have your table for two reserved till nine thirty,' he said. 'Bon appétit!'

'I suppose at half past nine we'll be chucked out on our ears,' Billy whispered to Laura as they sat down.

The maître d' returned and gave them a menu about the size of a school blackboard and showed them to their table. They decided to splash out and order a la carte. The menu was in French and listed such strange things as: *râble de lièvre, sauce poivrade; magret de canard quatre façons; canon d'agneau en croûte, sauce orientale.* What the heck was that all about? And why did they describe their courses with such pretentious phrases as *'Une symphonie de...'* or *'Un mélange de...'* A young family at the next table sat staring uncomprehendingly at the menu. 'They'd be better off buying Big Macs in the Arndale Centre,' Billy murmured to Laura.

The waiters stood around looking superior and bored as if it was beneath them to do such a menial thing as take an order for a meal. If they're so superior, Billy thought, how come they're doing the serving and we're the ones being served? If they ever get round to it, that is.

For the best part of twenty minutes, they were completely ignored even though Billy made several frantic hand signals, even whirling his napkin over his head.

'The snootier the restaurant, the more the waiters put you down,' he muttered to Laura. 'If they don't come soon, there won't be enough time to finish the meal.'

What with the appetizing smells coming from the kitchen and the sight of other diners guzzling, they began to feel hungry and his stomach started to rumble like an approaching storm. In desperation he stood up and waylaid a waiter hurrying by.

'We're ready to order now,' he announced, holding the man by the coat tails.

It did the trick, for one of the waiters engaged in conversation with his colleagues detached himself from his companions and sauntered over to see if they'd like to order any of the food on offer. For hors d'oeuvres, Laura chose *soufflé de Roquefort* and Billy opted for *mosaique de lapin*, both with *salade de cresson*. Despite their study of O-level French, they weren't exactly sure what they'd be getting but as long as it wasn't in any way connected with frogs' or snails' intestines, they weren't too worried. It turned out to be a sort of frothy whipped–up omelette for Laura and delicate slices of rabbit meat for him, both with watercress and served on gigantic charger plates.

'Why are the menus in posh hotels always in French?' Laura wondered.

'So as to disguise what the grub really is and so they can charge eye-watering prices. The posher the restaurant, the more incomprehensible the menu.'

'And why are the minuscule portions served on such big plates?'

'So as to make them look like edible works of art by Cézanne and to give the impression they're really special.'

For the main course, Laura selected *raie meunière avec petits pois* while he went for the *pavé de boeuf grillé avec pommes Dauphine*. Laura's meal turned out to be pan-roasted skate with green peas while his was grilled rump steak with mashed potatoes served in fancy patterns.

The wine waiter approached them and tried to sell them a 1976 white Bordeaux at £85 but though Billy was in a celebratory mood, it wasn't that celebratory and they settled for a bottle of Chateau Saint Floran Blanc at £12.95, which he thought expensive enough.

The wine waiter brought the bottle, uncorked it and with due ceremony poured out a little for Billy to sample. As was expected of him, he swirled the wine around the glass, then sniffed it like a connoisseur.

'Good,' he declared. 'It has good depth and a bright aromatic bouquet. We'll take it. It is a bon vin blanc.'

The waiter corrected Billy's accent.

'The French word *blanc*, m'sieu, is not pronounced as blank like that but should be said like this,' he pontificated, giving the word a ringing nasal twang. The supercilious bastard, Billy said inwardly.

'Thank you for putting me right,' he replied, even though his hackles were rising. 'I'll try to remember it, professeur.'

Laura stepped in quickly to avoid a confrontation by changing the subject.

'I wasn't aware that you were so knowledgeable about wine,' she said.

'I'm not,' Billy said, 'I know nowt about it. But I do know something about the humbug often used to describe the stuff. I once read a book entitled *How to Bluff Your Way in a Restaurant*.'

The waiter returned with their wine and placed it in the wine cooler.

'So, Billy,' Laura said, as she sipped her Bordeaux, 'what are you going to do with all the spare time you'll have now?'

'I thought I might help you in the kitchen.'

'Can't say that idea appeals to me very much, Billy. Some cynical lady said that she married her husband for better or worse, but not for lunch every day as well. I'm not used to you around the place during the day. Come to think of it, though, there are a hundred DIY jobs I could find for you, like putting up shelves, installing more electric sockets, decorating the spare bedroom.'

'I'll pretend I didn't hear that, Laura. But have no fear about me sitting around twiddling my thumbs. Things are going to be wonderful from now on. I've had a lot of time to think about it. There are thousands of possibilities, so many things I could take up. The world is my oyster.'

'Like for instance?'

'Well, off the top of my head, I could cycle round the world, learn to speak fluent German, play the guitar to concert standard, read all the classics like *War and Peace* and *Anna Karenina*, climb the Matterhorn. The list is endless.'

'Be serious. What would you really like to do?'

'Quite a question, Laura. I'd like to spend my time pursuing some worthwhile activity that gives satisfaction and offers a sense of purpose.'

'What about finishing that novel you were going to write? What was it called again?'

'You mean *Our Kid*. I made lots of notes, even started the first chapter but found there's an awful lot to writing a novel. People are always declaring how they have a wonderful idea for a novel but writing one is not as easy as they think. Maybe I'll look at it again some time but right now I have one or two other ideas in mind.'

'Sounds intriguing.'

They'd just about given up ever seeing any food when their main courses arrived and they became preoccupied tucking in.

'Knowing you, Billy,' Laura said as she spooned her outrageously expensive fish onto her plate, 'I'm sure you'll find lots to occupy you. But it's also important to keep yourself fit.'

'You're right, Laura. One thing I'm sure of is that I'm not going to get into the habit of watching daytime telly with those old black and white films featuring all the old stars, like Leslie Howard, Alastair Sim, and Margaret Rutherford. You find yourself saying, "He's dead. He's dead. She's dead." All the ads are for things like Steradent, surgical stockings, walk–in baths, stair lifts with Dame Thora Hird whizzing up and down, and personal loans (Why not cripple yourself by consolidating all your little loans into one massive debt?). And then to cap it all, on comes Misery himself in the person of that Frank Windsor fellah with the melancholy face to ask if you've made your funeral arrangements yet and do you want to be buried and, if so, what kind of box, wood or degradable cardboard, or what about cremation? Then follow loads of boring quizzes and games like *Countdown,* which I hate 'cos I can't do it.'

'You can play tennis with your old school chums in the afternoons now they've also taken early retirement,' she said brightly. 'Didn't you call yourself the Smokers' Club?' Anything to keep him out of the kitchen, she thought.

'That's right, Laura. The old Smokers' Club at Damian College. So called as that's how we became friends, puffing on our Park Drives in the toilets at break time. Funny thing is that none of us smoke nowadays but we've kept the name for old time's sake. Getting together for a men's doubles once a week is a good idea though they're not all at liberty to play. Poor old Olly is still beavering away in the Central Library but I think Titch, Oscar and Nobby should be available. It'll be great to have my old mates around for company. It was a miracle the way we all managed to get ourselves pensioned off early when the government went barmy making cuts right, left and centre.'

'Titch, Oscar, Nobby and Olly! I always thought they were such peculiar names,' she said as she cut into her fish. 'Remind me again. How did they come by them?'

Billy chuckled as his memory went back to that first day as an eleven-year-old scholarship boy at Damian College. He could remember it as if it were yesterday when he. and his pals had given each other nicknames. Norbert Nodder became Nobby; Oliver Hardy, Olly; Tony Wilde who'd fancied himself as an intellectual, Oscar; and

Richard Smalley because of his name and small stature was accorded the sobriquet Titch. As for himself, sometimes he was called Hopalong Cassidy but the one most people favoured was Hoppy.

'Amazing how the names have stuck all these years even now you're retired,' Laura remarked.

'Apart from tennis, Laura, I've been thinking of joining a sports centre and maybe even buying a bicycle.'

'No need to go over the top, Billy. You're not exactly a young man, you know.'

'Maybe not, but inside me there's a twenty-one-year-old trying to get out.'

'Then this young man's in for a disappointment when he emerges and finds he's got the body of an elderly gent.'

'You wait till you see me after I've got myself fit. I'll have to fight the ladies off,' he said, slicing a piece of steak. 'Tomorrow, I'll see if the others are up for a weekly game of tennis and then I'll look into joining a gymnasium.'

'One thing is sure,' she said, 'we'll have to start cutting down on expenses. You know what they say about retirement? "Twice as much husband on half as much money." I hope we're going to be all right financially.'

'We should be OK, Laura,' he replied. 'For a start there's just the two of us now the family's flown the nest. We have my retirement lump sum of fifteen thousand pounds and a pension of nearly five hundred a month.'

'We should be able to manage, though things will be tight. We still have big bills for gas, electricity, telephone and so on, as well as the mortgage hanging round our necks. Monthly standing orders alone swallow two hundred and fifty pounds. Then there's housekeeping on top of that, say two hundred. That leaves very little for all the other expenses like clothes, running the car, etcetera.'

'I know, I know, Laura. But not to worry because I have two cunning plans. The mortgage is five thousand pounds and we can pay that off from the lump sum. That's one big expense gone.'

He paused to refill the wine glasses.

'And the second cunning plan, Billy?'

'I shall take on private pupils. That should bring in a little extra cash to help eke out the pension. At first, I thought of doing supply teaching as I believe it's well paid nowadays but that'd simply be doing the same old job that I've been doing for forty years. No, I'm going to coach students.'

'Coach? English, I suppose.'

'Not only English. Music as well. I studied piano with my old friend Denis Glynn for a considerable time and don't forget that I once took singing lessons with your mother when I had polypi on the larynx. Why, I once sang a Mozart aria before an audience of two hundred women students in a Yorkshire college!'

'I haven't forgotten and I'm sure those students haven't either.'

'Don't be so sarky, Laura. Anyway, I could try teaching piano and singing. And as you said, there's always English. But not grammar, punctuation and that kind of thing. No, I'd like to try a different approach. I've always wanted to teach creative writing. You never know. I might find hidden talent in the back streets of Salford. A Charles Dickens or a Jane Austen.'

'Dream on, Billy. But that won't be much of a retirement for you, will it? I mean, isn't coaching the same as teaching?'

'Not quite, Laura. I shall be dealing with students as individuals instead of large lecture classes. Something I've always wanted to do but never had the chance. But all that's in the future. The first thing we should do is take a good holiday abroad while we're still in funds.'

'Abroad? Where did you have in mind? Australia, the Bahamas, South America?'

'No, none of those fancy destinations where you have to fly. Think of all the dangers you risk going to exotic places like that: cramped airline seats, travel sickness, claustrophobia, jet lag. And when you get there, food poisoning, stomach bugs, gyppy tummy, mosquitoes, malaria, and prickly heat.'

'Why do you always exaggerate, Billy?'

'I don't always exaggerate. Only when I want to win an argument.'

They'd now reached the coffee stage of the meal and to round things off Billy ordered liqueurs: Benedictine for Laura and Drambuie for himself.

'No, I was thinking of Ireland,' he continued, stirring his coffee.

'Why Ireland?'

'You might remember that before we married, I cycled round the Emerald Isle with my old friend and school colleague, Alex. We had a great time. You were staying with your uncle in Ayr at the time. Ireland was such a lovely place that I vowed I'd return with you one day to show you just how beautiful it is.'

'Yes, I remember. You sent me enough picture postcards to fill a whole album. We still have them somewhere. When you said a holiday abroad, I never thought of Ireland as "abroad" but it sounds like a good idea. I hope you're not thinking of a driving tour.'

'I wasn't but what would be wrong with that?'

'Because when you get into a car, you become a completely different person. You suffer from LPT, low patience threshold. You have a very short fuse and get easily rattled by people and things. As soon as you get behind the wheel, it's as if another personality takes over and it's like sitting next to Adolf Hitler, the way you go on. Everybody on the road is an idiot, except you. You should listen to yourself some time.'

'Well, it's true. Most of the drivers on British roads are dangerous maniacs who should be locked up. I wonder sometimes how many of them ever passed the driving test. I've even seen one bloke driving on a busy road and reading a map at the same time. And my hackles go up when I get stuck behind a caravan or some doddering old geezer driving down the middle of a country road at twelve miles an hour with a ten-mile tailback behind him.'

She laughed. 'You never know. Perhaps it was a retired undertaker who thought he was heading a cortege. You'll be on about women drivers next.'

'Did you know that in Memphis there's an old by-law which stipulates that women drivers must be preceded by a man waving a red flag? You must admit that most women don't know their right from their left. Ever seen one trying to read a street atlas?'

'Don't get me on to that subject. Never, never ask me to read one in a car for you again, Billy. When the car's bouncing about and we're going through a strange town, you expect me to find the *A to Z* and direct you to the exact street within ten seconds flat or you get all prickly.'

'That's because you say something like "Turn left at the next junction" and then you point to the right. Anyway, you'll be relieved to know that I have no intention of driving in Ireland. I was thinking of a coach tour.'

He'd visited a travel agent's and seen a brochure showing two young-looking filmstar pensioners sitting in a luxurious coach, raising their glasses of Dom Perignon and beaming happy smiles.

'Now, that sounds really sensible,' Laura said. 'Let somebody else do all the work and the worrying.'

'Leave it to me, Laura. Tomorrow, I'll go into Didsbury and arrange it all. Pay off a few invoices and fix up a holiday.'

They'd finished the meal and, with apprehension, he waited for the waiter to return with the bill. It was even more than he'd feared. Judging by the size of it, he wondered if they thought he wanted to put in a bid for the place.

'Mercy!' he said, looking over the various charges.

'The French for thank you, m'sieu, is pronounced *mer-see,*' said the same supercilious waiter, still anxious to correct his accent.

'I didn't mean thank you,' Billy said, studying the bill and handing over his credit card.

'Shall I add the usual ten per cent for gratuities?' the waiter asked.

'Non, m'sieu, let's keep that particular section *blanc,*' Billy replied with a ringing nasal twang.

The total cost of the banquet was enough to feed an African family for a month and would have given Billy's old mam and dad heart failure if they'd still been alive. And what did the meals amount to? Fish and peas for Laura, meat and potato for him.

'Next time we'll go to the local chippie for a takeaway supper plus a bottle of plonk from the outdoor,' he said as they rose from the table.

'Didn't you leave a tip?' Laura asked anxiously.

'I did not. At the bottom of the bill, it says "Service not included" and I certainly go along with that, seeing how they made us wait. They're the ones called waiters but we were the ones who did the waiting. Anyway, time to go home – that is, if you don't mind sharing a taxi with Herr Adolf Schickelgruber.'

'*Ja, mein Fuehrer* she answered sweetly.

Chapter Three

Shopping

Monday morning, the beginning of the week, and Billy's first day of freedom. What a wonderful feeling when he woke up and realized that he didn't have to go rushing off to join the traffic jams to work. Instead he could have a leisurely breakfast and do a spot of shopping with Laura. The only problem was that he hated shopping. The low patience threshold (LPT) syndrome that Laura had spoken of applied to that as well as to his driving. Perhaps that should be qualified. When Billy said he hated shopping, he didn't mean *all* shopping. He didn't mind going round the supermarket with Laura because in some ways it was like a sociological study.

That morning, he picked up a trolley and began pushing it, or tried to, because as usual he got the one with the wobbly wheel and a will of its own and a determination to turn right when he wanted to go left. He enjoyed wandering along the aisles as Laura selected sundry items from the shelves. Whenever her back was turned, though, he seized the opportunity to include one or two things that took his fancy, like pitted green olives, cambozola cheese, white lump crabmeat, Häagen-Dazs ice cream, pressed cod roe and prawns. The trouble was that as he put them into the trolley, she put them back on the shelf. However, she didn't see the Supercook Chocolate Ice Cream Shaker that he hid behind the vegetables.

'Shopping with you,' she said, 'always costs twice as much as my regular bill. You pick out items I wouldn't buy in a month of Sundays.'

'I suppose you're right,' he said. 'It's probably a reaction to having spent so many years abroad going without luxuries.'

Being in a supermarket and seeing all the activity going on around him invariably got him speculating. He liked to watch the people as they went about the business of making their selections from the bewildering display of goods on the shelves. Choice! That was the operative word nowadays. Seemed it was necessary to have fifty kinds of this and fifty kinds of that to choose from. Supposed to improve the quality of life but all it did was cause confusion. It wasn't enough that shoppers were offered, say, a few varieties of coffee. Instead a whole range from across the world was put out on display. How different from those far-off childhood days in Collyhurst when a thing like coffee had been practically unknown and a cup made from a bottle of chicory Camp Coffee, the one with the picture of the bearded and kilted Scotsman sitting outside his tent, was considered very special and the height of luxury a sure sign that a family was thriving. Only a few families were so fortunate. Billy's family was seen as prosperous since his father was a porter in Manchester's Smithfield Market and was able to bring home a wide assortment of fresh fruit, vegetables, and fish. Especially fish. Haddock, cod, or plaice. Fish seemed to feature at every meal.

'Silver 'ake! That's where our Billy gets his brains from,' his mam claimed when he'd passed the scholarship to go to grammar school. She had one or two strange ideas like that on the benefits to be derived from various foods. Porridge for strength (she was influenced no doubt by the picture of the hammer-throwing Scotsman on the packet), stew to put a lining on your stomach, and crusts for curly hair.

But families who had the wherewithal to go to the corner shop and pay for their groceries were a rarity. Living on tick or 'putting it in the book' was an accepted way of life. Even that was beyond a family where the father was on the dole and relied on Public Assistance. Such didn't know where the next meal was coming from and the kids often went hungry.

Collyhurst people's poverty, however, was as nothing when compared to that of the peasants of Machakos in Kenya where Billy had worked for five years as a secondary school teacher. There, peasants couldn't afford to buy anything in a store and for survival depended entirely on the meagre food they were able to cultivate on their 'shambas'. When they first returned to Britain, both Laura and he found a visit to a supermarket a traumatic experience, seeing so many trolleys piled high with groceries and luxuries. Mentally, they were still in Africa, a waste-nothing Third World, and they had great difficulty adjusting to a society where there was so much extravagance and excess. When it came to choice in Kenya, the local store had only a limited selection of goods on offer and shoppers who could afford them considered themselves fortunate to get even those. New-laid eggs, for example, were like gold and when news went out on the grapevine that Suleman's Store had received a consignment, there was a mad scramble to be first in the queue. And, if you were lucky enough to buy half a dozen, somehow they tasted better than when there was a glut.

Billy shook off this reverie and looked round the supermarket – and what did he see? A bunch of harassed husbands following their wives like a lot of trained puppy dogs while she tripped along throwing stuff into the trolley that he was pushing, stuff that he was going to have to pay for and carry when they reached the check-out.

Laura navigated the way in and out of the aisles, with Billy in tow. They were held up a few times because of bottlenecks caused by some dreamy old couple not knowing where they were. Why can't trolleys, Billy wondered, be issued with bells or car horns so as to avoid collisions? They'd have proved useful that particular morning in the clash between two bull-headed ladies who got into a blazing row over who had right of way. Give a certain kind of woman a shopping cart, he mused, and she became one of Rommel's panzers.

'Would you mind backing up so I can get through?' the big-breasted lady with the peroxide hair snarled. Obviously a tank commander.

'Why should I?' snapped the other woman, threatening to charge with her heavily loaded cart. 'I was here first. You back up.'

The busty lady responded by ramming the other's vehicle and, had it not been for the intervention of a male assistant, there'd have been a nasty case of trolley rage.

There are some pretty weird people wandering around, Billy reflected; though maybe the other people consider us weird. What he found fascinating about people-watching was that in many ways it was like seeing a cavalcade of one's own life at its different stages. Here was a young couple with a bawling kid sitting up on the front of the trolley, just like their own situation not all that long ago. Over there was an old couple bent double and using the trolley not simply to carry their purchases but as support to keep themselves upright. That could be us in a few years' time, he thought. Then there was the sight of a forlorn figure of an old lady or a lonely old man shopping for one. That could be Laura or me in the not too distant future. Best not to think about it today, he told himself. It'll happen soon enough.

So, Billy didn't mind the supermarket. It was the other kind of shopping he loathed. The kind which brought him face to face with a stroppy assistant.

The day after the supermarket visit, Billy walked across to Didsbury village.

His first visit was to the local Happy Returns Travel Agency where he paid a deposit for a six-day coach tour round the south of Ireland with Wolfhound Coaches Limited. The staff there were friendly and welcoming, as was only to be expected; after all, he was handing them money.

As he went down Wilmslow Road, it began to drizzle, the sort of Manchester drizzle that soaked you through and through, and to make matters worse, he hadn't brought a mac. His next port of call was the bank, and irrational though it may seem, banks made him feel apprehensive. His nervousness went back to the early fifties. In those far-off days, when Laura and he were flat broke, he could never borrow money from them, not even for a worthwhile purpose. As a young married man and father of a baby son, he'd applied to his local bank on Stockport Road for a loan of £20 to pay his fees at Manchester University where he was studying for a degree as an evening student. The manager turned him down because he felt that Billy was not a good risk because he'd married too young.

'In our bank,' the manager had preached, 'we do not encourage our employees to marry until the age of twenty-five as we consider marriage before that to be improvident. As you married at twenty-two, I must reject your application.'

Billy had had to go cap in hand to Duncan, his father-in-law, for a loan. Something he hated doing.

And if they'd been overdrawn by a fiver, they used to get a letter charging them £15, money they didn't have. Now they were a bit better off, the banks were always wanting him to take out a loan. He could have a loan, it seemed, as long as he could prove he didn't need it. A bank's a place, he thought, that'll lend you an umbrella when the sun's shining but will want it back as soon as it starts raining.

This morning the business he had with the bank was a simple transfer of funds from Scotland to his current account in Manchester. His savings which had recently been augmented by his pension lump sum were deposited in a Glasgow bank, an account he'd opened when he'd worked at a teacher training college in Kilmarnock.

He joined the line to wait his turn. Queuing was a thing that the stoic British had learned during the war. Then whenever you saw a queue, you automatically joined it even if you didn't know what it was for. Anyway, in this bank, there were two lady tellers on duty, one young, pretty and smiling, the other middle-aged, sour and frosty-faced. Of course he got the latter.

'Yes, and what can we do for you?' she asked.

'I've written a cheque on the Clydesdale Bank and I'd like to transfer one thousand pounds to my current account here. I've completed a paying-in slip.'

'You can't do that,' she said immediately. 'You can't do it without your passport.'

'Why do I need my passport? I'm not going anywhere.'

'How do we know you are who you say you are?'

'Because I've been a customer of this bank and of this branch for nearly twenty years and you should know me by now.'

'I'm from head office and I don't know you.'

'That's the trouble with banks today,' he said. 'Too impersonal. Everything's done by computers and cash machines. You've lost the personal touch. When I was a young man, I had regular, sometimes weekly, contact with the bank manager and he was always asking to see me. He was concerned about me and he knew my face well. Anyway, you have my signature on file so you can check that.'

'How do we know you didn't find the Clydesdale chequebook in the street? We must have proof of identity. We must have your passport.'

'Not everyone has a passport and, anyway, I could have forged one, for all you know. There are a lot of crooks about nowadays, if we're to believe what the papers tell us.'

Billy realized he was beating his head against a brick wall and it was useless arguing. There was nothing for it but to go and get his passport. He was dealing with a cold, impersonal robot and there was no use fighting it. He strode out, quivering with rage. Speechless and pale with the effort of bottling it up, he tramped back home through the rain, mumbling incoherently to himself. God is testing me, he thought.

As he stormed through the house to fetch his passport, Laura sensed that something was wrong. Perhaps it was the white round the gills that gave the game away.

'What's happened?' she asked anxiously.

'Don't ask,' he seethed.

After a frantic search, Laura and he found the passport amongst insurance documents and other old records in the chocolate-biscuit tin labelled 'Important Papers'. There were even his old wartime papers, and he wondered if the teller might like to see those too.

He trudged back to the bank and once more joined the line and waited for attention. Without a word, he handed the passport over to Frosty-Face. She examined it to make sure it was genuine and not out of date, then finally accepted his Clydesdale cheque.

'I wonder if you might want to see these documents too?' he said witheringly as he handed them over, his identity card, ration book and sweet coupons.

'No need to be sarcastic,' she said. 'Anyway, the cheque won't be cleared for another five days,' she added with a glint of triumph in her eye.

Billy left the bank fuming. So, this is what retirement's all about, he thought. Maybe my poky little office back at the college wasn't so bad after all. But I really will have to watch it, he told himself, I'm becoming a crotchety old man.

His next errand was the chemist's and after his fracas at the bank he was not in the best of moods. He wanted only a few items but had to wait while the assistants dealt with a crowd of people clutching prescriptions. Billy had been suffering from blocked sinuses and Laura thought she might be coming down with a cold, so he wanted to buy a few things to relieve the symptoms. Patiently he hung around until a middle-aged female assistant was free to deal with his requirements.

'I'd like a large packet of blackcurrant-flavoured Beecham's powder, a large box of paracetamol capsules and a Sinex nasal spray.'

'I can't serve you with all them items together, luv,' she announced as if addressing the village idiot. Billy wondered if she was in some way related to the lady at the bank.

'Why not?'

'It's dangerous to take all those at once, luv.'

'I haven't the slightest intention of taking them

67

all together, but what if I were? That would be my own business. Besides, what's to stop me from getting the forbidden items at the other pharmacy round the corner?'

'No need to get shirty, luv,' she said menacingly. 'Anyway, I'll have to consult the pharmacist for his advice.' Billy liked the use of that word 'consult', as if she was a medical specialist of some kind.

By now, the verbal exchange had attracted the interest of the waiting prescription holders who were becoming excited at the prospect of a bit of theatre.

The assistant called up to the pharmacist who had his pill-dispensing laboratory three feet above floor level so that he could look down on the inferior mortals seeking his ministrations.

'Can this old chap here be served with Sinex, Beechams, and paracetamol all at the same time?' she asked loudly.

From his eyrie, the chemist inspected Billy over his pince-nez to check that he was not a junkie, a drug peddler, or a potential suicide. Reassured, he gave permission for the purchases. Reluctantly, the assistant handed over the drugs, obviously thinking she was dealing with a moron and so Billy pulled a simpleton's face, mouth open, tongue hanging out.

'We have to make sure, luv. In this business, we can't be too careful. You do understand that you're not supposed to take them all at once.'

Apart from anything else, Billy strongly objected to being addressed as 'luv', as he didn't know the woman from Adam, or Eve as the case may be. A foreigner hearing this term of endearment would have assumed that he and the assistant were intimate friends or lovers. 'Luv' was not the only term he hated, though. There were other expressions of assumed intimacy adopted by all manner of people. Words like 'mate' or 'chum' or 'pal' for example. He was amazed at how many of these close associates he appeared to have acquired lately. The window-cleaner called at the house and asked, 'Could I have a bucket of warm water, mate?' He took his car to be serviced and the mechanic said, 'Right, mate, leave it over there.' It seemed he was mate to a vast array of workers and shop assistants. Had these people forgotten how to address their customers courteously with expressions like, 'Good morning, sir. How can I help?'

Still in the pharmacy, he turned his attention to the optician's section of the shop to make his next purchase.

'I'd like to buy a pair of spectacles, strength one point five,' he told the young lady assistant, 'but I've looked all round the counter and I can't see them for looking.'

'That's why you need glasses, pop,' she smirked, looking round the shop for appreciation of her scintillating wit. As she handed over the specs, she repeated the slight. 'There you go, pop.'

Billy paid for the glasses and got out of the shop quickly, still smarting from that word 'pop'. What did she mean? Pop! Sure, I've got silver hair – it runs in my family, my dad had silver hair before he went bald – but it's going a bit far calling me 'pop'. The cheeky young madam!

He crossed the road, and saw reflected in a shop window a decrepit old codger hobbling along, shoulders hunched. Now there's a man who deserves the title 'pop', he thought. On taking a closer look, he saw that it was himself. What's happened to that 21-year-old Adonis I carry round in my head? he asked. When did this happen? I must have aged overnight like the portrait of Dorian Gray.

The experience worried him for the rest of the day and when he got home later he solved the problem by steering clear of mirrors, so avoiding sight of his own reflection. In the bathroom, they had a large six-foot mirror which did nothing for his self-esteem, and he made a mental note to remove it. When it came to shaving, he concentrated on the particular part of the face he was dealing with and studiously refrained from looking at the face as a whole because when he did, he was horrified to discover that it was his own father looking back at him. And not the young version either but the old man with the bloodshot eyes and the furrowed face.

Chapter Four

A Healthy Mind in a Healthy Body

When Laura heard about Billy's disagreeable shopping expedition, she became concerned.

'You're in danger of becoming an old fuddy-duddy,' she said.

'What, me? An old fuddy-duddy? Never!'

'Then forget about shopping as you seem to end up in disputes. You need to occupy all your new-found leisure hours. What happened to the big plans you talked about when we went out to dinner the other night? Like getting yourself fit and all that.'

Laura was right. As usual. He *had* been dragging his feet in the matter of embarking on a keep fit routine.

The very next day, he determined to do something about it. He put on his new tracksuit and, bubbling with enthusiasm, sprinted to the new sports centre which had recently opened in the district. It was known locally as 'Juvenal's Gym' because over the entrance was written the poet's well-known Latin inscription, *'Mens sana in corpore sano'* (A sound mind in a sound body). Inside, it boasted an impressive array of state-of-the-art equipment.

'It will cost you twenty-eight pounds a month, or a mere seven pounds a week,' the gym manager told him. 'Surely worth it for keeping fit and raising your self-esteem,' he added. Billy signed the membership form on the dotted line.

Of course his sons couldn't resist making cracks about his latest effort to hold back the oncoming tide of old age.

'You too can have a body like mine,' said John, his youngest.

'All you have to do is neglect it for fifty years,' added Mark.

'So, what happened, Dad?' asked Matthew 'Have you been looking at the Charles Atlas ads? Are you the skinny guy who had sand kicked in his face?'

'It's easy to make cheap remarks,' Billy replied. 'You wait till you see the results at the end of a year.'

At the fitness centre, he was allocated a young lady with Nordic features – blonde hair, bright blue eyes, trim figure. She was to be his personal trainer and coach.

'My job,' she said, 'is to design an individualized programme for you. You have a most interesting body type.' She smiled, giving him the once-over. He wondered what his particular body type was. Maybe kyphosis-lordosis with a suggestion of scoliosis thrown in, or in other words a stoopy-droopy posture. At first, it worried him that a physical fitness expert should find his body shape 'interesting' until he learned that trainers at this centre had had only three hours' instruction to become qualified.

The gym appeared to be crowded with lots of lusty, vigorous young people bursting with health and dressed in the latest athletic gear: young men with bulging muscles in vests and shorts; ladies in skimpy leotards displaying their curves. I'm going to like this, he said to himself, though the latter may prove something of a distraction. But at £7 a week, it'd be worth it, if only as spectator sport.

That first day he was introduced to the various machines that were going to get him fit and give him back his youth. The last time he'd seen instruments like this was in the dungeon of Warwick Castle. The equipment looked more appropriate for torturing sixteenth-century heretics than for promoting fitness. There was the treadmill, the rack, the body stretcher, and a piece of apparatus that seemed designed for drawing and quartering. Nevertheless, for the first couple of days, everything went fine.

Then he received his bill. It was from some loan shark company in the Midlands informing him that he now owed them £336 plus £72 interest and administration charges, giving a total of £408 which would be collected at £34 per month. The fitness centre had charged him a whole year's fees and collected it via a finance company. It sounded like a scam and he complained to the fitness centre boss, but to no avail. It was all shipshape and above board, he claimed. Billy was now committed for a whole year, whether he liked it or not. If that's the case, he thought, then in true Lancashire style I'm going to make sure I get my money's worth by attending every morning session and twice at the weekend. He worked so hard at the gym that he found that at the end of every session he couldn't move for an hour or two and every muscle in his body ached. Long hot soaks in Radox baths plus a surgical knee support were the only things that kept him going.

After a few weeks of this punishment, he became tired of running on a treadmill in a sweaty gymnasium and he realized that if he continued along these lines, he was going to end up as the healthiest man in Southern Cemetery. It was time to throw in the towel. What was the point of killing himself when he could work out by simply running round Hough End fields in God's own fresh air? He wrote off the balance of his subscription and vowed to steer clear of these torture chambers. Instead he would go back to his two other loves – tennis and cycling.

He bought a new Kettler bike – regretfully German but there didn't seem to be any British bikes of good quality. This machine, which cost him £500, was the Rolls-Royce of bikes, with its own shock absorbers and the latest accessories. He started a routine of cycling round the district every day. Bloody dangerous, he found. You take your life in your hands every time you venture forth in a town like Manchester, he realized, and he was lucky not to get himself killed in the first week. Motorists, damn their eyes, allowed the cyclist about one inch of space when overtaking and his signals were completely ignored. He was invisible to them and in the end he had to buy a fluorescent reflective vest. He didn't wear a helmet and was thinking of investing in one until he read a research report that claimed that drivers gave helmet-less cyclists a much wider berth, judging them to be more stupid than their helmeted brethren. That didn't stop stationary motorists though from swinging their doors open without warning and it took all his forty years' cycling experience to avoid being knocked for six. Turning right was only slightly less hazardous than jumping out of an aeroplane without a parachute and he found it best to dismount and cross on foot. He read that in cities like Amsterdam, traffic arrangements were designed wholly for the welfare and safety of the cyclist. We could learn a lot from them, he reflected.

Each morning when he went out on the bike he noted that ninety per cent of private cars were occupied by a single person who believed that being surrounded by a lump of metal and being propelled by a mechanical device gave him or her a God-given right over the rest of mankind. And that was saying nothing about the fact that the average motorist contributed to the warming of the planet by pumping out thirty tons of carbon into the atmosphere. A Martian visiting Manchester during a morning rush hour would have been forgiven for concluding that the healthy minority of humanoids got about the place in the upright position by employing their limbs in a piston-like fashion while the sick majority were crustaceans seated in protective aluminium shells and could only achieve locomotion by means of a combustion engine.

It was a different kettle of fish, though, when Billy was out in his car and if there was one class of road-user that really got his goat, it was the bloke on the bike, especially the one in a blindingly psychedelic jacket. He wobbles around like

75

a drunk coming out of a pub on a Saturday night, he inwardly cursed, and he doesn't see the need for signals and thinks traffic lights are a leftover from the Christmas decorations. On the rare occasion when the biker stops on red, he occasionally maintains his balance by holding on to the roof of my car. I usually shake my fist at him and sound my horn and that makes him jump all right. The cyclist doesn't consider himself as part of normal traffic and he thinks that permits him to ignore road junctions, road signs and zebra crossings. Naïve pedestrians believe themselves safe by avoiding the main road. The poor, misguided devils! They've forgotten about the cycling lunatics who mount the pavement and pedal at breakneck speed at helpless old ladies who have to leap into the nearest garden hedge to escape being mowed down. There should be a law banning such psychopathic morons or, failing that, heavy taxation on all push bikers. Why should they get away scot-free? After all, they're making use of the roads and highways like everyone else. There'd be exemptions for pensioners like me of course, he reasoned.

Sadly Billy's cycling career on the Kettler did not last long. He was out shopping one day and had loaded up the front basket with groceries, including three bottles of red wine which had been on special offer. As he approached the local pharmacy, he raised his right leg to execute a wide arc to deck off. He considered himself to be still pretty fit. Unfortunately, the crotch of his tracksuit bottoms caught on the saddle and he found himself helplessly trapped as the bike keeled over and he hit the pavement with a crash. He didn't make a sound but several lady bystanders squealed and shopkeepers came running out to his aid.

'Are you all right?' they asked.

'Would you like to come into the shop and sit down? Have a glass of water?'

'I'm OK,' he assured everyone, but he knew he'd damaged something. His left arm and shoulder were out of action.

'Poor old bugger. They shouldn't be allowed on bikes,' he heard someone say, and that remark hurt more than the physical pain in his shoulder. Everyone put the accident down to age, which annoyed him. It was the sort of thing that could have happened to anyone, even a twenty-year-old. That put paid to the Kettler which was a 'gent's bike' with a crossbar. But it didn't stop him cycling. He bought a 'ladies' bike' which was easier to mount and dismount. He gave the German machine to eldest son Matthew who found daily use for it in that bicycle metropolis, Oxford.

Though he'd slightly injured his left arm, there was nothing wrong with his right and so, despite the accident, he continued to play tennis. He used to play a lot in Kenya and, although he never actually won any competitions, cups or anything like that, he thought he'd been pretty good. People talked about his whip forehand when he would stab the ball with such force that it whizzed across the net and was virtually unplayable. Sometimes, the ball was in the court. But his particular forte was his wind-up shot. He revolved his arm round and round like a windmill before imparting the accumulated force to the ball. Opponents cringed (and inexplicably so did his partner) when they saw it coming and were reduced to quivering jelly.

He had managed to fix up a regular Thursday afternoon game with his three old school chums, Titch, Oscar, and Nobby, even though they were not in the same league as those he was accustomed to playing with abroad and they didn't always appreciate how lucky they were that he'd agreed to play with them. After all, had he not once been on the Marangu Fifth team that played all over the colony (as Kenya then was)? Admittedly only as a reserve to be called on when they were stuck.

For a start, his three companions wore glasses. From their very first encounter they were constantly questioning his decisions whenever he called the ball in or out.

'You can't be serious,' he exclaimed, stealing John McEnroe's favourite expression. 'That was clearly out. After all, I'm the only one here with twenty-twenty vision and not wearing glasses.'

'Doesn't matter,' they said, 'you're outvoted. Besides, you're the only one here that *needs* glasses.'

Oscar had a really despicable tennis court habit. This was his tendency to mis-hit the ball with the handle, sending it spinning out of control but in the court. He would break out into high-pitched, maniacal laughter each time it happened. Oscar didn't take things seriously and obviously thought it was some kind of game. As for Oscar's partner, Nobby, he was insufferable. No matter how hard Billy delivered his whip forehand, Nobby returned it with a lob a hundred feet in the air. Infuriating! 'Lobby Nobby' they called him. An overhead smash would have put paid to his pathetic little game but Billy had never mastered that particular shot.

As for the normally placid Titch, *he* became a bad-tempered bastard once he got onto a tennis court. Although he'd taken up the game late in life after retirement, he nevertheless fancied his chances and imagined he was invincible. If he lost, which he often did, he invariably blamed it on Billy, his partner, with a flow of comments like: 'Tut. Tut. Tut. I may as well be playing on my own here' or 'Dear, dear me. That was hopeless. You were meant to go for that, Billy', etc., etc. It was this barracking of every point Billy went for (or didn't go for) that made him nervous and affected his game. Titch went too far one day and Billy stalked off the court in disgust.

'No one is going to talk to me like that, Titch. You can insult my wife and my kids but not my tennis!'

The others had to persuade him to go back on but it made matters worse, for now Titch remained shtum, no matter what errors Billy made. 'I didn't say a word,' he'd protest, his face a picture of innocence. He didn't have to – his expression was enough. Billy preferred his tutting. But that wasn't the only loathsome thing about him. When Oscar fired over one of his weird corkscrewed mishits, Titch invariably missed it and then stepped to one side and called out, 'Yours, Billy!'

Not long after Billy's bicycle accident, Nobby turned up and said he'd have to cry off as he'd twisted his ankle on a broken pavement. Not to be outdone, Titch replied, 'That evens things up then, as I have athlete's foot.' Oscar had to add his two cents' worth and complained that he'd been to a really good party the night before and was still groggy after numerous G and Ts. Billy reminded them of his fall from the bike but they pooh-poohed it.

'You hurt your left shoulder,' Oscar sneered, 'but since you're right-handed it doesn't affect your game. So stop moaning and get on with it.'

Despite their various infirmities, they played on, even though Billy could only serve underarm. Nobby was made to strap up his ankle and persevere. Titch and Billy played on Nobby mercilessly, knowing he could only hobble about, while Oscar was seeing two of everything. Billy had problems with his paralysed shoulder and missed a couple of sitters but that didn't stop Titch from subjecting him to a constant flow of 'tut-tuts'. Titch and Billy managed to win but only by a narrow margin. There was no quarter given in love, war and tennis.

As he lay luxuriating in his Radox bath afterwards, Billy thought how lucky he'd been that his fall from the bike had been on his left side. At least he could still play his tennis though the underarm serve was a definite weakness in his game.

Then God decided to play him a dirty trick by handicapping his right arm. Laura's sister Katie had moved to Freshfield, outside Southport, with her husband, Stuart, and Billy had agreed to help them settle in their new home by doing a few odd jobs, like painting, decorating and putting up shelves. Laura had opted to stay home that day in Manchester as she had a number of chores to attend to. He got to Freshfield all right and did his stint of helping out. It was on the way back that it happened. He decided to return via Liverpool Lime Street, and had to change stations at Moorfields, an underground station almost as deep as any on the London tube. Unfortunately the escalators had broken down and he had to descend by foot, carrying his tool kit. He managed to negotiate the first set of stairs without any problem but the second flight was steep and vertiginous, and he had to tread very warily. He had got halfway down when a young lady behind him asked, 'Are you all right, darling? May I help you with that case?'

Billy swivelled his head round to look at her and said, 'That's kind of you. But no, thank you, I can manage.'

He turned to continue his descent. And that was it. He tumbled down the rest of the way, head over heels, with his toolcase following behind. Oh no, not again, he mumbled to himself as he keeled over.

For a short while there was pandemonium and several people at the foot of the stairs came running to his aid.

I seem to be making this toppling-over business a habit, he reflected as he lay there. The young lady was distraught when she saw the result of her kind offer. She took charge of his tool kit and helped him into Lime Street station where she insisted that he go to Boots for first-aid treatment. The gash on his right hand was bleeding profusely and his right forearm had been badly bruised. The lady, whose name turned out to be Veronica, gave him her address, bought him coffee and organized a special trolley to take him to his train. Leaving him with his coffee behind Boots's counter, Veronica rushed off to catch her train. She was on her way, she told him, to attend a conference in Birmingham on the subject of health and safety.

When he finally got back to Manchester, his family wondered if he could be trusted out on his own. That of course was nonsense for it was the kind of mishap that could've happened to anyone.

'People are too quick to assume that if I have an accident, it's because of my age,' he protested. 'Besides,' he added, 'that escalator was stopped at a queer angle.'

'You could consider suing the station authority,' his son Mark commented, 'but I don't think you'd have a leg to stand on.'

'Huh, funny,' Billy replied.

The one long-term effect that concerned him most was that his tennis days were over for the foreseeable future. Now he couldn't even serve underarm or return the ball. He was sure his three companions would have been only too pleased to take him on now that his formidable whip forehand had been neutralized.

So much for retirement, he thought. Up to now, it's been one thing after another. Fallen twice, almost paralysed by over-exercise, and if I go on like this it won't be long before I'm on crutches. It was safer in my little cubbyhole at college. I really will have to look around for activities that don't raise my blood pressure or threaten to kill me with exhaustion. Meanwhile, how he looked forward to the coach holiday in Ireland.

Chapter Five

Round Ireland in a Tin Can

Billy was no good in the mornings. Come to think of it, he was no good in the afternoons and evenings either. But when he woke up, he was never in the best of moods and he liked to come to consciousness gradually, one eyelid at a time. For this coach holiday in Ireland, however, they had to be up at the crack of dawn. So he shook off his moroseness and got on with his packing, Laura having completed hers a week ago.

'What clothes should I pack for Ireland in August?' he asked

'Everything,' she said, 'but especially a mac.'

They dressed quickly in their smartest holiday gear and closed up their suitcases. As they were about to leave the house, Laura noticed that Billy had sprouted one or two errant hairs in his nose and ears and had developed eyebrows that rivalled Denis Healey's. There was nothing for it but to give him a final trim before setting out.

'We can't have you looking like an old man on this trip,' she said.

They took a taxi to Lower Mosley Street bus station where they boarded a minibus waiting to take them to a central joining point in Rainhill in Lancashire. They had been travelling about half an hour and were well on their way when Laura turned to him and said, 'Who will water the plants while we're away?'

'Laura, we're only away for a week and I think the plants will survive somehow.'

'And I think I may have left a pan of water boiling on the stove. It'll dry up and the place will fill with smoke. Can you remember? Did you see me turn it off or perhaps *you* turned it off?'

'Not a chance, Laura. You know I'm not allowed to meddle in the kitchen.'

'Then the pan'll burst into flames and the whole place'll burn down.'

'So we can look forward to coming back to find the house gutted or blown to smithereens. Not to worry though 'cos it's fully insured. Wait a minute. Did I renew the insurance? I forget.'

He received a sharp dig in the ribs for his pains.

At the assembly park, they found an impressive collection of around thirty buses ready to take their passengers to all points of the compass, to far-flung destinations in Britain and across Europe. It took them a little time to locate their coach but eventually they recognized it by the large notice stuck on the front window informing the world at large that this coach would be visiting Cork and Blarney Castle.

A young Irishman greeted them with a friendly smile.

'Good morning. I'm Colin Murphy and I'm going to be your driver and tour guide for the next seven days. Welcome aboard. I'll put your suitcases in the luggage compartment.'

They climbed onto the coach and were taken aback when they saw that the bus was already full and the only place available was a bench seat at the back. The bus had been designed to give maximum discomfort. Friends had warned them to avoid this particular seat.

'You'll be thrown around like the inside of a cocktail shaker,' they said.

As they made their way to the rear, giving friendly nods to their fellow passengers, one thing became patently obvious. This was no trip for the under-thirties seeking sea, sand and sex because the coach was packed to the gunnels with silver-headed seniors and there was a powerful pong of Sloan's Liniment and Vick's VapoRub. The two old girls in the seat immediately in front of them looked like a pair of nonagenarian twins out on licence from an Eastbourne nursing home.

'At least we'll have plenty of room,' he said to Laura in consolation. 'This seat can accommodate at least three so we should be able to stretch out.'

Then the last two passengers joined the coach. The two old codgers that wheezed up the aisle could not have been more dissimilar. One look at them and Billy realized that God had a subtle sense of humour after all. They were straight out of a Bertram Mills circus. Little and Large weren't in it. The thin one was a long streak of melancholy while his corpulent companion who seemed to have a clownish smile permanently etched on his features was a mountain of blubber. His shape – or lack of it – was reminiscent of the great glutinous blob in the Quatermass Experiment. And what's more, he was heading straight for Billy. He plonked himself down, right next to him. Politely

85

Billy hoisted up to make room and that was the last time he took a normal breath for the rest of the trip.

'I'm Stanley,' the skinny one said, 'and this is my brother Oliver.'

'Pleased to meet you,' Laura and Billy chorused.

Stanley and Oliver! Billy thought. Their parents must have been aficionados of the comic pair and named their sons after them.

The journey began on time at 10 a.m. and they were soon bowling along the M62 towards Holyhead where they were to board the three o'clock ferry to Dun Laoghaire. Through the PA system, Colin played the music of the thirties and forties, interspersed with nursing-home top ten favourites, like 'Dolly Gray', 'Lily of Laguna', and 'Nellie Dean'. Most of the passengers knew the lyrics by heart and sang out in their cracked voices.

'It looks as if things are going to go smoothly and on time,' Laura remarked. 'I hope you're not too uncomfortable there.'

'At the moment I'm squashed between Charybdis and Scylla but when I learn to survive without oxygen, I'll be fine,' he panted. 'At the speed we're travelling, though, it shouldn't be too long before we're in Holyhead.'

He spoke too soon because twenty minutes into the journey, they were overtaken by a police car signalling them to turn off at the Burtonwood service station which they were approaching.

'No need to worry, folks,' Colin called out cheerfully through his microphone. 'The traffic people simply want to carry out a routine check to make sure we're roadworthy, that's all. Shouldn't take too long.'

They pulled in at the section reserved for heavy vehicles and joined a line of buses awaiting inspection.

'You could give the old legs a stretch out here, if you like,' Colin continued.

It was only then that Billy came to full realization of just how old and decrepit his fellow wrinklies were. As they struggled to their feet, there was wheezing and creaking of joints. 'It's your knees what go first,' remarked a white-haired gentleman loudly to the other passengers who nodded and murmured in agreement. Meanwhile Oliver took out a hip flask of whisky and began guzzling.

'I only drink to forget I'm an alcoholic and to make people more interesting,' he explained.

'The inspection usually takes about an hour,' said the lugubrious Stanley. 'This is my fourth coach trip this year, so I should know.'

'Is it always Ireland you visit?' Billy asked.

'No, we go to different places. Maybe England, maybe the continent. We change about according to what takes our fancy.'

'Or what fancies he can take,' his brother smirked between tipples of Scotch. 'He collects souvenirs, you see.'

'That's interesting,' Laura said. 'I like collecting mementos of places visited. I hope to get one or two on this trip.'

'And so do I!' Stanley added, winking at his brother.

By this time, the bus had emptied and they were

able to join the other passengers who were sitting disconsolately on a low wall a few yards away. The evacuation had taken twenty-five minutes.

Stanley's estimate proved to be accurate as the police mechanics checked the electrical system, ignition, brakes, tyre pressures, windows and door security. The coach was given a clean bill of health but they were now one hour behind schedule and to make up for lost time Colin had to put his foot down. Before long they were in North Wales.

'Hold on to your hats, folks,' he said as they whizzed along the A55.

They made the three o'clock ferry but only just.

They drove straight onto the boat and into the lower deck parking bay.

'The crossing will take about three hours,' Colin told them. 'We should be in Dun Laoghaire about six o'clock. You must be back on this bus by half past five at the latest so that we can make a quick getaway. We're not allowed to linger and all vehicles have to leave in strict order. Remember where we are. B Deck.'

More wheezing, more creaking as they disembarked.

It was a smooth crossing and Billy relished being released from the crushing weight of his Brobdingnagian fellow traveller and the opportunity to stretch his limbs. Laura and he utilized the three-hour voyage enjoying tea and buns in the cavernous refreshment hall, circumnavigating the decks, standing at the ship's rail to breathe in the ozone, and gazing meditatively into the grey waters of the Irish Sea.

Promptly at five thirty they descended into the

bowels of the ship to find their bus and were relieved to find that by five fifty-five, their coach was ready to disembark. Shortly after that Colin drove off the ferry and up the long ramp to the main road where they halted for a final roster before setting off to their first night's accommodation, the Wild Geese Hotel.

It was discovered that the two old ladies were missing.

'Oh, my God!' Colin exclaimed. 'They must still be on the boat. They could be anywhere. I'll have to go back and organize a search party.'

There was an audible sigh as they realized that they were to be held up yet again. To make matters worse, it was raining. Nothing unusual in that, Billy thought. Not in Ireland. After all, how had it come to earn the title, the 'Emerald Isle'?

Colin came back after half an hour. 'We can do nothing now but wait. It's a very big boat and this may take some time.'

'Perhaps they've fallen overboard,' someone offered.

'Maybe they jumped or were pushed overboard,' Stanley suggested mournfully.

A little while later, the sirens of two Irish police cars were heard as the Garda arrived on the scene. One car drove straight onto the boat to investigate while the other parked next to their coach. Two officers came onto the bus and began questioning everyone as in an Agatha Christie thriller.

'Did anyone see the two old ladies? When and where did you last see them? Did they seem happy or depressed? Was there any talk about jumping overboard?' Billy looked around for Colonel Mustard and Miss Scarlett and the other characters.

No one could shed any light on the subject, though one passenger reported that the two old ladies had complained they were on the wrong bus and had been hoping to go on a pilgrimage to Knock instead of Cork, but the two places sounded so much like each other. 'Cork – Knock,' Billy whispered to himself. 'How could they get those two names mixed up?'

'Fancy wanting to spend your holiday on a pilgrimage,'

Stanley commented.

'Don't knock it!' Billy said.

Laura resisted the temptation to fall in the aisle helpless with laughter. Instead, she said. 'Did I ever tell you that you're corny?'

'Yes, every day since we married thirty-three years ago.'

Time dragged by. The hour turned into two. Then three.

'Ah, the poor old buggers,' Stanley said to his brother. 'Who'd have thought that two nice old ladies would have made a suicide pact because they'd got on the wrong bus?'

His brother didn't answer – he was too busy knocking back the duty-free Jameson's he'd bought on board.

Then the first police car emerged from the ship with the two old biddies sitting beside a cop at the back.

'They'd fallen asleep in a remote part of the boat,' an officer explained.

Shamefacedly, the two old dears returned to their places.

Outside, the police officers could be heard talking to Colin, their driver.

'You've got a right lot this time, Colin. Where in God's name did you get them?'

'Most of 'em look as if they've got one foot in the grave,' added his companion. 'Maybe you should just drive them straight to the knacker's yard at Glasnevin Cemetery and have done with it.'

'Ah, hah. But I'd be out of a work then, wouldn't I?' said their driver. 'I've found in this job you've got to be forever on the alert with old fogies like this. You never know what they'll get up to next. Anyway, thanks again, lads!'

Colin got back in the bus and they set off again. He ignored the officer's cemetery suggestion and drove them to their three-star accommodation just outside Bray. From the way the manageress Moira Maguire and Colin exchanged osculatory greetings, it was evident that their arrangement was more than a business one.

'Kissy-kissy kickbacks,' Stanley said with a wink.

'How do you mean?' Laura asked.

'Colin's reward for bringing the coach party here. Sometimes it's money; sometimes it's honey, like now.'

Despite the warm welcome accorded to Colin, they found they'd arrived too late for supper and had to make do with sandwiches which the kitchen staff very kindly made up. At least they could get a good night's sleep, they thought, so as to be ready for an early start the next day. But they hadn't reckoned on the ceilidh which was being celebrated in the bar below. As they were about to drop off, the fiddles struck up, accompanied by the thump-thumpety-thump of the bodhrán, penny whistles, and foot stamping.

'Beautiful fiddling,' Billy remarked. 'But when does that di dilly-i dum dum stop?'

In the early hours was the answer. Not a good start to their holiday.

Next morning at six o'clock sharp, they were roused from slumber by early morning telephone calls arranged by Colin, their solicitous warder. With much bitching and bellyaching, the company went down to a breakfast of bacon and eggs. This was one meal the Irish did not stint on. The rashers were big enough to feed a gang of hungry navvies.

'Come on, folks,' Colin said, ushering the stragglers along. 'No need to hang around here all morning. We've a long way to go today. We've to make Midleton by four o'clock.'

'This is supposed to be a holiday,' Billy muttered to Laura. 'If I'd wanted this hurry-hurry kind of pressure, we could have stayed home.'

It was still drizzling when they re-mounted their coach an hour later. Billy returned to his place between the two brothers.

'That stay was short and sweet,' Laura remarked. 'We hardly had time to catch our breath.'

'Breath! Don't talk to me about breath!' Billy gasped from his pinioned position.

'I really enjoyed the stay at that hotel,' Stanley declared. 'I got a lot out of it.'

'How do you mean?' Laura asked. 'Did you

take the soap, shampoos, and hair conditioner? I sometimes help myself to those. They're free and all part of the service.'

'No,' Stanley replied. 'I mean these.'

So saying, he produced three ashtrays and four coat hangers, all marked Wild Geese Hotel.

'That's his little hobby,' his brother explained. 'Now mine is to be found at the first stop after lunch between Youghal and Cork.'

At eleven o'clock they stopped at a roadside cafeteria for coffee and a visit to a craft centre.

'More kickback,' Stanley whispered. 'It's a racket.'

'I think you'll find Arklow interesting,' Colin told them, 'and you'll be able to buy good souvenirs at the shop. The place is famous for its knitted woollen jerseys worn by the fishermen.' Then with a broad grin, he added, 'By law, English tourists must buy a minimum of two, of which at least one must be green. You'll be checked at the docks and won't be allowed to leave the country unless you have the documentation for them.'

'I notice you never wear green, Colin,' Billy remarked as he disembarked. 'Why is that?'

'Reminds me too much of seven hundred years of national tragedies and also our Irish soccer teams.' Giving Billy a wink through the rear-view mirror, he said. 'Not only that, it doesn't suit my skin colour. Anyway, we'll be here in Arklow for forty-five minutes.'

It sounded like a reasonable enough time to order coffee and have a look round the shop but he'd not taken account of the time needed to unload and reload the passengers. This left them about ten minutes in the establishment. Billy thought this might be his big chance to change seats. After all, no one had actually reserved particular places. He nipped back onto the bus and took a seat about halfway down. It wasn't long before he heard the now-familiar, 'Time to get back on the bus! No dawdling!' from Colin who was beginning to sound like Lewis Carroll's White Rabbit with his 'No time! No time!' as he rushed around the shop gathering in the strays.

Billy sat defiantly in his new seat and awaited the consequences. It didn't take long. Two minutes later, a big, burly man with a menacing smile placed a callused hand the size of a shovel on his shoulder.

'You wouldn't by any chance have taken my seat by accident?' he said.

'Why is it your seat?' Billy protested. 'Did you reserve it or pay a special fee for it? Is it a family heirloom, or what?'

'I want no arguments,' the man said, tightening his grip on Billy's shoulder. 'You'll either get out of my seat or I'll break your face.'

At this point, Colin intervened to prevent a murder. Billy's.

'Please return to your own seat,' he admonished, 'before someone gets hurt.'

Reluctantly Billy got up and went to his place at the back. He still wasn't happy. 'By what right does anyone lay claim to a specific seat? No one told me you could reserve a particular place.'

'It's a case of first come, first served,' Colin replied. 'However, in the interests of justice, we'll have democratic choice.' He addressed the pass-

94

engers. 'Raise your hand anyone who wants the back seat.'

No one did.

'Next, hands up all those who would like to change their seats.'

Everyone did, except the old lady sitting immediately behind him.

'In that case,' Colin said, 'you'll all stop where you are. I'm not going to spend the rest of this tour trying to satisfy everyone's requirements.'

Billy had to resign himself to his place in the human vice. It'd been worth the try, though.

As they set off for the next leg of their journey, he said to Laura, 'When you consider how long it takes to debus, the best seat is the one just behind the driver at the front. The occupant is first off and last one back on.'

The seat he was referring to had been taken by a toothless old crone who at that moment was engaging Colin in earnest conversation, handing him handfuls of peanuts as she did so.

'That's very kind of you, Bridget,' said Colin. 'It's nice to have something to chew on during these long journeys. Helps to relieve the boredom.'

'So glad you like 'em,' the old dear rejoined. 'Here, have some more.'

For the next hour or so, she continued to ply Colin with what seemed like an endless supply of nuts.

Eventually, Colin felt he'd eaten enough.

'I won't have any more,' he said. 'I must have eaten about fifty peanuts already. But why don't you eat them yourself?'

The old lady rewarded him with a gummy smile. 'Shure I can't chew 'em 'cos I forgot to bring me teeth,' she croaked.

'Then why buy 'em?' he asked.

'Ah, I just loves to suck the chocolate offa dem,' she replied.

Appropriately for an Irishman, Colin turned green and for the rest of the two-hour journey was strangely quiet.

The man with the big hands decided to start a game of bingo and came round handing out cards. Laura and Billy had never played it in their lives and this wasn't the time to start, especially as they were passing through the most beautiful countryside. So they turned down the offer to join in. They couldn't see the point in spending so much money on a coach tour if they were going to spend it with their eyes glued down on a piece of paper crossing off numbers.

'Shure, it'll help kill the time,' said an elderly lady.

Lunch was celebrated at Kathleen's Cottage just outside Wexford. The company sat at four long tables, twelve to a table. Laura and Billy sat opposite their two companions, with the two frustrated Knock pilgrims next to them. In the few hours sitting on the coach, everyone had worked up a good appetite and when the starter course of Blarney Salad described on the menu as 'crisp lettuce leaves and crunchy pan-fried black pudding pieces topped with a soft egg mayonnaise' arrived, everyone tucked in heartily. Stanley and Oliver in particular ate ravenously, smacking their lips and even licking and sucking the prongs of their forks so as to savour every last morsel. The first course finished, everyone helped the waitress by passing down their plates and cutlery to the head of the table where they were stacked up neatly ready for collection. They looked forward to the main course described as 'delicious meat balls flavoured with onion and garlic, cooked in a thick tomato sauce with cabbage and potato wedges'.

'No, no,' the young waitress said when she saw the plates piled up. 'You weren't supposed to pass them down. You'll need to keep everything for the next course.'

The plates and cutlery were quickly passed back down the table but nobody was sure which items had been theirs. Laura and Billy suddenly lost their appetites and decided not to have the main course after all. The two brothers, however, did not seem fazed by the mix-up and ate not only their own food but theirs too. The ice-cream dessert, though, was a different matter as they were given fresh crockery and a clean spoon.

'Well, I didn't think much of those arrangements,' Billy remarked to Stanley on the way out. 'Why on earth did Colin choose such a dump? No, don't tell me. Kickbacks?'

'Dead right,' he replied, 'and from Kathleen herself. It happens on most coach tours. It's the only way the driver can make a decent living.'

Everyone processed back onto the bus and a couple of hours later they passed through an idyllic landscape in a beautiful rural setting. They turned off the main road into what looked like an industrial estate. Now they saw what Oliver had been getting at when he spoke of his own little hobby because they found themselves in the middle of an alcoholic's dream. This was Midleton, the location of Ireland's largest distillery.

'For me,' Oliver said reverentially, 'this is the little part of heaven that fell out of the sky one day. This place produces Ireland's finest whiskeys: Jameson, Power, Paddy and Tullamore Dew. "Give every man his Dew" is the advertising slogan.'

'We shall be stopping here for one hour and then we must leave on time. Stragglers will be left behind,' Colin informed the company.

Once again, he hadn't allowed for the off-and-on routine. There wasn't nearly enough time to look round, considering how complex the plant was, and they had to content themselves with the brief summary given by the general manager. He was in the middle of a sentence explaining the difference between Irish and Scottish whiskeys when Colin interrupted. 'Sorry, folks. No time now. Everybody back on the bus if we're to make the hotel at a reasonable hour.'

Everyone duly obeyed and settled back in the coach only to discover that Oliver was missing. Alarmed, Stanley alerted the driver. 'We'll wait a quarter of an hour and then we must go.' The fifteen minutes passed and Colin said, 'That's it. We've got to leave. He'll have to find his own way to Cork. He shouldn't have a problem as it's not too far and there's a local bus service.'

They checked in at the Ned Kelly Retreat in Cork and settled in for the night. The room was small but comfortable with its own tiny en suite bathroom. No doubt Stanley will stock up with free toiletries, they thought.

The hotel was nothing to write home about so they didn't. This time there was no ceilidh, thank the Lord, and they had a restful night after a couple of nightcaps in the bar. It was there that they saw how kind, conscientious and popular Colin, their driver, was. He seemed to know everybody in the hotels across Ireland. Billy offered to buy him a drink but he turned it down.

'Thanks a million,' he said, 'but I must say no. You see, I took the pledge when I was a young-ster. Anyway, it wouldn't do if your driver was caught drinkin'.'

Billy had to admit he had a point. The same considerations did not apply to a red-faced farmer who was putting it away like nobody's business.

'Now, Declan,' said Colin addressing him. 'I think you've had enough for tonight. You'll never get up for work tomorrow the way you're going on. I hope you're not thinking of driving home, the state you're in.'

'And why not?' Farmer Declan said. 'I have a special button on the dashboard marked "drunk driving". I have only to pull that and the car drives itself back.'

'And then you'll lose your licence, Declan,' Colin told him. 'Look, drink up and I'll drive you back.'

'That is very kind of you, Colin,' Declan splut-tered. 'But then how will you get back to the hotel yourself?'

'It's a lovely night so I'll walk back. It's only a couple of miles.'

'You'll do no such thing, Colin. I won't hear of it. I'll drive you back.'

As Colin said to Billy later, 'You couldn't make 'em up.'

Next morning, the travellers were free to explore the picture-postcard town of Cork. It was still raining but Billy didn't mind one bit as it meant a day off from the human clamp on the back seat and that was sufficient reward for him. Cork brought back memories of the summer holidays in 1948 when he and his good friend and fellow teacher at St Anselm's School had embarked on a cycling holiday round Ireland. They had 'cycled' from Dublin to Cork in just two hours and when they told the drinkers at the bar of their incredible achievement, they were treated to free pints of porter. Billy omitted to tell the barflies that they had picked up a lift outside Dublin for themselves and their bikes and had roared down the road at ninety miles an hour. Billy now showed Laura the places he and Alex had visited all those years ago: the numerous boarding houses named after saints and their despair at not being able to find anything despite going through the litany of the saints; the famous Skiddy Almshouse; and the beautiful St Finbar's Cathedral with its twin spires.

They got back to their hotel late that evening but there was still no sign of Oliver. Stanley had become truly worried though he still found time to show them the pair of luxurious bath towels he'd filched.

Next morning, Oliver turned up as they were about to set off for Mizen Head, the most south-westerly point on the Atlantic Ocean. He looked haggard, his clothes and hair unkempt and he had a bandage round his left hand.

'I became distracted,' he explained. 'When we went into that distillery, I thought I'd died and gone to paradise. After you'd all gone, I was taken on a tour of all the departments, malting, mashing, fermentation and distilling, and I sampled each of their famous whiskeys. At the end I bought a gift set of each one of them.'

'And what's with the bandage round your hand?' Billy asked.

'As I was coming out of the last distillery, some idiot stood on my hand. Anyway, I missed the last bus into Cork and had to sleep in a bus shelter. I caught the first bus out this morning.'

The journey to Mizen Head was a long one and Oliver soon fell asleep, snoring loudly and with his head on Billy's shoulder. As the coach bounced around, Oliver's head gradually slid down Billy's body till his face was precariously close to his crotch. If it slides any further, he thought, I'll thump him.

They drove on and came to the most dangerous leg of the journey. The roads through the mountains had not been designed to take modern coaches and were much too narrow. This section of the tour took them along a series of sharp hairpin bends with precipitous cliffs to their left. In order to get round the worst bends, Colin had to reverse ever so gently to avoid backing into a ravine and then edge forward gingerly to complete the turn.

'This is good practice,' he laughed, 'for when I take my driving test next week.'

He was joking of course. Or was he?

Colin also judged it to be the ideal time to sing Irish ballads and make wisecracks about death and mortality.

'I hope you've all made your wills and taken out accident insurance,' he guffawed as he negotiated a blind bend on the brink of a vertical drop with a panoramic view of the surrounding hills.

Nobody appreciated his humour.

Several passengers took out rosary beads, and the shrieks of the elderly twins, 'God help us, he's going to kill us all,' did nothing to boost their confidence. Billy's screams didn't help either.

'Now, aren't you glad you decided not to drive?' whispered Laura by his side.

She never misses a chance to put me in my place, he thought, which is in the wrong. But this time he had to agree.

As they descended from the vertiginous ride through the mountains, they were treated to a view of the lush green countryside. They reached Mizen Head a little time later and had a breathtaking view of the wild Atlantic Ocean dashing itself against the rocks.

'You'll get a better view if you disembark,' Colin suggested.

The exodus began. By the time they stepped out into the air, there were five minutes left to enjoy the scene.

'On the next coach holiday,' Billy said to Laura, 'we'll make sure we get the seat immediately behind the driver.'

Then he thought, next coach holiday? What am I saying? I must be going off my chump.

Oliver was oblivious to the glorious view as he was still snoring with a noise like an overfed hog while brother Stanley decided not to bother getting out of the bus.

'If you've seen one sea view, you've seen 'em all,' he proclaimed.

After their Mizen visit, they stayed the night in Bantry, made famous in the single line of the song 'Star of the County Down' – 'From Bantry Bay up to Derry Quay and from Galway to Dublin Town'. Next day they drove over to Blarney where inevitably they were expected to take part in the ancient custom of kissing the Blarney Stone which was supposed to endow the performer with the gift of the gab. The last time Billy had visited this place he'd carried out the tradition all right but later found out that what he'd put his hips to was an imitation stone placed there for unsuspecting tourists like him. The real one was high up in an inaccessible place and he was determined to reach it even if he broke his neck in the attempt.

'We'll see if it pays off if ever I put pen to paper,' he remarked to Laura.

No true Irishman would ever dream of putting himself out for such a stupid exercise because for him blarney was an inherited gift passed down through countless generations via his mother's milk. The word 'blarney', not unlike the Americans' 'baloney,' meant persuasive talk or humbug, the kind of thing Alex and Billy had met on their cycling tour in Galway when, being lost on a country road, they asked an old farmer for directions to Dunluce Castle.

'Well, now,' he said, wrinkling his brow and scratching his head, 'I've lived in this county for over sixty years and I can't say I've ever heard of the place.'

Alex and Billy cycled on. They had covered about a quarter of a mile downhill when they heard the old farmer yelling out to them. When they looked back, they saw that he'd been joined by another man.

'Perhaps he's remembered where the castle is,' Alex said.

Panting, they walked back to the pair, pushing their bikes up the steep hill.

'This is my brother,' declared the old farmer. 'He's lived around here for sixty-five years and he doesn't know either.'

They had met a similar example in their last hotel when the porter who picked up their bags said, 'Follow me, sir. I'm right behind you.'

They drove from Blarney to Enniskerry for their overnight stay before embarking on the Dun Laoghaire ferry back to Holyhead. Back in England, they boarded their coach for the final run to Lancashire. Oliver was still three sheets to the wind, having topped up with more duty free. Stanley, who was normally a regular bag of bones, seemed to have put on considerable weight overnight, which puzzled them for a while.

'I cannot remember ever enjoying a holiday as much as this one,' Stanley said as they left

Holyhead. 'I set off with just a toothbrush and comb and now my cup and case are full to the brim. I rounded it all off at that last hotel in Enniskerry. I couldn't resist the temptation of the soft woollen bathrobe and just before we checked out I helped myself to the silk curtains by wrapping them round my body. They should look good on my bedroom windows at home. I'm so looking forward to our next coach tour in Italy.'

'He'd have taken the television and the telephone,' his brother Oliver remarked, 'but he couldn't get them into his suitcase.'

'I really enjoyed that break,' Laura said when they reached home, 'and I'm especially relieved now that I know I didn't leave the pan on the stove after all. I feel completely refreshed, don't you?'

Billy grimaced. 'If you find being rattled around in a tin can with a lot of obnoxious people in the pouring rain enjoyable, then yes, it was. Now I need six months' complete rest to recover. That was the worst vacation I've ever had. It was like Alice in Wonderland complete with the Mad Hatter and the White Rabbit with his stopwatch. When we set off a week ago, I was a young middle-aged athlete and I've come back a doddering old man.'

Billy couldn't wait to tell his friends about it, though. He met up with them in their usual pub, the Pineapple, near Granada Studios. It was centrally situated and convenient for everyone and so they had become accustomed to meeting there. In addition there was always the added thrill of catching sight of a visiting television celebrity, such as a *Coronation Street* star. Years ago, they had seen Pat Phoenix and Violet Carson who had played the parts of Elsie Tanner and the hair-netted Ena Sharples. Today various well-known actors sometimes called in for a drink, like Johnny Briggs and William Roache who took the roles of Mike Baldwin and Ken Barlow. Knowing they had come in for a drink and to relax, the Smokers' Club gang made a point of not staring at them but treated them like ordinary blokes.

The evening began with the usual bellyaching. Titch opened the proceedings after returning from the gents.

'If there's one thing that gets on my wick,' he began, 'it's underpants with an aperture that's impossible to find. I nearly wet myself just now.'

'If that's all that's worrying you,' Nobby retorted, 'then you're lucky. I've just had a big barney with my tax inspector and what really burns me up are those little cartoons you see on telly, making out that the inspector's a nice friendly little bloke in a bowler hat who'll treat you kindly with a big smile and lots of jokes. I found mine to be a vicious buccaneer out to grab every penny he can.'

'Now, two kinds of people send up hackles,' Oscar said, anxious to add to the general squawking, 'and I cannot make up my mind which I despise the more,' people who corrupt our beautiful English language by adopting Americanisms from the television and the cinema. All around us we hear words like "lootenant" and "skedule", and if you're in a pub somebody orders

106

a whisky and soda "on the rocks", or in a restaurant "a coupla fried eggs, sunny side up". I can understand why the French moan about their language being mangled into Franglais. The other group of people who come close to giving me apoplexy are the philistines at symphony concerts who wait till we've reached the tender pianissimo passage of a violin concerto before deciding to crinkle a bag of toffees or those who hum the theme being played by the orchestra. Last week I was at a Hallé performance of Tchaikowski's *Pathétique* and some harpy behind me was humming "This is the story of a starry night". I ask you!'

Oscar turned to Billy for a contribution to the whingeing session.

'So, how was the holiday?' he asked, hoping to hear him sound off. 'A week incarcerated in a coach with a bunch of old fogies! You must have had a great time!'

Billy disappointed them by adopting a positive tone.

'A great time? Only the best holiday we've ever had, that's all,' he told them, lying through his teeth. Maybe that kissing of the Blarney Stone was beginning to work its magic after all. Besides which, who was going to come back after spending a fortune on a holiday and then tell everybody they'd had a lousy time?

'But what did you do? You were just sitting on a bus!' Nobby protested.

'True, but we enjoyed stimulating company. One man was heavily invested in hotel stocks and another man I became very close to was in whisky. And every morning we got up early and visited places. We saw the sights.'

'Where did you go?' from Titch.

'We went wherever we went.'

'And what on earth did you do after that?' Oscar sneered.

'We came back from wherever we'd been. And this was Ireland and I've never seen such colour. Forty different shades of green. Everything was green! The fields, the trees, the grass, the sky, even the faces of the passengers, and on one memorable occasion the driver.'

'If there's one other thing I really hate,' Oscar drawled, 'it's people who lie so unconvincingly about their holiday.'

But then, as my great hero Oscar Wilde once remarked, "If one tells the truth, one is sure, sooner or later, to be found out."'

So now the holiday was over and it was back to reality. So far, Billy's retirement had been a series of mini disasters. Shopping was out; he'd tried the get-fit routine, the sports centre, cycling, tennis, and nothing had really worked. Who knows? he thought. I may still have years and years of retirement ahead of me, and it's time I put my first cunning plan into action, namely coaching private students.

Chapter Six

Genius!

'Just stop for a moment there, Harry,' Billy said. 'Try to begin the *alla turca* movement with a little more verve, if you please. More stress on the first beat. Like this,' he said, beating time on his open palm with his index finger.

Six months had passed since their bus holiday and Billy was coaching a student in the subtleties of a Mozart sonata. On their return from Ireland, he'd placed an ad in the *Manchester Evening News* which had attracted a dozen young hopefuls. The present one, Harry Ramsbottom, was a young shop assistant at Lewis's store in central Manchester. He loved playing on their Broadwood and had shown unusual talent as both composer and performer. Billy found this amazing, because Harry had no piano at home and had acquired his musical skill practising on a piano accordion. Somehow, though, Billy couldn't see him becoming a famous concert virtuoso on such an instrument. In addition there was the matter of his name. If he ever became famous, they'd have to do something about it. He couldn't imagine anyone announcing him with, 'Tonight we proudly present a performance of Mozart's Concerto in A major played by Sir Harry Ramsbottom on the piano accordion.' It was a name not unlike the well-known fish and chip shop company.

No, we'll have to change it, Billy thought. Perhaps to something like Ramsey Harrison which has a more authentic ring. There was a precedent for reversing names in this way. The mayor of a Lancashire town had one introduced the BBC Symphony Orchestra conducted by Sir Malcolm Sargent with, 'I'm reet proud to present tonight's concert to be given by Sergeant Malcolm and his band.'

'Right, Mr Hopkins, got it.' Harry grinned cheekily, tossing his tousled red locks and repeating the passage. How Billy envied him! Not only for his undoubted musical talent but also for his good looks, bright blue eyes and ruddy complexion. Oscar Wilde had it right when he said that youth was wasted on the young.

Laura came in carrying a tray with two mugs of coffee and a plate of biscuits. 'Come on, you two maestros,' she said. 'Time for refreshment.'

'There's only one maestro here, Laura,' Billy said.

'You mean yourself, of course.'

'On the contrary. I mean young Harry here,' he said, sipping his coffee. 'I think I've found Manchester's answer to Mozart. Incidentally, what's happened to the chocolate biscuits?'

'You'll have to make do with digestives, Billy. We have to economize. I ran out of cash at the supermarket today. Most embarrassing as I had to put the chocolate biscuits back on the shelves and make do with these digestives.'

'Ta very much for the coffee and I love digestives, Mrs Hopkins,' Harry said tactfully. 'I

110

think your husband exaggerates a bit though when he talks about me being another Mozart.' He laughed.

'He always exaggerates, but not just a bit, a lot,' she replied.

Laura was forever accusing Billy of overstating his case and raising the students' hopes too high.

'So what's wrong with that?' Billy protested 'According to Robert Browning, a man's reach should exceed his grasp.'

'That's all very well, Billy, but I think you sometimes give your students unrealistic expectations, which can only lead to disappointment in the end.'

'Maybe so but one day you'll see this young man's name in lights.'

Harry felt it was time he said something. 'No sweat, Mrs Hopkins, I've got both feet planted firmly on the ground.'

Billy got really angry when he heard those words. 'Well, for heaven's sake, Harry, lift them off the ground,' he said vehemently. 'Let your imagination soar. Your latest composition must be the best thing you've done.'

'Hear, hear,' Laura said, agreeing with her husband for once. 'I heard it last time you were here. What exactly was it, Harry?'

'It was the slow movement from me piano concerto,' he said shyly.

'You should be trying to find a music publisher,' Billy told him, 'though there's not much chance of finding one here in Manchester. London! That's where all the big music publishers are.'

He recalled how his own son, Matthew, had

done something similar though his music hadn't been classical. Billy had been worried about him at first but he'd done well for himself down there in the end.

'If you did go to London, Harry,' Billy asked, 'how would your father feel about it?'

At the mention of his dad, Harry put down his cup and grimaced.

'Since me mam died, he's gone to pieces and been hittin' the bottle hard,' he replied. 'When he's not at his work on the docks, he sits at home mumbling to himself. As for music, he claims to have cloth ears. I don't think he gives a hoot what I do. I get fed up sometimes and, I tell you, I wouldn't mind gettin' away from it all.'

'Sorry to hear that about your dad, Harry,' Billy said, 'but you've got your own life to think of now. Your music shows great promise and I think if you could get some of it published, it'd greatly help your chance of winning a place at the Royal Academy next year. And you never know, that might cheer up your old man. Now, let's hear that slow movement again before we wind up the session.'

As Harry began to play, Billy sat with eyes closed, concentrating on the music. Meanwhile Laura had left to answer the doorbell.

Standing on the doorstep was Billy's next student, a pretty, dark-haired young lady, briefcase in hand. Laura's face lit up when she saw her.

'Oh, hello, Jane,' she said. 'You're early this week but it's always nice to see you again. Is it really a week since you were here last?'

'Hello, Mrs Hopkins. Yes, another week's flown

by. Time for my next English tutorial. Your husband's a marvellous teacher, you know.'

'Marvellous teacher maybe but half the time his head's in the clouds. Anyway, he's just finishing with Harry in there. Shouldn't be too long. Come and keep me company in the kitchen.'

'Thanks, Mrs Hopkins.'

The sound of the piano came through to them and Jane paused for a moment and cupped a hand to her ear. 'I know that piece. It's really beautiful, isn't it?'

'It certainly is. Harry's latest composition. Harry Ramsbottom. Yet another of my husband's so-called discoveries. Sometimes he thinks he's Hughie Green running the *Opportunity Knocks* show. Have you met Harry?'

Jane blushed. 'Why ... er ... yes, Mrs Hopkins. Our paths have crossed here on your threshold. When I arrive, he's usually just leavin'. Like ships passin' in the night.'

'But of course. How stupid of me! You couldn't help but meet each other. Harry's a very talented musician.'

The music faded in a beautiful diminuendo and then stopped.

'There, they seem to be finished now,' Laura said. 'Let's go through.'

Billy went into the hallway with Harry who was carrying the usual unstable pile of music books under his arm.

'That's fine, then, Harry,' he said. 'See you next week. Keep up the good work. Remember what I said about getting your music published.' Then,

113

spotting Jane, Billy gave her a friendly wave and introduced her to Harry.

'We've already met, Mr Hopkins,' she said coyly.

'Well, well,' Billy said. 'I'd no idea you two had made contact. I speak metaphorically of course.'

'How could they *not* meet?' Laura said. 'Coming here every week as they do.'

'Well, see you next week, Harry. Don't forget what I said.'

Laura was immediately suspicious. 'If he's been giving you advice, Harry, ignore it or pass it on to someone else.'

'Take no notice of Mrs Hopkins, Harry,' Billy said, tipping him a wink. 'That's our little secret, eh?'

Behind Laura's back, Harry gave him a conspiratorial thumbs-up. 'Right, Mr Hopkins. Mum's the word.'

Billy opened the front door and, still carrying his wobbly mountain of music manuscripts under his arm, Harry went off.

After he'd gone, Jane settled at the writing desk and Billy made himself comfortable in the easy chair by her side.

'Now, Jane. How's the novel coming along?' he asked. 'No writer's block, I hope.'

'Fine, Mr Hopkins. No, there's no writer's block. In fact, sometimes I sit down an' it's as if someone else were writing the book. I hope you don't think I've gone daft but it's odd, like another person dictatin' to me what to write an' I'm just the medium writin' it down, as it were.'

'That's the true meaning of genius, Jane. In Roman mythology, a genius was a protective spirit – a bit like a guardian angel that looked after a man from cradle to grave. So maybe that's who's giving you dictation. Let's hear how far you've got.'

'Right, Mr Hopkins. Last time I was here,' she said, taking her notebook out of her briefcase, 'we'd got to Chapter Five...'

'That's the one in which your young heroine and her mother were walking through Salford. Let's hear it.'

Billy was deeply moved by her writing and, as he listened to her account of the district where she'd been brought up, he told himself that retiring early from that meaningless job at the college had been the best thing he'd ever done.

She paused for a moment and looked up at him anxiously. 'Well, what do you think? Is it all right?'

'It's more than all right, Jane,' he said fervently. 'It's damned good! Now, I think it's time you looked for a publisher.'

'You said that last time I was here. But do you really think it's ready? It's only the first draft and I thought I might tidy it up later if I'm offered a place at Salford University this September.'

It's supposed to be the young who are impetuous but in this case Billy was the impatient one.

'I think it would be best if you tried to get it published before going off to university. What a feather in your cap that would be if you had your book already out.'

'But where would I find a publisher in Salford? Are there any?' she asked.

'I doubt it, Jane. No. London's the place.'

'I don't think my mother would be keen if I

went off to London. I have a younger brother, you see, and my mother depends on me to look after things at home when she's out at work.'

Billy asked her what she meant by 'looking after things' and was taken aback when she outlined the list of chores she was responsible for: cooking dinner at night, washing and ironing, and making the beds. Her father had left them some years ago for a younger woman and her mother, being an office cleaner, had to work long hours to pay the bills.

'Someone has to look after the domestic front,' she explained, 'and that's where I come in.'

'Fair enough, Jane,' he replied. 'If you want to stay home and play at being Cinderella, that's your decision. But just imagine how proud your mother would be if you got your novel in print! S'funny, though, that we should be talking like this about London and publishers. I've only just been suggesting the same thing to Harry, not twenty minutes ago. You two ought to get together.'

Jane went red.

'We already have, Mr Hopkins.'

Billy was a bit slow on the uptake and didn't get the message first time.

'Sorry,' he said. 'How...?'

'Harry an' I met here in your house by accident. In fact, at your front door almost a year ago. We've been goin' steady ever since.'

'Going steady, Jane? What does that mean precisely?'

Jane blushed for the third time that day.

'Put in its simplest terms, Mr Hopkins, it means we're in love.'

'But I never suspected for a moment that–'

116

His bewilderment was interrupted by Laura who came in with a tray containing biscuits and one cup of coffee.

'Refreshment time, Jane. None for you, Billy. You're drinking far too much coffee.'

'Thanks a lot, Mrs Hopkins. You're really very kind.'

'Yes, thank you, Laura,' Billy said, unable to keep the sarcasm out of his voice. 'I don't know what I'd do without you. But never mind the coffee, Laura. I tell you, this girl here has got real talent. Another Jane Austen.'

'Oh, I see, Billy. It's Jane Austen now, is it? One more genius to add to the list? She turned to Jane and smiled apologetically. 'Sorry about this, Jane, but he's forever discovering geniuses. A few months back, we had Enrico Caruso and Robert Browning. You can hear Caruso any Friday night singing in the Nag's Head. As for Robert Browning, he lives in a motor caravan now with a lot of others. Hippies, I think they're called.'

'New Age Travellers or Crusties are the correct terms, I believe,' Billy said, showing off his erudition.

'Well, whatever they're called, he was one of last year's geniuses. Now, *this* year, it's different. We've been honoured earlier with Wolfgang Amadeus and now you, Jane, you've been given the surname Austen. I'm half expecting William Shakespeare to turn up here any day now. Don't you be taken in by anything he says, Jane. You must take him with a pinch of salt.'

'You make me sound like a packet of crisps or a plate of porridge,' Billy said.

117

Throughout this exchange, Jane had been having a good giggle. 'I shall, Mrs Hopkins,' she said through her laughter. Then changing the subject, she turned to Billy. 'By the way, is it OK with you if I finish a little early today? Harry and I have a date.'

'Sounds mysterious,' he said. 'What's going on?'

'Now, Billy,' Laura said. 'Don't be nosy. You get along, Jane, and never mind his foolish notions.'

'OK, Jane,' he said. 'Don't mind me. See you same time next week.'

Jane hesitated a little before she answered. 'Yes ... er ... hope so. Until the next time then. Thanks for all your help and advice, Mr Hopkins. Especially your advice! As a teacher, you're the tops and I'll never forget you!'

Jane collected her belongings and Laura escorted her to the door.

Meanwhile Billy went to the piano and began playing Debussy's 'Clair de Lune' until she returned.

'Jane's such a nice quiet girl,' she said. 'Talented yet so modest and unassuming. That's what I like about her.'

He stopped playing and turned to face her.

'You're right, Laura. Her simplicity is one of her nicest qualities. But she's more than talented. She's outstanding.'

'Fair enough, Billy, but you really must be careful what you tell them. You have them almost believing they really are those great people. So many of them go off with high ideals only to flop when they get out in the real world.'

'That's the true test of character, Laura, when

118

they come up against the real world. One of these fine days, one of my students will make it to the top, you'll see.'

'That's all very well but I do wish you didn't have to take on quite so many of these private pupils.'

'No choice, Laura. On my pittance of a pension, we'd struggle if it weren't for my private work. We still have lots of bills to cope with.'

'As if I need reminding, Billy. I'm having to economize all the time.'

What a situation I'm in, he reflected. Now aged sixty having been made redundant at fifty-eight. How he hated that word 'redundant'! It meant superfluous. No longer needed. Written off. The strange thing was that, since retiring, he felt that he'd been doing something really valuable. His students came to him of their own free will and he felt happy and fulfilled teaching them.

'I may not make much money from private tutoring,' he said, 'but I love fostering talents that might otherwise go undeveloped and unnoticed. As Thomas Gray put it, "Full many a flower is born to blush unseen, And waste its sweetness on the desert air."'

'Well, talking of flowers blushing unseen,' Laura declared with a laugh, 'I'd better return to the kitchen and start preparing lunch.'

'Very droll,' Billy said, turning back to Debussy.

Later that evening, Laura and he were sitting in the living room. Laura was doing her embroidery of a Spanish dancing girl and he was immersed in Priestley's *Angel Pavement*. The TV in the corner was turned off as they'd developed the habit of

119

never switching on until well into the evening. Somehow, watching TV during the day or early evening seemed, if not immoral, then vaguely illicit. Perhaps it was because their upbringing had frowned on time-wasting during the daylight hours. Evening, though, was a different matter.

Laura looked up from her embroidery.

'I'll make some supper and then I see *Casualty* is on BBC later,' she said, 'Do you fancy a ham sandwich?'

'Fine, Laura,' he said, 'and I should love to watch *Casualty*. It'll certainly make a change from all the sex and violence we get nowadays. And I hope I don't sound squeamish but since it's about hospitals with lots of blood and guts and things, I'd rather have the ham sandwich *before* we start watching.'

As Laura made her way to the kitchen, the doorbell rang.

'I wonder who that can be at this hour. I'll see who it is,' she said.

'No peace for the wicked,' he rejoined.

A few moments later, she was back with Jane's mother who, judging by the tight-lipped expression, was simmering with anger.

'Excuse me for disturbing you like this,' she seethed. 'But I'm here about our Jane.'

His heart skipped a beat. 'Jane! Why, what's happened? Not an accident, I hope!'

'No. Nothin' like that. But she's flamin' well run away, that's what she's done. An' with one of your bloody students.'

'Harry!' Billy gasped. 'Surely not! I can't believe it! When did they... They couldn't have...

They wouldn't dare...'

'They bloody well have,' Vera Ford snapped. 'She left me a note sayin' she was goin' to London to get her book published or somethin'. She said you advised her.'

'But not in so many words and certainly not right away!' he blustered.

'Well, I blame you,' she retorted. 'People like you shouldn't be let loose on young people. Fillin' their heads with allusions of grandeur. It's left us in a right pickle at home, I can tell you. I don't know how we're gonna manage. I'll have to get some kind of home help an' that's gonna cost money. And another thing,' she was supposed to be goin' to Salford University this year.'

'There's no need to go on at Mr Hopkins like that, Mrs Ford,' Laura said, springing to his defence. 'It's not all his fault. He didn't exactly force her to go to London, did he? Jane's old enough to make up her own mind.'

'No, but it was here that she met that perishin' piano-playin' pupil o' yours. What's his name? Harry Ramsbottom. His dad's one o' them rough dockers and a lush into the bargain, I've heard. I wouldn't be surprised if his son weren't the same. What they'll do for money down there I really don't know.'

Once the idea of their running away together had sunk in, Billy began to see possibilities.

'So, they've gone together, eh?' he mused. 'Now that should be interesting. As a team, they could be formidable.'

These speculations didn't appeal to Vera Ford.

'Never mind all that,' she rasped. 'I'm holdin'

you responsible if anythin' goes wrong. I'll have you in court for abduction or false premises or summat. I'm goin' to stop your little game. I know some of the mothers of your pupils an' I'm goin' to warn them off you. By the time I've finished, you won't have a bloody student left.'

'There's no need to take on so, Mrs Ford,' Laura said, opening the lounge door to encourage an exit. 'I'm sure they'll be all right. They're both very sensible people. Trust in your daughter's common sense. Do let us know as soon as you hear anything. Come on, I'll show you to the door.'

Mrs Ford had to have the last word. 'It's that flamin' husband of yours,' she raged as she went out. 'He's a bloody menace. He shouldn't be around young people, fillin' their heads with stuff and nonsense.'

When Laura came back, Billy remarked, 'Did you notice, Laura, the way she used natural alliterative phrases like "perishin' piano-playin' pupil"? That's where Jane gets her literary talent.'

'Never mind all that, you silly man,' Laura chided. 'You've really set the cat among the pigeons this time.'

'But at least the pigeons are free,' he said. 'Apart from that, I'm going to have to look for two other pupils to replace them if we're going to go on eating biscuits, even if they're only digestives.'

'Will you stop going on about biscuits!' she said, exasperated. 'I only buy them for your whizz-kids. We'll get by somehow. We always have. I'm far more worried about those two youngsters you've sent down to London.'

'I did not send them down!' he protested. 'They

chose to go themselves.'

'I hope they don't end up living in cardboard boxes on the Embankment.'

'Nonsense. They'll come back dripping with success, you'll see.'

'I've lost count of the number of times I've heard you say that about your discoveries, Billy.'

'Anyroad, as my old mother used to say, they've buttered their bread, so they must lie in it. There's nothing we can do about any of it now except maybe pray that their true grit comes through and they make it down there in the smoke. We'll just have to wait till we hear from them. Now, what were you saying about a ham sandwich before *Casualty* begins?'

It was three months since Harry and Jane had absconded to London and little had been heard of them. Billy had received a brief note on a postcard about ten days after they left telling him they'd found 'a pad' in Pimlico and were looking for agents. But apart from that, nothing. Not even a phone call. He'd been desperate to learn more, to find out how their talents had been received but he had no way of contacting them. It was a complete mystery and his patience was stretched to the limit. Maybe, he thought, they were waiting till they had something definite to report. There was nothing to do but wait and get on with teaching his pupils even though he was down to only two after Vera Ford had worked her mischief. Today, he was coaching a particularly brilliant performer, young Mary Ann Morris.

'Well done, Mary Ann!' Billy said. 'The way

you played that prestissimo passage was superb. You get better each time I hear you.'

'Thank you, Mr Hopkins,' said Mary Ann.

'Did you know that Mozart had a sister called Maria Anna, nick-named Nannerl?' he asked his young protégé. 'By all accounts, she could play as well as Wolfgang himself.'

'I didn't know that, Mr Hopkins.'

'From now on, I think I'll call you Nannerl.'

'Thank you,' she answered shyly.

'But I think that'll do for today. Prepare the Scarlatti C Sonata for next week. Then we'll see about your Royal Academy exams.'

'Thank you, Mr Hopkins,' she said, putting her music books away in her satchel. 'Bye-bye for now. I'll see myself out.'

'Bye-bye to you, Mary Ann,' he called.

It was after his pupil had gone that Laura gave him the news. And it wasn't good. On the grapevine that only women seemed to have access to, she'd heard that both Harry and Jane were into the drugs scene and that the 'pad' they'd told him about in their postcard was a squat they were sharing with a dozen other hippies. Neither had managed to find an agent.

In music, Harry had become a public performer right enough but not on the concert platform. Instead he was playing his piano accordion busking in a passageway in the London Underground and for income relied on the coppers passers-by threw into his hat.

As for Jane, she'd taken up a writing career but not with a reputable publisher. Using the pseudonym Yvette La Rouge, she was turning out cheap pornographic novelettes for a pulp fiction printer. Her books, with titles like *The Lady Likes Nylon* or *Baby, Don't Turn Round*, could be found on any station bookstall and were recognisable by the lurid front covers of ladies with huge thighs and impossibly large cleavages.

'Things have not turned out as you'd hoped,' Laura said. 'Don't you feel sometimes, Billy, that it's been a waste of time trying to develop the talents of these young students?'

'Not at all, Laura. As I see it, my job is pointing young people in the right direction. I've tried to introduce them to the best that's been thought and said and to put before them a vision of greatness. If they turn their back on all that and choose the cheap and the tawdry, there's nothing I can do about it. Anyway, what we've been told about Harry and Jane is their behaviour in the short run. Who's to say what will happen in the long term? Education's like sowing seeds and sometimes we only see the true results after many years when the values we've tried to inculcate come to the fore.'

'Nevertheless,' she said, 'when you get depressing news like this there's only one thing to be done.'

'And what's that, may I ask?' As if he didn't know.

'Make a nice cup of tea, of course.'

'Typical!' he said. 'The English solution to all problems. I think I'd rather have a double whisky.'

He went to the cabinet and poured out a large measure of Scotch with a squirt of soda while Laura went into the kitchen to put the kettle on. He sat in his big armchair with his drink in his right hand and his chin in the other. He felt thoroughly dejected. As he sat there contemplating and wondering what life was all about, his reverie was disturbed by the sound of the doorbell.

'Someone at the door, Laura,' he called. 'I hope to God it isn't Vera Ford come to give me another tongue-lashing. I'll see to it.'

There on the threshold stood William Stretford, one of his youngest and most promising pupils. He had been coming to Billy for English lessons for just over three months.

'Oh, it's you, William!' he said, mollified. 'There's been so much going on, I'd clean forgotten it was time for your lesson. Come in.'

William was a fresh-faced lad, about twelve years old with big, innocent blue eyes. He was carrying his battered briefcase containing his notebooks. When Billy saw the earnest expression on his young face, his enthusiasm and his hopes began to return.

'Well, William,' he said gently. 'Did you finish those beautiful verses you said you would write for me?'

'Yes, Mr Hopkins,' he said, eagerly opening his case. 'I've got them right here.'

Billy looked at the boy and then paused for a moment.

'Wait there,' he said.

Then, going to the kitchen door, he called to Laura who was stirring the teapot. 'Laura! Laura!'

'Yes? What is it? What's happened?' she exclaimed, sounding alarmed. 'Not more trouble?'

'No, Laura. It's just that the man you've been expecting has arrived!'

126

'Man? Which man?' she called back, puzzled.

He laughed. 'The one they call the Bard of Stratford-on-Avon. William Shakespeare!'

Chapter Seven

Back to the Classroom

Billy was left with only the two young students. Both brilliant but the small income from their fees didn't help much in paying bills. Not only that, he still had lots of time on his hands. He had to find something else to fill in the hours, but what?

That year the newspapers were advertising for supply teachers to fill in the gaps left by the thousands of teachers who were absent, reporting sick. From the sound of things many schools, especially in the inner city, were desperate to recruit staff. Billy found this hard to grasp since teaching had always been considered a rewarding career choice. Though the pay was never great, life at the chalkface was seen as offering challenges and prestige. 'Besides,' people said, 'look at the holidays – three weeks at Christmas and Easter and six in the summer. It's the life of Reilly.' The daily rate of £60 a day being offered for supply teaching seemed generous and he thought he'd give it a try. At least his wards would not be running off to London to be corrupted by that swinging city.

He wasn't too keen on going back to teaching. In some ways it seemed like a retrograde step for he'd moved on since the days when he'd been a schoolteacher and it had been some time since he'd taught younger age groups. For the previous fifteen years his career had been spent as a lecturer with older people in teacher training. But he still retained fond memories of the years spent teaching adolescents both in England and abroad in East Africa. In Manchester he'd been particularly happy at St Anselm's Secondary Modern School in Longsight. The original school had been destroyed by the Luftwaffe during the Second World War and Mr Bill Wakefield, the headmaster, had set up his office at the back of Billy's classroom, with the result that for his first five years of teaching, Billy had the head listening to his every word. Not only that, there was always a stream of visitors to see the head and at times Billy found himself designing some of his lessons with the visitors in mind, in particular the finance officer from the local authority who appeared every Tuesday afternoon to collect the school bank money.

Mr Wakefield became a great friend, often participating in the lessons, and the two of them often indulged in Morecambe-and-Wise type verbal exchanges, to the amusement and entertainment of the top class. The pupils were a friendly, lively bunch of students, and had always been eager to learn and to make something of themselves. In addition the head was an enthusiastic scoutmaster and encouraged Billy to take his class on outdoor expeditions, hiking in the Peak District as part of map-reading and geography studies. The pupils learned not only geography however. Perhaps more importantly they acquired a genuine love and appreciation of Derbyshire and its beautiful countryside. Years later old pupils came back to visit the school and it was the part of their education that they remembered best. Their opening sentences usually began with something like, 'Do you remember the time we went to visit Longendale Reservoir, sir?' If I can get back to that kind of teaching, Billy thought, it'll be something to look forward to.

As for East African secondary schools, teaching there had also been a joy. Not only were the students anxious to learn, they were disciplined and respectful at all times. When a teacher walked into the room for his first lesson, the whole class would spring to their feet and greet him with, 'Good morning, sir.' Apart from being courteous, they were also highly motivated to succeed in their studies. Given homework, next day the students would present the teacher with thirty exercise books, the work beautifully and conscientiously done. And how could he ever forget his first day in class when he and the students had had to clear out a boomslang serpent before they could begin the lesson. Or the preoccupation (which amounted to obsession) of the school with athletics, when Billy had been required to teach javelin throwing (about which he knew nothing) to his Masai students. One of these Masai, who'd achieved excellent marks in English at the Cambridge School Certificate, went back to being a moran warrior in his home manyatta. Resplendent in traditional dress, face painted, hair daubed in yellow ochre, he was tending his cattle one day when he was approached by an American tourist family who were agonizing over an English/Swahili phrasebook and trying to find the way to Narok.

Imagine their shock when our young student laid down his spear and said in impeccable English, 'Can I be of any assistance to you people?'

Perhaps strangest of all, holidays were not welcomed by the students as they saw them as time-wasting and they resented days like Arbor Day when there was a compulsory holiday (which sounded like an oxymoron) from classroom work and they were required to participate in a tree-planting ceremony. Some boys would duck out of the ceremony and sneak back to their classroom where they could be found solving quadratic equations. This high level of dedication was understandable since education in Kenya was more than simply passing examinations; it was seen as a passport to a successful career and an opportunity to repay the family (and often their whole village) which had made great sacrifices to send a son (though rarely a daughter) to secondary school. The only discipline problem encountered was keeping their fervour within reasonable limits.

Remembering these halcyon days, Billy thought that perhaps he could win back some of this former happiness through working with younger people in school. Horror stories in the press suggested it was a tough job teaching in inner city schools but he loved his subject, English. Maybe he could use his skills and experience to kindle a love for learning and, who knows, even encourage creative writing like he had in the Manchester school where he had once got all the pupils writing novels, a co-operative exercise which involved not only English but art and handicraft skills also.

First chance he got, he phoned a teaching

agency and made an appointment to see one of their representatives the following day. They seemed particularly anxious to see him when he gave them a brief summary of his CV. Next day at their office, he completed a long and involved form giving details of qualifications and experience and told them he'd be willing to take the first temporary position that came up.

The gentleman who interviewed him was keen, to point out that most of the vacancies occurred in inner city schools, what he described as the more deprived and challenging areas of north-west towns.

'It is in these schools,' he explained, 'that teachers tend to go off sick, either short or long term. We do sometimes get requests for teachers in "good" schools in the advantaged districts, the so-called leafy lanes, but these are rare, except for maths and science. In those subjects, the scarcity is so acute, I think the only way we're going to attract graduates in these subjects is to offer a "golden hello", a signing-on fee like they do with top footballers. On the whole, though, schools in the well-off areas cover their vacancies from within their own staff and resources.'

'Is there much call for temporary teachers of English?' Billy asked.

'Not usually as such,' he said. 'In supply work, what schools are concerned about is the need to meet the statutory requirement of having a qualified body present. So you may be asked to fill in, or "sub" as it's sometimes called, for a colleague in any subject. Often, you won't even know what subjects you are covering until you

132

actually arrive at the school next morning.'

'But supposing it's a subject I know nothing about?'

'No problem, Mr Hopkins. Usually the absentee will have left material for the pupils in the form of worksheets and your job will simply be to supervise the class.'

'What if the teacher has gone off sick without notice? There won't be any work left for the class.'

'That's why we advise teachers on our books to have work ready to meet any emergency. Prepare something to occupy the pupils, regardless of the subject.'

'You mean "keep 'em busy" stuff?'

'That sums up the position admirably.'

On the Sunday evening following his interview, Billy had settled down to watch TV and was enjoying Arthur Negus on the *Antiques Roadshow* when the phone rang. It was the agency. Could he provide cover for a colleague at a boys' comprehensive school in East Manchester? Boys' comprehensive? Surely a contradiction in terms, he thought, as it couldn't be truly comprehensive if it was for boys only. The job would be for three days, covering for the regular teacher who was off suffering from a cold. The subject was mainly English and he'd be expected to teach all classes throughout the school. He accepted the offer as he'd spent a few days preparing worksheets in English, mainly comprehension exercises, word puzzles, and spelling lists. Enough material to keep any idle or restless class occupied for a few hours if need be.

On Monday morning, he arrived at the school

early at eight thirty. He parked his Morris Oxford in the car park and, as he walked across the main building, he noted the graffiti sprayed on the school walls,' 'Down With The Pigs', 'Burn the F–ing School Down', and wondered how long they had been allowed to remain there. As he entered the building, he was met by that un-mistakable smell forever associated with British schools, a mixture of floor polish, disinfectant, and school dinners. In the staffroom, he was surprised to find only one other teacher there. Not only that, this particular man appeared to be knocking on a bit. Certainly well past retirement age.

'My name's Murgatroyd,' he said, holding out his hand and giving Billy a cheery smile, revealing a black space in his front teeth, which made him look like a tramp or a circus clown. 'The rest of the staff should be here in the next twenty minutes or so,' he said, flashing a gappy grin. 'Meanwhile, let me make you a coffee. It's instant, I'm afraid.'

'That's fine,' Billy said. 'A coffee would be most welcome.'

'You're supply like me, aren't you?' the other grinned. 'Like half of us at this school. The regu-lar teachers are supposed to be off with colds and other minor ailments but most of them are away with nervous breakdowns. A bit like the neuras-thenia of the trenches in the First World War,' he chuckled.

As Billy sipped his coffee, the rest of the staff began arriving. He was surprised to see that a good half of them looked elderly like Murgatroyd. Obviously temporary replacements like him.

'This place relies on supply staff to keep going,'

Murgatroyd whispered, as if reading his thoughts. 'At the moment, we have two from Australia and one from South Africa. The maths classes have had ten different teachers in the last two terms. We temps are usually given the rubbish classes. If you're hoping to teach an examination class, you can think again.'

At five to nine, Mr Parry, the head, and Mr Warner, the deputy head, came into the staffroom for a final briefing. They both looked battle-weary and the head's words were less than reassuring.

'Good morning, everyone,' he began in a tired voice, giving the impression that his mind was on his retirement a few years hence. 'The start of another week and we still have six teachers absent and so we shall be continuing with the present complement of agency staff, I'm afraid. Today we welcome another, Mr Hopkins, who will be taking the place of Mr Hindmarsh who is away with a touch of the flu. Here is your timetable and a map of the school, Mr Hopkins. We don't want you getting lost on your first day here, do we?' he said in an attempt at levity. 'I hope you'll be happy during the short time you will be with us.' His good wishes somehow lacked conviction.

'Addressing the rest of you,' the head went on, 'I'm sure I don't have to remind you about avoiding any kind of discriminatory or racist remarks, no matter how innocent. And no matter what happens, do not lay hands on your pupils, even in jest. We live in a litigious age and you could quickly find yourselves in court. We might even have irate parents round again as we had last month and we certainly don't want a repeat of

135

that experience. May I also request this week that you avoid sending miscreants to me or the deputy head – we have enough on our plates without having to sort out your disciplinary problems.'

You're on your own, mate, Billy said to himself.

'Finally,' the head continued, 'do avoid expelling your troublemakers into the corridors where they only make further trouble. Last week three boys left the school premises and were picked up by the police in the city centre for shoplifting. Keep them in the classroom and at least we'll know where they are.'

As Billy listened to this list of dos and don'ts, he wondered what he'd let himself in for.

His first class, Form 1H, was a relatively easy introduction into the school routine. Or so he thought.

'Don't take any nonsense from them,' his self-appointed mentor, Murgatroyd, said as they left for their classes 'Form 1H shouldn't be so bad, though you're the fourth new face they've seen this term. Your main headache will be in Form Four which immediately follows in your second period. Watch out for Juddy Clayton, he's a thug and no mistake. That's how I came to lose this,' he said, pointing to the space where his incisor should have been.

'What happened?' Billy asked.

'I foolishly stepped in to break up a scrap and was given a Manchester kiss, or head-butting, by Juddy. I was tempted to thump the little sod but thought better of it.'

'I would have done,' Billy replied sympathetically.

'The one thing you're not allowed to do is fight back. They can swear at you or thump you but you mustn't retaliate, whatever you do. Touch any of 'em and in two shakes you'll have the Old Bill round with a summons for assault. I often think we should be given training in restraint techniques like they have at Ashworth special hospital on Merseyside.'

'But isn't that where violent criminals are held? Surely our pupils can't be compared with them?'

'Oh, can't they? Some of our most disruptive kids can resort to biting, scratching, kicking, and throwing things. We should be taught how to defuse a situation and, failing that, to restrain violent kids without hurting them or ourselves.'

Murgatroyd's words had Billy worried and he hoped that he wasn't going to meet a situation such as he'd described. He wasn't sure how he'd react if he did.

The corridors leading to his first class were carpeted in a hard-wearing cord material but the floors were littered with crisp packets, sweet wrappers, chewing gum and Coke cans. He passed a number of classrooms with groups of squabbling kids milling round the doors, waiting for someone to come and let them in. He reached the form room of 1H and found the place still locked but the waiting pupils seemed more concerned with their Snickers bars and drink cans than entry into the classroom. Eventually a janitor appeared and opened the door. There was a mad scramble to get inside, which almost knocked Billy off his feet. This is a long way from Marangu High School in

East Africa, he thought.

When everyone had found their place at the group tables, they began chattering like monkeys in a zoo. He clapped his hands to win their attention. No one took the slightest notice. This was something of a shock, for in the old days when he'd taught in school, there was hush when 'sir' called for attention. The teacher was the authority in charge. He wondered, too, about the sitting-at-tables arrangement. The idea of this was to get away from the old-fashioned talk and chalk teacher, with the kids sitting in rows listening to him. So what was wrong with that? he asked himself. He wasn't entirely convinced about this notion of sitting in groups for it seemed to him to encourage idle gossip and chit-chat.

He clapped once more and called out, 'Look this way.'

A few glanced lazily in his direction and went on chin-wagging. He had the feeling that if they'd had remote controls they'd have put him on 'Off', 'Pause' or 'Fast Forward' like Peter Sellers tried to do in the film *Being There*.

'What are you doing in English?' he asked a sensible-looking lad on the front row, one of the few who appeared to be listening.

'We're doing plurals and gender of nouns in the *Standard English*,' he replied.

Thank the Lord, he said to himself. The book was one he knew well.

'Where are the books?'

'They're in that cupboard,' the boy said, indicating the large bureau at the front of the room, 'but it's locked.'

138

'Who has the key?'

'Mr Hindmarsh,' he said gleefully.

Fortunately, Billy had prepared against this eventuality by bringing loads of worksheets on parts of speech: nouns, verbs, adjectives, and adverbs with lots of practise questions. He slapped the top of his desk forcibly and called in his best sergeant-major voice.

'Right, listen to me, you bunch of nattering old women.'

This did the trick; most of the class paused in their chatter and looked in his direction. He followed with oral questions of gender: actor – actress; prince – princess; man – woman; nephew – niece; bachelor – spinster. Next he revised a few plurals with a series of quick-fire questions: lady – ladies; child – children; goose – geese; son-in-law – sons-in-law. He wrote up the answers on the blackboard.

'Before you start work,' he said. 'Here's a joke.'

That seemed to get their attention. They're curious about my skill as a stand-up comedian, he supposed.

'A man wanted to start a zoo, so he wrote to the animal company. "Dear Sirs, I am starting a zoo. Please send me two mongeese." No, that doesn't sound right, he said to himself. He started again. "Dear Sirs, I'm starting a zoo, please send me two mongi." No, that doesn't sound right either. So he wrote, "Dear Sirs, I am starting a zoo. Please send me a mongoose. P.S. Please send me another."'

'Why did he do that?' asked a bespectacled boy on the front row.

''Cos he didn't know the plural of mongoose,

139

you bloody idiot,' said a big lad at the back.

'What's the correct answer, sir?' the sensible-looking boy asked.

'Some people would say mongeese but the correct answer is an exception to the rule, and is "mongooses".'

At least now he had them not only interested but laughing before they settled down to complete his worksheet, though a few spent the time doodling on the paper.

Later that night when he came to mark their papers, he found a fine collection of howlers, especially on genders and sentence completions.

The husband of a duchess was a duck or a dutchman; the masculine of heroine was kipper.

The wife of a duke was ducky; the feminine of manager was a managerie.

On Saturday mornings, my father cleans the widows.

The king wore a scarlet robe trimmed with vermin.

On the whole, though, the first lesson had been satisfactory and the time had passed peacefully. That was all very well but he had to face Form Four after the break. The warnings from Murgatroyd made him apprehensive. First rule, he told himself, is get to the classroom before the pupils so as to establish his presence. He stood beside the teacher's desk and waited for them to arrive. They swarmed into the room noisily, pushing, fighting, cuffing, swearing. His presence was ignored until somebody said in a loud voice, 'Not another f–ing supply teacher!'

The speaker was the biggest boy there and

there was no need to ask his name. This was the infamous Juddy Clayton.

'Right, settle down in your places,' Billy called in as confident a voice as he could muster. 'Mr Hindmarsh is away sick and I'll be taking his place for a few days.'

'You're the fifth f–ing teacher we've had this year,' the big lad sneered.

'Well, you've got me whether you like it or not,' Billy countered.

'I hate this f–ing school,' the youth snarled.

'I've heard a lot of swearing since I came into the school this morning,' Billy said, addressing the class. 'Why do you think people swear?'

'So as to sound tough,' one lad volunteered.

''Cos they don't know any other words,' added another.

'Right,' Billy said. 'But why f–ing school? What's it mean?'

'Means dead boring,' said Juddy. 'Dead f–ing boring.'

'Boring!' Billy said. 'Now that's a better word. I understand that. What other words could we use to mean we're fed up or bored with something?'

'What about "brassed-off"?' suggested a buck-toothed boy at the back.

Soon, answers were coming thick and fast. 'Cheesed-off, browned-off, chocker, down in the mouth, sick as a parrot, had it up to here.'

'You see,' Billy said, 'there are much better ways of saying "I hate this f–ing school". When we use a word like "boring" or "tedious" to des-cribe something, everyone knows what we're saying. Such a word is called an adjective. I want

141

you to think of as many adjectives or phrases as you can to describe something.' He began handing out worksheets on adjectives and phrases to express feelings. Most of the class got down to it but a sullen few decided not to co-operate.

Juddy began throwing a tennis ball across the room. One of his mates caught it and threw it back. This happened a couple of times and on the third go Billy caught the ball. At the same time he gently eased Juddy by the shoulders back into his seat and put the ball in the drawer of the desk.

'You can have the ball back at dinnertime,' he said.

'I could do you for assault,' Juddy said menacingly. 'You're not supposed to touch us.'

'You behave yourself and get on with your work,' Billy said, 'or you'll get worse than that.'

'Oh, yeah. You and whose army?'

Juddy knew that Billy was powerless, could do nothing. He was the emperor without any clothes. He could threaten, he could raise his voice (but not too much or he'd be accused of verbal abuse), he could try to persuade but in effect he had no sanctions. But some of the class wanted to do the work he'd set and he wasn't prepared to let this yobbo disrupt the lesson.

Then Juddy tried a different tack by making paper aeroplanes of the worksheet. Some of his cronies followed and before long the air was filled with their aeronautical productions. For some reason, Billy had left the classroom door open. Perhaps he'd left himself a ready means of escape. He saw Mr Parry, the head, scurrying past. Billy waylaid him and said, 'I wonder if you could have

142

a word with some of the boys here, Mr Parry.'

'Nothing to do with me. It's your class and your problem,' the head muttered, hurrying on.

Later Billy asked Mr Murgatroyd how Parry had come to be appointed head.

'Easy,' the other replied. 'He was the only applicant.'

Billy struggled through the three days he'd contracted for. No wonder Hindmarsh had the flu. Billy thought, if I'd been on the permanent staff, I'd have had pneumonia. But as a supply teacher he could only work within the rules set by the head. Naturally that school went on his blacklist and he never returned. Next thing you know, Billy mused, the school would have difficulty recruiting even supply teachers and then it would have real problems.

It was a fortnight before he heard from the agency again. His first reaction was to turn down any offer of work as his experience at the boys' comprehensive had left a bitter taste in his mouth.

'This one is quite different,' the agency man told him. 'Still inner city but it's a girls' school with a multiracial intake. Before going comprehensive, it used to be a prestigious, highly select-ive grammar school. Since it's all girls, it should be less problematic than a boys' school.'

Girls less problematic? Billy thought. This man obviously hasn't done much teaching.

Billy was persuaded, especially as it was only for a couple of days. Once again he turned up bright and early and was given his morning's allocation of classes. In the event he was simply required to babysit small groups of Asian girls who were busy revising for various exams. Supervision was hardly necessary but a teacher had to be there to fulfil the statutory requirement of having a qualified person sitting in with the class.

The afternoon session was different. He was to fill in for an art class of fourteen-year-olds. It didn't take long for him to find out that he was not welcome.

'Good afternoon,' he said cheerily to the fifteen students who sat weighing him up (and down).

'Where's Mrs Kershaw?' a big girl on the front row inquired testily. 'We don't want you. We want our regular teacher.'

'Sorry,' Billy said. 'Mrs Kershaw is off sick. So I'm afraid you've got me. Don't worry. I'm not as bad as all that.'

The first thing he needed was art materials if they were to have a lesson. And as was usual on these occasions, the classroom cupboard was locked. His own prepared worksheets were hardly appropriate for an art lesson. He told the disgruntled girl to go to the head of art who was taking another class in a different part of the building and ask for the key to the art stockroom. She was soon back and grinning from ear to ear.

'Miss Frost said she can't give the stockroom key to a supply teacher.'

'We shall soon see about that,' Billy said.

He marched determinedly to the office of Miss Fussell, the deputy head, knocked on the door, and walked in.

'If I am to take 3C for art, I need materials to work with. If your Miss Frost does not open the stockroom door in the next ten minutes and provide me with the materials I need, I shall be walking out of the school and she can take the class herself.'

It worked. Within ten minutes he had a supply of drawing paper, a selection of pencils, erasers and charcoal sticks.

Before they started work, he told the form about some of the great Renaissance artists.

'Artists usually began their great works of art by doing a pencil sketch,' he explained. 'Today, a rough sketch by da Vinci or by Rembrandt would be worth millions of pounds. Who knows? Perhaps the portrait sketches you are going to do for me today might be worth a fortune in years to come. Some great artists could produce a lifelike sketch at rapid speed. Giotto was once working with this teacher Cimabue when the teacher had to leave the room. While he was out, Giotto did a lightning sketch of a fly on the end of the nose of the portrait Cimabue was working on. When he came back, he tried to blow the insect away, so real was the sketch.'

Suitably impressed by the genius of Giotto, the class got down to the task of producing pencil portraits of each other and for the next hour peace reigned.

It was during the next period, the final session of the day, a double period, that the trouble began. Billy was down to supervise a non-examination class of fifteen-year-old biology students. The absentee teacher had thoughtfully provided elaborate worksheets with lots of boxes to be ticked. Normally such 'keep 'em busy' material lasted no more than ten minutes but he had lots of his own stuff in reserve, just in case.

The adolescent girls ambled into the room. A few sat down quietly at their desks and awaited instructions. The rest of the class stood around and embarked on loud and animated conversation about boyfriends, dancing and the latest fashions. They did not take their coats off, giving the impression that they hadn't the slightest interest in either biology or the work that had been left for them by their teacher.

'Sit down!' Billy called. 'Your teacher can't be here today but she's left you some work to be done during this lesson.'

He may as well have been talking to himself for hardly anyone paid him any attention. He soldiered on and distributed the worksheets. The quiet group began work immediately. The rest continued to gossip and stand around. That was it. Billy blew his top.

'Sit down at once!' he yelled. 'Get on with the work your teacher has left for you!'

The biggest girl in the class now approached him. 'Cool it, man!' she murmured. 'You're gonna blow a gasket if you ain't careful. An' we ain't gonna fill no f–ing stupid worksheets. No way.'

She screwed up the sheet and threw it at one of the others, who reciprocated by throwing her own at somebody else. That was the signal for the others to follow and before long the room was a snowstorm of paper projectiles.

That was as much as Billy was prepared to take. He sent an intelligent-looking Asian girl to Miss Fussell with a note: 'Please come down to see 5D who have gone berserk and are using the work-sheets left for them as missiles. Perhaps you have sanctions you can use to bring them under control.'

Five minutes later, his messenger was back with a verbal reply: 'Miss Fussell said to tell you that she doesn't have time to come down.'

This was the last straw. Billy collected his coat from the cloakroom and went home. Next day, he phoned the head and told her that since he had walked out, he would not be claiming his fee and he would not be returning for the second day. Nor would he be accepting further supply appointments at her school. As a temp, there was nothing he could do to establish control over an unruly, recalcitrant class. He could only work within the rules and regulations set by the head, and as far as he could see, there weren't any. In some ways, his philosophy could be described as Buddhist. If there was something he could do to change something for the good, he should do it immediately. If there was nothing he could do, best to waste no more energy in worrying but move on.

When his friends heard about his action, they forever referred to such precipitous action as 'doing a Billy'.

Billy made up his mind not to take on any more 'subbing' (temporary) jobs and he informed the teaching agency of his decision. But a month later he had a phone call from them appealing to his better or soft-hearted nature. They were desperate to find someone to cover for a teacher who was away for a couple of days attending a restraint techniques course at the Ashworth hospital.

147

'Look,' the man pleaded, 'I know you've had some rotten experiences in those inner city schools but you might find this one a challenge. It's an observation and assessments centre in deepest Lancashire. The classes are very small, no more than five in a class.'

Billy was intrigued. The following day he turned up at the centre and met the other three members of staff who welcomed him with open arms.

'Thank God you've come,' Mrs Nesbit, the deputy head said. 'We've been wondering how we were going to manage. The headmaster is rarely here nowadays. He's usually away giving a talk or running a course somewhere on how to run one of these centres. We have only eighteen kids but they are all special pupils who have been in trouble with the law and have been taken into care. Half the buildings are occupied by social workers who are responsible for their welfare and the boarding side of things while we have the job of educating them. Nearly all the wards are from broken homes and most of them have suffered unimaginable hardship and deprivation.'

Given these circumstances, Billy was glad to be of assistance. For his first duty, he was put in charge of a young thirteen-year-old boy named Pete Fleming and told to take him into the head's unoccupied office for English comprehension. The boy had lived in difficult circumstances, with an absentee father and a mother addicted to heroin. He himself had been arrested on numerous occasions for shoplifting and eventually been taken into care. Once or twice he had run out of the school and had to be brought back by the police who usually found him in town playing the fruit machines in an amusement arcade.

In the first lesson with him, Billy was to read and discuss *My Pal Spadger* by Bill Naughton. For some odd reason, his colleagues seemed highly amused by the task which had been given to him. Something was up and Billy wondered what it was. In some ways it reminded him of the time when as a callow seventeen-year-old copy boy at the *Manchester Guardian* he'd been sent on a fool's errand for 'the big stand' and 'the long weight', the words 'stand' and 'weight' having double meanings. He'd taken the newspaper job in the hope of becoming a journalist but found that even the lowliest reporters had honours degrees. And now as he went into the office with the lad, the staff were grinning mischievously just as the postroom staff at the *Guardian* had. It didn't take Billy long to find out the reason behind their Cheshire-cat smiles. As he began work, young Pete cleared his throat of phlegm with a loud, raucous har-rumph. Billy ignored it and started reading Chapter One. The boy har-rumphed again even more loudly. Billy went on with the lesson. By the time the boy had hemmed and hawked for the thousandth time, Billy was climbing up the wall and his blood pressure had risen to a dangerous level. The guttural rasping continued for the rest of the session and Billy heaved a sigh of relief when the bell sounded for the end of the lesson. When he emerged from the head's office, the waiting staff broke out into raucous laughter as they recited the famous ad of the time: 'Hoarse? Then go suck a Zube!'

Billy saw the joke and joined in the laughter.

In the afternoon, Miss Nesbit and he took a mixed group of pupils to the swimming baths. In the minibus on the way there, the pupils carried on a furtive discussion with each other in what sounded like a foreign tongue, with most of the words ending in the syllable '-kin'. The language was hissed through the teeth with such little movement of the lips that a professional ventriloquist would have been envious. It was the kind of skill that old lags acquired in prison after many years' practice.

In the baths, Miss Nesbit and he watched the class through the large windows of the observation room above. Billy was struck by the crazy, reckless way their wards leapt and dived into the pool, often missing the concrete sides by a matter of inches. It was a good job there was a lifeguard/first-aid attendant on duty. Billy wondered what the repercussions would have been had any of them suffered serious injury. One boy in particular, Ginger Jarvis, came so close to bashing his head, Billy couldn't understand how he'd survived so long without fracturing his skull.

The following day, Billy was put in charge of a small group of five – two girls and three boys – and told to keep them busy on some creative and constructive occupation. It was left to him to think of something. Ginger Jarvis, came into the class late, his right hand heavily bandaged.

Miss Nesbit told him what had happened.

'Last night, he was involved in a quarrel with one of the social workers over which television programme his house group was to watch. Ginger lost the argument and in frustration punched a brick wall with all his strength. He broke his knuckles and his wrist and had to be taken to hospital. Not an unusual occurrence in this centre.'

The night before the lesson, Billy had racked his brains to think of something to keep them occupied. Then he remembered the dozens of unused Letraset sheets he had left over from the time when he'd attempted to produce posh personal stationery. Using them was simplicity itself. You simply stroked the letters with a biro and hey presto! The result was instant professional lettering with illustrations. He wasn't sure how the idea would go down but it was worth a try.

Before his lesson could begin, the students had to entertain an ex-pupil who returned to the centre with her new baby. The young mother, now sixteen, had become pregnant while at the school. The father, also a former student, was serving a two-year sentence for housebreaking but hoped to join the girl when he was released. The girls of the centre gathered round the pram, oohing and ahhing and generally making a fuss of the little baby boy. For the teenage parent the assessment centre was her alma mater.

When the lesson began, Billy introduced the group to Letraset and it proved to be a great success. The appeal lay in the fact it was easy to use and results were immediate. Ginger's girl, Nell, was particularly struck by the notion. She ruled out her paper meticulously and spent the whole of the period transferring the letters. Her enthusiasm was infectious and before long the other four pupils, including Pete and Ginger, the latter being able to use his left hand still, were clamouring for their own sheets. As they worked on their individual projects, there was the quiet hum of conversation and purposeful activity. Billy rejoiced that he'd discovered something that absorbed their interest and kept them busy, not an easy thing to do. It was creative work with an end product that they could be proud of. This is what's been missing with these young people, he reflected. By the end of the period, Nell had produced the most impressive embossed stationery that he'd ever seen outside a professional printing agency. Nell glowed with pleasure as she showed her handiwork to Mrs Nisbet.

'Excellent, Nell. Congratulations!' the deputy exclaimed.

'May I please photocopy a few of these for my own notepaper, Mrs Nisbet?'

'Of course, Nell. Let's go and do a few now.'

So it was happiness all round for everyone, including Billy. He had the satisfaction of knowing that he'd engaged his pupils in a worthwhile pursuit. There was only one question gnawing him. What on earth had a nice girl like Nell done to deserve being taken into care?

A little later that afternoon he seized the opportunity to ask Mrs Nisbet.

'She's here,' Mrs Nisbet informed him with a wry smile, 'because she was found guilty of writing poison pen letters. Some contained threats and some to various married couples accused the husbands of being unfaithful with her. She made a great deal of trouble and was the cause of a few marriages breaking up.'

At least, Billy mused, in future her malicious pen letters would be executed on superb notepaper.

The afternoon brought his two-day commitment to an end and he decided that he'd had enough of supply teaching. He and Laura would just have to soldier on as best they could. Perhaps things will get easier in a few years' time, Billy told himself, when I'll be eligible for the state pension.

Chapter Eight

Country Crafts

It was while visiting a museum near Preston that Titch and Billy had the brainwave. Laura and Billy had invited Titch and his wife Elaine plus their two grandchildren on a day out to Ribchester. They'd spent the first part of the morning looking at the Roman fort built about AD 78. Titch and Billy had became engrossed in the history of the site but the kids, and the ladies, had been bored to tears by the whole thing, and so they'd moved across the street to the building which was the main purpose of their visit to the town, the Museum of Childhood. For the young ones, the place was a delight, a dream come true, for it was packed with every imaginable toy and game from all over the world, ranging from dolls and teddy bears to train sets and tricycles. But what eclipsed everything and captured the imagination of them all was Queen Mary's doll's house which was on loan from Windsor Castle. No two ways about it; it was a masterpiece and fit for a queen. It had been designed by Sir Edwin Lutyens and presented to Queen Mary in 1924 when she was fifty-seven years of age and so it was more a display thing than a kid's plaything. They certainly weren't allowed to touch any part of it and even photography was forbidden.

It was built precisely to the scale of one-twelfth and every detail of the furniture and fittings from the wrought-iron entry gates in the garden to the chandeliers in the bedrooms was exact. What's more, the equipment – the water system, electric lighting, and elevators, even the tiny gramophone – worked. The wine bottles in the cellar contained genuine vintage wines and there were more than two hundred miniature volumes of books by famous authors – some in their own hand: Kipling, Chesterton, Conan Doyle, Hardy and Barrie. In addition, the furniture had been built by the leading craftsmen of the day and the paintings were commissioned from well-known artists. Once finished, the doll's house was put on show at the British Empire Exhibition of that year and also at the Ideal Home Exhibition in 1925. Having once dabbled in his spare time in wood-turning and building doll's houses, Billy was mesmerized and could only gaze in awe and wonderment at the artistic genius of the workmanship that had gone into its creation. His own efforts had been amateurish and dilettante but he could recognize creative genius when he saw it.

'You know,' he said to Titch, 'I'd give my right arm to build something even a fraction as beautiful as this.'

'That might be difficult,' Titch grinned, 'trying to build something like this with only one arm but I take your point. If you ever decide to have a shot at it, include me in.'

'I know that look,' Laura said, gazing at Billy pointedly. 'I hope this exhibition is not giving you ideas.'

'Not entirely,' he replied, 'but if Titch and I worked together, we could produce some fine works of art, maybe not as good as this, but on a more modest scale perhaps. And our models wouldn't be merely for show but for children to play with. I still have the woodworking tools and equipment languishing in the cellar at home. Maybe the two of us could form a partnership and go into business together. Now that my private tutoring has more or less fizzled out, something like this might be the answer.'

'I wouldn't want to go through all that again,' Laura countered. 'And, if my memory serves me right, there was never any money in it.'

'Then it was just a hobby done in my spare time. This would be different. We'd run it on strict commercial principles. Work out costs, find the right market, and make it pay.'

'I remember the noise and the mess,' she said.

'I'm sure we can overcome that problem,' he replied.

To Billy's surprise, Elaine became enthusiastic about the idea.

'Building doll's houses could be a worthwhile occupation if they could find the right outlets,' she said. Elaine had long been looking for something that would take Titch out from under her feet.

Laura wasn't convinced. In so many ways, Billy told himself, I'm lucky to have someone like Laura as my wife. If we'd been a car, I'd have been the accelerator and she'd have been the brake. A good analogy perhaps, he reflected, but a car needs fuel, that is money, if it's going to move forward. At that moment, however, it was the brake

156

doing the talking.

'Where would you work and exactly where would you sell them?' she said doubtfully. 'I seem to remember that you could only move them at Christmas time. That wouldn't be of much use. What we need is a steady regular income. That's common sense.'

But Billy wasn't in the mood for common sense. The more he thought about this new idea of working with Titch, the more attractive it seemed and he wasn't to be put off by Laura's logical arguments.

'We could work in my workshop basement and maybe install a dust extraction system,' he said. 'As for outlets, we could try the craft fairs. They are held on a regular basis in various parts of the north-west and there's usually one being held somewhere every week. We could start by building small, simple houses and then as we get better, make bigger models.'

'Later, we could build miniature furniture and install lighting systems,' Titch added, becoming more and more excited. 'Let's go for it. I'm willing to put some capital into the enterprise. With Billy's manual skills and my brains, we can't miss; we're bound to go far.'

'How about Timbuktu?' Laura suggested.

On the drive home, Titch could talk about nothing else. He prattled on all the way back to Manchester.

'This could be the beginning of a large international company, Smalley and Hopkins,' he proclaimed.

157

'Don't you mean Hopkins and Smalley? Alphabetical order is the usual way of establishing a company name.'

'Why not think big?' Titch suggested. 'Best not to put all your eggs in one basket like doll's houses. Let's broaden the concept and include your other skills like wood-turning and wine-making?'

'Oh, no!' Laura sighed at the back of the car. 'Do you two learn nothing from history?'

'According to Henry Ford, history is bunk,' Titch said.

'Those who do not learn from history are destined to repeat their mistakes,' Laura countered.

It was no use. Titch and Billy were on a roll, and there was no stopping them. That's how their little concern, Country Crafts, was born.

For the first few weekends, Titch joined Billy in his basement, checking out the equipment. He pulled out the wood-turning tools from the back of the dummy cellar where they had lain for over three years. They'd become caked in dust and rust but they were all there still: the lathe, the gouges, the chisels, the chucks. Billy had almost forgotten what many of them were for. He gave Titch a Cook's tour of the parts and the need for safety precautions and they worked late into the evening cleaning up and lubricating everything.

'What's a chuck and what's it for?' he asked.

Billy explained patiently that a chuck was a metal faceplate usually screwed onto the wood in order to mount the work on the lathe.

Next Billy taught him the basics of doll's house construction though his own skills were limited in that respect as he'd never produced anything ambitious in his early efforts.

Undoubtedly the biggest cleaning job concerned the wine-making accessories, especially the jars and the demijohns, all of which needed swilling out and sterilizing. Most of the funnels or gurglers had to be discarded as they were beyond saving. Together they made a close study of C.J. Berry's *Wine-making for Beginners*.

'We are going to make a fortune,' Titch enthused. 'I only wish I'd taken up these hobbies earlier in life. I'd probably be a millionaire by now.'

Upstairs, Laura was still concerned about the clouds of sawdust that would be blowing into their lungs and throughout the house.

'I remember all this from years ago,' she said. 'Up above, the whole house was shaking, with books and ornaments falling off shelves. We had the impression you were building Noah's Ark down there. Not only that, there was a layer of fine dust on everything and it was a constant battle to keep the place clean.'

'No need to worry this time, Laura,' Billy assured her. 'Titch and I have ordered state-of-the-art respirators and a vacuum dust extractor. So there should be no problem.'

Titch was a quick learner and after three months they were up and running.

They had twenty gallons of the most delicious fruit wines fermenting: elderberry, peach, apricot, apple, gooseberry, rhubarb, and even carrot.

'This will be ready in another three months,' Billy told Titch. 'It's illegal to sell it but there's nothing to stop us offering it to customers at the

159

craft fairs as a bonus for buying our other products.'

On the woodcraft side of the enterprise, they had honed their tools and their skills. The only thing they needed now was wood in order to go into production. The hardwoods were expensive to buy new at the timber merchants and they looked round for alternative sources. Billy fell back on his old remedy when he'd been searching for bargains. The auction. And it didn't take them long to find one.

It was to be held just outside Bury and involved the sale of a complete carpentry and joinery business specializing in fitting out pubs and clubs. It seemed that the previous owner, a fifty-year-old Lothario, had run off to South America with his twenty-year-old secretary, leaving behind a wife and three grown-up sons. The enterprise, its tools, equipment and materials, was to be sold, lock, stock and barrel. Titch and Billy weren't too interested in the locks and the barrels but they were definitely in the market for any stocks of hardwoods that might be going.

On the Saturday morning, they got there early to secure a place at the front. The premises were crowded with dealers and artisans of all kinds, all looking, like them, for bargains. There were lots of miscellaneous pieces of exotic hardwood put up for sale: mahogany, teak, ebony, iroko, rosewood, walnut. The wood was seasoned and ready for working. The bidding was keen and Billy was in there with the rest of them, holding up his auction number. It was dangerous for him to attend an auction like this; in fact, dangerous for him to attend any auction, for like Oscar Wilde he could resist anything but temptation.

'I think we have enough now,' Titch whispered to him when he'd secured the twentieth batch of wood. 'There should be enough to keep us going for the next year.'

Titch was right. Anyway, there was no hardwood left. Most of it was now registered to them.

When the auction was over, they collected the wood, which was heavy, and packed it into the boot and back seat of the old Morris Oxford. Billy found that in addition to the wood, he had somehow bid for a mountain of boxes containing sundry plumbing and electrical accessories: wires, sockets, u-bends, T-joints, giant G-cramps, and lots of other things whose purpose stumped him. They were all his and they weighed a ton. They managed, only God knew how, to pack them into the Morris but the poor old car was now well down on its springs. The whole way back, it screeched and squealed in agony at the torture to which they'd subjected it.

At home, they unpacked the purchases into the cellar, leaving hardly any room to move. As Billy viewed the huge collection of wood and metal he'd bought, he felt like the old farmer in the Grimm Brothers fairytale: the one where he went out to buy a cow and came back with a turkey, or was it a donkey? Anyway, it was the wrong thing.

Before getting down to business in the workshop, they attended a wood-turning course in the Lake District – a sure sign that they were taking the whole thing seriously. They were the only two students on the course which was conducted by a master craftsman who had his workshop in a converted chapel deep in the heart of the countryside and away from other human beings. Surrounded by beautiful lakes, mountains and valleys, they began their woodcraft course. The first thing that struck them was that the floor of the workshop was two feet deep in wood shavings.

'My wife comes out to clean up the place about once a month,' their teacher explained.

'Why don't you work at home in Kendal?' Billy asked him. 'Why have your workshop here, five miles out of town?'

'The wife won't allow me to work at home.' He smiled ruefully 'She said it's too noisy and too messy and this old chapel was the only place I could find.'

It sounded ominous for his own chances working in the basement at home in Manchester. Apart from Laura's complaints, Dr Gillespie next door to them in Manchester had once asked Billy if he could turn off his drill as it was interfering with his television reception. Maybe when the business was up and running, they could rent premises in an industrial park but for the time being it wasn't on.

On their return to Manchester, they got down to work and found that there was something hypnotic about watching a piece of wood whirling round on a lathe and before long they were turning out all manner of objets d'art: wall plaques, clocks, barometers, bowls, pepper mills, serving platters and nutcrackers. This last item caused much mirth amongst Billy's male acquaintances, especially when they heard he could also offer a heavy-duty version.

Meanwhile Titch had begun producing doll's houses under Billy's instruction. He taught Titch everything he knew. First, they bought the blueprints of several models and came to the conclusion that the double-fronted pseudo Tudor type was the most impressive. It was also the most difficult but they were ready for challenge. Next, they visited a timber merchant and purchased large sheets of compressed wood which was easy to work with, especially as Billy was the proud owner of a deWalt bandsaw. They worked with modest designs at first and Titch soon picked up the routine. After a few weeks, Billy felt confident enough to leave him working on his own. He was proud to see how Titch used his new metal tape measure to check all his calculations. Billy was so sure about Titch's skill that when he suggested they install miniature lighting in the houses and even a front door bell, Billy went along with it immediately. As a final touch, they bought a few items of tiny Renaissance furniture plus one or two dolls and stood back to admire their handiwork.

'I think our problem,' Titch said, grinning happily, 'is going to be holding the crowds back at our first craft fair.'

'We must insist on orderly queues,' Billy added. 'And only one doll's house to a customer.'

When they had produced six models, it was time to bring in their sternest critic – Laura. If she liked their work, they were quids in. With a fanfare of trumpets, they brought her down to the basement to view their masterpieces.

'So, what do you think, Laura?' Billy asked,

removing the cover with a flourish.

'The wood-turned pieces look fine. I like the eggcups in particular but the pepper mills seem stiff and refuse to turn,' she said, trying one out.

'Just a few adjustments needed,' he said hastily.

'And then there's the barometer, it's not straight...'

'OK, OK, Laura,' he said testily 'I get the picture. Everything will be superb when we've done a little more work on them. But look at the doll's houses. You can't fault them, surely.'

She pursed her lips as she carried out an inspection, walking round the back of Titch's masterpieces. Finally she pronounced her verdict.

'They don't look quite right,' she said carefully. 'Was it part of the design to have the chimneys inclined at an oblique angle like that? At first sight, they look like authentic Tudor houses and are most impressive, but...'

Billy was half expecting this 'but'. It would have been unusual if she hadn't had a 'but'.

'Well, what is it?' he asked wearily

'They look kind of skew-whiff. A bit cock-eyed.'

'The houses have character,' he replied.

'You're right, Billy. They're certainly unusual. And what about the windows and doors? Are they supposed to slope like that?'

'OK, OK. So they're not perfect. But they look attractive. And little girls won't be measuring angles with protractors and plumb lines.'

'They can't be skew-whiff!' Titch whinged.

But Laura was right. The houses did look as if they had been affected by underground subsidence.

They were at a loss to explain it as Titch had been so scrupulous in his measurements. To be absolutely sure, he had even used two tape measures.

Billy checked the front and the back of the houses carefully and the discrepancy soon became obvious. The back was longer than the front. But how had that come about? That was the question. He decided to look at the tape measures Titch had been using. One of them was in feet and inches, the other was metric.

'We're always being told,' Titch wailed, 'that we must go metric and so I bought a new measure.'

'But you were not meant to use both,' Billy said. 'It was either one or the other. It's a damn good job you weren't working in the American space programme or NASA would be in serious trouble. The question now is: what do we do with these six houses after all the money we've spent?'

Laura had the answer.

'Why not make out that you've made them crooked deliberately? You could advertise them at the craft fairs as towers of Pisa or listed buildings or maybe illustrations of the nursery rhyme, "The House that Jack Built". Or maybe the House that Titch Built.' She laughed. 'You could sell each one under the title of "The House of the Crooked Man". You remember the jingle ends, "And they all lived together in a little crooked house".'

'This is no laughing matter, Laura,' Billy pouted. 'These houses cost one hundred pounds each in materials. We can't afford to lose all that money.'

Chapter Nine

Come to the Fair

Their first craft fair was in Liverpool at Lark Lane, formerly a police station. They arrived at nine o'clock and throughout the day a small procession of punters strolled through the fair.

Every craft imaginable was presented there: leatherwork, jewellery, glass, stuffed animals, ceramics, needlecraft, soap and candles, flower-arranging, the list was endless. And much to their anxiety, included two other wood-turners and one doll's house maker.

They set up their stall, making it as attractive as possible. It was illegal to sell their wine but there was nothing to stop them having a free wine-tasting session as an incentive. They sat behind their trestle table feeling like spiders in a web, waiting for unwary victims. Only two punters came and that was to try the free wine. They weren't connoisseurs, though, as it soon became apparent.

'That would make an excellent paint remover,' remarked one cheeky, spotty-faced youth. Billy hated him immediately, especially as he didn't buy anything.

The second one was a mottled old man who offered to buy a bottle of rhubarb wine.

'Sorry,' Billy told him. 'We're not allowed to sell it. You liked the taste, did you?'

166

'No,' he croaked, 'but I'm looking for an effective weedkiller for my garden.'

They sat there for hours without making a single sale. Several times it looked as if someone was going to approach to examine their merchandise. It was a test of nerves as they watched their potential customers wandering along the aisles.

'Keep your eyes down, Titch,' Billy hissed. 'For God's sake, don't let her see you looking at her but I think that lady over there is staring in our direction. I think she's coming towards us. Try to look nonchalant.'

The lady glanced at them and grimaced as she made her way to the knitwear stand next door.

Late in the afternoon, they caught the attention of a little girl with her mother and father.

'Oh, Mam, look at those funny cock-eyed houses. They're called Crooked Houses. I want one.'

'Come away, Doris,' the father scolded. 'Don't touch anything. You'll break something. Them chimneys don't look too safe.'

Titch and Billy sat there for a whole day. At five o'clock they counted their takings. Five shillings for the sale of one pepper mill. Petrol to drive there and back had been nearly five pounds.

They tried several other craft fairs after that with similar results. Lucy, in London and now married to Steve, took pity on them and tried to sell one on their behalf. In their struggle to carry it into the house, they managed to drop it, making it even more crooked and causing injury to Steve's foot. For several weeks, he hobbled around, his foot in plaster. Lucy did not tell them the actual wording of the imprecations he used to describe their endeavours. But since he was an advertising copywriter and a wordsmith by profession, it was no doubt creative and colourful.

They'd managed to get rid of most of the wood-turned objects to unsuspecting customers but when Laura discovered that Billy's favourite African hardwood, iroko, was carcinogenic, she soon put the kibosh on any further wood-turning. They still had capital tied up in half a dozen crooked houses, however. There was nothing for it but to advertise and this they did by placing an ad in *Practical Gardening*, thinking that maybe some kind-hearted grandparents might think of buying one for a granddaughter. Even there they had more or less given up hope and resigned themselves to being stuck with the remaining houses. Then out of the blue they had a phone call all the way from someone in Salisbury in Wiltshire.

'I am very interested in buying one of your Tudor mansions,' a voice with a Farmer Giles dialect said. 'I hope they're not all gone.'

Billy was able to reassure him on this point.

'I shall be driving up with my wife this afternoon,' he said. 'It may be late evening when we get there. I hope this will be all right.'

Billy was jubilant. Maybe it was only a single house but it would mean one less to worry about if the stranger bought one.

It was ten o'clock at night when the couple arrived but they didn't mind a little inconvenience. Anything to move these leaning towers. The middle-aged pair looked tense and worn out after their long journey, the lady complaining of a bad

168

headache. Laura was able to offer relief with a cup of tea and a couple of aspirins. Then it came to the part where they were to inspect and select a house and now it was Billy's turn to have a headache.

'They look a little bent,' their visitor remarked, examining the offerings.

End of sale, he thought.

Then to their surprise he said, pointing to a house, 'But that don't matter none. I'll take this one. Now, if you don't mind, we'd like to get off as we have a long journey ahead of us.'

Without haggling, he paid the asking price of two hundred pounds in cash. Ten twenty-pound notes which Billy counted out in the kitchen. Without more ado, the customers were gone and Billy was left flabbergasted but overjoyed in the knowledge that at last their work had been appreciated. Though it was late, he phoned Titch and gave him the good news. Like Billy, he was hardly able to take it in.

'At last,' he exclaimed, 'someone has recognized the skill, artistry and industry that I have put into these creations.'

Next morning, Laura took the money to the bank as their first business deposit and came close to being arrested. All the notes were forgeries and not very good ones at that. There was nothing for it but to take them to the police station which they did together.

'I'd like to make a donation of two hundred pounds to the Policemen's Christmas Party Fund,' Billy said to the sergeant on duty.

'That's very kind of you, sir,' the officer replied happily.

But he didn't seem to appreciate the humour when Billy explained they were forgeries which had been foisted on them. Instead the policeman laboriously subjected them to the filling out of an interminably long form requesting precise details of the deception. Not that they were able to tell him much as they had no name, address, or phone number. They'd been well and truly swizzled.

Next day Billy remarked to Titch that their Farmer Giles character had said the houses were bent but he was the one who'd proved to be bent in the end.

They still had five houses left and they thought of handing them to a gang of boys collecting firewood for Guy Fawkes Night. Then son Mark, the estate agent, came up with a brilliant idea.

'Most building societies I know have the most unimaginative displays in their windows,' he declared. 'They usually have boring brochures about interest rates for loans and savings, and advice about surveys and valuations. These houses could give them a focus of interest.'

He approached a building society with whom he had professional dealings and, after employing his persuasive techniques, they took the lot at £250 each.

The following week their sloping houses could be seen in the windows of the building society with the ominously-worded warning:

A HOUSE IS THE BIGGEST PURCHASE YOU WILL EVER MAKE. BEFORE YOU INVEST, HAVE YOUR HOUSE SURVEYED PROFESSIONALLY OR YOU MIGHT END UP WITH ONE LIKE THIS.

ASK FOR DETAILS INSIDE.

That left only the wine, of which they had fifteen gallons. Despite the negative responses at the craft fair, Titch and Billy were not discouraged and continued to offer it as gifts to their friends and relatives. They lost most of their friends and a few of their relatives steered clear of them. They offered a prize to their own families for the most attractive names which they could use for their labels when they came to bottle it. The entries weren't as attractive as they'd hoped but at least they were original.

SAUTERNE D'AUF (SO TURNED OFF)
GRAPE EXPECTATIONS
VIN À GARE
VIN PLONK
SHATTERED NERVE DU PAPE
NASTY SPEWMANTI

That was enough. They got the message. And when foreign, professionally-produced wines in the supermarkets became cheaper than their own, they abandoned their careers as vintners and poured their surplus stock down the drains. For some time afterwards, the district was infested with a plague of inebriated rodents.

Meanwhile Billy looked around for fresh inspiration. It was amazing how time hung heavy when he was not busy and he didn't have a routine. He'd ended up in the situation that he'd been dreading. Nowt to do, at a loose end – and one he'd been warned about in the books about retirement. He still remembered one poignant contribution written by a lady whose husband had become 'lost' after taking early retirement.

'He's spent his whole life working and now he doesn't know what to do with himself,' she wrote. 'He goes for a walk in the park in the morning. He keeps rabbits but they don't take up much of his time. He used to be hale and hearty but not any more. He just mopes round the house getting under my feet. I wish he'd join his mates in the pub but he reckons they have nothing to talk about except football and betting on horses.'

Billy was resolved never to become like that or, if he did, it wouldn't be for long. Twiddling his thumbs or staring at the wall were never his forte. Something had to turn up and soon if he was to remain compos mentis.

Chapter Ten

Some People have All the Luck

They say that bad luck comes along, like London buses, in threes but Billy didn't go for that superstitious mumbo-jumbo. When he'd nearly set the kitchen on fire, it was an accident, not an omen or a sign of bad luck. Laura had gone to town to do some shopping and he'd been left to make his own lunch. Something simple, so he thought he'd boil a couple of eggs. He'd just put them in the pan and lit the stove when the phone rang. It was Titch. He was a real chatterbox and kept him talking. When Billy got back to the kitchen he found the place thick with smoke. The pan had boiled dry and the smoke had ruined the wallpaper and the ceiling tiles. The eggs were as hard as rocks but he hid them in the bin and made a peanut butter sandwich. No big deal. Could have happened to anyone. He switched on the fan but it didn't deceive Laura.

'I can't leave you alone for a minute,' she said. 'The kitchen will need redecorating.'

'It's the first time it's happened,' he protested.

'What about the time you were running a bath and went to answer the doorbell. That cost us a pretty penny to clean up the mess.'

Sometimes he wished she didn't have such a good memory.

Laura never accused him directly though. She usually made snide remarks like, 'Somebody left the tap running in the bathroom' or 'Somebody left the fridge door open' or 'Somebody forgot to lock the garage door'. Since there were only two of them living in the house, the 'somebody' could only be one person. Billy!

When their ancient Morris Oxford broke down and required serious and expensive work on it to get it through its MOT, he thought that maybe there *was* something to the three-in-a-row luck theory after all. Although the car had given reliable and faithful service for many years, a major repair job was inevitable to keep it on the road. All the same, it was money they could ill afford and there was no alternative but to keep it on hold. They hoped there were no more big expenses around the corner.

Shortly after this, it was their wedding anniversary. They usually celebrated by going out for an a la carte dinner in a city restaurant but this time they thought they'd do something different. They booked a bus trip to Blackpool where they planned to walk along the famous Golden Mile and perhaps do a spot of shopping in the area around the Winter Gardens. The newspaper headlines that morning seemed pretty depressing, all about some Russian nuclear reactor at a place called Chernobyl being on fire. But then Russia seemed an awful long way off and not really their concern. Besides, they were so looking forward to their day at the seaside. They boarded the single-decker bus and were surprised to see that there seemed to be only two other passengers that day.

Blackpool held so many memories for them. For Billy it was a mixture of good and bad associations. There had been the wartime evacuation to Bispham where he had shared a billet with Titch and Oscar and where the landlady, Mrs Mossop, had helped herself to some of their rations to feed her own family; there had followed the move to the headmaster's bungalow at Cleveleys where the food was better. Then later in life in the fifties, Billy and Laura had brought their young family for a happy week's holiday at the Squire's Gate holiday camp.

'I remember that week so well,' Laura said when he reminded her. 'On the first morning, the manager announced that we had to wear the camp badge at all times as proof that we were bona fide residents.'

'And two-year-old Matthew lost his on the sands,' Billy laughed, 'and was sick with worry for the rest of the week, fearing he wouldn't be allowed back into the camp. He wasn't happy till we got him a new one from the camp office. All water under the bridge now,' he sighed.

Their anniversary trip went like clockwork. It was a lovely day, the bus was on time, and within the hour they were dropped off outside the famous tower.

'I shall collect you at this same spot at three thirty,' the driver told them. 'Please don't be late and I shall have you back in Manchester by around five o'clock.'

Their day at the resort was most enjoyable. They did their shopping and in the market picked up many bargains, including of course the com-

175

pulsory stick of Blackpool rock; they had lunch in Hill's Restaurant where many years before Billy had once dined with his old father during the war. It had been 1941 and Billy found that thinking about it brought a whole lot of memories flooding back. It was amazing how a particular smell or piece of music could so evoke a scene and the associated emotions. In his head, he could still hear the voice of Deanna Durbin singing, 'Waltzing, waltzing, high in the clouds'. He recalled that the purpose of the old man's visit had been to bring a precious gift for the headmaster, Brother Dorian, namely two dozen eggs to be shared by the dozen evacuees living in the billet. After their lunch, there had followed a crazy vertiginous ride on the Big Dipper, his father still clutching the bag of eggs. The priceless cargo eventually reached the Brother's hands intact but none of the evacuees got to see a single egg.

Their day in Blackpool was soon over and it was time for Billy and Laura to make their way to the rendezvous for the journey home. Anxious not to miss their bus, they were in the agreed place at three fifteen. It began to rain but they couldn't complain because it had remained fine for most of the day. Three thirty came and went but there was no bus. Furthermore, there was no sign of the other two passengers who had come with them.

'Perhaps they were Blackpool residents returning home on a single ticket,' Billy said.

At three forty-five they became concerned; at four o'clock they began to worry. When four thirty came round with still no sign of their transport home, they reluctantly gave up. The bus wasn't coming. There was nothing for it but to walk the two miles to the nearest bus station in Talbot Road where they found there wasn't anything back to Manchester that day until 8 p.m. What to do with the time until then as it was still raining? Billy remembered there was an Odeon cinema on nearby Dickson Road and they decided to while away a couple of hours watching whatever film was playing there. Ten minutes of the movie was enough to fill them with horror. To say the theme was warped and bizarre was an understatement. The plot concerned a lover who was so obsessed with a girlfriend who had jilted him that he cut off her limbs one by one, leaving her as just a torso with a head. As they came away to catch their bus, Billy couldn't help remarking, 'That film was sick, sick, sick and so is the world that could think up such a plot. If there's such a thing as reincarnation, I pray to God that He'll send me to another planet next time around.'

Later they were not surprised to learn that critics had lambasted it as 'the worst film ever made'. Nevertheless it was hardly the ideal way to end their anniversary celebration. It was the fourth piece of ill luck on the trot. Surely things had to change for the better soon.

Chapter Eleven

Shocks and Scares

It was all Maggie Thatcher's fault. She was the one who lured Billy into the stock market. In 1979 she became the first woman prime minister and, as a dedicated believer in free markets and private enterprise, one of her first actions was to put Britain's public utilities up for sale. Everyone was to become a stockholder and part-owner of the nation's wealth. Council house tenants were encouraged to buy their houses instead of wasting money on rent and everybody was offered shares in the nationalized industries. The country's assets were to be put up for auction and no one was to be left out of the chance to acquire a slice of the cake. Privatization became the new buzz word.

For a number of years, Billy had been in the habit of meeting up with his old school chums – the Damian College Smokers' Club – and they usually got together on the last Friday of each month in the Pineapple, close to the city centre. Doris, formerly the barmaid and now the land-lady, had made the place cosy by providing a log fire in the winter and by laying on a good selection of sandwiches when called for. In the early days, the gang, comprising Titch, Oscar, Olly and Nobby, had been accompanied by wives or partners but for some time now, as the members had grown older, the get-together had developed into males only, like one of those male bonding peer groups you read about in Margaret Mead's anthropology books. Perhaps wives had become only too glad to see the back of their partners for an hour or two. Be that as it may, the men had come to regard their regular rendezvous as a refuge from family cares and a forum for discussion of personal problems. Whatever the reason, they looked forward to their monthly chinwag and the exchange of news and views. The one thing that had not changed was the fact that they saw the gathering as an opportunity to show off their wit and verbal dexterity. Apart from sharing news of latest family developments, their usual topics were women, sex, experiences at work, and jokes about these. To the list of subjects was now added stocks and shares or, as Oscar liked to call them, shocks and scares. In particular, they wanted to hear each other's opinions about Maggie's first offering, British Telecom. Should they join the capitalist class and become stakeholders in Britain? Olly, who'd been their Mister Know-All since the age of eleven when they'd all been in the same form, was soon pontificating and dispensing his 'considered advice'.

'It's the opportunity of a lifetime,' he said. 'We should fill our boots with as many shares as we can lay our hands on.'

Even Nobby whose expertise lay in the realms of women and sex was enthusiastic. 'It's money for jam. The government's selling off the family silver and we'd be fools not to apply for some of it.'

'You think we should become investors in Great Britain plc?' Billy asked.

'Hell, no!' exclaimed Olly. 'You don't invest for the long term. You buy the shares and sell the very next day, putting the profit in your pocket. It's vital that you don't ever become emotionally involved with shares of a particular company. You've got to be cold-hearted and take your money the first chance you get.'

'In that case,' added Titch, 'you should submit your application through a stockbroker. That way, you don't need any money Which is just as well because I haven't got any.'

'Don't need any money? How do you make that out, Titch?' Billy asked.

'The document which I've received from Harold Lumgair, the broker, says, "Tick here to buy but if you tick this second box, we shall sell them for you as well." They simply send you your profit.'

'Free money?' Billy said. 'That makes nonsense of the old maxim that there's no such thing as a free lunch!'

Their friend Oscar who fancied himself as a something of a wit and a cross between Noel Coward and Oscar Wilde had to put his oar in. 'This meeting of ours is beginning to sound like Fagin's den of thieves with all this talk of money and profits.'

'Don't you want to double your money?' Olly asked.

Oscar smiled indulgently as he said languidly, 'The safest way to double your money is to fold it and put it in your pocket.'

A week after their meeting, British Telecom was floated on the market. The public were so crazy to get their hands on the shares that the two million applications received had to be rationed to eight hundred shares per customer. Nevertheless, each member of the Smokers' Club – with the exception of Oscar who felt the business was beneath him and rather vulgar – were a few hundred pounds to the good.

'You know, Laura,' Billy said when he reported his success with the British Telecom shares, 'since retiring I've tried numerous things: private coaching, supply teaching, woodcraft, and each one has turned out a bit of a flop. I've been on the lookout for a new interest in life, something that will absorb my surplus energy. Maybe dabbling in the stock market is the answer, especially if we make a few quid out of it.'

Laura was her usual cautious self 'You've made a couple of hundred pounds, Billy, on one speculation. One swallow doesn't make a summer. There's no guarantee that you could make a steady income from buying and selling shares.'

'No one said I was going to go into it full time. But wouldn't it be good if I began making money by investing?'

'Investing? You mean speculating. To make money that way, you may as well roll a dice or consult a gypsy fortune-teller. What I find weird is that when one man sells a share, another one buys it and they both think they're clever. Somebody wins and somebody loses. Besides, you don't judge a man's success by the size of his wallet. Probably your best investments will be the ones you don't make.'

'I think you're being overcautious, Laura.'

'I know you, Billy. You tend to go over the top once you become interested in something, like you did with your private students. Remember what my father used to say. Moderation in all things.'

'I think the Roman poet Horace said it before him, Laura, but never mind, I take the point. But if we're going to quote sayings, don't forget the old Russian maxim: "He who risketh not, drinketh not champagne."'

'Sometimes I'm convinced you're mad,' she said.

At the next meeting of the Smokers' Club, his friends were euphoric. They'd all made a few hundred and the way they rejoiced, you'd have thought they'd pocketed millions.

'I think you've all got things out of proportion,' Billy told them. 'Our profits won't exactly change our lives.'

'Maybe not, Hoppy,' Olly gloated, 'but it's like finding a five pound note in the street. That flyer gives more satisfaction than a hundred we've had to work for. It's the same with making a profit out of shares, it warms the cockles of your heart.'

'What *is* all this talk about profit?' Oscar drawled. 'As far as I'm concerned, a profit is a religious bloke who talks to God.'

'There's plenty more where that came from,' Nobby enthused, ignoring him. 'Maggie Thatcher has a whole bunch of industries lined up for flotation: gas, water, electricity. We're going to be rich. I'm thinking of ordering my Roller now.'

'Lucky you!' said Titch. 'The few quid I made went to pay off some of my overdraft. I have what the accountants call a cash flow problem. When I was out shopping the other day, the shop assistant told me that they took credit cards. "Too late," I said. "Mine have already been taken."'

'If we go on making easy money like this,' Billy said, 'our money worries will be over. I still have some of my pension lump sum left and I wouldn't mind doubling that if I could find the right shares to invest in.'

'What is happening to us?' Oscar asked, looking round at them all. 'Our little band of brothers who used to discuss literature, poetry and politics has become a right-wing investors' club talking about nothing but filthy lucre and how we can make more of it. And what's all this talk about cash flow. As far as I'm concerned cash flow is the movement of your money going down the toilet. We've become a bunch of philistines, anxious to get our snouts in the trough. You're all on a roll at present, but I warn you, it won't last because it never does.'

Despite Oscar's misgivings, their little flutter on the stock market had whetted their appetites and had them hooked. Especially Billy. He was thinking about going beyond speculating in new shares and dipping a foot in the main stock market. If he could make a few hundred profiting from the new privatizations, he thought, how much more could he make in the big market. Already he'd ordered delivery of *The Investor's Chronicle* and had begun studying form like a gambler at the racetrack. There were one or two shares that he fancied, like BAT (British and American Tobacco), Fisons, Beechams, the London Brick Company, but he didn't tell the others about them because they preferred to bet on the new flotations, not old-established companies. Besides, he didn't think they had as much capital as he had to invest. Following the stock market became an obsession and he found himself reading books on the history of the London Stock Exchange and price movements. He even began drawing wall graphs of economic trends in commodities. He felt as if he'd at last discovered his true talent. He was an investor!

Billy was the youngest child in his family and for many years had been considered the 'baby'. In serious discussion among his brothers and sisters his opinions had tended to be discountenanced as the views of a youngster even when he had passed the age of forty. There had originally been six children in the family and today only he and his brother Les remained. His brother Jim had been killed in the merchant navy in 1943, his two sisters Flo and Polly had died some years ago, while Sam who had lived in Belfast had passed away five years earlier. His brother Les, who was four years older, had now retired with his wife Annette to an idyllic country cottage in Lancashire. He had formerly worked in the rainwear industry where he had earned a good living, his earnings in the early days being always more than Billy's meagre salary as a teacher. Les had also gone into politics and had been a Labour councillor on Salford City Council. When Billy told him about his interest in the stock market, Les was not impressed but when Billy mentioned that he'd been buying shares in Thatcher's recent flotations, he hit the roof.

'You're betraying all our family's working-class

principles,' he stormed. 'The old man would be spinning in his grave if he knew that you had gone over to the enemy.'

'I can't see anything wrong with making a few bob,' Billy protested. 'Maggie Thatcher is trying to create a shareholding democracy. The nation's assets will belong to the ordinary people instead of the bloated plutocrats.'

'Nonsense, Billy. What she's doing is having a car boot sale and selling off the family possessions for much less than they're worth. No doubt she'll use the proceeds to reduce income tax. What she's really doing is emasculating the trade unions by making the working man a capitalist.'

'Sorry, Les. I can't see it that way. People will take a much greater interest in public affairs if they have a stake in it. And it will also give them a chance to share in the profits of the big industrial concerns instead of lining the pockets of the millionaires.'

'Rubbish, Billy. The stock market is a casino for the filthy rich who create nothing but simply push bits of paper around and the whole thing is driven by two emotions: greed and fear. When greed is uppermost, you have a bull market and everyone is making lots of money and everything in the garden's rosy. Then suddenly there's rumour, say of possible war in the Middle East and the price of oil is going to rocket. Then everyone rushes for the exits and you have a bear market and the price of your shares will plummet and you'll lose your shirt. Speculators are like a herd of sheep and sheep get slaughtered.'

'You're too pessimistic, Les. At the moment,

everything's going great now Maggie's in charge.'

'Sure, Billy, we have a bull market at the moment but the stock market is a dog-eat-dog world, a bit like trench warfare. Everyone is trying to forecast what's going to happen next but you'd be better off looking in a crystal ball. Speculators always remind me of a massive swarm of hungry sardines who dart one way in greed then turn tail in terror at the mere shadow of a shark. At the moment, the governing factor is avarice. When historians look back on the eighties, they'll associate the period with greed and selfishness, each man out for himself. Your Iron Lady says there's no such thing as society, only individuals.'

'So are you telling me, Les, that you're not tempted to dabble in the market and put a few shillings away?'

'That's right. I'm not tempted in the least. Annette and I have enough to live on and we're content with things as they are.'

'But what do you do with yourself now you're retired?'

'I have a number of hobbies. For example I enjoy working on my allotment. I do oil paintings on canvas, mainly scenes of Manchester, and I play bowls at my club.'

'Those should keep you busy, Les. So tell me your day's routine.'

'I sleep a little late; in the mornings tend my allotment (I've won prizes for my cucumbers); take a nap at dinnertime; in the afternoon stroll over to the bowling club, have a pint with my mates and practise my bowls. I now play for Lancashire. Then each evening I relax with my oil

186

painting. That's my life more or less. Simple and no worries.'

'I've seen your paintings, Les, and I think they're every bit as good as L.S. Lowry's. If you could get them exhibited at the Salford Art Gallery, I'm sure they'd soon be recognized as the masterpieces they are.'

'What then, Billy?'

'Maybe you'd have exhibitions in a West End gallery in London. Maybe you'd become rich and famous.'

'And then?'

'You'd have thousands in the bank.'

'And then?'

'You'd be able to come back to Lancashire, buy a little cottage, and take things easy.'

He laughed. 'Perhaps I could even have a little allotment, do a bit of painting, and take up bowls.'

The talk with Les had left Billy feeling a little uneasy, even a bit guilty. Was it immoral to want to make money by buying and selling shares – by, as Les had put it, moving bits of paper around? It was a relief to meet up with his fellow speculators at the Pineapple. They shared a common interest and enthusiasm for 'making a quick buck'. He had to come clean with his friends, though, and admit that he'd bought shares in the regular market and hit a rough patch. He'd been losing money on the shares of the big companies. But no one offered him sympathy.

'The whole idea of investing,' Olly preached, 'is to make money, not lose it. You buy when the price is low and you sell when it's high. Simple.'

'Easier said than done,' Billy replied. 'I seem to

187

have the unusual gift of always making the wrong move. As soon as I buy a share, its price goes down. Then after I've sold it, the price goes up. Last week, I bought shares in four established companies and I lost money on all of them.'

'That's terrible,' Titch exclaimed. 'How did you sleep at night?'

'Like a baby,' he replied

'With all that worry! How do you mean, like a baby?' Titch asked.

'I sleep for a couple of hours and then I wake up and cry for a couple of hours.'

That got them all laughing.

They're a heartless lot, Billy said to himself.

'It's good to see you haven't lost your sense of humour; Hoppy,' Olly said. 'But you'll never make a fortune betting on the old companies. The big money is in the small, up-and-coming firms that are relatively unknown. Take one called Polly Peck. If you'd put say a hundred pounds into it a few years ago, your holding would now be worth one hundred thousand. The firm was originally a tiny insignificant clothing company until a Turkish Cypriot called Asil Nadir used it as a shell company and poured all his huge business interests into it, electronic, fruit, hotels, and God knows what else.'

A hundred pounds becoming £100,000! When the gang heard this, they were all ears.

'But how do you recognize it when a tiny company like that comes along?' Billy asked.

'You need to have inside information about developments before they take place,' Olly replied. 'Then you buy in on the ground floor when the price is at rock bottom. And it so happens that Nobby and I have such information about a small company that is about to take off literally and metaphorically I hand you over now to my learned friend, Norbert Nodder, who will tell you all about it'

'Thanks, Olly. Now, I've got a company,' Nobby began.

Oscar said, 'You sound like Prince Honolulu at the racecourse. "I gotta horse! I gotta horse!"'

'This is a better bet than any horse, believe me.' Nobby laughed. 'It's a cast-iron certainty – a sure thing!'

'No such thing,' Oscar declared. 'Wasn't it Benjamin Franklin who said that nothing in this world is sure except death and taxes?'

'Let him finish,' Olly protested. 'Maybe Nobby is going to tell us how to make our fortune.'

'You've all heard of Bond?' Nobby went on.

'You mean James Bond? Double oh seven, shaken-not-stirred Bond?' Titch asked.

'No, this is a different Bond,' Nobby said. 'This is Alan Bond, formerly British but now an Australian millionaire. Over there he's a hero for beating the USA and winning the Americas Cup for his country. While he was racing the yacht, *Australia II*, he noticed that the event was being filmed from an airship above and he became interested in it as a possible business investment.'

'Surely you don't mean we should put our money into blimps?' Billy asked incredulously. 'Weren't there disasters a few years back? I seem to remember reading about the British airship R101 which crashed, killing nearly everyone on board, and then later the German Hindenberg which burst into flames on landing.'

'That's right,' Nobby said, 'You sure know your history but I have a good friend who is an expert and a pilot in the RAF and he tells me that things have moved on since those early days in the nineteen thirties. Then the blimps were filled with combustible hydrogen. Today, they're filled with non-flammable helium and are safe as houses.'

'So you think these airship shares will rise?' Oscar drawled, unable to resist a witticism.

'They ought to if they're filled with helium,' Titch chuckled. 'So what's the deal, Nobby?'

'It's a British firm that runs these blimps,' he replied. 'Airship Industries, and they were about to go under until Alan Bond stepped in and bought half the company. At the moment, the share price is a mere five pence but they should soon go up.'

'But what use are airships?' Oscar asked. 'Surely they're nothing more than glorified antiquated barrage balloons belonging to the Second World War.'

'Nonsense!' Nobby replied fervently 'The airships today have dozens of uses. Think of filming and televising sporting events like football matches or the Olympics, and when it comes to security work or detecting drug trafficking, they can be a permanent eye in the sky. Better than helicopters because they are invisible to radar and can float silently over a scene for twenty-four hours. If, for example, the Royal Navy had used them in the Falklands War, they could have spotted those Exocet missiles earlier coming over the horizon, so saving many lives and ships.'

'Furthermore,' Olly added, warming to the subject, 'they use little fuel and they don't require expensive airports to operate.'

By this time Billy had become really interested. Perhaps this was the answer to all his prayers, his big break. Maybe it was another Polly Peck! He could see himself with £100,000 in the bank. How he'd be able to help his family with a sum like that! He could set them all up for life. As Olly was expounding on the subject, he became determined to find out more and buy while the shares were still cheap. He still had eight thousand pounds left in savings, mainly the residue of his pension lump sum, but he wasn't going to speculate with that until he was one hundred per cent sure.

On Monday morning, he phoned a small but reputable stockbroking firm, Sherwell Securities, in London and inquired further. What Nobby had told them was accurate and on the strength of this he bought 50,000 shares at 5 pence, costing him £2,500. He deemed it best not to mention any of this to Laura as he knew she would pour cold water over the idea and caution against it. In his buoyant frame of mind, he wasn't in the mood for doubt or having second thoughts.

By the time Friday rolled round he was in seventh heaven for the price had risen to 8 pence and the shares were worth £4,000! He'd made a profit of £1,500 in his first week. He simply had to tell Laura.

'It's a paper profit,' she said. 'It's not a true profit until you have the money safely in the bank.'

Typical canny Scot, he thought.

'Have faith, Laura,' he said. 'We're on a winner. We're going to be rich!'

Laura, who had been born in Dumfries in the same year as himself, 1928, was the eldest in a family of four children. Her family upbringing had been loving, safe and secure, and great store had been set on the virtues of prudence and economy. Thrift had been the family's watchword, which was a great contrast to Billy's impetuous disposition.

That afternoon, he contacted Sherwell Securities and bought another 50,000 at 8 pence, costing him £4,000. He now owned 100,000 shares and had £6,500 invested in blimps. For several months, nothing exciting happened. The price went up and down by a couple of pence and he came to know what a neurotic speculator he was. When the price rose ever so little, he was ecstatic but when it went down by a similar sum, he was down in the dumps. One evening Laura and he went to see *The Pyjama Game* at the Opera House in Quay Street but the two pence fall in airships that day cast a shadow over everything and he couldn't enjoy the show. He kept thinking that in theory he'd just lost £2,000.

'On paper!' Laura insisted.

No use, he was inconsolable.

He had to wait a whole year for the good news. In the newspaper, he read that there was a possibility that the Fuji Film Company might sign a contract to advertise their product on the sides of the airships. It would be a 200-foot long advertisement, the newspaper said. On the strength of the rumour, the share price rose by ten pence. Once again he was on Easy Street. Should he sell or buy more?

'Sell!' Laura said. 'Get your money out! Cash is king!'

'Buy more!' his Friday night discussion group advised.

The latter view prevailed and he bought another 50,000 at 20 pence, costing him £10,000, for which he had to take out a second mortgage on his house with the Bank of Scotland. He was now more nervous than ever but the gamble paid off for the airship price rose to 25 pence and his holding was now valued at £37,500. His dreams had come true! Almost. They were rich but he still had that Polly Peck company in mind. If he could only hold his nerve, his airship would come in and his investment would reach greater heights. Who knows perhaps the share would reach £1 and that would be the time to pull out and cash in his chips.

It was at this time that shareholders were invited to take a free ride in a Skyship 600 airship across London and Laura and he decided to take advantage of the offer. They drove down to an airfield just outside Watford from where the flight was to begin. There was a large crowd of people gathered there waiting their turn. Many of the men with their handlebar moustaches looked like typical Battle of Britain types and Billy and Laura caught various snippets of RAF lingo: bloody good show, damned fine kite, strong cross wind today, old boy.

In their numerous trips to Africa, Laura and he had flown many thousands of air miles by conventional aircraft but this was to be a strange and exciting experience. Eventually it was their turn to board and eight passengers waited until the airship ground crew pulling on the ropes held the skyship steady enough for them to climb into the gondola. The crew released the ropes and gently and silently they floated into the sky. Travelling at fifty miles an hour above the ground they were afforded spectacular views of the surrounding countryside. The experience was nothing like that of a normal aeroplane. No seat belts, they could walk around, they could slide back the windows and, strangest thing of all, the airship could go into reverse and did so several times. Soon they were looking down on London from a height of a thousand feet. Gracefully, they floated over the capital's landmarks: Trafalgar Square (how strange the fountains looked from above), the Houses of Parliament, Tower Bridge, and the West End. People stopped, looked up, and pointed to them. They were like gods looking down on mere mortals. An hour and a half later they were back at the airfield and (thank God!) the ground crew was waiting to grab their ropes and bring them back to Mother Earth. What courage the job required! Billy remembered seeing a film of a tragic airship accident in the early days when a sailor had been carried up helplessly to several thousand feet, from where, unable to hold on any longer, he had dropped to his death. On this occasion, the landing went smoothly and they clambered out gratefully but hardly able to believe that they had just passed across London in a blimp.

In the assembly tent, there was a souvenir shop

with a wide selection of mementos: photographs, shirts, badges, airship history books. Billy bought a small penknife decorated with the engraving of an airship. Wherever he went afterwards, he proudly showed off this little item and bored people to death by telling them about their airship ride.

When they got back to Manchester, he said to Laura, 'Olly once said that you should avoid becoming emotionally involved with your investments but after that wonderful, once-in-a-lifetime ride, how could we be otherwise?'

A week later, he threw caution to the wind and acquired another 50,000 shares at 27 pence by borrowing a further £13,500 based on the equity of his house. He now owned 200,000 shares and he owed the bank over £25,000, which was about a third of the value of their home.

For a year after their airship flight, things ticked over. Nothing dramatic happened on the blimp scene. The price fluctuated a little as people bought and sold and Billy swung between despondency when it was down and euphoria when it was up. Laura had long since given him up as a bad job and couldn't make up her mind whether he was a lunatic or a brilliant tycoon. Exactly the way he felt about himself. Call it gypsy superstition or what you will but he had a hunch that big news was going to break one day and so he hung on grimly.

Then it happened as he guessed it would.

The US Navy announced that it intended awarding a multimillion-dollar study contract for the building of a fleet of giant airships to guard the American coast against possible enemy incursions and to watch for drug runners and illegal immigrants. These airships, which would remain stationary for long periods and would carry state-of-the-art radar and surveillance equipment, would form a ring of defence round the States in preference to Star Wars technology. It was to be a two-horse race between the American giant Goodyear and the tiny British company Airship Industries.

The clever money was on Goodyear because it was a US-based company and it had greater experience of airship technology, having been building them at Akron in Ohio since 1919. It was part of the American establishment and no doubt had powerful lobby groups in business and trade unions exerting pressure in Washington to keep the work at home. This was obviously what the market expected as the share price of Goodyear rose dramatically on the strength of these considerations.

Despite this, the shares of Airship Industries rose to 30 pence on the remote possibility that it just might be awarded the contract.

'Surely now's the time to get out while the going's good,' Laura urged.

'We've come this far, Laura,' he said. 'I'd hate to pull out now. Life's a funny thing and sometimes the unexpected can happen. I'd never forgive myself if we got the navy contract and I'd sold out.' Perceptive readers will notice that he was now talking about the company as 'we'. He had become inextricably emotionally involved with 'his' company.

For the next few weeks he was on tenterhooks waiting for the United States Navy to make up its mind. If the decision went against Airship Industries, he stood to lose several thousand pounds, but if it went in its favour... His mind boggled.

Then on Saturday, 10 August 1985, against all the odds, the unexpected happened. He learned the news from a simple announcement in the press.

'Airship Industries said today it had been awarded a $200,000 study contract by the United States Navy that could mark the return of the airship to the American air fleet. "This is without a doubt the most important development in the company's history," said the British firm's founder and technical director, Roger Munk.'

On Monday morning the shares hit an all-time high of 60 pence. On paper he was rich beyond anything he'd ever imagined. He was the proud owner of 200,000 shares worth £120,000, that is, about twenty times his teacher's pension. He could not wrap his mind around it. So after all the early mishaps, at last he'd got something right. It was 12 August, their thirty-fifth wedding anniversary and they celebrated it in style with a champagne dinner at the Midland Hotel. They ordered the works with no expense spared.

'What will you do now, Billy?' Laura asked, sipping her champers. 'Will you sell?'

'I'd be crazy to sell now, Laura. This is only the beginning. The company has won only the contract to study the feasibility of these goliaths and when they actually start building them, the sky's the limit. Sure the price will drop slightly as the timid take some profits but in the long run we can't miss.'

Amongst his friends in the Smokers' Club there were different reactions.

'You're right to hold on, Hoppy,' Nobby advised. 'My aeronautical friend reckons they've some way to go yet. They should soon reach a pound.'

'It's a bit of a gamble,' Olly said, 'but if it pays off you're going to be a very rich man. My instinct is to wait till the price goes higher.'

'Being broke as I am,' Titch said, 'I'd be inclined to cash in, if not all my holdings, say half.'

As usual, Oscar was contemptuous of the whole business. 'For the life of me, I cannot see the sense in investing good money in balloons. The idea is fatuous.'

It was interesting to hear their views but Billy had already made up his mind. He was in for the long term.

A whole year passed and the value of the company fluctuated a little as was to be expected as the shares were bought and sold. These fluctuations didn't worry him in the least. He'd become a hardened speculator.

Then things began to go wrong. Inexplicably, the share began to go down significantly until it reached the level it had been before being awarded the big contract, 30 pence. He was puzzled as he'd heard nothing untoward about the company. A few weeks later, the reason for the fall became apparent. The finances of Airship Industries were published and they were in deep trouble with liabilities far exceeding assets. In other words, the firm was in the red, the biggest debt of half its value being to the Bond Corporation in Australia.

'I think you should get out now,' Laura pleaded, 'before you lose the lot.'

Billy was concerned but still optimistic. It was bound to recover because when all was said and done, it still had the big deal with the US Navy. Other speculators obviously didn't agree with him because the price continued to drop. When it reached 20 pence, he thought maybe Laura was right and he'd better pull out whilst he still could. Then fate intervened. With a vengeance.

On Friday, 16 October 1987, a viewer rang the BBC and asked Michael Fish, the weatherman, if there was going to be a hurricane. He laughed off the suggestion. Within hours, south-east England was being lashed by winds of 110 mph causing greater havoc than any other storm in the twentieth century. The storm killed seventeen people and left a multimillion-pound trail of damage from Cornwall to the Wash. Hotels and houses collapsed, road and rail communications were paralysed, power lines were down. The London fire brigade was inundated with thousands of emergency calls, and hospitals were filled with casualties from flying debris. The Meteorological Office apologized with the understatement of the century.

'Our forecast was somewhat inaccurate,' a spokesman said.

On the Monday following the weather turmoil, the bottom fell out of the international stock markets and also out of Billy's world. The two events may or may not have been connected but their effects were equally devastating. There was a tidal wave of selling and the day was dubbed Black Monday. Stockbrokers spoke of financial meltdown as billions of pounds were wiped off the value of the London exchange. Thousands of dealers and investors were ruined overnight.

Billy of course was not exempt from any of this. He read the news in the *Financial Times*. The value of Airship Industries – a mere minnow in the stock market ocean – was wiped out and he found himself the owner of worthless bits of paper. His spirits hit an all-time low and that was saying something. Could he not get anything right? Everything he touched turned to ashes. Whatever the opposite of King Midas was, he was it. He was not the suicidal type but he could sympathize with those speculators who topped themselves when they found they were ruined.

His friends were not slow to voice their opinions.

'You became too emotionally involved with airships,' Olly told him. 'And you made the fatal mistake of putting all your eggs in one basket.'

'Most unfortunate,' Nobby said, 'but it must be some comfort to know that you weren't the only one to go under.'

It didn't seem much of a comfort to him.

Titch said, 'I hate to be a told-you-so type but I did advise you to get half your money out. You gambled and you lost.'

There was no sympathy from Oscar. 'You pays your money and you takes your choice. I have no time for fortune hunters on the stock exchange.' Billy had the feeling that Oscar was not without a sense of *Schadenfreude* and was enjoying a certain amount of malicious pleasure at his misfortune.

'I never cease to be amazed,' Billy said, 'that in the matter of hindsight, so many people are blessed with twenty-twenty vision.'

His brother, Les, was more philosophical about the disaster. 'The stock exchange is nothing more than a gambling den for high rollers. And gambling is for losers, you can bet on it. Did you manage to salvage anything at all from your investments?'

'The only thing I have of any value, Les,' he said ruefully, 'is a small penknife with the outline of an airship engraved on the holder.'

Billy still had Laura to face. She had advised him a dozen times to sell the shares and get his money out while he still could and he had ignored her. How deeply sorry he felt that he should have caused her such anguish. How would he ever be able to make it up to her?

When Laura heard the news of their loss, her first reaction was anger and she was ready to blow her top. Billy had squandered a fortune on his ill-considered investment despite her constant plea to cut his losses. But when she saw how pale and distressed he looked, she had second thoughts and decided to bite on her tongue. She'd read, too, in the newspapers that a number of ruined stockbrokers had taken their own lives and even the remote possibility that Billy might contemplate such a drastic step filled her with dread.

'Laura, how can I ever apologize enough?' a distraught Billy asked. 'It was all my fault. You were right and I should have listened to you. It was because of my stupid conceit that we've ended up in this situation.'

With a sudden intensity he'd never seen in her before, she said, 'I don't mind what happens now as long as we face it together.'

She tried to console him with a stream of positive thoughts. 'Money isn't everything and it's not the end of the world. At least you've still got your health and strength. We'll get by somehow. We always have.'

But he didn't feel like being consoled. He only knew that for a few brief moments in their lives, they'd been rich and now he'd lost the lot. Greed had been his downfall. Having had money and then losing it was worse than not ever having had it at all. Furthermore, he still owed the Bank of Scotland a tidy sum, about equivalent to half the value of their house.

'Are the shares completely worthless?' Laura asked sadly.

'The shares, Laura, are worth less than an Andrex toilet roll. In fact, I'm tempted to cut the certificates up into squares and hang them on a nail in the toilet as we used to do when I was a kid long ago and our lavatory was in the backyard.'

Laura sighed. 'In that case, there remains only one question to ask ourselves. Where do we go from here?'

Chapter Twelve

I Do Like to be Beside the Seaside

'Where do we go from here?' Laura had asked.

Southport was the answer and it came from Laura's younger sister, Katie, who was a nurse at the local hospital there. She had gone to live there with her husband, Stuart, after their grown-up son, Robert, had gone to work as a teacher in Barcelona. Billy and Laura had visited Southport several times and had come to love the place. When they expressed an interest in moving to the area, Katie began house hunting for a smaller and less expensive house for them. Apart from anything else, the one in Manchester with its six bedrooms had become too big for two people. The resort was located on the Lancashire coast about twenty-five miles north of Liverpool and was popular with the citizens of that city because of its proximity. It was popular also with other people from the north-west because it had a carefully cultivated reputation for gentility, offering a sedate atmosphere as a holiday resort and a retirement town, as evidenced by the number of homes with names like 'Dunroamin', 'Rose Cottage' and 'Home At Last'. Generally speaking, it was seen as less flashy than rival Blackpool with its rumbustious pleasure beach and its brash Golden Mile. One wag had described Southport as 'Blackpool with O levels' and it was the butt of many jokes about the sea being a long way out.

'I saw the sea once at Southport,' said a lugubrious comedian as an opening to his act. 'It's in the *Guinness Book of Records*. And it's such a lifeless place, they don't bury the dead. They stand 'em up in bus shelters with a bingo ticket in their 'and.'

All nonsense of course, since it was a beautiful town and an attractive shopping and recreation centre for east Lancashire. And it may have been their imagination, but the weather seemed better, the skies bluer and more open. It was definitely cleaner and less congested than dear mucky old Manchester.

Billy and Laura made the forty-mile trip several times to inspect various houses but none was quite what they were looking for. One had excellent accommodation but backed onto a busy main road; one turned out to have dry rot, another serious subsidence.

Then one day Katie phoned, all excited. 'I've found the perfect house for you,' she said. 'It's a corner house set back from the main road and the side entrance is on a quiet avenue lined with trees. It has three large bedrooms, two entertainment rooms, beautiful gardens, double garage suitable for a car and a workshop.'

They drove over to look at it and they loved it from the start and agreed to buy. It would involve a temporary bridging loan on top of the loan Billy already had with the bank. It didn't present a major problem since the sale of the Manchester house would clear the debts and once more they'd be in the black. There was a niggling negative thought at the back of his brain, however. Supposing the Manchester house took longer to sell than they thought or, horror of horrors, didn't sell at all? He'd be up that familiar creek without a paddle. It didn't bear thinking about. In addition, the Southport house needed a few minor repairs which the owner's young daughter obligingly pointed out, much to the chagrin of her mother.

'The back gate doesn't close properly,' the young girl said, 'and it needs a new lock.'

'All right, Marlene,' said her mother, looking daggers at her. 'That's enough. You go inside and do your homework.'

'Already done it.'

'Well, go and do it again.'

They had the impression that the young girl didn't want to move house as she continued to make them aware of the flaws.

'Our dog's put millions of scratches on the paint-work of the kitchen door; it does that when it wants out. You can see them there. Another thing: we're next door to my junior school and there's always lots and lots of noise coming from the playground. At four o'clock the side road outside is always parked up with cars and you can't get in or out.'

But these adverse comments didn't matter. Nothing could put them off. This was exactly the house they'd been looking for and with a little money spent on it would be perfect, or so they thought. They hadn't bargained for the major survey which pointed out a number of serious repairs that were required: the need for pointing and painting, the renewal of gutters, and replacement of some window frames, new pathways. The value of the Southport house was much less than their own in Manchester, but it was still necessary to take out a small mortgage of £3,000 as the bank insisted on the most serious of the repairs being carried out as a condition of the loan. They went ahead with the purchase although completion had to wait until the building work had been finished. The less important repairs like gates and fencing had to be put on hold for the time being.

Meanwhile they had to sell their own house. Mark still worked at the Manchester estate agency and advised them to save on commission charges by selling it themselves privately He supplied them with the usual estate agent jargon: attractive property affording spacious accommodation of six bedrooms, two magnificent entertaining rooms, capacious dry cellars, large mature gardens and so on. The surveyor who inspected the property spotted some slight subsidence on an outside wall but nothing too serious. They had never noticed it themselves and they hoped it wouldn't put people off.

The surveyor valued the house at somewhere between £75,000 and £80,000.

'But there's no such thing as intrinsic value,' he told them. 'Any commodity is only worth what someone is prepared to pay for it. So the value of your house may be a little lower or even a little higher. Who knows? Ask for eighty-five thousand and let the buyer beat you down to the price you're hoping for. That always makes him feel good and he congratulates himself on what a wonderful bargainer he imagines himself to be.'

They placed an ad in the *Manchester Evening News* and soon had a stream of interested purchasers on the phone making appointments to inspect. For several weeks, they found themselves repeating the same old spiel over and over again until they'd memorized it. They had lots of visitors but no takers. Until one day a young man who introduced himself as Mr Andrews came with his wife and three young daughters. He had a secure job at the Education Offices in Manchester and the family glowed with pleasure and murmured approval as they visited and examined each room.

'Exactly what we've been dreaming of,' the wife said. They were loud in their praises as they discussed how they would allocate the various bedrooms. They, the parents, would have the large bedroom and the girls a bedroom each. One of the rooms would be reserved for the wife's mother.

Laura and Billy exchanged glances. If the visitors had already begun imagining themselves in the house, then it was practically sold. At the end of the tour, the young man turned to Billy.

'Consider the house sold,' he said, holding out his hand. 'Let's shake and make a gentleman's agreement here and now that you will not offer it to anyone else. As soon as we have seen our solicitor, we'll be back and make the whole thing formal with the necessary deposit.'

When their visitors had gone, Laura and he rejoiced. They'd soon be in a position to make final arrangements on the Southport house and, most important, clear their debt with the bank.

They had several more inquiries but they turned them away with apologies. 'Sorry,' they told callers. 'The house is sold.'

Mark warned them not to be so optimistic at this early stage of the negotiations but they felt he was being overcautious and typical of someone working in the estate agency business.

Ten days passed and, hearing nothing more from their prospective purchasers, they began to be seriously concerned. Then much to their relief they received a phone call from Mr Andrews, still as friendly and affable as ever.

'We'd like to come and make a final inspection with the wife's mother, if that's OK,' he said breezily. Of course they readily agreed.

One afternoon, he arrived with his whole family, wife, three daughters and mother-in-law. Billy didn't like the look of the latter one bit. Unsmiling and sharp-featured, she walked through the house slating everything her eye alighted on. Nothing escaped her censorious tongue.

'The windows are stuck with old paint,' she snapped. 'The doors are skew-whiff and do not close properly. The floorboards creak and that's something I could not live with. The whole house needs redecorating.'

Next day, they were not surprised to hear that the sale was off and they were back to square one.

Through a contact at the Education Offices, Billy learned later that what had really happened was that Andrews had been turned down for a mortgage because of inadequate salary. His mother-in-law had come to pull his chestnuts out of the fire by picking holes in everything that came under her scrutiny.

'I did warn you,' Mark said philosophically. 'At least you've learned something we estate agents are only too aware of never count your chickens until they're hatched and you have formally and officially exchanged contracts.'

A few weeks passed by, things went quiet and the inquiries dried up.

They were despondent. There they were, just the two of them, in a big house with six bedrooms, and a huge debt at the bank. This couldn't go on and Billy saw debtor's prison looming. Surely their luck had to change!

Then it did. Out of the blue, like the proverbial cavalry, the aptly named Catholic Rescue Society came riding onto the scene when it began buying big houses like theirs for conversion to nursing homes. The organization first bought Dr Gillespie's house next door and then it was their turn. Two smartly dressed men, one young, the other elderly, came round, not primarily to inspect but to negotiate. Billy took them on a tour of the house from cellar to attic.

'Not really necessary,' the younger one said. 'We've already seen Dr Gillespie's and it's more or less the same kind of accommodation.'

Billy thought he'd be honest and tell them about the reported subsidence. 'Best to tell them, Laura,' he said. 'They'd have found out later in any case when their own surveyor inspected.'

'Minor subsidence doesn't matter in the least,' the older man said. 'We've no choice, we've simply got to have this house in order to complete our plans for the block.'

His younger companion threw him a withering look. 'Not quite true,' he said. 'Our plans are still flexible and we have other properties to look at.'

They adjourned to the lounge and Laura went into the kitchen to make tea for everyone. There then followed a great deal of irrelevant chit-chat, about the weather, the virtues and drawbacks of the Manchester football teams, City and United, about the pieces of antique furniture that Laura had inherited from her parents.

It was only after tea and biscuits that the guests came round to the real point of their visit. From thereon, it was like a game of poker.

'So, what figure did you have in mind, Mr Hopkins?' asked the younger one.

'Dunno really. How much are you prepared to offer?'

'That depends on the figure you have in mind.'

'We've got to have the house, no matter what,' the old bloke added, putting his foot in it once again.

His companion scowled at him. 'We don't *have* to buy this particular house; we do have alternatives, if need be.'

This verbal interplay went on for some time while they drank more tea and ate more biscuits.

What figure should I go for? Billy asked himself. I don't want to overplay my hand and so blow the deal. But then the old bloke did say they had no choice and they had to have the house as part of a bigger plan. But who will blink first?

'So how much are you offering?'

'So how much do you want, Mr Hopkins?'

This subtle interaction continued for another

half hour, neither of them willing to show his hand.

This can go on forever, Billy thought. So, losing patience, he decided to throw in an unrealistically high figure to start the haggling off.

'We won't take a penny less than eighty-five thousand,' he declared.

As soon as they heard this, the eyes of the visitors lit up. Joy and relief flooded their features. And Billy knew he'd asked too little. Hadn't the senior man said they had to have the house to complete their plans, no matter what? He could have asked for £90,000, even £100,000, and he had the feeling they'd have paid it. This became only too apparent later in the year when the Rescue Society began building a huge extension which must have cost around half a million.

'Business was never your forte,' Laura said.

To save money on the removal, they hired two large trucks from Salford Van Hire to be driven by Matthew and Mark. They gave away many items of furniture to the family since they were moving to a smaller house. Then it was all hands to the pump as they loaded up the vans.

'Whenever I see the sign for this company,' Mark grinned, 'I always think of the great Dutch masters like Van Gogh, Van Dyck, Van Eyck. And now this one, the great Salford Van Heeré.'

Came the sad day when they said goodbye to their old home. Though they'd be exchanging the built-up area of Manchester for the blue skies and open spaces of the seaside, it was still a sorrowful occasion. Moving after twenty-one years from a house they had come to love and

211

with which they had so many associations was bound to be a melancholy business. They looked back and remembered the years they'd spent there: the glad times like when they'd first moved in and the whole family had rolled up its sleeves and got down to painting and decorating; the sad times when young John had been seriously ill and they'd feared leukaemia; the bad times like the airship fiasco; and the mad times when the kids had got up to crazy pranks on April Fool's day, John ending up with a saucepan stuck on his head and having to go to hospital to have it removed. The kaleidoscope of memories flowed through their minds, and as they reversed out of the driveway, Billy felt a lump in his throat and the tears rolled down Laura's cheeks.

'The end of an era,' she sighed.

'A turning point in our lives and a fresh start,' Billy added, his voice a little choked.

For the first few weeks in Southport after the family had departed, they felt lost, just the two of them in their new, strange surroundings.

'It's not as if we were abroad, Laura,' Billy said to console her. 'We're only forty-odd miles from Manchester and we'll have plenty of visits, especially as we now have the added attraction of living at the seaside.'

The family did enjoy their trips to see their parents at the coast. Rather than descend en masse, they decided among themselves to stagger their visits so they could meet up on a regular basis. However, big occasions like Christmas, Easter, birthdays, Mother's and Father's days were different. On these occasions they got together and went to Southport in a body.

Billy and Laura kept themselves busy putting the house in order: arranging furniture and allocating knick-knacks to the various rooms. Laura did the planning and the designing; Billy followed orders, lugging stuff around and hanging and rehanging pictures. Reproductions, of course.

'I think we'll put Monet's Waterlily Pond in the hallway and Holbein's Ambassadors in the lounge.'

Billy obeyed the commands, including those relating to the extremely fine adjustments required to ensure the pictures were hung with precise horizontality until she changed her mind, as he knew she would.

'No, put the Ambassadors in the hall and the Waterlily Pond in the lounge.'

'*Ja, mein Fuehrer.*'

When it came to the garden, Laura was not only in her element, she was the boss. It was beautifully laid out with several trees and bushes whose names Billy could not remember though he did know that one of them produced sour green apples. They made several visits to the local Ladygreen Garden Centre and came back with dozens of plants and flowers whose names were all Greek to him. Laura had green fingers and whatever plant she tended, flourished. Billy had red fingers and whatever he touched tended to wither on the vine. Understandably his job was confined to turning over the soil in preparation and cutting the grass with their new motorized lawnmower. He could see that when the Southport Flower Show came round in the summer, he was going to be kept busy as Laura would no doubt come home loaded up with all kinds of exotic plants.

In the evenings, though, when he relaxed under a cloudless blue sky on the new sun lounger with a glass of cold Chardonnay in his hand, he thought that he'd died and gone to heaven.

As for the Southport town centre, Katie was most anxious to boast and show off the high-class and expensive shopping facilities along the tree-lined boulevards. Especially Lord Street with its Victorian arcades and passageways, and the fact that its three-mile length was covered by glass and iron canopies.

'It's a little known fact,' Katie enthused, 'that Louis-Napoleon Bonaparte once lived in exile on Lord Street before becoming Napoleon the Third, Emperor of France in eighteen fifty-one. A year later he set Baron George Haussman the task of redesigning Paris. Much of the medieval centre was replaced with broad, tree-lined boulevards, covered walkways and arcades, just like Lord Street. It may be mere coincidence but it has been claimed that the redevelopment of Paris may have been inspired by his memories of Southport's town centre.'

'Tell me another,' Billy laughed. 'I find that story a bit hard to swallow.'

'It's certainly true that he stayed in Southport,' Katie giggled, 'though maybe the claim that Paris architecture was influenced by what he saw here is a little over the top.'

'Still, it makes a good story,' said Laura.

In those early days they developed the habit of

going into Southport together, sometimes by car but more often by taxi as parking had become something of a nightmare with the recent introduction of 'Pay and Display' parking meters which had sprung up like mushrooms all round the town.

If there was one group of people in society that was despised, apart from lager louts who littered the streets with empty beer cans and the yobs who spattered the pavements with their discarded chewing gum, it was traffic wardens. In the town centre there seemed to be dozens of them swarming on the streets where police officers were rarely seen since most of them were busy back at their station desks filling out forms. The wardens appeared to take a perverse delight in slapping tickets on cars the moment they overstayed their time. No excuses and no mercy. It was not unknown for them to give a ticket to a waiting funeral cortège or a wedding limousine outside a church. Stop for a couple of seconds to post a letter, say, and before you could get back to your vehicle there'd be a penalty notice on your windscreen. This was supposed to avoid congestion and keep traffic flowing but there was a strong suspicion among motorists that the real rationale behind it was to raise revenue for the local authority which seemed to regard it as a licence to print money.

In his naïvety, Billy accompanied Laura and Katie on their window-shopping expeditions. Big mistake. As the reader is aware, Billy hated shopping but if there was one kind of shopping for which he retained a particular loathing, it was window-shopping. He'd never been able to understand the concept; in Laura's and Katie's case, it involved examining every garment and every shoe shop along the length of Lord Street without actually buying anything. The word 'examine' is used in its loosest sense since Laura and her sister had a compulsion to feel and finger the texture of every article of clothing hung up on every rack in every store. Billy suspected, though Laura denied it, that he once saw her carry out a nasal inspection of a woollen jumper by sniffing at it. Without the slightest embarrassment, the pair were prepared to ask a harassed shop assistant to show them fifty pairs of shoes and then decide that none of them suited after all. How different from a man like me, he reflected, who will ask to try on one pair of shoes and if they fitted, buy them without more ado.

'But aren't you going to try on other shoes?' Laura would ask.

'Why should I? These are comfortable. Why complicate matters?'

The two ladies may have been captivated by the clothing shops but for Billy, Southport's biggest attraction was the book shops. While the ladies wandered through the emporiums along Chapel Street, he found his happiness among the books. As well as the usual Waterstone's, Hammick's, and W.H. Smith, Southport boasted a number of superb antiquarian book shops, and one of his chief delights was browsing through the hundreds of second-hand and fine old books and magazines displayed on their shelves. When not perusing the book shops, he was equally attracted to the 'gadget and gizmo' shops that stocked the most ingenious but useless items that eccentric inventors had dreamed up in their backyard workshops. He never purchased any of the articles but was intrigued by the notion that somewhere, someone thought that the world was waiting for such things as: a desktop singing football; an ashtray that coughed when ash was deposited in it; a Poweriser with springs that enabled you to leap six feet in the air and run with nine-foot strides; an inflatable referee costume; and perhaps most fascinating of all, a book with the suggestive title of *101 Things To Do In A Shed* which promised 'hours of fun in your little safe haven'. He almost bought it but decided against it in the end. Justifying it to Laura might have proved too much of a problem.

One day he came out of the shop just in time to see a traffic warden about to slap a ticket on the car parked outside. He consulted his watch and checked the time on the paid display ticket. The car was seven minutes overdue.

'Surely you're not going to impose a fine for a mere seven minutes?' he said. 'Have a heart! Show a bit of mercy.'

'Rules are rules,' she said, continuing to write out the ticket.

'That is pernicious,' he said. 'You obviously have a nasty streak in your personality. Maybe you were dropped on your head as a baby.'

'Not only is the time up,' she said, looking more closely at the windscreen, 'the display is upside down and that means an extra fine for failing to display the payment in the accepted manner.'

'This is nothing but petty bureaucracy,' Billy snapped. 'You ought to be ashamed of yourself.'

Then she noticed that the tax disc was a month out of date.

'I shall have to report this expired tax disc as well,' she said triumphantly.

'I give up,' Billy seethed. 'The country's gone to the dogs.'

He stalked off angrily.

Thank the Lord, he said to himself, that we came into Southport today by taxi but I can't help feeling sorry for the poor bloke who owns the car.

Billy usually met up with the ladies for lunch in a small café overlooking the promenade where they favoured the baked potato with a selection of fillings and he went for the Welsh rarebit. In the afternoon, they explored the antique shops with which Southport was abundantly provided. Once or twice they almost bought something.

Ainsdale where their home was located was a delightful village which catered for their immediate needs. It had one main street leading to the railway station on the Southport-Liverpool line. The village had the usual amenities: churches of the major denominations, two banks, a couple of supermarkets, pharmacies, travel agents, hairdressers, a DIY/garden centre, medical and dental practices, a public library and a police station. What made the place distinctive was its friendly, sociable atmosphere where people knew each other and actually exchanged greetings in the street, something that would be almost unknown in a big city. This neighbourliness was brought home to Billy on one of those rare occasions when he went out to do the shopping. Outside the greengrocer's he hesitated before the fruit section, undecided as to whether he should buy Conference or William pears.

'Your wife always buys the Conference,' said the greengrocer, coming to his aid.

He was taken aback. He didn't know the lady knew him or that he was married to Laura and that she had a preference for a particular kind of pear. Small world. But he liked it.

Window-shopping and browsing in Southport were all very fine and for the first few years, they were in clover. But as time went by, the novelty, that first flush of moving and exploring their new surroundings, began to wear off a little, at least for him, and the old craving or 'divine discontent' began to manifest itself. Sitting in the garden sipping wine and browsing through musty old books was all very well but there remained the big question of what he was going to do to keep himself not only busy but challenged. Laura didn't have this problem; she was happy looking after house and garden, she had her art and had recently taken up playing the recorder as well.

'How am I going to spend my leisure hours?' he asked. 'I've tried private tutoring, supply teaching, woodcraft, and dabbling in the stock market. All came to grief.'

He had recently watched the film *On Golden Pond* and, like the old character Norman, played by Henry Fonda, was ready to admit defeat. What's the point in trying? he asked himself. Everything I touch turns to dust in my hand.

'Why not continue with that autobiography you began all those years ago after your release from hospital?' Laura suggested. 'It looked most promising and you have the memory of an elephant. Who knows? It might lead to fame and fortune.'

'You mean the one I entitled *Our Kid?* I started the first chapter and then gave up.' While twiddling his thumbs in his cubbyhole that had served as his office in his last college, Billy had begun penning his memoirs but hadn't got very far with that idea either. At the time, he couldn't see the point of taking on such a Herculean task.

'Then forget about fame and fortune,' Laura urged. 'Write it for the family and our descendants. I'd give anything to be able to read the written memoirs of our great-grandparents on either side of the family. To know what they thought, what they felt, what worried them, and what made them laugh.'

'You've got a point there, Laura. I've often wondered myself what their concerns were and what kind of thing amused them. Maybe you're right and I should write my memoirs at least for our children and grandchildren. But who's to say I have the talent for tackling such a hefty piece of work?'

'I'm sure you have,' she said. 'After all, have you not kissed the Blarney Stone?'

Billy still wasn't too confident about the idea of undertaking a lengthy piece of writing at his age – after all, he was approaching his mid-sixties. But Laura's positive manner sowed a small seed somewhere in his brain and got him thinking. Maybe he really could write his autobiography – but for family only. Why, he didn't even have to show it to anybody if he didn't feel like it. So what was the harm in having a go?

Part Two

'I start off a book by writing the first sentence.
For the second and those which follow, I rely on
Almighty God.'
Victor Hugo

Chapter Thirteen

Collyhurst Memories

It was a sunny weekend and they were both in the garden, Laura tending her beloved flowers and plants, Billy sitting in his deckchair with eyes closed, meditating. What he was really doing was writing his book in his head by running over background material that he could possibly use in his story. He fell into a brown study and began to relive the scenes of his childhood, trying to organize the episodes into a coherent sequence. It was like watching a mental movie of his life. After visualizing a particular scene, he hurried inside to type it up before he forgot the details. In this way he began building up a comprehensive account of life in Collyhurst during the thirties.

His thoughts carried him back to the tenement Collyhurst Buildings in Manchester where he'd been born in 1928. The block had been put up by the Disraeli government in 1875 under the Artisan's Dwellings Act and had been hailed as a piece of enlightened social reform at the time. In the district, it was known simply as the Dwellings.

The accommodation which they shared with the cockroaches and the occasional water rat from the nearby River Irk consisted of two bedrooms and a stone-flagged living room with bare walls streaming with damp. There was no kitchen as such, but in one corner of the room there was a slopstone with a cold water tap and a gas ring. Most cooking, however, was done on a coal fire in the grate of the large iron kitchen range which had an oven for baking and heating up pans. The range had to be black-leaded every week with Zebo – so named after its black and yellow striped packaging – until it was gleaming. There was a large iron kettle permanently on the hob so that visitors could immediately be given a cup of tea. Sometimes people ran out of coal and it was not uncommon for a housewife to go round her neighbours asking for a 'loan' of hot water to make a pot of tea. No one resented it as people knew they might need the same favour themselves one day. Overhanging the fireplace was the mantelpiece decorated with a fringed velvet pelmet, on which stood the chiming clock and the framed photograph of his Uncle Danny who'd been killed at the Somme. Round the hearth was a brass fender with a fireside companion set comprising poker, tongs, brush and small shovel. Beside the fender was a peg rug which Mam replaced every Christmas Eve with a brightly-coloured new version she had painstakingly created during the year, always a joyous sign for him that the festive season really had begun.

Furniture was minimal, comprising a built-in cupboard, a huge wooden table with a cover of rich red chenille, four hardback chairs, a horsehair sofa and a huge mirrored dresser on which were displayed one or two holy statues – the Sacred Heart, the Virgin Mary, and St Joseph – under protective glass domes. Under one of these shades, as they were called, was a small wooden doll's shoe which his sister Mary had been clutching when she'd died of diphtheria at the age of five in 1916. On the small landing or balcony at the back was the lavatory, placed perhaps appropriately next to the rubbish shute. The only light in the tenement was provided by a gas mantle attached to a wall bracket in the living room. There were no lights in the bedrooms which meant getting undressed in the dark or by the light of a candle if there was any spare money to buy one. Perhaps it was as well that they got undressed in the dark since the bedroom was occupied by two adolescent sisters, Flo and Polly, and four boys, Jim, Sam, Les and himself.

Poor though the people of Collyhurst were, it would be wrong to describe their homes as slums, if that word is taken to mean squalid or wretched. Certainly the accommodation was limited and hopelessly inadequate but the people who lived there were extremely houseproud and made the most of what circumstances had bestowed upon them. Housewives who fought a never-ending battle against the grime and the particles of soot which rained down on them from the numerous factories and house fires in the district seemed to be forever on their knees scrubbing the stone floors, cleaning the windows, polishing the brass, black-leading the grate. Since there was no such thing as a washing machine, the laundering of clothes was a manual chore that took up most of the day, involving boiling, pummelling, scrubbing, mangling, drying, and ironing the family linen. At the same time, Mam prepared a meal for the family coming home at night. Throughout his childhood, Billy associated Monday with washing day and delicious home-made lentil soup prepared from stock from the weekend joint. Refrigerators were unknown which meant daily shopping. Being a housewife was a full-time job, which explained why few working-class mothers went out to work.

At the back of the Dwellings was a huge railway sidings known as Red Bank where trains were serviced and made up for their onward journeys, so that every night they were lulled to sleep by the sound of shunting locomotives. People on the Dwellings were often short of coal mainly because they could seldom afford it and also because coalmen were reluctant to lug heavy bags up the stairs. Coke was a cheaper alternative and this meant regular trips for Billy and his brothers to the Gould Street gas works to have one or two bags filled up. And an even cheaper alternative was to be found by climbing the railway fence and rooting in the debris of spent fuel discarded from the trains' tenders. The sidings thus proved to be a godsend as they were a rich source of cinders, and the kids, with a few unemployed men alongside, would sometimes spend the weekend scrabbling on the tip like worm-seeking hens in a farmyard. After supplying their own families, they would usually sell the clinkers (euphemistically called 'coke') at threepence a bag. Unearthing a piece of coal, or better still a cup bearing the LMS logo, was like finding the Koh-i-noor diamond. They had to be always on the alert, however, for the sudden appearance of the Railway Police who

were ever ready to give chase and arrest tres-
passers. The scavengers became skilful at vaulting
the six-foot railway fence and Billy could never
understand why no one from Collyhurst had ever
entered for the Olympic gymnastics.

In front of the tenement was the River Irk,
known locally as the Cut, which was not only
home to huge water rats but a repository into
which people dumped their rubbish – decayed
mattresses, rusty bikes, discarded furniture, and
dead dogs and cats. And when the fetid odour
which arose from the Cut (especially in the hot
weather) merged with the smells emanating from
the bone works, the Phillips rubber company and
the Coop tobacco factory, the foulness of the
stench defied description. The river changed
colour every day as the dye works upstream
added its waste so that the Collyhurst people were
treated to a technicolour display ranging from
crimson red to sickly yellow. The tenement was
connected to the main Collyhurst Road by an
iron bridge and when it rained heavily, residents
became marooned like poor Ben Gunn in *Treasure Island*.

This was the environment in which Billy grew
up. It was a world of dimly lit stairwells with
courting couples spooning on the cold stone
steps, the only place they could find privacy; a
world of gaslit streets and lamplighters making
their evening rounds, switching on at dusk and off
at dawn; a world of trundling trams and roads
cobbled so that horses' hooves could get a grip. As
he sat in his Southport garden on that lovely
summer afternoon, he visualized the Collyhurst

227

scene: hard-faced, hefty women gossiping on the doorstep; First World War veterans, many of them maimed and crippled, sitting on wooden chairs at their doorways, mug of tea grasped in both hands, taking in the malodorous Collyhurst air, staring out vacantly and thinking of the days that used to be; old women – Ena Sharples lookalikes – with chipped jugs hidden under their shawls, shuffling in their clogs to the local snuggery for a quick gill and to collect their daily ration of Boddington's best mild; pallid men chopping mountains of firewood to eke out their dole money. Sometimes men were so ashamed to admit they were unemployed, they'd dress and pretend to go out to work. But of course they couldn't keep that up for long.

Billy's family lived in poverty and it was a matter of always having to share; it was hand-me-down toys, hand-me-down clothes and sharing a bed, top and tail, with two or three brothers. It was only when Billy got married that he got to sleep in a bed by himself.

Opposite the Dwellings was the much-frequented pub, the Dalton Arms, his dad's local on weekday evenings though he never stayed late; being a porter at Smithfield fruit market, he had to be at work at 4 a.m. He worked a five and a half day week and his real drinking came around noon after pulling a heavily loaded cart for eight hours. Then he would retire to the Hare & Hounds on Shudehill and down six or seven pints of best bitter. Despite this daily consumption of ale, he did not carry an ounce of surplus flesh, never weighing more than nine stone, testimony perhaps to the tremendous output of energy his job entailed. Next door to the Dalton Arms on Collyhurst Road was the Rechabite Temperance Mission whose avowed purpose was to promote the virtues of Adam's Ale amongst the denizens of Collyhurst. If ever they'd come near to succeeding in their mission, Billy would have begun looking for pigs flying past his window.

In those days, people could leave their doors open, partly because of neighbours' honesty and partly because nobody had anything worth pinching, though Billy had read somewhere that during the depression of the thirties, doors became locked again as people became so desperately poor that they resorted to stealing from each other.

In the district there was great community spirit and people genuinely cared for one another in times of need, though to a certain extent the price of this was loss of privacy as neighbours thought nothing of popping in and out of each other's apartments. It was a price that most people were prepared to pay. Children could wander freely, play in the street and walk to school unharmed; old folk were never left to suffer or die alone, as was the case he'd read about in modern times when an old lady injured herself in a fall and remained immobilized alone in her home for a week before anyone noticed. Even that case paled by comparison with that of an old woman whose corpse remained undiscovered in a London flat for two whole years. Did no one miss her during that time? Did she have no caring neighbours?

In the Collyhurst of which he was thinking on

229

that beautiful day in his Southport garden with the birds twittering all round him, this would not have been possible because people were always there for each other. The arrival of an ambulance would cause a gauntlet of tut-tutting women to form at the invalid's doorway; perhaps they were nosy parkers but they were also genuinely concerned for their sick neighbour. And whenever there was a funeral, there'd be a collection for a wreath and sympathizers would gather at the cemetery gates. Every street and tenement block had its complement of amateur specialists, whether midwife ready to deliver a baby, undertaker to help wash and lay out a corpse, judge available to resolve disputes, scholar ready to help in the writing of a letter or the filling out of an official form. His own Mam, Kate, became adviser in the baking of bread during the bakers' strike of 1926. 'All very well,' she said, 'teaching them all to bake bread but they were using my oven and my coal!'

If a man was lucky enough to have a job, a 'knocker-up' might be employed to ensure that he was awakened in good time. 'Come on, let's be having you up on this lovely morning!' And he would wait a little till he got a response. The term 'knocker-up' always caused great amusement among American friends when they learned that a man with a long pole was employed to go around the district every morning knocking people up. In Collyhurst, another important function was fulfilled by the pawnbroker, known affectionately as 'Uncle'; Catherine Cookson's 'In and Out' shop where the master's suit could be deposited on a Monday to help through the week until Friday pay day when hopefully it could be redeemed. If a family was desperately short of money, nothing of value was left lying around the home unpawned. The symbol of the three balls displayed outside the shop is attributed to the Medici family of Lombardy where pawnbroking was supposed to have begun, but in Collyhurst it was popularly understood to signify that there was only a two to one chance of the depositor ever getting her stuff back.

For entertainment, there was perhaps a weekly trip to the second performance at the pictures, the so-called 'second house', though this tended to be favoured by women, men preferring the pub if they could afford it. Films favoured included Charlie Chaplin in his epic *Modern Times* and the many gangster films which Hollywood produced as if on a conveyor belt around that time and starring such people as Edward G. Robinson, George Raft, or Humphrey Bogart. The undoubted favourite was James Cagney playing the part of a reformed gangster in films like *Angels with Dirty Faces*, co-starring Pat O'Brien as the kindly priest with the heart of gold. It was interesting to note that in a Hollywood lifetime award ceremony, Cagney claimed that he'd never once used the expression, 'Take that, you dirty rat,' though his many impersonators believed it to be his accepted catchphrase. Other favourites around the time were Spencer Tracy and Katherine Hepburn and Joan Crawford. Mam was something of an addict when it came to a visit to the first-house pictures

which began around 6.30 p.m. and, as a youngster, Billy took full advantage of her weakness.
He had only to say, 'I see that Robert Taylor's in
a fillum called *His Brother's Wife* at the Riviera,'
for her to cave in and take him along for company.

For those short of money, there was always the
wireless which ran on battery and accumulator.
Despite the possibility of spilling acid on his legs,
it was Billy's regular job to take the accumulator
to the shop when it needed exchanging. On the
wireless they listened to favourites like *Henry Hall
and His Guest Night*, Jack Payne and his
Orchestra, or Arthur Askey and Richard (Stinker)
Murdoch. Billy's family would sit in a semicircle
round the fire while his dad operated the controls
and passed judgement on the various acts which
were broadcast. Henry Hall and Jack Warner were
'in' but performers like Vic Oliver and his violin,
or the public-school drawling Western Brothers
('Keep it up, you chaps. Keep it up') were definitely 'out'. These evaluations stayed with Billy for
the rest of his life. An outsider viewing the scene
would have concluded that Dad ruled the roost,
and in matters like this it was certainly true. The
family was nervous in his presence and when the
wireless was on, strict silence had to be observed,
especially at news time. But the real power behind
the throne was definitely Mam. She was the
ultimate authority and if her opinions on vital
matters clashed with Dad's, it was usually her
views that prevailed in the long run. The hous-
ehold revolved around her and if she happened to
be absent when a member of the family returned

home, the first question asked was always, 'Where's Mam?'

For the really well-off there was the wind-up gramophone. Billy's family must have come into this category because they possessed one, with a picture on the lid of a dog listening to its master's voice. In their house, nobody but Dad was allowed to touch this piece of amazing technology when, on very special occasions, he brought it down from the top shelf of the built-in cupboard. They had only a few 78 rpm records: Sousa's 'The Stars and Stripes Forever' played by the Royal Marines, Waldteufl's 'Skater's Waltz', Harry Richman's 'King for a Day', and others featuring celebrities like Gracie Fields ('The Biggest Aspidistra in the World'), Sandy Powell ('Can you hear me mother?'), George Formby ('Leaning on a Lamp-post'), Flanagan and Allen ('Underneath the Arches' and 'Hometown').

In 1934, when Billy was six years old, they 'flitted' from Collyhurst Buildings to Honeypot Street on the other side of the Red Bank sidings. It may not have been far measured in distance but in terms of facilities and accommodation, it was a different world. For a start, it was a three-bedroomed house with a parlour, a living room, and a scullery. But what made it special for the kids was that it had a cellar, a backyard and a tiny front garden. All the Honeypot houses were terraced with a front door that opened onto the street, except for three which were set back a little from the pavement and were approached by six steps. And they had the middle one of the three houses which Billy supposed gave them a certain amount of status.

Living in a street was a different kettle of fish from living in a tenement block, especially for the young. Little traffic came down the street and so there was space for all kinds of games. Kids invented their own and, in the absence of sports equipment, adapted whatever was to hand: jerseys became goal posts and full use was made of any street features available, like walls, steps, drainpipes, lamp-posts, and the pillar box. He could not remember ever hearing one of the kids complaining that he or she was bored or that there was 'nowt to do'. The games and activities changed with the seasons. There was Queenie O-Co-Co, hopscotch, kick-can, whips and tops, conkers in the autumn, fishing for tadpoles in nearby ponds, weak 'orse leapfrog against a wall, garfs or hoops involving propelling a bicycle wheel with a stick (you were seen as upper class if you had one with a pumped-up tyre). There was the game of alleys – marbles to posh people – blood reds being considered the most valuable. After school, the street outside St Chad's became like a medieval market with crowds of boys trying to win alleys from each other by throwing or thumb-flirting at targets set up in the cracks between the cobbles. Boys were adept at making 'guiders' or go-carts from discarded planks and pram wheels, using a red-hot poker to bore the hole for the steering bolt. At one time, the yo-yo was all the rage and another time pea-shooters and fibre-firing guns were fashionable. The latter involved shooting fibre pellets – these same pellets resembling today's All Bran.

Girls preferred playing 'doctors and nurses', especially if one of them had received a nurse's uniform for Christmas; boys scorned such frivolities though it is perhaps worth noting that, for some odd reason, the boys became interested in such games when they reached adulthood. Other games favoured were 'shop', using broken pot for money, or 'house' which involved building a square of bricks, and if a real live baby could be borrowed as a prop, so much the better. The lamp-post provided a useful anchor for a rope swing. Individual skipping was often of such a high standard that many a professional boxer would have been envious. Group skipping, with a washing line tied to a drainpipe, was the most popular, however, and girls skipped to such socially and historically relevant rhymes as:

Who's that coming down the street?
Mrs Simpson's sweaty feet.
She's been married twice before.
Now she's knocking on Eddie's door.

Or

Red, white and blue,
The Queen's got the flu
The King's got the belly ache,
And doesn't know what to do.

One game Billy invented with his next-door neighbour pal involved riding side-saddle on a big sit-up-and-beg bike (known as a bone-shaker). His mam who was passing on her way back from

235

the corner shop called out, 'That's dangerous, our Billy. If you break your legs, don't come running to me moaning about it.'

Since they were given freedom to play in the street, there was always the danger of accidents, especially among the boys. His older brothers Les and Sam were members of the Stanley Street gang and along with their companions were forever having some mishap or other which required hospital treatment. These street gangs kept Ancoats Hospital busy. The accidents varied from minor to major, from cuts and bruises to the time Mick Scully, the boss of the Stanley Street gang, fell through the glass roof of a garage and was nearly killed. Billy himself suffered a few injuries even though his brothers would never let him join in any of the gang's activities as he was considered, unjustly he thought at the time, to be 'a mama's boy and a telltale'. 'Tell your kid to go home,' Mick Scully commanded. 'He's a blabber mouth.' 'Scram, our kid,' ordered Les. 'You'll tell on us.' 'I won't, honest,' Billy would protest. It was no good. He was rejected.

Nevertheless, he had his share of mishaps, one when during horseplay he bashed his head against a door bolt and had to have stitches, another when he was climbing over the garden of an empty house when the wall collapsed and he suffered a greenstick fracture, giving his left arm a strange banana shape. He was treated at the Elizabeth Street Hospital. Although it catered for the general community, it was known locally as the Jewish Hospital or simply the Jewish, having been built in 1904 for the Jewish immigrant community and the name had stuck. Chloroform anaesthetic was necessary to return the arm to its normal contours. Surprisingly, the landlord of the empty house paid Mam five pounds' compensation. Needless to say, Billy didn't see a penny of it which, he supposed, was fair enough since Mam had the job of looking after him. The most serious accident he had was when he was sitting cross-legged on the back of a 'guider', going fast downhill, and the rusty back wheel cut a slice out of his right knee, leaving a hole resembling the inside of an orange. Dad had to be wakened from his afternoon snooze to carry him to Ancoats, which didn't please him too much. The hospital was a terrifying place permeated by an obnoxious chloroform/iodine smell and with shelves holding an ominous collection of violet and purple bottles containing God knows what concoctions, probably poisons, but all no doubt excruciatingly painful when applied. The severe-faced nurse in her starched headdress seemed to be eight feet tall and merciless. 'I hope we're going to be very brave,' she said, holding him down as the doctor put six stitches in his leg without anaesthetic. Naturally Billy screamed the place down. As a reward for being 'brave', kids were usually given an ice-cream cornet from Frascati's van waiting purposely outside the hospital for deserving cases such as his. His brother Les claimed that he used to look forward to having stitches because of the ice-cream reward afterwards, but Billy thought that, given his age, his memory was beginning to fade. The scar the accident left on Billy's knee featured later in life when he had to fill in a passport application and under the heading 'Distinguishing Marks' he was able to write, 'Scar on right knee.' Billy didn't know how many such marks his older brothers had sustained but they probably ran into double figures.

Billy didn't receive pocket money as such. Most kids in the district had to earn their own spends by doing odd jobs, like running errands or doing a paper round, as was the case with his brothers, Sam and Les. In Billy's it was chopping and selling firewood to earn a few pennies. Their next-door neighbour was a rag-and-bone merchant, and his son ('Henery') and Billy were often the recipients of the rich pickings of his trade. His two older sisters Flo and Polly also had a side-line. They worked at Northcotes, a furrier on Oldham Street, and, being allowed to take home any unwanted remnants, had started a profitable business in mittens and fur hats. The latter were especially popular when people realised the hats could double as tea cosies.

Another source of income for Billy from the age of seven to eleven arose from being an altar server at St Chad's Church on Cheetham Hill Road. If you served a full week's complement of services (Mass and Benediction), the priest rewarded you with sixpence which was enough to buy a bar of Cadbury's Fruit & Nut as well as a Caley's Double Six. Weddings and funerals were another source of income though funerals were best as they meant not only generous money rewards but a ride home in a luxurious limousine from Moston Cemetery.

Billy also lit fires on Saturday mornings for the Jewish people in the district. They referred to him as their 'goy boy'. The job involved arranging paper, wood and clinkers, lighting it and then creating a draught by putting up a 'blower' of a newspaper across a shovel. He had to be careful though not to get carried away by reading the paper when he had it in position since it was likely to burst into flames – as it did on many occasions. Another branch of religious work amongst his Jewish brethren involved turning up at the synagogue at 9 a.m. and switching on all the lights for the rabbi and returning around 1 p.m. after the service to switch them off again. For this he was paid sixpence, which was a fortune. The easiest money he'd ever earned.

He once asked a Jewish lady customer why her religion had such strange taboos. She told him there were thirty-nine things that were to be avoided on the Sabbath, including untying bundles and lighting a fire or a gas stove. Billy thanked God that as a Catholic he was not subject to strange rules! Not much!

How did they spend the money they earned? Mainly on toffees, comics or at the pictures.

There was a wide variety of toffees available. There was a chewy sweet called Black Pete which made your teeth black and left a black ring round your mouth. Bubbly Gum could be used to annoy adults by stretching it out of the mouth or by blowing bubbles and popping them. There was Hollands cream toffee which was broken off a large slab with a toffee hammer and weighed on brass scales. It wasn't always easy to eat it as it was often sold in large triangular pieces which almost pierced the cheeks and, if you tried to speak to someone, caused you to emit jets of toffee juice in all directions. There was liquorice, called Spanish, which could be bought in many kinds of shapes like bootlaces or pipes, and when supplied as embossed medallions were known as Pontefract cakes. There were sherbet dabs, a kind of lollipop which was dipped into the fizzing sweet powder and gave the most delicious taste in the world. Near their local cinema there was the Toffee Apple shop which supplied not only the toffee apples (to accommodate which you needed a mouth the size of a hippo) but also homemade sweets like acid drops or pear drops which were fine but gave you a monumental thirst.

Is it any wonder that school dentists of the time despaired?

They also spent their earnings on comics. Every week, they waited impatiently for the latest editions of comics to appear on the newsagents' shelves. Comics like *Beano*, *Film Fun*, *Dandy* were read hungrily as if the survival of the universe depended on the outcome of the exploits of characters like Korky the Cat, cow-pie chomping Desperate Dan, Lord Snooty (alias Lord Marmaduke of Bunkerton) and Pansy Potter, the strongman's daughter. A few years later, they graduated to D.C. Thomson's Big Five: the *Rover*, *Skipper*, *Hotspur*, *Wizard* and *Adventure* which included a few complete short stories plus one or two serials. The standard of writing in these was very much higher than the comics and each week they devoured the stories about Red Circle School with its public school ethos and heroic teachers like Dixie Dale and the villainous Mr Smug. For excitement, they had daring characters like Strang the Terrible and the Wolf of Kabul. They also read about Billy Bunter in *The Magnet* where they were introduced to the strange (and to them foreign) upper-class language of the public school with dialogue that went:

'I say, Bunter, you fat blighter, do pass the jam tarts or I shall be compelled to give you a Chinese burn.'
'I say, you fellows, cut it out! Yarooh! Wow! Crikey!' yelled Bunter.

They had been introduced to this alien world in the infants school when learning to read from primers which were about typical middle-class families where Daddy wore a suit with collar and tie, Mummy a flowery silk dress, and they drank lemonade with their daughter Kitty in a beautiful garden. They had a pedigree dog called Rover to which they gave the order, 'Run, Rover, run!' They were very proud of their dog's achievements for they repeated over and over again, 'See. Rover is running.'

They could also spend their hard-earned cash on the penny crush at the local 'bug hut' on Saturday afternoon where the scene was utter bedlam with kids yelling and screaming, the air filled with missiles of orange peel and apple cores. They saw mainly shorts featuring characters like Popeye with his girlfriend Olive Oyl plus their thuggish enemy, Bluto, whom Popeye invariably beat up after imbibing a can of spinach. (Billy was always impressed by the power of this spinach and though he often requested it at home, it was a vegetable that never appeared on their dinner table.) And there were the Three Stooges, (Larry, Curly and Mo), Laurel and Hardy, Leon Errol, Harold Lloyd, and poker-faced Buster Keaton. They also managed to see some of the great children's classics of the day, like *Treasure Island* starring Wallace Beery and Jackie Cooper who was Billy's hero and role model, David Copperfield with Freddie Bartholomew and Basil Rathbone as the wicked Mr Murdstone, but his favourite film was *Boys' Town* with Spencer Tracy and Mickey Rooney. The kids' matinee usually finished with a serial featuring Ken Maynard, Buck Jones, Tom Mix or Hopalong Cassidy (real name William Boyd), Roy Rogers and his horse Trigger, and finally Gene Autry, the singing cowboy on his white horse, Champion. Though Autry often became involved in brawls and rolled around in the sawdust on the bar-room floor, his immaculate outfit never seemed to get dirty. You knew where you were in those days because roles were clear-cut. 'Goodies' were clean-shaven and wore white hats while the 'baddies' had black hats and a moustache. Kids made their feelings known by booing and cheering loudly in the appropriate places. The serials always ended on a cliffhanger (often literally), with the hero or heroine tied to the railway track before an oncoming train. But they knew that he or she would escape miraculously the following week.

Billy's brothers had their own pursuits. Sam and Les spent most of their time going round with the Stanley Street gang whose members occupied themselves exploring derelict buildings, like the church on Red Bank that was being demolished; standing at the corner telling each other stories and dirty jokes, plotting with military precision their various forays and fights with rival gangs, especially around the time of bonfire night when wooden boxes and baskets were at a premium. His hero and eldest brother, Jim, worked as a warehouseman on Salford Docks where he saw the big ocean-going ships arriving and departing for exciting, faraway places. Seeing these every day made him restless with the wanderlust and he talked about joining the Royal Navy. He spent his leisure hours going out dancing with his mates and chasing the girls, or going to the pictures. He was also fond of playing 'pitch and toss' with his pals on a remote part of Barney's waste ground – remote because it had to be well away from the prying eyes of the 'rozzers', or coppers, since gambling in public was against the law. Occasionally, Jim employed Billy's services as a dog-out or look-out – for a small fee of course.

Their greatest entertainment, however, was free as every street and tenement block was a theatre in itself. There was always something going on: a chimney on fire or what the police referred to as 'a domestic' as a husband and wife fought like cat and dog; perhaps a fist fight after the pubs closed, between two men or better still between two women who would scream abuse and pull

243

each other's hair out over suspected infidelity. There were regular street ceremonies like weddings and funerals (perhaps involving the aforementioned fights) but always including largesse in the form of cakes and money which would be thrown by inebriated celebrants to the kids waiting around expectantly. And every day there would be a parade of itinerant tradesmen: the 'club' or insurance man, the tally man come to collect the weekly payments, the muffin man with his large basket of barm cakes and crumpets; the horse and cart of the milkman with his huge metal churn from which he ladled out your requirement into your jug – they always gave the milkman's horse a sugar butty and it became so used to having it that it refused to go on without it; the rag-and-bone man who would exchange your old iron or clothes for a donkey stone or a windmill on a stick; the knife and scissor sharpener with his foot-operated carborundum wheel; the gypsy with her ragged, snotty-nosed kids selling paper flowers or clothes pegs and God help you if you didn't buy any for she'd put a curse on you and your family for generations to come. They were treated to musical entertainment when Franco Granelli arrived pushing his barrel organ and began churning out tunes like 'Sweet Rosie O'Grady' or 'Daisy, Daisy, give me your answer do'. He made the handle-turning seem like an art by cocking his head and listening with a critical expression to the musical production and varying his speed as if conducting an orchestra. Sometimes he'd let the kids have a go at the handle-turning while he went round knocking on doors collecting odd coppers from anyone who could spare them. They also had the visiting street singers who would simply throw down their collecting caps on the pavement and, without more ado, burst into melody with a semi-religious ballad like 'Because ... God made thee mine' or a sentimental song such as 'I'll Take You Home Again, Kathleen'. Many of them were simply after beer money but occasionally one of them manifested genuine talent, for example Arthur Tracy, who achieved national fame and a BBC contract by this route.

This was Billy's boyhood background and it is easy to imagine the trauma he experienced when, in 1939, he 'passed the scholarship' and went to a grammar school. There he became immersed in its middle-class culture and ethos. The mid-Victorian school had a house system, organized games, the study of classical languages, and it insisted on received pronunciation. Richard Hoggart talked about the scholarship boy being at 'the friction point of two cultures' and this described the conflict admirably. Billy found he had to live in two worlds, with two sets of values and two languages. He had to be extremely careful not to get the two worlds confused. At home, he spoke fluent Collyhurstese and reserved his attempts at received pronunciation for school so as to avoid, the accusation of snobbery. Being stuck-up or getting too big for one's boots was regarded as the cardinal sin in working-class culture. He learned received pronunciation the hard way, through the ridicule of teachers and a few fellow pupils from more privileged backgrounds. He learned that the thing you put your head on at night was a pillow and not a 'pillar'; that the day after today was tomorrow and not 'tomorrer'; that a large truck was a lorry and not a 'lurry'; that it was incorrect to say 'pass me them books'; that instead of 'Scram!' or 'Shift up, you!' it was preferable to say, 'I do wish you would go away,' or 'Excuse me, would you mind moving up a little?' He learned to aspirate and to say such things as 'In Hertford, Hereford and Hampshire, hurricanes hardly ever happen.' His English teacher once remarked to him, 'Hopkins, you have a distinct talent for language. Pity it isn't English.'

His mam and dad were totally bewildered by these strange goings-on in this alien world. The confusion was illustrated when Mam was showing off his erudition at a family gathering and said to his uncle, 'At this posh school, he's learning all kinds of new things and foreign languages. Come here, our Billy, and say a few words in algebra for your Uncle Eddie.'

The headmaster, Brother Dorian, did nothing to ease the process of adapting to the new school for he was a frightening, awesome figure. Every morning he put the fear of God into their hearts when he addressed the school at morning assembly. He swept onto the stage, a giant, majestic figure in black cassock and wearing thick, horn–rimmed glasses. He gazed down on the boys as if they were ants and you could have heard the proverbial pin drop. The new boys in particular were petrified and watched his histrionic performance as if hypnotized. He took out a small silver box, sprinkled a little snuff on the back of his wrist and, still looking down on the assembly, slowly and deliberately sniffed the powder up each nostril. Then from somewhere deep within the folds of his cassock he extracted a huge silk handkerchief into which he blew his nose with a deafening explosion. Then he glared at his juvenile audience. Fastidiously, still gazing down on the mortals beneath, he proceeded to fold the handkerchief into a long sausage shape and, in a sawing movement, polished the underside of his nose. Lingeringly he put the handkerchief back, removed the heavy spectacles, fixed his eyes gravely on the insect-like kids and addressed them in ringing Churchillian tones.

'I give you solemn warning now. Be under no delusions.'

Thinking that a delusion might be some kind of Damocles sword, Billy looked up anxiously at the ceiling to make sure he wasn't under one.

This was the world Billy called to mind and wrote about. It included the war, being evacuated with the school to Blackpool in 1941, being bombed out of their home in Manchester, the rebellion of early adolescence, the awakening of his interest in the opposite sex and his first girl-friend, his ballroom dancing days, his first job at the Inland Revenue, and acceptance at a London teacher training college. At the end of a year, he had written nearly a hundred thousand words. Perhaps it was time to let the family look at his effort.

Chapter Fourteen

Critics

The boys of the family were the first to look at it. Mark gave his opinion.

'You know, Dad, you've got something in common with Charles Dickens.'

'You really think so, Mark?'

'Yes, Dad. His surname ends in "s" and so does yours. Once I started reading it, I couldn't put it down.'

'Thanks, Mark.'

'Yes, Dad, you must have used super glue.'

Matthew was next. 'From the minute you sent me your manuscript, Dad,' he said, 'I couldn't stop laughing. Now I must read it.'

And from John, 'Thanks for letting me see your memoirs, Dad. I lost no time in reading them.'

By heck, Billy thought. If my own children dismiss my work like this, what chance will it stand if I send it to a publisher?

The two ladies in his life, Laura and Lucy, were more charitable.

Laura said, 'I think this is as good as anything of Catherine Cookson's.'

'I agree with Mum,' added Lucy. 'It's a fascinating account of life in Collyhurst in the thirties. I think with more work on it, it could form the basis of a good novel.'

Billy bridled when he heard this. 'How do you mean, with more work on it? What more needs to be done?'

'Don't get me wrong, Dad. I think what you've written so far is wonderful,' Lucy said quickly, 'but it's only background stuff. Now you need to put something in the foreground, to superimpose a gripping story onto it. Your account so far could serve as a backdrop to a piece of fiction based on your life. It needs organizing into a dramatic sequence, that's all. Many autobiographies are boring because they are simply set out in chronological order – first this happened, then that happened, and so on. A bit like young children in an infants school telling you about their school day.'

'I know what you mean, Lucy,' Billy said. 'Many autobiographies by celebrities read like that. Some of them amount to no more than a name-dropping exercise. They write: "Before I went on stage, Sir John called in my dressing room to wish me luck. Afterwards, Sir Larry came round and congratulated me on my performance." But for an amateur like me, converting my memoirs into a novel is a tall order, Lucy. What training have I had as a novelist? Some writers claim that they simply sit down and without more ado or any kind of plan start writing and the stuff simply pours out. I don't understand how they do it without some kind of plan or structure. Writing up this autobiography was difficult enough but writing a novel is a different kettle of fish.'

Laura said, 'But you've been teaching creative writing to all those students of yours, like Jane

Ford, the one who ran off to London to become a writer.'

'And look what happened to her! She preferred pornography to literature. But Laura, there's a big difference between teaching a thing and actually doing it. We don't expect an Olympic swimming coach to take part in the competition himself. Remember what George Bernard Shaw said: "Those who can't do, teach." Maybe I can teach others but have no talent for it myself.'

'I've often thought you can spin a good yarn, Billy,' Laura said. 'That's the Irish blarney in you.'

'Maybe so but I think there's a high degree of skill and technique to writing a novel. I've read a few how-to-do-it manuals with titles like *How to Write a Blockbuster in Ten Easy Lessons*. But it doesn't mean I now know the secrets of how to write the good novel. It's like saying, "I've visited a few art galleries and seen a few masterpieces in my time, so I think I'll sit down and dash one off this weekend?" There's a lot more to it than that.'

Lucy laughed. 'You're absolutely right, Dad. It just so happens that I attended a course on writing a few months ago. It was first-class and I cannot speak too highly of it. I think you would gain a lot from attending it when it's repeated in London next month.'

'Tell me more, Lucy. I'm always willing to learn.'

'The course is run by Alf Buttershaw and he gives it the title "How to Write a Good Novel".'

'Buttershaw? Can't say I've ever heard of him. Who is he when he's at home?'

'He's a British writer with a few bestselling novels to his credit, a couple of which have been featured on the BBC's *A Book At Bedtime*. He's a down-to-earth northerner, a bit of a rough diamond, you might say, but you'll learn an awful lot from him.'

'Did I hear you say featured on the BBC? It sounds a bit too high-powered for me. I simply want to write up my memoirs as a tale that will interest my family and maybe our descendants.'

'Then Buttershaw's your man. His seminars teach the basic principles of writing a novel. It's an intensive weekend course that will have your head spinning but at the end you should know how to organize your story.'

'I bet it's expensive.'

'Around two hundred pounds, I think.'

'That's a hundred pounds a day! That *is* expensive! Add on railway fare and hotel and I shan't see much change from three hundred. I can ill afford to spend that kind of money on a vague hope. We have many repairs on the house still waiting to be done and then there's the car still not through its MOT. I'd be crazy to chuck my money away on a writing course.'

'But, Dad. It could mean a new way of life, a change in career and a higher income. Who knows where it might lead?'

'Probably to the workhouse.'

Laura said, 'You're always telling me that I'm a canny Scot but on this occasion I think you should go for it. After all, what have you got to lose?'

'Most of our remaining bank balance, that's all.'

The two ladies, Laura and Lucy (he was tempted to call them the two Ls), were persuasive, and in the end Billy relented and signed up for the course but not without misgivings. Who the heck do I think I am? he asked himself. And why am I chucking my money away on a writing course? I should have my head examined.

Chapter Fifteen

Looking for Inspiration in London

Billy couldn't explain it but whenever he arrived at London's Euston Station, he felt vaguely awkward and gauche like a peasant down from the grim north visiting the big city. Perhaps memories of his first visit to London in 1945 when he'd been a callow, seventeen-year-old student still lingered. And he remembered also the dire warnings his dad had given him about going to some lah-de-dah college in London where he'd be sure to pick up a lot of bad ways from the 'toffs down there'. The old man had been certain that the capital was heaving with thieves and vagabonds out to take advantage of innocents abroad, lads like Billy from north of Watford. The war had not long ended and he, along with half a dozen fellow students, had arrived to take up places at the St Mark and St John teacher training college in Chelsea. He'd felt overwhelmed by the sheer size and complexity of the city. For him it had been the centre of the universe and of civilization – thirty cities in one, they'd been told in school geography lessons. It was the nation's metropolis, home of parliamentary democracy and the world's commercial and trading centre. Even after a world war and despite the bomb damage, the city's history and tradition was almost palpable,

253

its ancient past preserved in so many beautiful buildings and monuments. As for the West End, every street and every theatre was world-renowned and brought a tremor of excitement at the thought that he might even have the chance to visit one or two of them. Now, forty years later, as he wheeled his suitcase along the platform and up the ramp which led to the vast central hall, those feelings of inferiority came flooding back. He was a country bumpkin once again and everyone around him seemed so urbane, so purposeful as they hurried hither and thither, as if concerned with mighty affairs of state. Except of course for the odd drunk and beggar who lay in wait for yokels like him.

'Got any spare change, guy?' one of these derelicts asked, recognizing Billy's provincial provenance.

'Yes, thanks,' he answered. 'Plenty. Nice of you to ask though.'

As he crossed the concourse, he was joined by a well-dressed young man who fell into step alongside.

'Just in from Liverpool?' he asked with a broad smile. A Scouser, Billy thought, recognizing the accent.

'Why, yes. How did you know?' Billy said.

'Saw you get off the train. I love that city. Liverpool's my home town, you see.'

'I never would have guessed.'

'I came down here a month ago looking for work but no luck. I've been waiting all morning for my brother to arrive from the Pool but no joy so far.'

Alarm bells were sounding in Billy's head and his antennae went on red alert.

'Sorry to hear that,' he said sympathetically. 'Maybe he'll be on a later train.'

'No. There's no chance of that now. There's a bit of an emergency at home, you see, back in Toxteth.'

Billy didn't say anything. He wasn't going to take the bait and ask the nature of the 'emergency at home'.

'Yeah,' the Liverpudlian continued, answering the question Billy hadn't asked. 'My mam's ill and my brother was coming down with my train fare so that we could go back together.'

A likely story, Billy thought. 'That's tough,' he said, trying not to sound too sympathetic.

'The old lady's dangerously ill,' the other went on, adopting a sorrowful expression. 'At death's door, they tell me. I've just got to get back somehow.'

Billy continued walking in silence, waiting for the punchline, for the other to put the bite on him. He hadn't long to wait.

'Look,' the young cadger said ever so politely. 'I hate to ask you this, but it's like this. I have most of my train fare but I'm five quid short. Could you, as a fellow Liverpudlian, see your way to loaning me a fiver so that I can get back to the Pool? We can swap names and addresses and all that and I can pay you back as soon as I get home. Honest to God.'

Now it was Billy's turn to come up with a story. If he was to be a writer, he had to start getting in some practice in the use of imagination. He continued walking as he replied.

'I wish I could help but, sad to say, I'm stony. You didn't ask why I was down here in London. You see, my old dad's desperately ill and hasn't long to live. I've got to get across to Chelsea before it's too late. And another thing, I'm not a Liverpudlian. I'm a Mancunian and a keen supporter of Manchester City and Manchester United.'

The tout saw that Billy was playing him at his own game and came up with a swift response.

'Then you can f... off, you Mancunian bastard. I hope you and your whole family rot in hell,' he added as he marched off to look for fresh quarry.

I may be gauche, Billy said to himself. But gullible I am not.

He was on a tight budget but nevertheless decided to splash out and take a taxi to his accommodation, the Lewis Carroll Hotel, which was within walking distance of Welbeck Hall where the course was to be held. It was an old hotel, small and inexpensive in an expensive city, not fancy but adequate. It was rumoured that the Victorian author and humorist had once stayed there. Billy didn't know a great deal about the Oxford don but his encyclopedia told him that his real name was Charles Dodgson, that he'd been born in 1832 and had died in 1898, that his 'Alice' books, along with his nonsense poems, were regarded as great children's classics.

He reached the hotel just after twelve noon, which left him enough time to register, lug his suitcase up to his room – there was no elevator – grab a quick sandwich and take the tube for a two o'clock appointment at Highgate Cemetery.

He'd chosen the Lewis Carroll Hotel deliberately for what might be considered bizarre reasons. He had the notion that Carroll's spirit might somehow still be in residence and floating about the place. And if so, that, by some process of osmosis he, Billy, might absorb some of the surplus artistic genius and wit that the rhymster had not used up in his lifetime. Mind you, Billy didn't fancy meeting him wandering along the corridor in the small hours when he, Billy, was paying a visit to the toilet. No, he had in mind the idea that he might find himself sleeping in the same room, and, who knows, even the same bed that the poet had once slept in. In which case, perhaps the great man would whisper a few bon mots in Billy's ear while he was enjoying sound slumber.

Many writers of fiction claimed that some of the characters they had invented appeared to acquire a life and a will of their own, almost making up their own dialogue and their next move in the plot. An eminent writer, Hilary Mantel, and a distinguished concert pianist, John Lull, attributed much of the inspiration for their work to the presence of guiding spirits. If it happened to them, Billy thought, then why not to me?

'I think you're going barmy,' Laura said, when he outlined his theory. Her opinion of his mental state would have been confirmed had she known that, in his search for external inspiration, he'd taken it one step further. He'd heard about the famous authors who were buried in London's Highgate Cemetery and he wondered whether

257

any residual talent might be hovering about their mausoleums. After all, these writers had had such prodigious talent, they must have had lots of unused material in their heads when they finally shuffled off their mortal coils. Maybe they could somehow pass some of it on to him. So he'd booked an extra day in London to visit their graves on one of the guided tours he'd seen advertised.

At 1.45 p.m. he found himself part of a group of about twenty people waiting outside the main gate of the western side of the celebrated cemetery. They were an international party consisting of German, Japanese, Scandinavian, and American tourists. At two o'clock precisely, their guide appeared.

Billy could scarcely believe his eyes. It was Alistair Sim in the flesh but, since he'd died in 1976, it had to be his double. He had the same long-faced, long-toothed face, with doleful and anguished expression, which brought to mind the ghoulish personality of Sim's famous dramatization of Scrooge. This seemed ideally suited for a cemetery, as did his Scottish brogue.

'Ma name is Ben McBogle and I'm to be your guide today in the western section of the cemetery I tak' it you've all paid for the admission tickets and, if that's the case, we'll proceed. However, if you're lookin' for Karl Marx, he's in the other cemetery in the eastern section.'

'Karl Marx in Highgate Cemetery!' Billy remarked to his German neighbour. 'It's just another communist plot.'

Sadly, the humour was lost on him.

'Some things I'll warn you aboot,' their guide announced. 'First, the tour is approximately one hour's duration and turning back isn't permitted as you'll certainly get lost without my guidance.'

Then looking vaguely in Billy's direction, he said, 'Secondly, surfaces are uneven and much of the tour is uphill, so I do hope that any elderly folk among ye are fit enough to undertake a strenuous tour like this. We don't want anyone expiring on the way up.'

Then pointedly turning his gaze on Billy, he made his last pronouncement. 'I must warn you that there are nae toilet facilities on the tour. If you're caught short, you must go to adjacent Waterlow Park. Very well, if you're all ready, let's go.'

So saying, he set a blistering pace along the path that led into the cemetery. The Scandinavians seemed to have their own agenda for they stopped at various graves and carried out private discussions about the inscriptions. Not a good idea.

'Do come along, you folks. You must keep up,' the guide commanded.

Despite his brusque and intimidating manner, he knew his stuff and gave them a pen portrait at the graves of some of the famous people buried there: Bronowski, Cruft, Faraday, Rowland Hill among many others. But it was the writers that interested Billy most: Christina Rossetti, Mrs Henry Wood, and Charles Dickens, though the great novelist himself was buried in Westminster Abbey. However they stopped at his magnificent memorial and the graveside of his wife and children. The Japanese took out their video cameras and posed for each other's pictures with the mausoleum as backdrop.

Ben McBogle became incandescent. 'You must'na tak' pictures' he stormed. 'It is clearly against the rules. D'ye no understand plain English?'

Evidently they didn't, especially when spoken with a strong Scottish accent.

As for Billy, at each graveside, he whispered the same entreaty. 'If by any chance you have any unused talent or surplus material you'd like to get rid of, and you would like an earth-bound amanuensis, I'm your man. Ready and waiting.' He was quite hopeful as Dickens had died at the relatively young age of fifty-eight when still working on *The Mystery of Edwin Drood*, while Mrs Henry Wood had been a prolific novelist, having turned out fifteen novels in seven years, though admittedly only one, *East Lynne*, was remembered.

The last grave they came to was that of Adam Worth, master crook and named on his headstone 'The Napoleon of Crime', He was considered by scholars of Conan Doyle to be the basis of Sherlock Holmes's nemesis, Moriarty. With my kind of luck, Billy thought, it'll be his talents that I'll inherit though I haven't asked for them.

Billy returned to his hotel in the early evening and then went out for a stroll. He visited a fast food restaurant where he consumed a Quarter Pounder, which, though not epicurean fare, satisfied his hunger. If you were on a tight budget, as he was, a quick burger was the answer. Apart

260

from that, Lucy had warned him that the Butter-shaw course was pretty demanding and as preparatory reading he had been told to study Terence Rattigan's play *The Winslow Boy*. And so, all things considered, he opted for a hot bath and an early night. If he was to get his money's worth from the course he had to be fresh and alert.

He liked the Lewis Carroll Hotel. It was small, quaint, and attractive with colourful hanging baskets decorating the walls around the doorway. The internal décor was fascinating and unusual. Examples of Carroll's verses and illustrations were liberally displayed about the place. There was the Jabberwocky:

Beware the Jabberwock, my son!
The jaws that bite, the claws that catch!
Beware the Jubjub bird and shun
The fruminous Bandersnatch

And:

'The time has come,' the Walrus said,
'To talk of many things:
Of shoes – and ships – and sealing wax–
Of cabbages – and kings–
And why the sea is boiling hot–
And whether pigs have wings.'

In his own room, he found his favourite nonsense song, 'The Lobster Quadrille', pasted on the wall opposite his bed. It was the one he'd learned at St Wilfred's Infant School, oh, so long ago!

'Will you walk a little faster?' said a whiting to
    a snail,
'There's a porpoise close behind us, and he's
    treading on my tail.'
Will you, won't you, will you,
Won't you, won't you join the dance?

It brought memories of his childhood flooding
back and made him feel at home. He slept
soundly that night and, if Carroll had responded
to his petition, he was not aware of it.

Billy went down to the dining room for his English breakfast which meant a cholesterolly rich
fry-up of eggs, bacon, beans, sausages, tomatoes,
mushrooms and fried bread. Why it was called
'English breakfast' he'd never been able to understand because most people in Britain started their
day on a modest fare of cereals like Kellogg's or
Shredded Wheat, and maybe a piece of toast. The
English breakfast that hotels liked to boast about
in their brochures was a myth and probably
derived from the William Cobbett era when the
squire liked to breakfast on a gargantuan feast
before going out on a fox-hunting expedition.
Still, Billy ate the hearty breakfast offered by the
hotel as he wasn't sure how much energy the
course would require nor when and where he'd
get to eat again. The hours of attendance were
9.30 a.m. to 8.00 p.m. for each of the two days of
the course. It sounded formidable.

Chapter Sixteen

How to Write a Novel

Suitably fortified, Billy made his way to the Welbeck Hall which was a mere ten-minute walk across Holborn Street. He arrived at nine o'clock and found there was a crowd of around three dozen people already there, milling about in the reception hall. He registered at the secretary's desk, paid the balance due and was handed a spiral-bound booklet entitled Alf Buttershaw's *How to Write a Good Novel*, along with his name badge. Thus equipped, he wandered into the hall to collect his complimentary cup of coffee. As he stepped through the doorway he was met by what sounded like the buzzing of a giant apiary, the hum of many individuals all talking at once in animated discussion, each trying to get his point of view across. As he stood there, coffee in hand, he felt lost, a fish out of water, a shrimp in a large pool. He looked around for a friendly face but could see none. A quick glance at the lapel badges of the people around offered no information other than name.

Billy swept the room with his eyes to check for the presence of stars or celebrities in the crowd but couldn't see any, at least any that he recognized, though generally speaking writers' faces, except for people like Somerset Maugham or

George Bernard Shaw, are not well known. But what on earth was he doing here on a novel-writing course? He hadn't written any kind of book or play. He cast a look towards the exit and wondered if there was still time to go to the organizer's desk and confess that he was an imposter, that he'd made a mistake and please could he have his money back? No use. He'd committed himself and there was no going back. He finished his coffee and went into the lecture theatre where he chose a seat at the back so as to remain inconspicuous and also, perhaps more importantly, because it was next to the exit for the toilets.

Suddenly, conversation ceased, a hush fell over the hall and all eyes turned towards the stage. The great Alf Buttershaw sauntered to the front of the rostrum and met the audience's gaze head on.

'Why you lot waste your bloody money on this course, I'll never know. It's all in 'ere,' he barked, holding up his book, *'How to Write a Good Novel'*, 'and it costs twelve ninety-nine. You must be as daft as a brush.'

He spoke with a broad Yorkshire accent, which for some strange reason Billy found reassuring. Nevertheless he wondered if he'd heard him right. Had he just told them they were wasting their bloody money? Apparently he had.

Billy looked more closely at Buttershaw. He would make a great character in a play like *I, Claudius*, he thought, for in some ways he resembled a Roman emperor with his billiard-ball scalp, leonine head, big bushy eyebrows, and the fervent, orator's gleam in his eye. He wore a white shirt, though a toga and a laurel crown might have been more appropriate. Billy sensed they were in for a virtuoso performance by a man devoted to the art of story-telling.

'Now before we begin, a few ground rules,' Buttershaw announced. 'Let me warn you that this course is tough. It's a ten-and-a-half-hour day and there'll be one hour for lunch and three fifteen-minute breaks. There's no smoking in the hall and if you're daft enough to want to commit suicide, you'll have to wait for the breaks when you can then smoke yoursel' to death. I know from your application forms that you all have books on the go and you'll be wanting to talk about your own particular work but there's three dozen of you and there just isn't time for me to give you individual tuition. So instead of just listening to me spout words of wisdom, seize the opportunity to talk over your masterpiece with the friends I hope you'll soon make on the course. You'll probably learn more from them than from me. Having got all that out of the way, let's begin.

'If you've come on this course hoping to learn how to win some hoity-toity literary award, you're on the wrong course. If your aim is to produce a literary gem that will impress the intelligentsia and get you a review in the *Times Literary Supplement*, best you go home now as this course is not for you. My aim is to show you how to construct a good story, how to write a synopsis and present your work to an agent or publisher.

'How do you tell a good tale? You could do worse than reread a few fairy tales by Hans Andersen and the Brothers Grimm. They knew how to spin a yarn and they usually began their tales with "Once upon a time, there was..." With this opening, we are thrown in at the deep end into a story about a hero or a heroine with whom we can identify. Then something happens, there occurs some pivotal event that kick-starts the story and we're off. Crucial questions are soon raised. What does our hero want? What is there to stop him? How does it all end? Does he get what he wants or not?'

Billy was hooked. He settled back to enjoy listening to a master at work. Time seemed to melt away as Buttershaw introduced them to the art of spinning a good yarn, how to present it to an agent, and how to avoid common pitfalls.

Billy found that Buttershaw's notion that the students would learn from each other was entirely accurate. Over coffee, the hum of conversation became animated as people discussed the first session and exchanged ideas and experiences. Billy found there was a wide variety of subjects being covered in the students' novels. Several men were writing 'whodunits', a number of ladies romantic fiction, one or two family sagas, a few historical dramas, and one man was writing about his experiences as a Spitfire pilot during the war. In the one-hour break allowed for lunch, many of the students retired to a nearby snack bar on Fetter Lane where the discussions continued over coffee and sandwiches. Several students had already finished their books and had stories and advice on the best ways of submitting work to publishers.

The course, though gruelling, was so enjoyable that the weekend whizzed by and Billy found himself spellbound by Buttershaw's hypnotic style and powerful message. Billy had never fully appreciated before how much skill there was to telling a good tale.

On the final day of the course, Billy said good-bye to the friends he had made; everyone shook hands, wishing each other luck and promising optimistically to keep an eye on the bestseller lists for each other's books. As he walked back to his hotel on the Sunday evening, he felt drained. It had been the toughest course he'd ever attended, as there'd been so much to absorb. He decided to celebrate by treating himself to a steak dinner at a Park Lane restaurant and drank a whole bottle of burgundy. Needless to say he slept soundly that night.

Next morning he caught the eleven o'clock train back to Liverpool and, although he dozed much of the time, in his waking moments he ran over the course in his mind. What had he learned? How did it apply to his own story of a kid growing up in Collyhurst? As the train went past Watford Junction and picked up speed, so did Billy's brain. First, what did the kid want out of life? To survive and to better himself, that's what he wanted most, though he may not have been able to put it in so many words. That was the theme of his story and, no matter what, that had to be kept at the fore-front of his mind. He determined to print it out in capital letters and pin it to the wall near his typewriter. That way it would always be before him and if ever he was tempted to wander off the point and lose direction, it would be there to remind him to get back on track.

The next important thing to decide was the pivotal moment in the kid's life that set up an urgent need in his heart. Was it the death of his hero brother, Jim, in the merchant navy? No, it was something much less dramatic. It came in a chance remark by his friend, David Priestley, when on the way back from serving Mass. He'd said, 'I've passed my scholarship and next year I'll be going to a grammar school.'

From that moment, Billy's life changed. He didn't know what a grammar school was but if his pal was going, then that was what he wanted to do as well. What seemed like an insignificant encounter changed the direction of his life forever: his education, his job and even his future wife and family.

The next big question to consider was: what was to stop the kid from achieving his heart's desire? What were the pitfalls along the path? Maybe not demons like those in Greek legends but there was the poverty and tradition of the area. Few Collyhurst kids went on to grammar schools mainly because their families couldn't afford the expense. Not only that, the rare few who did make it were likely to be subject to social sanctions, like being accused of becoming too big for their boots or getting ideas above their station. This had been the outlook of his own dad who'd held a strong 'us' and 'them' attitude. For him, going off to a grammar school meant join-ing the toffs, going over to the enemy and being a traitor to your class. And there was so much more in the story to tell: the war and evacuation to Blackpool, his first job, going to college...

As these ideas flowed through his mind, Billy became excited, sensing that maybe he'd got a good yarn to spin. He could hardly wait to get home to start writing it.

Chapter Seventeen

Modus Operandi

When it comes to the actual business of writing, authors have their idiosyncratic ways. Robert Louis Stevenson, Mark Twain and Voltaire, among others, did most of their writing in bed. A.A. Milne, best known as the creator of Christopher Robin and Winnie-the-Pooh, preferred working at the bottom of his garden in a shed from which children were strictly forbidden. Philip Pullman insisted on doing his writing on special narrow-lined paper with blue margins and he, too, worked in a hut which, by his own admission, was dusty and cobwebby. Jeffrey Archer advised renting a cottage in the country away from distractions, and writing solidly until the work was finished. Joanna Trollope liked to write on an A4 pad, sitting at the right-hand corner of the kitchen table. Alan Bennett said that, when writing, he acted things out, pacing about the room and saying dialogue out loud, and for that reason he liked to work in an empty house. Perhaps the strangest modus operandi of all was that of Thomas Wolfe who, being extremely tall, wrote standing up using the top of a refrigerator as a desk. As he finished each page, he tossed it into a cardboard box on the floor.

How long it would take to write a book like his

was a question Billy often asked himself. It seemed like forever as it made glacier-like progress with the addition of a few paltry words each day. How he envied those writers like James Hilton who wrote *Goodbye Mr Chips* in four days and Robert Louis Stevenson who wrote *Dr Jekyll and Mr Hyde* in just three, thanks mainly to a nightmare which, he said, presented him with the entire plot. On the other hand James Joyce took seventeen years to complete *Finnegans Wake* while Flaubert needed eighteen years to write *Madame Bovary*. As for those writers like Anthony Trollope and Larkin, who turned out books during their leisure hours while pursuing demanding careers, Billy took his hat off to them.

Exactly *when* writers did their writing also varied widely according to personality and circumstance. Some preferred to stay up late or get up very early to take advantage of the small hours when things were nice and quiet. Not Billy. He liked his beauty sleep. Not only that, he never wrote in the morning because his brain was usually too heavy with sleep and needed time and innumerable cups of coffee to bring it round.

He had formed the habit of using up the first part of the day devouring caffeine and the *Daily Telegraph* right up to the very last page, including the obituaries in order to check on his own shelf life, that is, on how long he possibly had left to live. Then he rounded off the a.m. by solving the easy clues of the crossword, much to Laura's annoyance as she was left with the hard bits, though he suspected that she secretly enjoyed the challenge. The real reason he spent so much time

271

on the newspaper was not hard to fathom. Anything to put off the evil moment when he'd have to sit before that typing machine and think of something interesting to say. If anyone ever tried to tell him that writing was easy, he knew right away that such people had never tried it.

Finally, after lunch, Billy had a Churchillian nap and then he could postpone the moment no longer. He went to the typewriter but before he began, he switched on some music, Handel's Chandos anthems for preference because the anthems seem to offer familiarity and security. Finally he plucked up courage and began, which was always the difficult part. And then the strangest thing of all happened; once he was sitting at the machine, it wasn't too bad and one or two ideas that he didn't know he had came floating up to the surface. He tried to write something every day, even if it was only a couple of hundred words. Five hundred words were usually his aim and if he managed a thousand, he reckoned he'd had a successful session, even if what he'd written was gobbledegook, as it usually was. It was a thousand words he didn't have before and they could always be worked on, amended or even deleted later. After all, they were not written in aspic.

Whoever writes in aspic? it occurred to him to ask himself. And come to that, what exactly was aspic? He looked it up and found it was an aromatic oil, a poison, or a meat jelly. Who was the nutcase who sat down one day and said to himself: 'I'm fed up writing in ink. Today, I shall write using aromatic oil. I shall use aspic and no one will ever be able to delete it.' Billy had to give up.

In the early days, his office was a converted bedroom and he knocked out his script on a portable Remington. He worked every day, converting his memoirs into a novel, applying the principles he'd learned on the Buttershaw course.

Though it was based on his true life story and many of the events had actually taken place, he used poetic licence in fictionalizing characters, embroidering the story and altering the time frame. At the end of six months, he had turned out over one hundred thousand words in twenty-nine chapters under the pseudonym Tim Lally. At last, he thought, after all the wrong turnings and the cul de sacs I've been down, I've found something I can do reasonably well. This is how I'll spend my retirement – writing! Eureka!

He hated it on those occasions when he struggled to produce the next sentence or paragraph and he found himself staring at a blank piece of paper. But there was nothing like the satisfaction when the work was finished and he could finally write 'The End'.

One day Laura asked, 'Why the pseudonym and why Tim Lally in particular?'

'Charles Dickens called himself David Copperfield in what was really his autobiography. Lally was my mother's maiden name and Tim Lally was a distant cousin of hers long since deceased. I liked the sound of it as my nom-de-plume.'

It was time to give the book an airing and to get some reaction. Was it trash or did it have any merit? But who to ask? Who was his ideal reader who could give him an objective assessment? He used the immediate family as guineas pigs by passing it around, though all the writing manuals advised against it.

'Don't show it to your family,' they said. 'If they criticize it, you're likely to blow your top that anyone would dare to suggest that your *oeuvre* is less than perfect. On the other hand they may be afraid of hurting you and you are liable to receive unwarranted praise.' Not from his kids! If they thought it was garbage, they wouldn't hesitate to tell him.

'This is a really great read,' said Laura when she had turned the last page. 'Well worth publishing. It has the makings of a bestseller.'

But was Laura the best person to exercise objective judgement? Nevertheless, that initial reaction pleased him no end as it was a welcome relief to learn that it made sense to someone else. When a writer finishes a long piece of work, he's been so close to it that he's never sure how it's going to be received. As for the word 'bestseller', he wasn't sure what that meant. Top ten? Top twenty? Or, as is the case with pop music, top fifty? His dictionary didn't help much either for it defined bestseller as 'a book that has sold many copies, overall or in a given season'. Furthermore, there was no guarantee that anyone actually read the bestsellers in question. Some people bought books simply for display and to show off to their friends.

Lucy was next to read it and she was equally enthusiastic. 'The title alone will hook the readers, Dad. It's like that famous old Charlie

Chaplin film *The Kid*. What exactly does the expression "our kid" mean?'

'It's the nickname I always received in my family. In the north, it means a brother or a sister. In the north-west, it can be a younger or an older sibling but it's always a term of affection, signifying, "You belong to this family no matter what you do, whether you've robbed a bank or committed a murder." It can also be used when a telling-off is due, for example, "Scram, our kid. Go home." A friend from northeast England told me that in his part of the world, the term had a slightly different connotation. He wrote: "In Geordieland, *our kid*, or in the vernacular *wor kid*, means the *eldest* son, so the Geordie youngster who, when bullied, shouts, *I'll set wor kid on ye!* he means I'll get my big brother to wallop you!"'

This interpretation was confirmed when Billy heard Bobby Charlton, talking about the 1966 World Cup, say, 'So, I passed the ball back to our kid,' meaning his big brother, Jack.

'Thanks for the lecture, Dad.' Lucy grinned.

'Well, you did ask.'

'Are you sure no one else has used the title?' Laura asked.

'It doesn't matter, Laura, even if they have because there's no copyright on titles. However, I checked it out and could find only one *Our Kid* and that was written by Ann Pilling in nineteen eighty-nine. It was a very different kind of story.'

The boys were next to read the manuscript. Considering their reaction to his memoirs when they'd made so many cracks, it took him aback and threw him off his stride when they said they liked it. He thought maybe he preferred it when they were abrasive adolescents because at least he knew where he was with them. Now the two youngest, Mark and John, were sure he was going to win fame and fortune.

'Publishers will scratch each other's eyes out to publish this,' Mark said. 'You might get to number one in the bestseller list, Dad, and become a millionaire. We're always reading in the papers how some unknown author was discovered and went on to make his or her fortune.'

John had even grander dreams of success. 'Freddie Forsyth, Wilbur Smith, Tom Clancy, move over and make way for Tim Lally. Where will you moor your yacht, Dad? St Tropez or Monte Carlo?'

Billy laughed. 'And pigs might fly. Dream on, you two. The media love to pick up on cases where some unknown has been paid half a million or more for a first novel. Rags to riches stories like that are meat and drink to them. A favourite example is someone like Colleen McCullough who was a lowly paid nurse until she wrote *The Thorn Birds*, for which she was reputedly paid over a million dollars. The tabloids love to exaggerate and talk about the immense wealth of novelists but it's only writers like Catherine Cookson, Danielle Steel, and John Grisham that make it to the top and such cases are rare. I should think my chances are somewhere between zero and nil and I stand more chance of winning the lottery. I read somewhere that the great majority of writers are on the breadline and few can make a living from it.'

Matthew had a different hope. 'Apart from the money, Dad, you might achieve a literary reputation and be written up and reviewed in the highbrow newspapers, like the *Guardian* or *The Times*. Now that would be something.'

Billy grimaced. 'I want my book to be read, enjoyed and understood by the ordinary man in the street. In general, your average readers aren't looking for novels of literary merit; they want a good story to read on the train or on the beach, something that'll appeal to their imagination and keep them turning the pages.'

Lucy nodded. 'Dad's quite right when he says few make a living out of writing. When I took it up, the best advice I ever received was: don't give up the day job. That's why I continue with my art therapy. Fortunately, Dad has his pension and doesn't need to rely on writing.'

Things were going too fast for Billy's liking. 'Whoa!' He laughed. 'We're running ahead of ourselves here. Who said anyone will be interested in my book? Who wants to read the ramblings of an old codger like me? Not only that, publishers will probably think that, as an OAP, I'm a one-book writer when what they're really looking for is a young person who can turn out dozens of books, like a sausage machine.'

'You never know, Dad,' she replied. 'You might just swing it. The first thing you need to do is win the enthusiasm of an agent who will pitch your book to a publisher and get you a contract.'

'Why do I need an agent? Why can't I pitch it myself to a publisher?'

'You can, but publishers prefer it to come

through an agent who's done the spadework for them, sifting and weeding out likely manuscripts from the thousands that are submitted. Some scripts are illiterate tripe, and it saves publishers a lot of time and trouble if someone goes through them and picks out likely winners. But agents are like gold dust and not easy to get. I've heard it said that it's easier to get a publisher than an agent as they take only a limited number on their lists.' Lucy chuckled. 'I like the story of one naïve writer who came to London clutching his manuscript thinking he'd interview a few agents and then choose one. He told them what a great Hollywood movie his novel would make and he warned them that there would be fierce competition to become his agent. They should therefore make out a case for being his representative and then phone him to make an appointment. The boot's on the other foot though. There are too many writers chasing too few agents.'

'I have a feeling,' Billy grinned, 'that the gentleman in question is still wondering why he hasn't received an answer to his generous offer. In time, he'll come down to earth no doubt. But then how do agents pick out potential bestsellers from the mass of manuscripts received in their post bag?'

'I think it's largely a matter of guesswork. Nobody really knows what's going to be the next big winner. Could be a boy's book of adventures or even a book on English grammar or spelling. Who knows what the public will go for next?'

'I doubt the last two.' Billy laughed. 'Somehow, I can't see Joe Public going for a book about punctuation. But I do wonder sometimes what criteria agents use to sort the wheat from the chaff.'

'There was an article recently in a Sunday review section,' she said. 'It said agents have their own particular foibles. One said he can judge a script in thirty seconds flat.'

'How on earth does he do that?' Matthew gasped.

'He looks at the submission letter and if it's written on tatty paper, full of spelling and grammatical mistakes, he doesn't need to read any further. Also if it's written in stilted language.'

Mark laughed, 'You mean like: "Esteemed Sirs, Following on my telephonic dialogue with your amanuensis, I should deem it an honour if you would deign to scrutinize the enclosed transcription." We get letters like that all the time at the office. I can almost hear the literary agent dismissing this submission with a curt, "Next!"'

'Exactly.' She laughed. 'Agents have their own idiosyncrasies and prejudices. On a course I attended, one agent, probably speaking with her tongue in her cheek, claimed that she automatically rejected stories with unpronounceable foreign names, children's tales as they were not her cup of tea, extravagant science fiction containing technical gobbledegook because she didn't understand it.'

It was John's turn to join in the merriment. 'So Tolstoy and Dostoevsky are out, so are *Alice in Wonderland* and *The Hobbit*, along with *Hitch-hiker's Guide*.'

Lucy was obviously enjoying this exchange because she went on, 'One agent does not like books that have the name of the protagonist on the first page. Another hates titles with an exclamation mark.'

'There goes *Moby Dick* with its "Call me Ishmael" on the first line,' Matthew said.

'And it's goodbye to poor old Charles Kingsley with his *Westward Ho!* and Lionel Bart with his *Oliver!*' Mark chortled.

'Enough of this banter,' Billy said. 'How do we go about finding an agent?'

'The best way,' Lucy said, 'is to go through the *Writer's Handbook* and pick out a few. But not any old agent. Avoid those who ask for a reading fee and it's pointless choosing those who specify special interests like poetry, horror, crime or religious works. We must look for those interested in your kind of work: family sagas and that kind of thing.'

Together they combed through the lists and identified the names of thirty agents and publishers who might be prepared to consider memoirs or family histories. Then Lucy said that she'd heard that some of them can take as long as six months to answer.

'In that case,' Billy said, 'it'll take around fifteen years to get round them all if I write to them one at a time. I'm not sure I have that much time left! I'll write to them all at the same time and accept the best offer, if any, that comes along.'

'Is that an acceptable practice, writing to so many at once?' Laura wondered.

'It is, Mum,' replied Lucy. 'According to the Society of Authors it's quite ethical to make multiple submissions without necessarily mentioning that copies have been sent to other agents.'

It was a mammoth task producing thirty photocopies of a synopsis and the first three chapters of the book, together with a one-page covering letter telling about himself and his previous experience of writing. After three weeks' hard graft of addressing and packaging, his desk was piled high with thirty crisp Jiffy bags. It cost a small fortune to post them out with return postage but finally it was done. Then there was nothing to do but cross his fingers and wait.

Chapter Eighteen

Thanks but no Thanks

Six months later, the Jiffy bags started to come back. For a week or two Billy became all too familiar with the squeaking sound of the letter box opening and the thud of his manuscript landing on the doormat. Twelve were returned and eighteen disappeared down a black hole, for he heard nothing more about them.

Many of the rejection letters were simply postcards with a few simple standard phrases, for example: 'Many thanks for offering us your manuscript but we regret that on this occasion we are unable to accept it and return it herewith. Please Note: A stamped addressed envelope should accompany every submission.'

Nearly all intimated that there was no market for his kind of book. His submission had been read with interest but the list of this particular agent was already full and they were unable to take on any further writers. In returning his three chapters and synopsis, one told him that in future submissions, he should enclose three chapters and a synopsis. Some of the rejections, however, were worthy of a book in themselves.

One said that, in order to promote a work, she had to 'love it' and that unfortunately in his case she did not and therefore regretfully had to reject it. One took the time to write him a whole paragraph: 'What a charming story *Our Kid* is!' she said. 'What a pity you are not a little girl as I am sure I could have done something with it then. Why not rewrite it and pretend that you are?' Billy wanted to be published but was not prepared to undergo a sex change to achieve it. He was keen but not that keen.

The second refusal said simply, 'You should learn to write sideways.' This puzzled him somewhat as the only time he'd had to write sideways was when writing on the blackboard in a tough school in the Ardwick district of Manchester where turning your back on a class was a sure way of inviting missiles from recalcitrant pupils.

Another agent told him, 'There's no demand for kitchen sink tales about northern slums and "trouble in t' mill". Such stuff is passé.' So much for Catherine Cookson and *Coronation Street*, he thought.

The next letter gave the family some difficulty as it consisted of illegible scrawl on a tatty scrap of paper and they only managed to decipher it with the aid of a magnifying glass and after prolonged debate. It said, 'Someone left this stuff on my desk. I don't know why but I certainly don't have time to read it. I'm swamped.'

Many of the letters contradicted each other. 'Too much conflict in this story,' and 'Too bland – not enough drama.' Or, 'The story did not click.' So the comments continued, the rest being standard replies along the lines of, 'not right for our list' and 'has potential but not quite what we are looking for'.

Lucy, who'd had similar experiences of rejection, told him that he was lucky to receive any kind of comment as most agents, if they replied at all, answered with, 'Thanks but no thanks.'

Nevertheless, these rejections were a rude awakening and a severe blow to his self-esteem. At first, he was down in the dumps as he found them a bitter pill to swallow. Was writing to be like the other enterprises he'd attempted? Lots of effort but no reward. After all, he'd attended an expensive course, spent hundreds of hours putting his heart and soul into the story and rebuffs were not easy to take. In his innocence, he'd believed that, since it was a labour of love, it was bound to be published. When people asked him how long it had taken him to write the thing, he always replied, 'About sixty-five years', because that's how much thought had gone into it. He began to feel that maybe the book was worthless and he was ready to throw it in the bin. What's more, he thought that maybe he was worthless as a writer. He said as much to Laura but she would have none of it.

'Nonsense,' she exclaimed. 'You must remember that agents probably receive dozens, maybe hundreds, of manuscripts every week. How are they going to pick out your masterpiece from that lot?'

Then he began to get mad about the cavalier treatment he imagined he'd received.

'How could these agents be so blind?' he ranted. 'Didn't they recognize a work of merit when it landed on their desk? To be given the boot once or twice would be bad enough but to be rebuffed twelve times! That must mean there's no market for my kind of stuff. Who's going to be interested in the memoirs of a nobody, some old bloke living in the wilds of Manchester?'

'Mum's right,' said Lucy, who'd come round to commiserate. 'Agents do receive hundreds of submissions. You can't expect them to read them all; it'd take up nearly all their time to get through them. Remember, agents have mortgages and grocery bills like everyone else and they can't afford to go chasing after unknown writers in the remote possibility that they'll find a masterpiece among the dross. In accountants' language, it's not cost effective.'

'I hope you're not calling my book dross, Lucy.'

'No, it's just that when publishers and agents are looking at the work of new writers, it's dodgy trying to make predictions about what'll sell. They'd rather put their money on sure-fire things like established writers with a track record, and who can blame them?'

He couldn't help adding, 'And also famous TV celebrities and sporting personalities with their ghost writers who tell us details like what they eat for breakfast and how many fillings they have in their teeth.'

'But those are the books that get onto the best-seller lists!' Laura exclaimed. 'So obviously the public wants to read about such details. Such books perhaps tell us more about the readers than the writers. Besides, the profits on them probably enable publishers to print quality books that don't sell too well.'

'Anyway,' Lucy said, 'being turned down isn't so

285

bad; it's happened to me often. I'm thinking of papering the walls of my room with rejection letters but I take comfort in knowing that we're in good company. Many famous writers had their work rejected many times before they succeeded.'

'Who, for example?' he asked.

'Almost every famous writer you can think of has been refused at some time or other. But for starters, how about George Orwell's *Animal Farm* which was declined with the comment "impossible to sell animal stories", or *Moby Dick* condemned as being "very long and old fashioned"? And one of my favourite writers, John Grisham, had his first novel *A Time to Kill* rejected fifteen times. So there's no need for you to get depressed or think about giving up.'

'That's all very well, Lucy,' he replied, 'but it doesn't then follow that if you've been rejected twelve times, you're going to be famous later on. Besides, I've been rejected thirty times since eighteen haven't even bothered to answer. I wonder what happened to those, manuscripts.'

'Probably in their office slush piles.'

'Slush piles?' He grinned. 'They sound like a revolting case of haemorrhoids.'

'They're the heaps of unsolicited manuscripts that pile up in some agents' offices. Horror stories report that some of them are six feet high.'

'No doubt there are some precious jewels hidden in the mud.'

'Sure,' she said, 'along with all the dross, the badly written, badly typed (or even scribbled), badly punctuated, badly spelled and probably on cheap, flimsy paper.'

'Anyway, Billy, I'm glad to see that you're cheering up,' said Laura 'Having your manuscript returned is not the end of the world. If I know you, you won't give up so easily.'

'You're quite right, Laura. I could throw the manuscript into a cupboard, forget all about it and hope that my great-great-grandchildren find it and enjoy it. Or I could take up another hobby like playing the trombone but I'm not yet ready to throw in the towel. I can still recall my brother - in-law many years ago quoting a Churchill speech when I failed to get into the London college. It went like this: "Never give in! Never give in! Never, never, never! In nothing, great or small, large or petty. Never give in except to convictions of honour and good sense. Never yield!" We should make it the family motto: "Never give in!"'

'So what will you try next?'

'I've seen those adverts in writers' magazines inviting writers to submit their work for private publication. "New authors wanted. All subjects invited," they proclaim. Might be worth a try.'

'You mean pay to have it published?'

'Why not? We can recoup the costs by selling lots of copies.'

Chapter Nineteen

Vanity

In the writers' magazines that he consulted, there were many ads offering publishing services. In the end he plumped for one that asked for quality manuscripts – all genres considered.

He sent off for the 'free' brochure and had it back almost by return post, inviting him to submit his manuscript for consideration by their Editorial Board.

How much warmer and friendlier he found this response after so many cold and heartless rebuffs, he thought. He was captivated and he had his stuff in the post to them the next day.

The company was as good as its word because two weeks later, he had their reply and it warmed the cockles of his heart to read it. He couldn't believe it when they told him that their selection committee had read the sample chapters, loved them, and would he be so kind as to send the whole book as they were of the opinion that he had written a masterpiece.

He packed up the book carefully, all twenty-nine chapters, and sent it off by registered mail. The post office staff were becoming good friends.

'We'll soon be inviting you to our staff dances,' the head clerk joked.

He hadn't long to wait for the company's

answer. How different from the mainstream agents and publishers! No hanging around for months awaiting their verdict. Their reply was with him within three weeks and the first part of their letter set his heart racing with joy. They told him the Board had read his book with great pleasure and it was unanimous in recommending it for publication as they felt the work was of outstanding literary merit and on a par with the work of Charles Dickens. Furthermore, it had great potential as an adaptation for television.

On a separate section, details of the cost of publication were appended. It would be a joint effort and if he would kindly send his share of the costs for 5,000 books, i.e. £10,000, they would begin work immediately after a design for a cover had been agreed.

'Well, it certainly tells you all the things you've been longing to hear,' Laura chuckled when she'd read the letter. 'Now I know why it's called vanity publishing. The next Charles Dickens indeed! But the question is, what are you going to do about it?'

'That's easily answered, Laura. First of all, I don't have ten thousand pounds to chuck away. Secondly, what on earth am I going to do with the five thousand copies of my book when they're dumped on the doorstep? They'd fill up the whole garage. No, I'll write to the firm and tell them what they can do with their offer.'

'You can't just abandon the book, Billy.'

'I don't intend to. I know how to type and I don't see why I can't publish the bloody thing myself. But not in the thousands. I'd like to produce just enough to let family and friends read it.'

He sent off his letter to the company. How he enjoyed writing it! This time, for a change, he was doing the rejecting. He thought he'd heard the last of the company but not so. Six months later it was announced in the press that the company had gone into liquidation and it was apparent that the 'Editorial Board' had consisted of one member.

Shortly after his brush with vanity publishing there was a lively television campaign conducted by the Amstrad Electronics manufacturer. Several times a day, they were treated to the spectacle of Alan Sugar turfing typewriters into a giant skip. 'Typewriters are history,' the ad proclaimed. 'Chuck them in the bin and replace them with an Amstrad word processing computer.' It sounded like the answer to his prayers and Billy hurriedly made his way across to the Comet warehouse to purchase his first computer, an Amstrad 8256.

It came with everything necessary: word processor, printer and a standard QWERTY keyboard which was the only part which resembled a conventional typewriter. It was a whole new world and involved him in hours of cursing and frustration before he got the hang of clicking and double-clicking a 'mouse' and taking in new concepts like CUT, COPY, PASTE and PRINT. Gone was the need for Tippex corrector fluid and India rubbers; whole sentences and paragraphs could be shunted around at will. He was soon boring everyone at the dinner table spouting esoteric terms and abbreviations, like, floppy disk (the 'floppy'), software and hardware, multitasking, DOS, RAM, CPU. The list seemed to be endless and it wasn't long before family members who happened to be visiting melted away and he found he was eating alone, still jabbering to himself in this recondite language.

For several months, his head was left spinning as he tried to absorb so many new operations. The task of getting his book, all 100,000 words of it, into the computer seemed daunting until he found a firm that was able to scan it and transcribe it for a reasonable fee. He found it hard to believe that the whole book fitted easily onto one 'floppy' with lots of room to spare. Two years' work on one little three and half inch disk! But even the miraculous Amstrad processor didn't last and it was soon superseded by a more versatile machine when Bill Gates came along with Microsoft Windows.

It was simpler to use but after a while Billy developed a love/hate relationship with this electronic monster and at times had the eerie feeling that it was really an alien being trying to take him over. When it behaved itself and worked efficiently, he loved it and blessed the day he'd bought it. Things didn't always go so smoothly, however, and on those occasions he loathed the thing and was ready to chuck it out of the window. On one occasion it accused him of breaking the law. He'd been working happily and steadily and was in the process of moving a block of text over to another file when out of the blue he received the message:

YOU HAVE PERFORMED AN ILLEGAL OPER-ATION!

Guilty without trial. He half expected the CIA or MI5 to come around with handcuffs but when nothing happened, he thought maybe he'd got away with it. Wrong! His punishment followed immediately:

YOU WILL BE CLOSED DOWN WITHOUT SAVING!

Duly chastized, he booted up again, though inwardly he felt like booting **it** up the backside. A few days later he decided to erase a page of text which he deemed irrelevant. First, the computer double-checked that he hadn't gone completely round the bend:

ARE YOU SURE YOU WANT TO DO THIS?

when he confirmed that he really did, it came right back at him with:

YOU DO NOT HAVE PERMISSION TO CANCEL THIS!

He wondered whose permission he should have sought before deleting. He searched through his paperwork to see if Bill Gates or someone at the White House was available but could find nobody with sufficient authority. That was not the end of it, for a little later he did something it didn't like by opening too many programmes at once. Without warning, the whole system crashed and switched itself off. 'Uh-oh,' he said to himself, 'I've really done it this time. I've committed some heinous act and done irreparable damage. My computer will never forgive me.'

Fearing the worst, he switched on again and was relieved to see that it was booting up again successfully. But before it would let him back into the programme, he received a serious reprimand.

DON'T EVER DO THAT AGAIN!

He waited for a hand to come out of the box and slap him on the wrist.

He continued formatting and typesetting his manuscript into book form while Lucy provided him with cartoon drawings to illustrate various scenes. He printed out three copies and for the umpteenth time proof-read the text. Unbelievably he found another half-dozen errors that he'd missed first time round. They're like little gremlins, he thought, that creep imperceptibly into your work when you're not looking. For example, 'I wish to express my gratitude to Marion Smith became 'Martian' Smith, while the omission of a 'k' after 'week' made all the difference to the meaning in the sentence: 'Billy thought about it carefully, and after a wee, decided to resign.'

He found, too, that care had to be taken before instructing the computer to replace one name with another. He decided to change the name of Brother Matthew to Brother Dorian and ordered the computer to change all occurrences of Matthew to Dorian throughout the text. He didn't expect the bizarre results it produced, viz: 'The whole congregation rose to its feet when, in clear, ringing tones, Canon Calder announced: "A reading from the Holy Gospel according to Dorian."' Perhaps worse, in a passage describing his dad's dexterity in pulling his cart through Smithfield Market, the text changed from 'Like Stanley Matthews streaking down the wing' to 'Like Stanley Dorians streaking down the wing'. It didn't do to fall asleep when editing a manuscript. Then Laura gave it a final once-over and found yet more errors that he'd overlooked. From that day forth, though she tried to turn down the honour, she was promoted to be official editor and proof-reader. Now he was ready to go into book production.

He consulted Yellow Pages to find a reputable bookbinder. There were a fair number of them and, since he had no personal knowledge of any of them, it was like buying a pig in a poke. He eventually plumped for Thomas Loughlin Ltd of Liverpool. He was wary and wondered if he'd made the right choice. He drove over to Brunswick Business Park where they were located and there all his concerns were dispelled, for standing at the counter receiving a finished book was no other than the Most Reverend Derek Worlock, Archbishop of Liverpool. Billy greeted him politely with, 'Good morning, Your Grace.' He hoped that was the correct form of address. The archbishop returned his salutation warmly and shook Billy's hand. I'll never wash my hand again, Billy vowed to himself. After the prelate had departed, Billy asked the assistant what the archbishop had used to bind his book.

'Leather,' the clerk informed him.

'Then I'll have the same,' he said.

'It's rather expensive, sir. It'll be fifty pounds per book.'

'That's fine,' Billy said, hardly able to believe what he'd just said.

Then he thought, in for a penny, in for a pound. In this case, one hundred and fifty pounds for three books.

Four weeks later, Billy returned to collect the

finished products. Nothing, but nothing in this world could ever equal the joy of first seeing one's first-born child. But the sight of those three books bound in leather with their gold-blocked lettering came very close to it for him. It was like the adrenaline rush an actor must feel when he first sees his name in lights, he mused. He held the books tenderly in his hands as if holding Chinese porcelain. He turned them over and over, examining the front, the spine, then the contents. Never mind the quality of the story within, he thought, what I'm holding here are three works of art. OUR KID by TIM LALLY they boasted in glittering golden capitals. He congratulated the manager of the firm and happily handed over his cheque. Now he was an author and here was the proof of it for all the world to see.

With lots of warnings and caveats about taking care of the precious volumes, the books were distributed around relatives and friends for comment. Needless to say, he heard nothing but high praise both for the quality of the product and the story content. They vied with each other for superlatives. But in the immortal words of Miss Mandy Rice-Davies at the trial of Lord Astor, 'Well, they would say that, wouldn't they?'

Now he had to decide on his next move. Should he leave this venture into publishing at three books for family consumption only and consider them simply as heirlooms to be passed on down the line of the generations?

Then his old friend, Fate, stepped in. Like a bolt out of the blue there landed on his doormat a letter from a literary agent in Winchester.

Dear Mr Hopkins,

I must apologize for not replying sooner to the submission of the manuscript of your novel but I have only just seen it as it had fallen behind a radiator and only came to light when my office was being redecorated recently. I absolutely love the story and have been deeply impressed by your three chapters. It is a great pity that I did not see it earlier as I am sure I could have done something with it.

Sincerely,
Madge Monaghan

With great excitement, he rushed off one of his new leather-bound books to her by registered post. That should impress her even more, he thought. At last he had found an enthusiastic agent who was in love with his book and would begin offering it to mainstream publishers. Surely one of them would recognize its worth! With trepidation, he waited. And waited. And waited. Three long months passed before they got the news. Madge Monaghan's little agency had gone bust. As for his fifty-pound, leather-bound book, he never saw it again.

Chapter Twenty

D.I.Y.

'Damn, damn, damn!' Billy cursed. 'I'm tired of trying to persuade people out there to publish my book. I'll produce and market the bloody thing myself. After all, I have a computer and I know how to use it. It can't be that difficult to have a hundred copies printed and bound.'

First, he had to decide on the dedication of the book. Not entirely an easy matter because, in many ways, the whole family had contributed to it with their comments, criticisms, and support. He was tempted to use an unusual or bizarre dedication similar to those used by one or two famous writers. High in the running was P.G. Wodehouse's dedication to his daughter, Leonora, without whose never failing sympathy and encouragement, he said, the book would have been finished in half the time.

A close second was that of the writer e.e. cummings who not only wrote his name in lower case letters but had dedicated his appropriately titled book *No Thanks* to the fourteen publishers who had rejected it and also to his mother, who had paid for its printing. And third, that of Nikolaus Pevsner who expressed his gratitude by dedicating his work entitled *Bedfordshire, Huntingdon and Peterborough* to the inventor of the ice lolly.

297

In the end he thought it best and perhaps safest to dedicate it to his wife, Laura, for her great patience in listening to his idiotic ramblings when the book was in its embryonic stage.

Lucy and he designed a cover using the only picture he had of himself as a kid, taken at the home of a well-to-do family whose son he used to play with. In Billy's family, possessions did not run to a camera, not even a humble Kodak Brownie. So now he had the book and its cover and all that remained was to find a reputable company to print it. Going through various trade magazines in the Manchester Central Library, he found a London firm by the name of 'In-Type' which agreed to produce a hundred copies at a unit price of £8 a copy. He decided to go ahead and, six weeks later, after almost emptying his bank account, he was the proud owner of ten packages containing his first paperback book. It looked good with the picture of the slum kid in the rundown street with the old lady in the background. All he had to do now was sell them.

'Advertising is the answer,' his son Mark declared, 'but not any old advert in any old magazine. You have to focus your publicity at your target readers.'

'But who are they?' he wondered.

Lucy had the answer. 'First, the older generation, and since the story concerns a kid who was an altar boy, Catholic readers.'

He took their advice and, using the last few pounds left in his account, placed ads in *The Oldie, Practical Gardening, Choice,* and finally *The Catholic Pictorial.* He also sent a round robin to the library authorities in the north of England. He priced the book at £12 (or £11.99 as that seemed to be the accepted practice) which just about covered the cost of printing, postage and advertising. Little or no profit in the exercise but at least it would get the book out there being read.

The ad was made up of the front cover of the book, a blurb saying what it was about and a few comments written by the first set of readers, mainly friends.

The response was overwhelming and the first run of a hundred books sold faster than a pint of best bitter going down his old man's throat. On the basis of this initial success, Billy splashed out and had a further five hundred copies printed.

'I hope you know what you're doing,' Laura remarked. 'You haven't forgotten what happened with the airships?'

'Hardly likely,' he replied ruefully.

In the event, the reprint went just as fast as the first lot. The books were selling in their hundreds, which was better than anything he'd expected even in his wildest dreams. He was perfectly content and would have been satisfied to have remained in this situation. Then something that he found mysterious and hard to understand changed everything.

Sometimes things that are happening elsewhere can have a crucial effect on developments in your life. Such events may involve other people and be so remote from your own circumstances that you're hardly aware of them. Some call it luck or chance but Carl Jung called it 'synchronicity', by which he meant that cosmic events beyond your ken could sometimes coincide and change your destiny. Like what happened to a few film stars in Hollywood. William Goldman in his book *Adventures in the Screen Trade* told how certain movie stars became big as a result of a mistake made by even bigger names at the box office. He quoted the examples of Robert Redford who might have remained an unknown extra had he not got the part of the Sundance Kid after it was turned down by Marlon Brando, Steve McQueen and Warren Beatty. And if Albert Finney had not spurned the role of Lawrence of Arabia, nobody would have heard of Peter O'Toole. And most astonishingly of all, Humphrey Bogart only got the part of Rick in *Casablanca* after George Raft had said no thanks. This was synchronicity at work.

At a more modest level, a similar set of circumstances occurred for Billy when his daughter Lucy attended a writing class in London run by Reginald Holmes. At the end of the course, Lucy gave him a copy of *Our Kid* and asked for his opinion. He read it, liked it, and changed Billy's life.

Chapter Twenty-One

Red Letter Day

Reggie Holmes was an interesting character with the most impressive credentials. As well as being the author of several international bestselling novels, he'd worked as a screenwriter and script analyst at every major studio in Hollywood during his thirty years in the film industry. He had also participated as creative consultant in a number of highly successful television series.

Happily for Billy, Reggie Holmes agreed to take a look at the book. Shortly after Lucy had completed his course, he wrote a letter which said:

28th December 1997
Dear Mr Hopkins,
It was very kind of you to let me see a copy of your book. Reading it was a very emotional experience. I was born in the North-West area in the thirties; was educated during World War II at a Lancashire Grammar School; often stayed with an aunt who lived on the coast. So you can understand how touched I was by your beautifully written, deeply moving and heart-warming reminiscences.

Many congratulations!

Perhaps we will meet one day and be able to reflect at length on growing up in such a unique area, at such an unusual time in history. I do hope so.

All best wishes,
Reginald Holmes

Billy had to read the letter several times over to grasp its import and that he was not dreaming and that it really was happening. After all those rebuffs, someone as celebrated as this had actually said he found it 'heart-warming'. Reggie Holmes was a well-known and respected figure in the publishing world, and most important of all for Billy, he was a friend and colleague of Geoff Lewis, senior partner at the Lewis/Travers Literary Agency.

A fortnight after receiving Reggie Holmes's letter, Billy was visiting Mark in his Manchester estate agency office when his phone rang.

'It's for you, Dad,' he said, offering him the phone, his hand covering the mouthpiece.

'Me?' Billy exclaimed, a trifle puzzled. 'Who can it be? Who knows I'm here in Manchester? Who has your phone number?'

Mark grinned. 'Probably passed on by Mum, who does know you're here visiting me. Why not take the phone and find out?'

Billy did as suggested and, as he listened, he went into total shock and had difficulty understanding what he was hearing.

'Good morning, Mr Hopkins,' the voice said. 'My name's Margaret Harrison and I'm an agent at the Lewis/Travers Literary Agency here in London. Your wonderful book has been passed on to me by our senior partner, Geoff Lewis. I love the book; I'd love to try and sell it on your behalf and send it out to some editors. Do I have your permission to proceed?'

'Permission?' Billy mumbled. 'By all means, go ahead. I'm so glad you liked the book!'

'There are no guarantees, of course,' she continued, 'but, if *I* have read it in one sitting with delight, then I am hoping an editor will do the same. I shall be in touch again if I have any news.'

In a daze, Billy returned the phone to its cradle. Finding it hard to believe what he'd just heard, he had to ring Laura right away.

'Laura, Laura,' he babbled into the phone. 'The call you passed onto me was from a London agent, and she said she likes my book! Actually likes it! No, correction. Loves it and is going to offer it to one or two editors to see if they are interested in publishing it! We've cracked it!'

'Wonderful news!' Laura replied. 'But calm down, Billy. She didn't say someone was going to publish it, did she? She simply said that she was going to try and interest a publisher. You know how many times your hopes have been raised only for them to be dashed at the last moment. Remember what happened to your leather-bound volume. Keep your elation on hold. Believe it when you see it.'

Laura was right. As usual. But the fact that a reputable, experienced agent had said she loved the novel had to mean something. The eternal optimist, Billy had the gut feeling that it was the real thing this time and not a bit like the situation where the manuscript had fallen behind the radiator.

Then followed an agonising wait for news. Day after day, he was on tenterhooks, sitting by the phone willing it to ring. A great author, when once asked what inspired him to write his novel, replied, 'The phone call.' Billy knew what he meant. What would it be this time? Rejection again? Or would someone out there be willing to take a chance on the book?

The four weeks that followed seemed like eternity. Then Margaret Harrison rang again. The tone of her voice said it all.

'Good news!' she enthused. 'Wilbraham Press would like to publish your book! First in hardback and then later in paperback. They are prepared to offer an advance of three thousand pounds and, if you would like us to proceed, I shall put our agency contract in the post and we can take it from there. Perhaps you would let us know if you find this acceptable. May I conclude by offering you my heartiest congratulations!'

Did he find it acceptable? What a question! To be taken on by a leading agency and to be offered an advance by a mainstream company! Three thousand pounds! He'd have been happy with thirty pence if they'd agreed to publish it. After all the heartaches and setbacks! His book was going into print and with a top publisher!

Billy was dumbfounded. Normal speech deserted him. It was like being told that he'd just won the lottery. After all those years writing and trying to get published, the dream had become reality. His book had been recognized and was to be made available to a wider public. Furthermore, the publishers were going to pay him money! This was a special moment and a once-in-a-lifetime experience. He didn't have a single coherent thought for the rest of that week.

In the days which followed, he felt punch-drunk. He signed all kinds of documents, not really knowing what any of them were. But who cared! He was going to be a published author! Dealing with the correspondence which came through his letter box, he became familiar with various arcane publishing terms, like 'shoutline', 'blurb' and 'buzzword'. A further flow of letters followed and Billy found himself having to approve dates of publication and jacket design. It was agreed that the cover should be similar to the original Tim Lally edition featuring a schoolboy in uniform in the foreground with a working-class scene in the background. They advised him, however, to drop the pseudonym Tim Lally and use the name Billy Hopkins instead. What a wonderful feeling of relief Billy experienced knowing that the many issues involved in the book production were being handled by a professional team. Issues that he had had to resolve himself not very long ago.

When the hardback came out, both agent and publisher sent him bouquets of the most beautiful flowers, which touched him and at the same time embarrassed him. In the working-class culture of Collyhurst in which he'd been raised, it was not the done thing for a male to receive flowers, not unless he was dead. And certainly not if he wanted to be considered an example of virile manhood. He was grateful of course but a bottle of Dimple Haig might have gone down better. Some time later, however, he was relieved when he saw a famous concert pianist receive a bouquet at the end of his performance. Billy had entered a new world and he had a lot to learn.

Since he was an unknown, first-time author, Wilbraham Press were not sure how the book would be received. Experience had taught them that it was wisest to err on the side of caution since many first novels sold under one thousand hardback copies which were usually taken up by libraries and book clubs, so they set the print run at a thousand copies. This was a huge quantity in Billy's world and he was as pleased as Punch.

Then he was invited to give an interview about the book on the radio. He felt flattered when producer Nicola Newson asked him to attend the BBC Radio Lancashire studios in Blackburn, but his first instinct was to turn it down. I'm getting out of my depth here, he thought. Me on the wireless! Who do I think I am? Nicola Newson's persuasive manner, however, convinced him and he duly turned up at the Darwen Street studios.

As he sat in the ante-room waiting to be called, he could hear the voice of Betty White, the interviewer, telling her half million audience how she would be shortly talking to popular Lancashire author Billy Hopkins. As he listened to this announcement going out on the air, he was petrified. What if he couldn't think of anything to say? Or became tongue-tied? Or couldn't answer her questions? Or made an idiot of himself? A vast multitude out there, including many relatives and friends who were tuned in, would be witnesses to his stupidity. He was tempted to make a run for it there and then but, too late, a young secretary was ushering him into the semi-darkened studio.

He needn't have worried. Betty White proved to be an experienced interviewer and soon had him at ease. Before long, they were sharing jokes and the fact she'd read the book certainly helped things to run smoothly. Radio Lancashire's involvement did not stop there. They decided to serialize an abridged version of the book and employed the services of John Spencer, resident reader at Blackpool's library service. Every afternoon for five weeks, excerpts from the book were broadcast and demand in the north-west soared. After the first episode had been read, their telephone went, in the words of Betty White, into meltdown. The run of a thousand hardback copies was soon gone and Wilbraham Press had to print an extra five hundred but these, too, soon sold out. Disappointed listeners were advised to wait for the paperback edition which was due out six months later when there would be plenty of copies available.

The first intimation that sales of the paperback had taken off came when a senior partner at Lewis/Travers contacted him with the brief message: 'I don't know if you've seen the *Observer* yet today,' she said, 'but *Our Kid* has entered the top twenty paperback bestseller list at number nineteen.' The book rose later to reach number twelve, just short of the top ten, and for a brief time Billy found himself alongside Andy McNab's *Crisis Four* and Thomas Harris's *Hannibal*.

After that, things began to happen so fast he was overwhelmed. A whole new world was opening before him. Whereas previously, when self-publishing, he'd thought in terms of a few hundred, now the talk was of thousands. In his mail he received copies of various internal memos from Wilbraham staff announcing nonchalantly that so-and-so had sold *Our Kid* to a UK book club for a print run of 6,500 copies for their club edition. Or that another staff member had sold rights for a special promotion by a major supermarket who would take 15,000 copies. So it went on and he felt that he was being swept along on a tide of events beyond his control.

He discovered, too, the advantages of being represented by a well-connected London agency. There were spin-offs that he'd hardly imagined possible. Crescent Books bought the large print rights for a flat fee and then an auction between Rowntrees and Sikia for the right to produce an audio version began to take place. Bidding began at £1,000 and rose in increments of £100. Laura and he went out to Safeways to do the weekly shopping and when they returned found that the auction had been finally won by Sikia of Hartlepool. The book was read by Chris Shuttleworth, ex-BBC, and was published in fourteen audio tapes at a cost of £44. When Billy listened to the finished version, he was more than happy to note that the narrator not merely read the story but acted out each part in authentic voice and accent.

Another unexpected source of income came from the library service or Public Lending Right scheme which was set up by the government in 1977. Under the scheme, writers received payments from a central fund for the free borrowing of their books from British public libraries. Each time a book was borrowed from a public library, the author received four pence, which didn't sound like very much but when the number of borrowings over a year ran into thousands, the sum could add up to a considerable figure. There was a maximum of £6,000 set on the amount paid to any given writer to avoid the lion's share of the grant going to the most popular writers, like Catherine Cookson or Jacqueline Wilson. In Billy's first year, the sum paid to him came to £620, which meant that his book had been borrowed from libraries across the country 15,500 times, a figure which he found mind-blowing.

Popularity of the book received another huge boost when an international book club chose it as their star book of the month.

It wasn't long before the success of the book began to pay off in money terms though not on the lavish scale envisaged by his sons when they talked of buying a yacht. Royalties were more modest. Not sufficient to change their lifestyle in any dramatic way but enough to carry out the much-needed repairs on the house: new gutters, garden fencing and gates, pointing, roof for the garage. One urgent need was for another car because the old Morris Oxford had finally pegged out. Much to the disappointment of the younger end of the family, Billy couldn't afford a Roller or a Bentley but he was able to buy a glittering white, ten-year-old Mercedes 190 in good condition and with full service history. His one concession to a luxury item was to buy a personalized number plate. He spotted it in

Autocar and was immediately tempted. The number was K1 DGO, thus spelling out KID GO, and was on sale at £500. The older and more sensible half of the family, Laura, Matthew, Lucy, said no, the idea was crazy and a complete waste of money. The less responsible half, Mark, John and Billy himself, said 'Go for it!' The latter view prevailed, and so he went for it. As soon as his children saw the gleaming white saloon they mockingly named it the Pimp-Mobile.

'Why?' Billy asked.

'Because it's the kind of car,' Matthew replied, 'that you expect to be driven by a pusher wearing big sun shades, a loud T-shirt, and a gold medallion slung round his neck.'

Despite the sarcasm of his sons, the Mercedes proved great to drive as the previous owner had cared for it, but Billy nearly wrote it off in his first week of ownership and he wasn't proud of the incident. 'Incident' being the operative word, not 'accident'.

Lucy was coming up from London to visit them and Laura and he were due to collect her at Lime Street Station in Liverpool. It was a route he knew like the back of his hand as he had driven it many times before. On this day, however, there were numerous roadworks and innumerable diversions and he ended up in an unfamiliar part of the city centre. Lucy was due to arrive within ten minutes and it was imperative that they be there as she'd have been bewildered had they not been on the platform to meet her. Billy found that the complex system of one-way streets had forced him along a main road until he reached a large roundabout. As he drove round it he saw to his dismay that he was being drawn into the Mersey tunnel leading to Birkenhead, which would have made them hopelessly late to meet the train. What to do? He glanced in the driving mirror and saw that the road behind was clear, with not a single vehicle in sight. He decided to take a chance and turned off the roundabout and crossed over two pavements.

Laura screamed at him as he executed the manoeuvre. 'What are you doing, Billy? You'll get us both killed!'

He made it safely into an adjoining car park where he stopped to catch his breath and to allow his heart to slow down.

'We were being sucked into the Mersey tunnel, Laura. God knows when we'd have been able to get back to collect Lucy. I made absolutely sure the road was clear before I pulled off the round-about. So there was no real danger.'

As they were talking, a police car drove into the car park and a traffic cop got out. He knocked on Billy's window.

'The video cameras have just reported a white van driving the wrong way round the round-about,' he said. 'Did you happen to see it by any chance?'

'I think it may have been me, officer,' Billy replied ruefully.

'So what happened?' the policeman asked.

'We've come to collect our daughter at Lime Street. You see, we're from Southport and–'

'So which side of the road do they drive on in Southport, pop?'

There was that 'pop' word again. Billy ignored it and explained about the many diversions and how he'd lost his way but the policeman was no longer listening. He was talking into his radio to a fellow officer.

'Yeah. Some old bloke from Southport. Got lost. Was heading towards the Birkenhead tunnel and didn't want to go in there.'

Billy thought he was for it but the policeman was indulgent.

'I'll not book you this time but when you come to Liverpool, keep to the rules of the road no matter what they do in Southport. Then you'll come to no harm.'

'How do I get to Lime Street from here?' Billy asked. 'Our daughter will be waiting for us.'

The officer didn't merely tell them. He stepped into the main road, held up his hand to stop the traffic and waved them through. They met Lucy as she came along the platform. From that time on, the family never trusted Billy to drive long journeys or in strange towns. He didn't object too strongly as he didn't mind at all being chauffeured about.

Chapter Twenty-Two

Promoting *Our Kid*

Reviews of *Our Kid* appeared in local north-west newspapers and magazines, including a superb piece by Alan Beaufort in the *Warrington Guardian* and one by Roger Alkrington of the *Manchester Evening News*. The biggest boost came in the *Daily Telegraph* in a full-page article by Cyril Ainsworth who, under the banner headline, 'BILLY THE SLUM KID COMES OUT ON TOP,' began his piece with: 'This is the story of a bright young literary agent (Margaret Harrison), an experienced Hollywood screenwriter (Reginald Holmes) and Billy the Kid from the slums who became a top-selling author in his seventies.'

It was only later that Billy learned that Margaret Harrison had not only two master's degrees in English and Linguistics from Dundee but was also a prize-winning poet. It was about this time, too, that he was invited to the Lewis/Travers office in London where he met up with her.

'Did you know,' she smiled, 'that your book has resulted in a new genre in our office? It goes under the initials OMM.'

'OMM? What's that?'

'It stands for Old Men's Memoirs, and since the success of *Our Kid* we have been inundated with OMMs.'

313

They took a taxi across to Wilbraham Press in Bloomsbury where they signed the register at the security desk, received their ID badges and took the lift to their plush offices on the eleventh floor with their panoramic views across Central London. They were greeted by Susan Munro, senior editor, who introduced them to Roberta Reid, Wilbraham's managing director.

Billy was taken into a meeting of the staff who had gathered for coffee. Roberta made a short speech congratulating him on his book and then announced that she had just received news that sales had passed the 100,000 mark. Billy made a short speech thanking them for their hard work, at the same time expressing his appreciation of their skill and professionalism. He'd had special celebratory pens manufactured with the inscription OUR KID BY BILLY HOPKINS. PUBLISHED BY WILBRAHAM PRESS SEPTEMBER 1999, which he gave out to the staff. There followed a lunch in an upmarket Italian restaurant with selected members of staff directly involved in the production and distribution of the book. He felt like a film star and as he sat there surrounded by publishing executives, five young ladies and three men, he found it difficult to take it all in. He'd come a long way since the days of Collyhurst Buildings, Red Bank railway sidings and the Cut. Any moment now, he thought, I shall wake up and find it's all been mere wishful thinking.

At the end of the meal, they said goodbye with continental kisses – happily not the French variety, but the sort involving pecks on both cheeks. This practice was one that had been imported into the country recently and had even reached outposts in the grim north where many regarded it with anxiety and saw it as distinctly foreign. Up there people rarely indulged in kissing each other, not even with their wives. Billy was relieved to find that the men in the luncheon party did not indulge in the practice.

Letters from readers from all over Britain and from other parts of the world began to arrive, from Australia, New Zealand, South Africa, Canada, and even a couple from the Falklands. Readers were from a wide cross-section of the community: housewives, students, teachers, headmasters, doctors, even nuns and priests. It was evident that the book had touched a nerve for many readers, who said they'd been emotionally moved by the story. The youngest reader was a fourteen-year-old boy from Manchester and the oldest a lady aged ninety-four writing from a nursing home in West Sussex.

One common theme running through the letters was that of identification with the characters portrayed in the book. 'That story,' so many people wrote, 'was *my* own family's story, for there are many aspects where your life and mine coincided.'

Out of many hundreds of letters, only one sounded a sour note and oddly enough it was the one Billy remembered best. The letter, *not* from Disgusted of Tunbridge Wells, was in response to a very warm review in the correspondent's local press where the reporter had written:

If you start reading *Our Kid* on Christmas Eve, your family won't see much of you until the New

Year. I read it on the train between Liverpool and Manchester and I laughed so much I was getting funny looks off my fellow passengers. In his life, the writer has been known as Tim Lally, Billy Hopkins, maybe Shakespeare. Never mind the name, just buy it.

The correspondent who took umbrage wrote:

Dear Sir,
    I bought your book in a bookshop and I nearly had heart failure when I read it for it contained a lot of filthy talk and bad language. I did not ask the shop for a refund as it was well worth the money to find out what sort of book it was so that I could warn my friends not to buy it.
    I will be complaining to my local newspaper that advertised such a book.
    A disgusted reader,
    Miss I.M. Merseyside.

Billy's family was not only taken aback to receive such a letter but puzzled as to where the filthy talk and bad language appeared in the book. After a careful check, they could only assume it was the libidinous comments of the fifth form adolescents at Damian College in their pathetic attempts to spice up lessons.
Life became hectic as Billy was invited to so many radio interviews in Lancashire, Greater Manchester, and Merseyside. He was no longer nervous as they were becoming routine with the same questions being asked. Did he always want to write? Why did he wait till he was old before

beginning? How long did it take to write the book? How much of it was fiction? Would he be writing a sequel? His favourite presenter was Fred Campion of BBC Greater Manchester Radio for he had an easy-going manner and it was like talking to an old friend at the dinner table. The two men found they had much in common both in their school backgrounds and their strategies for surviving in a poor, working-class district of Manchester. Billy appeared on his Sunday programme several times to discuss their mutual childhood experiences.

While in Manchester for a book promotion, Billy managed to get across to the Pineapple pub for a rendezvous with his old chums. Since moving to Southport, he had missed their regular Friday night meetings but here was a rare chance for a get-together.

'After all your false dawns, your country crafts and your airship disaster,' Nobby said, 'at last you've turned up trumps. I'm surprised you're willing to come down from the lofty heights to talk to lesser mortals like ourselves.'

'Come off it, Nobby,' Billy replied. 'I've made a few bob but hardly enough to change my life-style. But we higher-ups don't mind forgoing our busy schedule once in a while to slum it and have a brief word with hoi-polloi like yourselves.'

'Very noble of you, I must say,' Titch grinned. 'All the same, I suppose it's drinks on you from now on.'

'I'll get my round in, like always,' Billy said, 'but no more.'

'Then you can make mine a double Pimm's

Number one,' Titch answered.

'And mine will be a double Napoleon brandy,' added Olly, 'and in return I shall recommend your book to punters at the Central Library.'

'Thanks, Olly. Very good of you. That'll certainly add to my riches seeing how it'll save your borrowers from buying the book and I'll receive fourpence each time it's taken out. That should help me on the way to my first Roller.'

'All the same,' Titch said. 'Lots of fourpences soon add up.'

Billy got the round in and the five of them settled down before the log fire to enjoy their drinks.

'I never had you down as a writer,' Oscar remarked. 'I seem to remember that when we first went to Damian College, our language teacher, Miss Barrymore, said that for you English was a foreign language.'

'And that went for the rest of us,' Billy countered. 'We all spoke fluent Mancunian, did we not?'

'Anyway,' Titch said, 'what's this busy schedule you spoke of? I suppose it's seeing your accountant and your business adviser about your investments.'

'Nothing of the sort. I'm run off my feet giving talks all over the place, being interviewed on radio, and tomorrow I'm due to appear on television.'

His four companions put their fingers to their noses and adopted snooty expressions.

'Look,' Billy protested. 'Success hasn't spoiled me.'

'No,' quipped Oscar, 'you were always like this.'

'The drawback to success,' said Billy, 'is that it annoys all your friends.'

'Come on, everyone,' Titch said, 'that's enough ribbing. Hoppy's still one of the Damian Smokers' Club and always will be.'

'Agreed,' said Oscar. 'Enough fooling about. On the subject of writing, let me quote my idol's experience. The great Oscar said that after writing one of his books, he decided to spend a whole morning on editing and after long deliberation he removed a comma. Then after a good lunch and a nap, he went back to the task and decided to put it back.'

'And that story brings us to the next stage of *our* deliberations,' laughed Nobby. 'Time for the next round. My twist, I believe.'

Billy may have become accustomed to radio interviews but when it came to the television programme he'd told his friends about, the collywobbles really made themselves felt for not only was it television, it was *live*. So there was no possibility of corrections by means of an edited recording. The programme was *In Manchester Today* with Declan McCleary.

'How big is your audience for this programme?' Billy asked a young Granada executive before they went on air.

'Not too big as it's a midday programme. Say half a million, give or take a few thousand.'

When he heard this, Billy's heart did a double take. Half a million! That's enough to fill Wembley Stadium five times over. Just enough for him to demonstrate what an inarticulate idiot he was.

The seriousness of what he'd agreed to was brought home most forcibly when he was ushered into the make-up room.

'I have a spot on my forehead,' he whinged.

'No problem,' the young cosmetician replied. 'One pat of a powder puff and abracadabra it's gone! By the way, all the ladies in the studios here are quite excited about this particular edition of the programme.'

'Why is that?'

'Because of who is appearing, of course.' She smiled.

Billy blushed with embarrassment. He had no idea that he was that well-known and that his appearance would cause a stir among the ladies. He was conducted to the set and soon realized his mistake. The first guest on the programme was no other than heart-throb Nigel Havers of *Chariots of Fire* fame.

That'll teach you to jump to conclusions, he muttered to himself.

He was introduced to the celebrity and they shook hands warmly. That's a second reason for not washing this hand, Billy thought. First an archbishop and now a film star. Whatever next!

His own interview went smoothly enough though Declan introduced him with: 'And now we have the remarkable story of a pensioner from *Stockport* who has written a bestselling book in his retirement.' Billy put him right quickly as he didn't fancy being lynched by the good citizens of Southport.

After the broadcast, he found himself being invited to give talks at various venues. The Society of Authors had a recommended scale of charges for such events but the groups to which he was invited certainly couldn't afford such fees. His rewards for delivering talks were usually made up of a free lunch and travel expenses. In most cases he charged nothing, considering the talks as ideal opportunities for promotion, and at the end of such sessions he usually sold a respectable number of books.

His first engagement was at Bolton Town Hall and organized by Sweetens, an independent book shop. Billy turned up expecting half a dozen people with whom he could have an informal chat. He couldn't have been more wrong for when he got there he was met by his hostess who conducted him into a room not unlike the lecture theatre at the Royal Society where about a hundred people were already waiting. He hadn't prepared anything formal to say but his forty years as a teacher, and maybe the kissing of the Blarney Stone, had given him the gift of the gab which held him in good stead. He determined there and then that if this kind of thing was going to continue, he'd have to have something better prepared. After the session, Sweetens sold over a hundred paperbacks, all of which Billy signed.

'You'll soon be needing a bigger sized hat,' his son Mark remarked when he read an account of the talk in a Bolton newspaper.

'Just remember who you are, Dad.' Matthew grinned. 'You're Billy 'Opkins from Collyhurst Buildings.'

'And you sell firewood on Saturday mornings,' added John mischievously. 'So don't go getting too big for your boots.'

'Why all this sudden concern about size of hats and boots?' Billy chuckled.

'Ignore them, Dad,' Lucy countered. 'We're proud of your achievements.'

'Yeah, not bad for an old geezer,' Mark laughed.

Laura didn't know what to make of all the publicity. She had a reserved nature and didn't like being in the limelight.

'I don't mind all the fuss,' she said, 'as long as I'm never asked to appear or speak in public. I'll see to it that you're fed and you have a clean shirt but I'm happy to stay in the background. I only wish my mother and father were alive to see you become an author.'

'I've written one book about my childhood in Collyhurst, Laura. That doesn't exactly make me Somerset Maugham or Graham Greene.'

His next invitation was to a large primary school in the extreme north of Lancashire. He resisted taking it on this time because he didn't think his book was suitable for such a juvenile audience. In addition, the place was miles away and he didn't fancy getting lost in the maze of minor roads in that part of the county. He hadn't forgotten what happened the last time he'd become lost in unfamiliar streets in Liverpool. The teacher however was not easily put off and rang several times. It was one of those sponsored weeks that the government foists on the nation from time to time. Particular weeks were chosen by some obscure quango and then everyone was supposed to devote their attention and energies to some cause or other. So the country was landed with resolutions like Plant-a-Tree Week, Keep-Fit Week, Kind-to-Animals Week. Billy thought the whole idea was not only barmy but self-defeating. Did it mean everyone was to be kind to animals for seven days after which they could go back to kicking the cat? When the teacher phoned, it was to celebrate Read-a-Book Week and she was so persistent, he relented, especially when she volunteered to collect him and take him home again afterwards. He got to the school at 10 a.m. and, after a quick cup of tea, was taken straight into the large assembly hall where he found he was faced with a huge crowd of children sitting on the floor.

'How many children are there?' he asked.

'About two hundred and fifty. The lower half of the school. You'll meet the upper half after break.'

'Have they read my book?'

'Doubt it, but some of their parents might have.'

'So they won't know me from Adam.'

'No, but you're a writer and seeing it's Read-A-Book Week, they'll love you.'

He talked to the children about his childhood and related anecdotes like how he was mugged by the skenny-eyed kid on the way home from school. Meanwhile, the teachers had seen his presence as a golden opportunity to have a free period and had nipped off to the staffroom for a brew and a fag. The children were good listeners and their questions were refreshingly blunt.

'Are you rich?'

'Are you famous?'

'Are you on telly?'

'Have you ever been to Hollywood?'

'Do you know the real Billy the Kid or Clint Eastwood?'

After a short break and a quick cup of staffroom tea, he had to face the upper half of the school. The talk followed the same pattern. At four o'clock, he was glad to be on his way home as the day's ordeal had served as a powerful reminder of why he'd taken early retirement. He charged the school nothing for the event but the head expressed his gratitude just as he was leaving.

'Thanks,' he said curtly. That was it. A bit abrupt, Billy thought. After all, the head had just had his whole school occupied for the morning without having to pay a visitor's fee.

On the way back, Billy hummed quietly to himself his favourite ditty from Barnum. 'There is a sucker/Born every minute.' And a little voice in his head kept repeating: 'So, this is retirement! It was easier when you had a full-time job!'

As the book became better known, he found himself giving talks and doing book-signings in towns all round the northwest of England from Manchester and Salford to Lytham St Anne's and Blackpool on the coast. Some of these sessions were to Women's Institutes, libraries or as part of civic or literary festivals; others to specialized groups like the W.H. Smith Store Assistants (the people working at the coal face and, as such, a mighty powerful group!), Ainsdale Civic Society, the Cumbrian Literary Group, and one with a name that John Betjeman would have loved – the Chorlton-cum-Hardy Townswomen's Guild.

Billy found the idea of talking to certain bodies

nerve-racking because of the composition of the group. The Romantic Novelists' Association was one that fell into this category because it was made up of well-known, experienced writers. What could he say that would possibly interest them? It was a good lunch, however, and afterwards they exchanged news and views about their relationships with their publishers and the state of the book trade in general. There was lively debate about story endings and they were highly amused by the *New Yorker* cartoon which Billy presented. It showed a frustrated writer sitting at his desk surrounded by overflowing ashtrays, gin bottles, and balls of scrunched-up sheets of paper. The caption said: 'Oh, sod it! Then a lot of shots rang out and they all fell dead.'

The assembly seemed put out when Billy asked them why they invariably ended their romantic stories on a 'lived happily ever after' note.

'Because our readers demand it,' they chorused.

The next occasion was perhaps more daunting still because of the importance of the occasion. He'd been invited to be the after-dinner speaker at his old school, Damian College. Many bigwigs were to be present, including a knighted member of parliament and a literary critic on several prestigious publications, the current principal of the college, many civic dignitaries, and perhaps most formidable of all, his own school chums. Against all his expectations, the occasion proved to be a pleasurable one because after dining and downing several glasses of wine, his listeners were in jovial mood and ready to laugh at anything, including his feeble witticisms and his corny jokes about early schooldays.

Without doubt the most intimidating affair was one which he accepted without fully understanding its implications. The association was called Literary Events – not a literary society as such but one that organized an 'event' every two months. It involved two days at a snazzy Lancashire hotel, the Hot Pot House Hotel, and took the form of an evening dinner on the first day, and then luncheon on the second with an entirely different audience. The list of distinguished speakers who had appeared on previous occasions was enough to put the wind up people like Billy: Frank Muir, Fred Dibnah, Kate Adie (of whom it was said that no war could start until she got there), former cabinet minister Neil Hamilton and his wife Christine. There were two speakers scheduled for Billy's visit, the other one being Tricia Stewart, or Miss October on the famous Rylstone WI calendar and one of the leading lights behind the Calendar Girls. Helen Mirren had played her part in the film.

The evening began with a sumptuous dinner, the hundred and fifty guests dressed most elegantly in their finery and obviously looking forward to being entertained by after-dinner speeches. The elderly lady sitting next to Billy at the high table told him that Frank Muir had seemed so nervous before his performance that he hadn't been able to eat a thing. Billy sympathized with him. What made the situation worse was that Tricia Stewart proved to be an excellent speaker and it was evident that she had given her entertaining talk many times before. Follow that, an inner voice whispered to him when she sat down. It would have been so much easier if she'd been a lousy speaker and then he could have got away with his own paltry effort. He gave his talk and brought out all his best jokes and the audience seemed to laugh in the right places and he earned some applause afterwards. He retired to his room, which was the bridal suite and part of the fee, he supposed. Sad to say, there was no bride as Laura had been unable to accompany him on that occasion. Next day at lunch, the exercise was repeated, the only difference being that the audience had increased to two hundred and fifty and partitions had had to be rolled back to accommodate the huge crowd.

The thought did strike him that it was most unfair to expect writers to be entertainers, speakers, comedians, raconteurs. Their expertise lay (or was supposed to) in their writing, altogether a different talent, and yet so often they were put into difficult situations requiring public speaking skills, not always their forte. Certainly writers like Lewis Carroll, Arnold Bennett, Somerset Maugham would have been unhappy if thrown into such a position because they had speech impediments and problem stutters.

Finally Billy came to his last group and the one which really threw him off his stride. It also brought home to him the need to be sure about the kind of group he was due to address.

He should have learned his lesson from a doctor friend of his, Dr John Fleetwood, who had written a most interesting and learned book entitled *The History of the Irish Body Snatchers.*

He'd been so busy doing public speaking here, there and everywhere, that his secretary had got things muddled. She informed him that his talk on the Body Snatchers was to be to a group of historians but because of a mix-up, he ended up giving it to a group of pensioners who were expecting a session on 'Geriatric Health Problems'. Only after he'd shown the third gruesome slide did he realize from the sounds in the dark that something had gone wrong.

Billy made a similar mistake with one of the talks he was due to give. He'd received an invitation from the BRITISH WIZO to be guest at their luncheon and to give a talk afterwards. There was no phone number and the only address given was that of the assembly hall. But what was WIZO? On a visit to Southport, his family sat around the dinner table trying to guess the kind of organization it might be.

Matthew suggested that it might be simply an expression of delight, as in, 'We're going to the cinema! Oh, whizzo!'

John thought it was a slang word for pickpocket but that didn't make sense either in this context. Surely he wasn't down to address a bunch of pickpockets!

Mark said, 'I looked it up in the Oxford Dictionary, Dad, and it means to urinate. Perhaps the Wizzos are makers of fine porcelain urinals. Or perhaps a group noted for its prowess and skill in urinating.' His notion was rejected out of hand by everyone.

Lucy maintained it was an abbreviation of Wizard and that the group was probably a bunch of conjurors and magicians. This seemed the most plausible explanation and with this in mind, Billy began preparing his talk by rooting out all the funny yarns about conjurors that he could find. Such tales were thin on the ground but he came across one or two appropriate stories, his favourite being:

'There was this conjuror doing his act on a cruise ship but a parrot from a previous act kept butting in with comments like "It's up his sleeve" or "It's down his trousers" or "It's under his hat". Queering his whole act. Just then, without warning, the ship's boilers blew and the ship started to sink. Shortly after, the conjuror found himself alone on a raft in the middle of the ocean with just this confounded parrot. And the parrot was cocking its head from side to side and looking at him quizzically. Finally the parrot spoke up. "OK, I give up. What have you done with the ship?"'

On the appointed day, Billy took himself along to the assembly hall in Liverpool, ready and fully prepared to deliver his talk. On arriving there, he was caught completely on the wrong foot and had to do a rapid volte face. WIZO stood for Women's Institute of Zionist Organizations. His audience was entirely made up of Jewish women, mostly widows. As he ate lunch, he mentally ran over all his boyhood anecdotes about fire-lighting on Saturday mornings in the Cheetham Hill area of Manchester, switching on and switching off the lights at the synagogue. After lunch, as he was about to begin, a sharp-featured lady came up to him and said, 'I hope your speech isn't going to be too long because we're due to play bridge straight after lunch and we don't like to be kept waiting.' He gave his talk which, surprisingly, was well received for afterwards he sold over a hundred copies of his book. He'd learned his lesson though. 'Always make sure you know who you're down to talk to.' One old lady came up to him afterwards and thanked him profusely for bringing back so many happy memories of the good old days when she'd lived in the Strangeways district of Manchester and employed a 'goy boy' on Saturday mornings. It made up for the rudeness of the bridge-playing lady.

Chapter Twenty-Three

Sign Here

The other aspect of promotion was book-signing sessions at many book shops across the north-west area. The timetable was organized by Wilbraham Press and involved much travelling. On a few occasions, Billy took a crowded train often with no toilet facilities, which was a serious omission for an old bloke like him. On one of these occasions, he alighted but could still see no facilities and was forced to relieve himself down a secluded back street near the station. A good job I wasn't spotted, he thought. He could see the nightmare headline: BEST-SELLING AUTHOR ARRESTED FOR URINATING (OR SHOULD THAT BE WIZZING?) IN BACK STREET. And after all that, when he arrived at the book store in that particular town, he was told that they hadn't been expecting him. The manager who arranged these things was absent on leave. Furthermore, they already had a well-known, local soccer player signing books on the ground floor. Billy was allotted a tiny room at the top of the building with a pile of stock to sign and no one knew he was there. His isolation was eased occasionally when a lost aficionado popped his head round the door and inquired: 'Sociology Section?'

'Second floor next to Philosophy.'

'Thanks a lot.'

Then another. 'Where do I find Shakespeare?'

'Try English Literature on the ground floor. Failing that, the theatre-booking office.'

He didn't know where any of these departments were located of course but he didn't like to let these book-lovers down with a negative, 'Haven't a clue, mate.'

'Sorry about that,' the deputy manager apologized at the end of the session, 'but we've had so many local celebrities here lately signing books – footballers, rugby players, boxers – that we completely forgot you were coming and so we didn't publicize your event.'

Most of the book-signing tours, however, were straightforward and ran like clockwork but there were one or two bizarre encounters.

One Saturday morning, he turned up at Waterstone's on Deansgate, Manchester, and was delighted to find a long queue that snaked from inside the store and right round the building. He had no idea that he'd become so popular. He spoke to an elderly gent in the line.

'The book must be very much in demand,' he said to him.

'Oh, it is,' the old chap replied with enthusiasm. 'No one can write like David Attenborough.'

That put him in his place all right, which was bottom of the heap. He thought he'd better find his rank in the pecking order by asking an assistant.

'Oh, yes. Billy Hopkins! You're due to sign books round the corner at the St Anne's Square branch.'

He strolled round to his rightful place and was

gratified to see a file of around twenty-five people waiting, a more modest queue than David Attenborough's perhaps but clearly his fans as they were all clutching copies of his book.

Billy took his place at the table in the front of the shop. He was pleased to see the Wilbraham Press rep, Anna Bell, there and grateful for her help in streamlining the operation by turning the books to the flyleaf ready for his signature. On his computer he had printed out several hundred signed and personalized bookmarks to be inserted into every copy sold. The Waterstone's staff kindly provided him with a glass and a carafe of orange juice, with a large reproduction of the *Our Kid* book cover behind him. He took out his Waterman pen and was ready to demonstrate his best calligraphy with a flourish. He'd often been puzzled as to why people went to such trouble to collect all these signatures. What possible use were they? Did they take the books out at home and say to their friends, 'Look, Billy Hopkins really does know how to write his name! And see, no blots or scratching out.' At the end of his first signing session, however, his puzzlement was resolved and he found out in no uncertain terms why certain people were keen to have his moniker.

He learned there were genuine readers and there were speculators. The former liked to have their copies personalized with their name, a brief inscription and the date, for example: 'To Mary, With Best Wishes, Billy Hopkins, July 8th, 1999'. Some asked for an extra message like 'Keep Smiling' or 'Hope You Enjoy the Book' or chose one from the list of supposedly amusing comments he'd prepared ('If you think no one cares for you, try missing a couple of payments'; 'Eat, drink and be merry, for tomorrow we diet'; 'Behind every successful man, there stands an amazed woman'; 'Always remember you're unique, like everyone else'). Most people liked them and picked one out.

Not so the speculating clients who insisted: 'No inscription, please. Just your signature and the date.' Such people were usually buying the book not to read but as an investment, knowing that books were worth more if they were simply signed without any kind of message. One of these, a silver-haired lady, came up to the table bearing half a dozen copies of the hardback edition wrapped up in cellophane. At first he thought she'd bought them perhaps for her grandchildren but when she came out with the usual, 'No inscription, thank you. Just your signature,' and when she added, 'Could you please add nineteen ninety-eight as that was the year of publication,' he knew she was in it for the money. He obliged her but she'd raised his curiosity and so he asked, 'Aren't you taking a big risk buying so many hardbacks? Suppose the value drops.'

'No risk. In America, the hardback of *Our Kid* is already valued at one hundred and fifty dollars. Six signed first editions in mint condition must be worth a lot more. But they've got to be pristine and unread.'

He'd never thought of books as long-term investments. If he had, he might not have lost his capital on blimps.

'Yes,' the lady continued, as if reading his mind,

334

'books can be valuable assets in the long run and more reliable than stocks and shares. A signed copy of Beatrix Potter's *The Tale of Peter Rabbit*, for example, is worth a small fortune and if you had a signed copy of James Joyce's *Ulysses*, you'd be very rich indeed.'

'Same with Graham Greene's *Brighton Rock*,' said a young gentleman behind her, holding a couple of copies of Billy's book, 'and if I had an original copy of Conan Doyle's *The Hound of the Baskervilles*, I could retire tomorrow.'

Most of the people in the queue were not book-gamblers, Billy was relieved to see, and he spent the rest of the morning adding his autograph to what seemed like an endless conveyor belt of books presented by a steady stream of fans. Most people coming forward were straightforward and, aided by Anna Bell, he must have signed well over a hundred books but there were also a fair number of strange and unexpected encounters.

'When I read your book, the hair on my head stood on end,' said a grizzled old man. 'You said you were born at Number Six Collyhurst Buildings. That was the address my old grandmother moved into in nineteen thirty-four when your family moved out. Talk about co-incidences!' he muttered as he wandered off with his paperback.

One earnest young man who presented him with a thick wad of manuscript paper had obviously not come to buy a book but to talk about his 'writer's block' and to seek advice for his own creation.

'I've written half this whodunit and now I'm stuck. Would you mind reading it through for me and telling me how to put it right so I can submit it to an agent, preferably yours?'

Billy didn't wish to sound unfriendly and remote for hadn't he had the same problems not so long ago? But he had to tell him that he was not a script surgeon who operated on sick manuscripts, especially whodunits, about which he knew nothing. As for recommending him to his own agent, that was a no-no as he'd only just been accepted himself.

Lots of customers presented themselves at the table by standing to attention and simply stating their name, which he took to mean that they wanted him to dedicate the book to that particular person. If someone gave his handle as John Smith, he immediately began writing 'To John Smith...'

A well-known book-signing story that had become legend was that told by Monica Dickens when she was in an Australian bookstore. A lady handed her a book and Monica politely asked her if she wanted it dedicated to anyone in particular, to which the lady replied, 'Emma Chessit.'

'Fine,' Monica said. 'I've got the name Emma but how do you spell the surname Chessit?'

'No, no,' the lady protested. 'That's not my name. I'm asking you. How much is it?'

Billy had a similar case when a man announced himself as Ivor Czech. He wrote, 'To Ivor...'

'How do you spell your surname? With or without a "z"?' he asked.

'No, no,' the man protested. 'That's not my name. I'm telling you I want to pay for it and I have a cheque. My name's Jack Tollit.' That was a book ruined of course unless someone called Ivor came along wanting a book. Unfortunately, no one did.

One young lady came up to the table and stared at Billy for a while.

'Yes, do you want a book signed?' he asked.

'No, no, thanks. I don't want a book. But how much is it for a glass of that orange juice?'

One wild-eyed woman brought him her tatty, dog-eared copy of his book and thrust it at him. The copy must have been read by at least a thousand people because the gold foil on the title had been completely worn off.

'Write "To Jez with love,"' she demanded. He did as she'd commanded and she went off. An hour later, the woman was back. 'I've just phoned me daughter,' she said. 'And now she wants it made out to somebody else. So cross out "Jez" and put in "To Clint" instead.'

'Why not buy another book?' Billy suggested. 'Only five ninety-nine.'

'Oh, I'm not doing that. She can just bugger off. She'll have a different feller next week and she'll be changing the name again.'

The last encounter of the day was the one that threw him most. An old man who had been hanging back now sidled up to the table and looking at Billy from behind thick pebbled lenses placed his copy down. Billy signed it for him and then the man gave Billy a jolt by remarking, 'I saw you in that horror film as Hannibal Lecter and I thought you were bloody fantastic. Just fantastic.'

Billy stared back at him and made hungry, lip-smacking noises. He saw no point in setting him

337

straight. If he wanted to go home and tell his friends how he'd talked to Sir Anthony Hopkins, who was Billy to destroy his illusion?

As he came away from the last book-signing, Billy couldn't help reflecting how his life had changed in the past year or so. One moment, the days were going by slowly; he'd been wondering how he could possibly occupy his time and which hobby he should take up next. Today he knew what life was like in the fast lane and there were hardly enough hours in the day to meet the demands being made upon him. Now he understood why some pensioners laughed when asked how they were enjoying their retirement. Retirement! Which retirement? they retorted.

Chapter Twenty-Four

Translated at Last

While all this fuss was being made about his book, Lucy had been quietly writing her teenage books which had been selling well, especially in the USA. What was more, she had been translated into more than twenty languages, including Latvian. Billy was extremely proud of her achievements but he couldn't help feeling slightly miffed because his own book was in only one language – English.

It wasn't for want of trying on the part of his agent. Margaret Harrison had made great efforts to have his book published in another language, even American. But to no avail. Through sub-agents, she tried several US companies – Simon & Schuster, Crown Publishing, Dial Press, Doubleday, Picador, John Wiley, Henry Holt. The answer was always the same, 'Thanks, but no thanks.' The same old story of one rejection after another. He'd been down this road before and he was used to the routine. Looking over the replies, he had the impression that American publishers decided to turn the book down as it was financially safer to say no than take risks on some unknown Limey writer. Next, they thought up pretexts to justify the decision they'd already settled on. Most of them began by praising the book, 'charm' being a favourite term: 'Found the book quite charming but could not shake off my worry that it would suffer from the inevitable Frank McCourt comparison, both in terms of review attention and sales potential. I just didn't think we could make this work.' Or, 'Billy Hopkins charmingly captures a childhood in Lancashire during Britain's war time. However, in spite of these and other merits, I was not able to fully participate with the author in the local humour and idioms found throughout. I'm afraid it would present a challenge to successfully transfer those warm thoughts to the American audience without sacrificing the book's character. Therefore, as good as it is, I am going to pass on it.'

Margaret tried to ease the pain of rejection by pointing out the nice things the American publishers said about the book. Fair words, however, buttered no parsnips and Billy became reconciled to the fact that his book, like good wine, did not travel well. His story was too regional and people from other cultures did not understand it or appreciate it. The humour was over their heads. In those immortal words attributed to Shaw, 'We are two countries divided by a common language.' For Americans, his book, it seemed, was double Dutch. Billy found this puzzling and disappointing because he loved American humour in all its forms but, according to these agents, it seemed the feeling was not reciprocated by potential readers across the pond.

Then, out of the blue, came an offer from a publisher in Bruges. Maybe readers in Belgium would make more sense of it. Congratulations,

Margaret wrote, on your first foreign deal. Laura and Billy went out to dinner that night to celebrate the momentous event. They could not find a Belgian restaurant as such but they did round off their meal with a Mandarine Napoléon, a popular Belgian liqueur. A box of Belgian chocolates completed the celebration.

His joy was short-lived, however, for several weeks later, the company's editorial board retracted its offer. Maybe the original deal had been struck by an over-enthusiastic commissioning editor after downing too many Belgian beers, though the probable reason was that he had moved on to another company, leaving the book without a champion. Whatever the reason, Billy had learned an important lesson. In the book trade as in the buying and selling of houses, never count your chickens before they've hatched.

A number of readers had suggested that the story would make an ideal television series. Of course Billy was in full agreement. Every novelist believed his book was perfect television material. Geoff Lewis sent it out to several TV companies but there was nothing doing. The plot, they said, was too anecdotal and lacked sufficient drama to make it onto the small screen. Geoff then passed the book to one of the agency's most successful and prolific scriptwriters to see if he was interested in doing an adaptation that would help sell it to television. Though his answer was in the negative, Billy found his observations useful and insightful. In returning the book, he said he found it 'frighteningly authentic and familiar. Billy Hopkins certainly captures the flavour of wartime Lancashire. The central problem with the piece, whether seeing it as a two-hour film or a serial, is the time frame. Even if you picked up the story just before the outbreak of war and finished it in 1945, there would still need to be a lot of difficult re-casting, not just of Billy himself but of most of his family and young acquaintances as well, since you would be dealing with them at a period of their lives when they were changing at a most amazing rate.

'There is much to admire in the book; it took me right back there. But I don't think this is one for me as I cannot see as much as a chink in my schedule for months ahead.'

Billy valued these comments and felt most touched that a well-known writer had considered his work at all. It also helped him to accept once and for all that perhaps his book was a Lancashire tale and too localized to be fully appreciated by people outside the north. The latest rejection had been a gentle let-down with lots of positive and encouraging remarks. But it was still a rejection, no matter how it was dressed up. He had no cause for complaint however. *Our Kid* was still selling well and holding its own in the bestseller charts.

A year passed before anything else happened and when it did, it came in the form of an e-mail. Laura and he had just returned from a day's trip to the Lake District and, as was his wont, Billy went to his computer to check for mail. And there it was, an e-mail from Margaret Harrison.

Billy had often wondered what his mam would

have made of this notion of mail coming as it were by magic over the ether into his home. No doubt she'd have exclaimed: 'Eeh, isn't it marvellous what they can do nowadays?' It was her way of expressing not only fascination but bewilderment at the latest scientific findings. Many young people today, he felt, took things for granted and had lost much of this sense of wonderment. He recalled how people had been filled with awe when Neil Armstrong had made his famous 'giant leap for mankind' on the surface of the moon in 1969. Not so today's youth. Billy had pointed out the television images of the momentous event to his children. 'Very nice, Dad,' Lucy had replied, 'but they're not very good pictures, are they?' How different from his mam's perpetual amazement at the changes she was witnessing – an outlook which the family had viewed with amusement. After all, she was an old lady, they thought, and these developments were beyond her comprehension. After expressing her bafflement in the usual way, she'd once asked his dad how the wireless worked. After tracing all manner of complex patterns in the air, Tommy had declared, 'You wouldn't understand it, Kate. It's too complicated.'

'Oh, aye,' she'd said, giving him an old-fashioned look.

Come to think of it, Billy reflected, most of the things around us are beyond our ken. We accept and enjoy the fruits of the breathtaking research taking place in our world, for example television, computers, the Internet, laser technology, even the motor cars we drive. But how many of us understand how they work? Outside a scientific and technical elite, very few. So when faced by the Web and e-mails which send communications whizzing round the world in milliseconds, we can only think like my old mother: 'Eeh, isn't it marvellous what they can do nowadays?' and leave it at that.

The e-mail that day from his agent read, 'Viva España! I have wonderful news for you. Publicaciónes Especiales would like to publish a Spanish edition of your book with world Spanish pocket rights. I hope you'll be as delighted as I am. I knew we'd crack it eventually and hope this leads to others following suit. Warm wishes and congratulations.'

Great news indeed. It was quite something to be published in another language! And in Spanish! In the table of most widely spoken languages, it ranked third after Chinese and English. Apart from Spain, there were all those South American countries, the West Indies, and the Philippines. He had to restrain himself in case his delight got out of hand. Past experience had taught him to be wary and to keep his emotions under control. This time there'd be no jumping for joy nor a celebratory dinner until he was sure the deal was signed, sealed, and delivered.

Then a month later his doubts were resolved when he had an e-mail from a young lady in Chile.

My name is Maria Carreras and I am a Spanish literary translator. I am writing to let you know that I have been commissioned to translate your novel *Our Kid* into Spanish (I am currently

344

engrossed in it). I just wanted to thank you for your wonderful account of childhood and friendship, and for making this undertaking an exciting and fulfilling experience. I enjoy my job, I love translating, but it is not very often that I come across such a thrilling account of life experience and struggle against the hardships of war. And with a good sense of humour, as well!

Before long, Billy was receiving three e-mails a week and Laura was beginning to wonder who the mysterious lady from Santiago was. At first the inquiries were about the meaning of a number of idiomatic English expressions, like a mixed infant, a bacon hoist, a milk bar, Vimto, dancing in the dark.

He decided at this point to learn Spanish so that he could read the finished version and with this in mind began devoting two hours a day to it until he could read it reasonably well although he never expected to learn to speak the language apart from simple expressions, like 'Thank you', 'I like it', 'You're welcome', 'Goodbye'.

The first problem was the title of the book, *Our Kid*, which was a particularly northern phrase that was impossible to translate accurately. There was no equivalent phrase in Spanish. Together they thought about *Nuestro niño* or *Nuestro chico* or *Nuestro hermanito* (Our Child; Our Boy; Our Little Brother) but none of these seemed quite right. They eventually settled for *Nuestro pequeño Billy* – Our Little Billy, which his sons immediately translated as Our Peculiar Billy.

Maria made a fine job of translating the book

(he read it twice in Spanish) preserving the light-hearted style and the working-class atmosphere. For example in the scene where little girls are skipping in the street to the rhyme:

Who's that coming down the street?
Mrs Simpson's sweaty feet.
She's been married twice before
Now she's knocking on Eddy's door.

Maria translated it into a Spanish situation:

Who's that coming round the corner?
The sweaty feet of Josefina!
She's already had two husbands
And now she fancies Gustavito.

As their e-mail correspondence developed, so did their friendship until they found themselves exchanging photographs and details of their families. He found that Maria was from Toledo and married to a university teacher in Santiago. She and her husband would be moving to Valencia that August for a year's secondment. At the end of May, Maria finished the translation and sent it off to the publishers with its attractive, even heart-rending, cover.

The icing on the cake came later when the publishing house invited Billy across to Spain for a promotional tour. Once again, the Happy Return Travel Agency organized his itinerary to Madrid and Barcelona.

On a bright Sunday morning in October, feeling like a celebrity, Billy took a taxi to Liverpool's John Lennon Airport. The taxi was a sign of his new-found status for normally he'd have taken the train. As his dad used to say, 'Taxis are for toffs.' He paid the driver £35 and then, feeling like Rockefeller, gave him a £5 tip. He wheeled his suitcase over three main roads to the main concourse where he joined a queue for the EasyJet flight to Madrid. Laura had given a final check to his turnout, his Sunday best suit, dark raincoat, and his new fedora hat (made in Ecuador). He caught a glimpse of himself in the glass doors of the airport. He'd become the Don in the Sandeman sherry advert and he must have looked like a VIP because a young lady who accidentally brushed against him apologized with, 'I'm so sorry, SIR!'

He was flattered to be called 'sir' by a stranger but he wasn't too sure about it as it made him sound quite old. But you are old, you idiot, an inner voice told him.

Immediately in front of him was a line of adolescent schoolgirls accompanied by two lady teachers. The young ones were in festive mood and so were their teachers.

Billy asked the girl in front of him why she was going to Madrid.

'To see David Beckham of course.'

'But not his wife Posh Victoria,' her companion added. 'We can't stand her.'

'Careful what you're saying,' Billy said, 'You never know. I might be Beckham's father or even Victoria's.'

'Can't be,' the girl declared. 'You've not got the right accent.'

'Why are you really going?' he persisted.

''Cos we're studying Spanish at school, that's why,' the first girl replied.

'What can you say in Spanish?' he asked.

'*Que tal?* And that's about it. Anyway, why are *you* going to Madrid, I'd like to know.'

Never one to miss the chance of a sale, he said, ''Cos I've written a book and it's been translated into Spanish and I'm going to launch it in Madrid. It's called in English *Our Kid*. Ever heard of it?'

'Yeah, we had to read it in our English class. It's a belter.'

The girl rushed forward to tell her friends and teacher. Everyone looked back at him as if he were some kind of alien, a silver-haired bloke in a Mafia capo's hat, who had written a book that they'd been required to read. Evidently they'd liked it because they smiled and nodded in his direction. He felt chuffed. After all, hadn't the girl described his book as a 'belter'?

He reached the check-out desk and passed his suitcase through and was given the third degree.

'Did you pack it yourself?'

'Yes, of course.' That was a lie because Laura had done it. She knew he couldn't be trusted to do such a complicated task as packing a suitcase.

'Have you packed any combustible materials, like gasoline, matches, firelighters or bombs?'

He reassured her on these matters. She handed him a boarding pass and he put it with his air ticket, his credit card, his Euros and his passport.

Laura had organized him down to the last detail and he could put his hand on all these important items immediately. It's so important to be efficient in these matters, he thought, as you're expected to produce them instantly on demand and it's vital to have them ready so as not to hold up the line waiting to board. He noted with satisfaction that he'd been given easyJet priority boarding along with the handicapped in wheelchairs and on crutches, families with young kids, the very old, and those who looked like babbling idiots. He wasn't too sure which of the two latter categories he fell into; hopefully the 'very old', which was all very nice but a bit of an insult because inside his head he still felt, despite the images of himself that he spotted from time to time in shop windows, like a 21-year-old.

He went through security checks along with the other priority passengers. He was hoping he might be frisked by the pretty lady but instead was pulled out of line by a burly, bald-headed guard who ordered him to empty all his pockets and to remove his fedora in case he was hiding sticks of dynamite in it. On the orders of the big man, Billy walked through the door frame and set off the electronic alarm and had to be called back. In the top pocket of his jacket was a small nail file which he had to surrender. He felt like a shoplifter caught red-handed leaving the store with stolen goods. He was released on the other side of the security fence and given his belongings back higgledy-piggledy. The items which Laura had packed so carefully and so logically were now a jumble and he hadn't a clue where to find any of the items he'd need. Where was his passport? His boarding pass? His credit card? His money? He stuffed them all into his raincoat pocket, hoping he might get a chance to put them back in order when he reached Madrid.

This being a budget airline, there were no reserved seats and it was a case of each man for himself. He boarded the plane and secured a place near the window. Mistake! The best position for someone his age was an aisle seat giving easy access to the overhead locker and the toilets. He learned this fact the hard way. He settled into his seat and tried to switch off mentally for the two-hour flight. No use. After half an hour, he needed the toilet and had to squeeze past the corpulent, middle-aged couple in his row. Thirty minutes later, he needed the locker in order to get the sandwiches Laura had prepared and his money to pay for the coffee that would be coming round later. In his previous experiences of flying to Africa, he'd been acquainted with economy class but, this EasyJet flight could only be described as double economy. Maybe he should have brought his own cup and saucer as they used to do as kids for the school Christmas party. But then, he thought, the fare had been particularly cheap and so what else could he expect? After some time, the stewardesses came along with the goods trolley. This was their last opportunity, the tannoy told them, to buy perfumes and aftershave lotions at knock-down prices. Thinking he might reward Laura for all her work, her careful planning and eagerness to see him off to Spain, he decided to buy some exotic perfume.

'How much is the Estée Lauder?' he asked.

'Twenty-one pounds.'

'Twenty-one pounds! You said it was cheap!'

'It is,' she replied. Then, studying his grey hair and his wrinkles, she asked, 'When did you last buy perfume for a lady?'

'Nineteen thirty-nine, he said, causing laughter among the other passengers. 'But, OK. I'll take a chance on a set.'

A little time later they landed at Madrid and passengers began to disembark.

'Don't forget your perfume!' his fellow travellers called as they got their things together.

First to get off the plane were the twenty schoolgirls.

'I've read your book,' one of the girls called out as she disembarked. 'It's smashin'.'

'Now read it in Spanish,' he called back.

'No chance,' she replied as she went down the steps.

When he emerged into Madrid airport, there waiting to meet him was Maria and her brother, Luis, a barrister. Although they had swapped photos in their e-mails, he didn't recognize her but she knew him straightaway. There weren't many old blokes like him on the flight. She was much smaller than he'd imagined but there was no denying her dark Spanish beauty.

'*Bienvenido a España,*' she said, kissing him on both cheeks.

Billy was relieved that her brother settled for a simple handshake.

They drove him across to his first hotel, Hotel

Suecia, a name which worried him at first since the Spanish word for 'dirty' is *sucia* but his hosts soon put him right. 'Suecia' meant 'Sweden' and the hotel was so named because it had been opened by Prince Bertil as a place of cultural exchange. But what excited Billy most was the hotel's connection with Ernest Hemingway who had been a regular guest there in the fifties whenever he came to Madrid for the bullfights and to visit the nearby Museo del Prado and Arts Centre. This was even better than the Lewis Carroll hotel in London as a possible source of inspiration. Surely something of his spirit and genius was floating around the rooms and corridors. Maybe he'll appear to me in my dreams and offer me an idea or two, Billy hoped. He told himself that if he found himself writing declarative sentences like, 'He arrived at the river. The river was wide. The day had been hot,' or 'The road was long and dusty and uphill,' he'd know who to thank.

Maria and Luis dropped him off at the hotel having helped him to check in and to find his room. He was most impressed by the hotel which deserved its five-star rating with its avant-garde decorations and its antique Swedish furniture. Luis took Billy's suitcase from the car and lugged it up to his room. Billy was a little embarrassed and stuck for words to thank him, for it was the first and only time in his life that he'd seen a lawyer carry anything, especially belonging to him. He was grateful, too, that they had thoughtfully given him a few hours to unpack and settle in. When they'd gone, he helped himself to a whisky and soda from the little refrigerator, sat at the edge of the bed, and looked around. Opulence everywhere from the swish brocade curtains, the luxury sofa, the king-size bed, to the immaculate en suite bathroom. The Artisans' Dwellings and Honeypot Street in Manchester seemed aeons and millions of miles away. He felt a surge of elation and a lump in his throat as he thought how proud Mam and Dad would have been had they lived to see all this. At the same time they'd have worried about it. Possibly his dad would have seen him as a bloated plutocrat while Mam would have said something like, 'Eeh, our Billy, this is much too posh for the likes of us. I do hope you're not getting ideas above your station.'

A few hours later in the early evening, Maria came back with a colleague from the publishers, Ana Merino, a larger than life character who would be responsible for organizing the promotional campaign.

'You've written a great book and I like it a lot,' Ana declared 'It makes me think of Alan Sillitoe and Stan Barstow.'

She couldn't have said a nicer thing to him and from that moment on, he loved the lady.

They had drinks in the cocktail bar and Billy was introduced to tapas, a light meal consisting of Spanish omelette, cheese and salad.

'Tapas are only small portions,' Ana explained. 'There's a wide variety, including seafood, ham, and potato. Because they are small snacks, some people order several to make a meal.'

Billy decided to try one or two of them but felt it wise to let the ladies do the ordering on his behalf.

As he tucked in, they outlined the programme arranged for his visit. They looked surprised, and perhaps a little relieved, when he told them he was in the habit of retiring early. He'd heard about the tendency for Spanish people to start eating supper late at night and continuing into the early hours. After seeing the timetable they'd fixed up for him, he thought early nights were advisable.

At nine o'clock next morning, Maria arrived by taxi to take him to the publishing offices of Publicaciónes Especiales where he was presented to the managing director, Isabella Hidalgo, who gave him a warm welcome and introduced him to the members of staff who'd been involved in the production of the book. Billy handed round the pens he'd had specially made in Britain and inscribed with the legend NUESTRO PEQUEÑO BILLY, BILLY HOPKINS, PUBLICACIÓNES ESPECIALES.

After these formalities, they piled into cars and went round to the 8½ Libros de Cine book store for the 'book presentation'. This was a working lunch with journalists from the major newspapers and magazines (perhaps the lunch was provided as an incentive) where Alfonso Perez, a young, well-known Spanish historian who had read the book, introduced the work and gave his considered opinion of it. Then with Maria sitting by his side to translate, Billy told his story of how the book came to be written and how he self-published after being rejected by thirty publishers.

During lunch he was bombarded with questions which gave him little chance to enjoy the delightful lunch that had been laid on for his benefit.

After the meal they pushed their chairs back and the questions began. Questions not unlike those the English school kids had asked.

Had he always wanted to be a writer? Why did he write an autobiography in the third person? How much of it was true and how much fiction? Was he still writing? How did he explain the popularity of his books? Did he like the work of Dickens? Was he famous? Was he rich?

He half expected someone to touch him for a loan.

What was the moral – the message – of the book? This seemed to be important for the Spanish. He told them that they should read it as an entertaining story and only that. If they were looking for a message, they should try the *correos*, the post office. Which they seemed to find funny.

Articles appeared in a number of magazines like *El Periódico de Catalunya*, *Epoca*, *Negra y Criminal* (!) and the main Spanish newspapers *El Pais* and *El Mundo*. He liked the way the latter newspaper referred to him as *El bisnieto de Dickens* – the great-grandson of Dickens! – a distinction which he'd certainly not claimed.

After a one-day break which gave him a chance to see something of Madrid with Maria as guide, he flew across to Barcelona for more of the same. He was met there by his nephew, Katie's son Robert, who had lived in Barcelona for many years, having married a Spanish girl there. He was fluent in Spanish though Maria who'd spoken with him on the telephone told Billy with an amused smile that he spoke with a strong Catalan accent. At the various book presentations, Robert translated for him and, judging by the audience's laughter, none of the humour was lost. They particularly liked the part where Billy's two older sisters produced Russian fur hats which the Collyhurst people loved when they discovered that they also doubled as tea cosies.

He was also interviewed for radio (Radio Nacional de España) and two Spanish TV programmes. The main one (*Continuerá*) said they would be interspersing the interview with shots of old Manchester. The two ladies interviewing him had not only read the book but appreciated both the humour and the sadness.

It had been a hectic week in Spain and for that brief period he'd enjoyed his Andy Warhol 'fifteen minutes' of fame. From the moment that he'd arrived in Spain, he'd been wined and dined like royalty. No, better than that, he maintained, like David Beckham, hero of the Real Madrid football team! Apart from the generous hospitality, what impressed him most in Spain was the fact that nearly everyone he met spoke good English, having learned it at school and spent time as students in Britain. It put to shame Britain's own record in linguistic achievement and the tendency of youngsters to give up language studies at an early age.

The other thing he noticed at these functions was that nearly everyone smoked, often between courses. It seemed that the message of how dangerous both active and passive smoking could be had not yet reached that part of Europe. Or if it had, few had taken it seriously It was a great contrast to Britain where a blanket ban on smoking was being enforced and smokers had been accorded near-pariah status.

Despite this misgiving, he'd had a wonderful time and came to have the deepest respect and affection for all things Spanish. Nevertheless he was looking forward to returning to dear old England, if only for a rest. Before leaving Spain, Billy and his nephew paid a visit to El Corte Inglés, the large department store in Barcelona, where Billy bought gifts for members of the family and ordered a special plaque to be delivered to England later.

He almost didn't make it out of Spain. The day before he left, he was waiting in the foyer of the Hotel Majestic for his minder Ana to take him to the next venue when he was approached by an attractive Mexican lady who was a resident in the hotel. She remarked, in good English, how elegant he looked. (He was dressed in his Sandeman sherry outfit, complete with fedora.) One couldn't imagine that happening in Britain and such an approach would probably be misinterpreted. Ana explained to the lady that he was a British writer who'd come to Spain to promote his book. Next morning, Conchita, this being the Mexican señora's name, approached him at the breakfast table and asked him to sign a copy of the book which she had been out specially to buy. Billy gave her one of his pens, a bookmark, and a signed photograph. She said she would read the book on the flight back to Mexico and would promote it there. Then she invited him back to her home in Mexico. Billy thought it wise to report all this to

Laura later and sadly she wouldn't let him go. Shame about that, he thought.

When he got back to Southport, there was a piece of news waiting for him. And it was one that gave him more delight than anything that had happened since he'd first heard that his book was to be published. The news came in the form of a letter from a Liz Farrell, a reader development assistant at the National Library for the Blind, telling him that his book was to be transcribed into Braille. She asked him if he'd be willing to write a piece for their magazine *Read On* and also to give a talk to a blind and partially sighted reading group at their headquarters in Cheshire. He felt moved by these invitations and agreed happily to do both. For the magazine article, he wrote:

Thank you for inviting me to contribute to your magazine, *Read On*, which I consider a great privilege. My book has been translated into Spanish but I consider it a much greater honour to have it transcribed into Braille for it has given me a chance to communicate and share experiences both of joy and sorrow with you. Joseph Conrad put it better than I when he wrote:
    'My task which I am trying to achieve is by the power of the written word, to make you hear, to make you feel – it is, before all, to make you *see*. That – and no more, and it is everything.'

Mark drove him to the NLB in Cheshire and, after a light lunch, Liz Farrell took them on a conducted tour of the impressive library facilities. The huge shelves housing the great classical works in Braille were as numerous as any Billy had seen in any large city library. They were fascinated, too, by the demonstration of the processes by which a work was transcribed from plain text into Braille. But it was the talk itself that Billy found most unusual and emotional. In describing the procedure, two words sprang to his mind – dignified and civilized.

He stood at the entrance to meet individual members of the audience as they came through in pairs, one the visually impaired person and the other the helper. Introductions were quite formal.

'Allow me to present Terry Prater... Steve Binns... Tarnia Canham...'

Billy had often said that, if necessary, he'd be willing to talk to one man and his dog and when a reader accompanied by a golden Labrador came through the door, it looked as if he was going to get his wish. It was an extremely hot day and before they could begin, they had to make sure the dog was supplied with a bowl of water. His listeners proved to be one of the best audiences he'd ever addressed. They had all read the book, one of them having finished it in two days flat. They paid him close attention and most rewarding of all for Billy was the fact that they laughed in all the right places. One or two made incisive comments, for example, when he spoke of the Victorian habit of putting the coffin on display in front of the parlour window so that family and neighbours might come and take a last look at the deceased.

Terry Prater commented with a grin, 'They wouldn't do that today, of course.'

'Why not?' Billy asked.

'Because of central heating.'

There was further evidence that they'd retained their sense of humour. Before he departed, he asked them how they'd found reading the book in Braille.

'I felt as if I were really there in Collyhurst,' Steve Binns said.

'Very touching indeed,' Tarnia Canham commented.

Mark and he drove away from the NLB feeling very humble.

Chapter Twenty-Five

What's Next? Sequels

So that's the story of how *Our Kid* came to be written, rejected, published, promoted, translated and transcribed.

Some authors write only one book. Like Harper Lee who wrote *To Kill a Mocking Bird* because some friends dared her to. There was speculation that she was writing another, the subject of which was a well-guarded secret, but nothing materialized. Margaret Mitchell produced just one book in her life, *Gone With the Wind*, and most people would consider that writing a masterpiece like that was enough for one person's lifetime. She might have written a second book but was prevented from ever doing so when she was killed in a motor car accident at the age of forty-nine. Some writers did manage to write several books but were remembered chiefly for their magnum opus. Bram Stoker was forever associated with *Dracula*; Mario Puzo with *The Godfather*; J.D. Salinger with *The Catcher in the Rye*; Mary Shelley with *Frankenstein*; Joseph Heller with *Catch-22*. While not for a moment classing himself with these illustrious writers, Billy wondered if he'd finish up being dubbed a one-book author known only for *Our Kid*. When he wrote it he hadn't had a second book in mind. His reason for putting pen to paper had been simply to occupy his leisure hours following the various disastrous pursuits he'd undertaken on first retiring.

But no sooner had the paperback been launched than there was demand for a sequel. A flow of letters demanded to know what happened next.

'We've had the main course,' wrote Dennis Cunnington, an Oldham reader who described himself as Number One Fan. 'Now, what's for dessert?'

There wasn't any. Publicizing the first book had been a full-time job and Billy had found himself involved in an endless round of promotional talks, readings, signings, lunches. There had been little energy or time for writing another book. Not only that, he didn't really consider himself a writer. He'd penned the story of his Collyhurst upbringing mainly for his family and possibly great-grandchildren yet to be born. But him an author? He was nothing of the sort. If anything, he was a fraud and he couldn't go on getting away with it. One of these days there'd be a loud knocking at his door. It'd be the literary police come to get him and cart him away for taking money under false pretences.

As for a second novel, what could he write about? He'd poured so much of himself into the first novel that when he finished the last chapter, he'd felt a sense of loss, like a bereavement. What was more, there was little or nothing more to be said. He'd used up his stock of anecdotes and funny stories. So, what was left? Though they didn't say it in so many words, one or two friends felt that *Our Kid* had been nothing more than a flash in the pan, a fluke. If he wanted to prove himself, then he had to produce a sequel.

Easier said than done. In so many writing magazines he'd read of the difficulties in writing a second book and so he couldn't say he hadn't been warned. He'd come across ominous phrases like 'the second book syndrome' or 'the curse of the second novel'. One author described it as like having to sail around Cape Horn. If you can get through that, your writing career is plain sailing. Billy mentioned the problem to Titch who, as usual, offered no sympathy.

'Second book syndrome? You should try my problem, the no-book syndrome. You've only got this so-called headache because your first book was successful and it's a hard act to follow. If it hadn't been such a big seller, nobody would touch you again, no matter what you wrote. But seeing that it was a hit, they'll publish you, no matter what rubbish you write.'

'Thanks for those few words of encouragement, Titch, I must say. What worries me is that a second book will prove a big disappointment. Can I keep up the standard? My reputation's at stake. Am I to be known as a one-book wonder, a one-trick pony?'

'As I see it, Hoppy, there are three possible solutions to your dilemma.'

'I'm all ears, Titch.'

'First, you could tell your agent and publisher to get lost and to find somebody else to write their books for them. Second, you could do like that writer you once told me about, John Kennedy O'Toole who wrote *A Confederacy of Dunces* and

363

then committed suicide. Or, thirdly, you could write an even better book. Consider the first book as a practise run in order to learn the business of novel-writing. You've sharpened your technical skills and there's no reason why your next book shouldn't be more accomplished and polished than the first. Go out there and wow 'em.'

'I would, Titch, if I knew how. *Our Kid* came to me as a gift and I don't know how I did it. I haven't the first clue as to why it was a success. Writing it was a relaxed affair.'

'Well, do the same with the second book. Stay relaxed.'

'Can't, Titch. This time it's not the same; it's panic stations. With the first book, no one was waiting for it; there was no deadline and no one gave a tinker's cuss if I didn't finish it. But with the next book, it's different, it's no longer fun. The honeymoon's over. Lots of people are waiting for it and my reputation's on the line. Instead of second book syndrome, I may find I have last book syndrome. Everyone's expecting the second book to be as good as the first.'

'I'm sure it will be, Hoppy.'

'You hope. I can see the prophets of doom now honing their ready-made phrases: "A disappointing second book" or "ill thought out and pumped out too quickly", or worse still, "a carbon copy of the first book".'

There was no point agonizing about it. He simply had to get on with it. Maybe Titch was right; maybe the first book was a learning experience, a sort of rite of passage to becoming a writer. Perhaps the first book was to show that he could do it and the second to prove that it wasn't simply beginner's luck. Maybe the second would do better than the first. But then he thought: the readers out there couldn't care less about sales figures. What they were interested in was a good story, well told and one that they could relate to.

Choosing the theme for the second book was not as difficult as he first thought. Readers' letters made it clear what was expected.

'Do you have plans for another book?' a lady from Berkshire inquired. '*Our Kid* is so fascinating that I'd like to know what happened to him, his family and the boys of Damian College Smokers' Club.'

'You left us where young Billy has just gone off to college,' wrote a lady from London. 'Now I have high hopes for a sequel and can hardly wait to read the next instalment.'

Reading the many letters in this vein, who was he to resist? The second book would continue the story of Billy at college and his subsequent experiences. As for a title, the London lady's letter had supplied it: *High Hopes*.

It consisted of two words only, like his first book; it was short and snappy and, for him, said it all. The story was about Billy and his high hopes to do well at college and become qualified; to succeed as a teacher despite his class of unruly pupils; to win the hand of Laura in the face of the opposition of both her father and his own dad.

He checked at the public library for other works with the same title and found there were twenty, including one about Bill Clinton's presidency, and a play by Mike Leigh, also one by comedian Ronnie Corbett who used the title as wishful thinking because of his short stature. Although there were so many books with the same title, there was no problem since there was no copyright on titles.

He started work. The words came slowly and hesitatingly at first but as he dug deeper into his memory bank they began to flow. Writing about college was relatively easy though he wondered who, apart from fellow teachers, would be interested in the course of training that teachers had to undergo to become qualified. Then followed his account of his first teaching post, the resistance of his pupils who had been the first 'victims' of the raising of the school leaving age to fifteen. He was able to recall the details of each member of his class, their names and personality foibles and the struggle to win them over. In this he had been aided by the liberal attitude of the head, Mr Wakefield, who'd allowed him to adopt a radical timetable which included not only the traditional subjects but also ballroom dancing and outdoor hikes in the Peak District.

Writing about school thus presented no problem. It was a different kettle of fish when it came to describing his meeting with his future wife, Laura, and the need to overcome the resistance of her father, Duncan, who entertained higher ambitions for his daughter. Maybe female authors in the Romantic Novelists' Association found describing love and romance straightforward. Not so, Billy. Perhaps it was too intensely personal.

How different from writing *Our Kid* which, relatively speaking, had been a piece of cake. He soldiered on, however, not to the bitter end because the conclusion of the story was a marriage, a happy ending. Laura, his 'volunteer' proof-reader, subjected the manuscript to a thorough edit, amending and correcting numerous errors, and at the end of the year he was able to write 'The End'. Champagne and celebration all round? Not yet. Uncertain of what the outcome might be, he sent it off to Wilbraham Press with fingers crossed.

After a few weeks, the manuscript came back from Susan Munro, the senior editor, saying how much she'd enjoyed reading the manuscript. Her letter was accompanied by ten pages of detailed and shrewd notes on how the story might be improved, together with a list of things that needed attention, like unclear passages, non-sequiturs, and inconsistencies. Billy got down to work addressing her concerns and at the end of a couple of weeks, there it was. He'd made it! A second book! He was a writer!

Wilbraham's graphic artists found a superb picture of a young man on a bicycle for the cover and things began to come together. A few months after that, it appeared in hardback and went into the libraries and the book stores. Though the book did not outsell *Our Kid*, it went on to reach the top ten in the *Sunday Times* list of bestsellers. The local press gave it good reviews and even the staid old *Times Educational Supplement* described it as 'a good read'. One or two people wrote to tell him they'd liked the second book but with reservations.

Typical was the reader who commented: 'My wife and I both read *High Hopes* with enjoyment. That being said, we felt it was definitely a second book which does not come up to the high standard of *Our Kid* despite its high hopes.'

This seemed to imply that, *because* it was a second book, it couldn't be expected to be as good as the first. Not all readers agreed. Understandably many teachers and other educators preferred the second book since it was about teacher training and the experiences of a new teacher. This from a lecturer in education: 'I read *Our Kid* some time ago and I loved it but not nearly so much as *High Hopes*. I shall look forward to your next book.'

The successful launch of *High Hopes* gave Billy confidence for a third book – not a sequel but a prequel. It was a book that practically wrote itself. Before the death of his dad, his parents had lived together in an old folks' bungalow on the Langley estate in Middleton about ten miles north of Manchester. For many years, Billy and Laura visited regularly on Sunday afternoons, taking the children who enjoyed listening to Grandma's yarns of 'the good old days', which she usually amplified with lots of dialogue, for which she had an uncanny memory. The tales were related in Collyhurst dialect which their children found strange when they first heard it after returning from East Africa.

'Gran'ma,' Lucy, then aged ten, said, 'It's not "to-morrer", it's "tomorrow"!' Lucy had won a prize for elocution back at her Kenya junior school.

'Well, I speak Lancashire,' Gran'ma replied. 'So, there!'

Billy's dad, Tommy, also found the visits enjoyable because they always took him a couple of bottles of Boddington's Bitter, his favourite tipple.

After Tommy's death, Billy's mam managed to get by for a number of years, especially since she had a special friend in Mrs Martha Evans who lived a couple of doors away. Kate and Martha did their shopping together, and took one or two charabanc rides with the Union of Catholic Mothers to Walsingham. A few years went by and Kate's eyesight began to deteriorate rapidly and by the time she reached the age of eighty-nine, the problem had become serious. She was having accidents, like burning her arm on the cooker or tripping over things. When it became evident that she could no longer cope on her own, Billy and Laura provided her with a granny flat in their home.

Passing by her room one day, Billy overheard her having a dialogue with an imaginary friend.

'Oh, no,' she was saying, 'don't you try to tell me that our Flo and Polly are consumptive. Your kids have seen more dinner times than dinners.'

Billy realized that his mam was acting out her life story. He was eavesdropping on living history told in her own authentic voice and she had a heart-rending tale to tell. She'd been born in 1888 and had led a hard and eventful life. The next day, Billy took a tape recorder into her room and asked her to tell him her story.

'What was it like when you were a little girl,

369

Mam?' he asked. 'Were you happy or unhappy?'

It was as if she'd been waiting to be asked such a question.

'At first,' she said. 'I was very happy but when I was twelve, my dad died and things changed. From then on, I was very unhappy because I loved my dad. Life became one long struggle.'

She was off! She hadn't kissed the Blarney Stone but she told her tale as if she had. Her account filled four tapes and became a family heirloom. Here was a story ready-made. It ranged over a period from 1897 to his own birth in 1928. It needed much research to fill out details of the Victorian workhouse, domestic service in Edwardian England, and the 1914-18 war, the flu epidemic of 1919, and the roaring twenties. Apart from that, when Billy began writing the book in 1999, he had the uncanny feeling that what he was really doing was taking dictation from his late mother. The result was *Kate's Story* and this, too, joined the bestseller charts with sales almost equalling his first book. Many correspondents said they were able to identify strongly with the story since they or their mother or grandmother had suffered similar adversities.

For many, *Kate's Story* became their favourite novel. Billy thought the picture on the front had an interesting provenance. It wasn't easy to find a photograph of a young working-class girl around the turn of the last century for the simple reason that poor people did not possess cameras. Most photos available were of well-to-do families taken in stiff, unnatural poses beside the aspidistra. However, it was Lucy who, when browsing through London archives, found the photo they'd been looking for. It had been taken by a Reverend Frank Swanson who had toured the East End of London in 1911, taking pictures of street children. The little girl on the cover of *Kate's Story* had obviously posed for him in her best Sunday hat.

Shortly after he sent off the manuscript to Wilbraham Press, Billy and Laura celebrated their golden wedding anniversary. If there was going to be a celebration, they wanted no fuss, no special festivities, but their children had other plans. Early on Saturday, 12 August 2000, Mark collected them in Southport and drove them across to Manchester in time for early Mass at St Anselm's Church. It seemed surreal that they should be back at exactly the same time, at the same church, fifty years later. Billy could remember with great clarity that day in 1950. The church had been packed with extended family members on both sides, old friends, and pupils and staff from the school where they'd both been teachers. Today's Mass was a normal occasion for the parishioners though the young priest had been told of the special event for he referred to it in his sermon from the pulpit.

'In the church today,' he said, 'we have an elderly couple who married here half a century ago today. They are present here together with their four children and two grandchildren and so we congratulate Mr and Mrs Hopkins on their golden wedding anniversary; they are truly blessed in that they have both survived and are able to be here together, a joy not shared by every married couple where one of the partnership has passed away. And in this age when divorce and separation are only too common, it is a cause for great rejoicing that their marriage has been strong and able to weather the trials and tribulations to which they have no doubt been subjected over the years. Let us remember them in our prayers today.'

The brief homily had the tears sparkling in Laura's eyes and Billy had to suppress a sniff or two.

After Mass, the family drove across to the Water Park at Sale where a magnificent lunch was enjoyed, particularly by Billy when he found he didn't have to foot the bill. From there, they drove across to Mark's house for the presentation of anniversary gifts.

On the table in the front room, the gifts were beautifully laid out and then one by one given by the family members. From Matthew came a framed print of San Francisco's Golden Gate Bridge by K. Stimpson; from Lucy, a hardback copy of *Memoirs of a Geisha* by Arthur Golden; from Mark, a pair of golden candlesticks complete with golden candles; from John, a thousand-piece jigsaw puzzle of Francis Drake's ship *The Golden Hind*.

'You had me wondering what was next,' Billy said. 'I thought you were about to pleasantly surprise us with a golden retriever. Or better still with gold shares.'

'I had thought of buying you a tube of Glister whitening toothpaste,' grinned Mark.

'So what stopped you?' Laura asked, realizing

too late that she'd left herself open for his punch-line.

'Because it suddenly occurred to me that all that glisters is not gold.'

'Very funny,' Laura said, unable to stop herself from laughing all the same.

'Wait, wait. There's more,' Lucy gushed, pulling back the tablecloth to reveal a wide collection of miscellaneous objects.

'There are fifty altogether,' said John proudly.

Billy and Laura were taken aback to see on the table a veritable cornucopia of items all bearing some kind of a gold motif: Gold Blend coffee, gold leaf cigarettes, golden vegetable soup, gold churn butter, Golden Wonder crisps, golden syrup. The list went on and on.

'You've certainly used your imagination on the theme of gold,' Billy chuckled, counting up the articles, 'but I make it only forty-nine objects. So you're one gift short.'

The family looked nonplussed. They each put a finger to their lips and stayed quiet for a whole minute, which, for the Hopkins family, was a long time.

'Come on,' Laura smiled. 'What's going on?'

It was Matthew who spoke first. 'That's our fiftieth present. A minute's silence.'

'I don't get it,' Billy said. 'Why a minute's silence?'

'Easy,' said Mark. 'Silence is golden.'

'Very funny,' said Billy. 'You've all got a twisted sense of humour.'

'I wonder where we get it,' replied John.

It was time for Billy to bring out his gift of gold,

373

as a memento of fifty years of marriage and one that might serve as a family heirloom in years to come. For their twenty-fifth, he had bought a silver tea service which now had pride of place in the display cabinet; for the fortieth, a telephone table with a ruby-coloured velvet cover for the seat. For this, the fiftieth, he had specially ordered a damascened plaque in twenty-four carat gold made in Toledo by craftsmen and depicting Don Quixote and his squire Sancho Panza mounted on their steeds.

'I ordered this from El Corte Inglés in Barcelona just before I left,' Billy said. 'I hope you like it.'

'Like it?' Laura exclaimed. 'I love it and shall value it as long as I live.'

'And so shall we!' the family chorused.

Billy felt that he ought to make some kind of speech.

'Mum and I have been most moved by this little reception and the magnificent lunch you bought for us. It is hard for me to address you on an occasion such as this because you have already heard my stories and I'm afraid you might award me Olympic scores as you've done in the past. Mum and I married and we have the marriage lines to prove it on the day that grouse shooting began. For fifty years, I've done the grousing and she's longed to do the shooting. Being in St Anselm's Church this morning brought so many memories back. When I repeated after the priest the words, "With all my worldly goods I thee endow," my old mother, your gran'ma, said in a stage whisper that could be heard by the whole

374

church, "There goes his bike!" By the way, Laura, what happened to that bike?

'The big question now is, if we had our time over again, would we still go through with it? I think you know my answer. If you want Mum's, you must ask her. But she's still here by my side. It's a daft question anyway because in the immortal words of Duncan, your late grandfather, whose wedding speech must be among the shortest on record, "It's too late now."'

In the evening in the local parish centre, there was a reception complete with a buffet supper, also paid for by the children who had truly gone out of their way to invite people from past and present. It is said that a drowning man sees the whole of his life pass before him in a flash. The faces they beheld that evening came from every stage of their lives. But Billy and Laura weren't drowning. Just the opposite; the reception was one of the happiest they would ever remember.

From Laura's side of the family there was an impressive contingent: her sister, Jenny, and husband Hamish down from Edinburgh with their two daughters, both accountants and accomplished amateur musicians; Hughie, now registrar at a Staffordshire hospital, and still single; Katie with husband Stuart over from Southport; plus innumerable Caledonian cousins whom Billy could not remember.

Members of the extended Hopkins family were there in force. Nephews and nieces belonging to his late sisters Flo and Polly (or Florence and Pauline as their husbands had preferred to call them) were represented. Polly's oldest son, Oliver, whom Billy had entertained when the young lad had been five years old, had travelled over from Durham where he worked as a post office engineer. Hardly now the youngster Billy remembered as he was approaching sixty. Where had the time gone? Billy asked himself. Kevin, son of Billy's late brother Sam, had made the trip over from Belfast. Finally his brother Les and his wife Annette were there with their grown-up children.

Lucy's friends from the ashram had also put in an appearance. Still devotees of the Bagwhan Serpa Shanyassi but no longer full-time as they'd been when they'd taken over the upper floors of Laura and Billy's Manchester house. They met Mary Feeney and Sally Simpson, Lucy's old school friends, now forty-five years old. Still attractive but no longer the gawky schoolgirls they remembered from the seventies. Both ladies were now primary school teachers.

Billy's non-smoking Smokers' Club were there in strength. Oscar was accompanied by his soul mate, Derek; Nobby and Olly brought their wives, Prudence and Cordelia; Titch came with his wife Elaine and their two grown-up sons, the grandchildren having been left with a babysitter.

Music was provided by Matthew's old group, the Aquarian Angels, with Matthew on piano and his erstwhile renegade chums Tom Stephens on drums and Dessy Gillespie on trumpet.

'They seem to have learned to play together in tune at last,' said a voice behind Billy.

He looked round at the speaker; it was Dr Gillespie, his former next-door neighbour. Together the two men had provided free transport for the band and their equipment to their various gigs in church halls around the north-west of England.

'A definite improvement on the old days.' Billy laughed, shaking the doctor's hand. 'I once inquired of the doorman at one place if the band was ready to go. "As far as I'm concerned," he replied, "they can go any time they want. The sooner the better."'

Not that the quality of the music on the golden wedding night mattered, for the orchestral sounds were drowned by the buzz of conversation around the hall as everyone seemed intent on catching up on each other's news for the last thirty years.

The biggest surprise of the night came when Mark appeared with, of all people, old Uncle Eddy, aged 104 and one of the last remaining survivors of the Battle of the Somme. For some years, high-ranking army officers had been going out of their way to pay homage to Billy's veteran uncle and so Billy and Laura felt honoured that he'd managed to attend their celebration, even if it was only for an hour. Mark had secretly organized this surprise visit by chauffeuring the old man to and from his nursing home in Blackley.

'That school you taught at on Hyde Road, Billy,' Eddy said. 'What was it called again?'

'You mean Holbrook Hospital School?'

'That's the one. In the Great War, it was used as a casualty station for the wounded sent home from the trenches. When I got hit on the Somme in nineteen sixteen, that was the place they sent me to.'

Eddy's mind was as sharp as ever and there was nothing wrong with his memory either. It was the last time Billy saw him, for within six months of the party, he was dead. Still, not a bad innings, he reflected.

The golden wedding celebration went on to midnight and Billy and Laura came away happy but exhausted. Also somewhat confused as they had talked to so many people; it was going to take several months to get their thoughts in some kind of order. They were deeply moved and impressed by the way their children had organized the event and brought so many of their friends and relatives into one place.

Shortly after he had finished *Kate's Story*, ideas for a fourth book began hatching in Billy's mind. *High Hopes* had ended with the wedding of Billy and Laura – always a good event with which to conclude a story. Then readers began demanding to know about the early days of their marriage, how they coped and how they brought up their children. The result was *Going Places*, an account of the struggle to raise a family on the meagre salary of a young teacher and then the move to Kenya in search of a better life.

Billy thought that was it. He could hang up his pen or switch off his computer (whatever it is that retired writers were supposed to do) and put his feet up. But things couldn't be left there when a reader wrote to him: 'Come on, Billy. You can't leave us stranded in mid-air somewhere between Nairobi and London. We want the next episode in the life of the Hopkins family.'

No peace for the wicked. He sat down and spent a year producing a fifth novel, this time entitled *Anything Goes*, in which he tried to describe the challenges and heartaches of bringing up a young adolescent family during the swinging sixties when traditional values had been thrown into the melting pot.

So that's how Billy spent his retirement. He read somewhere that Cervantes was so depressed after *Don Quixote* that he simply went on adding to the novel so that the classic story was in effect his first, second, and third novels rolled into one. Not for a moment did Billy compare himself to the Spanish genius but something similar seemed to have happened to him. He'd set off thinking he was penning his memoirs for his family and ended up writing five full-length novels. Perhaps it was wrong to talk of five novels because what he had produced was one story in five episodes. Six, if the present one was included.

Chapter Twenty-Six

The Old Man's Not Asleep

If you were looking for a message from this book – and such a thing would no doubt appeal to a few Spanish readers – it would be this. If, when you reach the age of seventy, people write you off, think you've lost your marbles and that maybe it's time for you to take up the role of Shakespeare's slippered pantaloon, remember that by no means is it over. On the contrary, it could be the beginning of a new lease of life, a golden age. It's entirely up to you.

Remember Robert Browning's Rabbi Ben Ezra: 'Grow old along with me, the best is yet to be.'

One last point. If you ever find yourself in Southport and you happen to pass a garden where an elderly lady is tending her flowers and plants while her husband is dozing in his deck-chair, you could be forgiven for saying, 'Look at that old man over there lounging in his chair, the lazy so-and-so. Obviously he has switched off from life and left his wife to do all the hard graft.'

But hold it right there! Don't jump to conclusions! That old man apparently dozing in the chair could be Billy Hopkins, thinking up his next novel.

The publishers hope that this book has given you enjoyable reading. Large Print Books are especially designed to be as easy to see and hold as possible. If you wish a complete list of our books please ask at your local library or write directly to:

Magna Large Print Books
Magna House, Long Preston,
Skipton, North Yorkshire.
BD23 4ND

This Large Print Book for the partially sighted, who cannot read normal print, is published under the auspices of

THE ULVERSCROFT FOUNDATION